ADVANCE PRAISE

"In this thought-provoking and moving tale about interplanetary cooperation and the search for peace, . . . David Brown has taken the intergalactic invasion tropes of discovering other societies out there in the cosmos and done something truly inventive with them that I've never seen in a work of science fiction before. From the outset, this work of sci-fi, dystopia, and high drama keeps a laser-sharp focus on morality, ethics, and justice, and the poignancy of these topics makes it a highly relatable and credible read. I would certainly recommend *A Gigantic Leap: First Contact* for fans of intelligent, emotive, and well-considered science fiction everywhere."
- K.C. Finn, award-winning author

"I found *A Gigantic Leap: First Contact* by David Brown very exhilarating. There was nothing I disliked about the book; I enjoyed every bit of it. The book is quite exciting, and the suspense doesn't end until the last page of the book. 5 out of 5 stars!"
- Mercy Udeokeke, author

"*A Gigantic Leap: First Contact* is an engrossing page turner and the perfect book for our times. It is a race against time and an insightful probe of human nature, with an assortment of compelling characters in an uplifting science fiction adventure filled with action, intrigue, and aliens. And it's one fun read! I read the entire book in one sitting. I honestly can't wait for the sequel."
- Steven Reich, Emmy award-winning writer and producer

"David Brown's sprawling volume, *A Gigantic Leap: First Contact*, has an impressive imaginative arc, taking topics as varied as corporate intrigue, alien abduction, and the innate qualities of humankind. It offers an engrossing and imaginative take on the "judgment of humankind" science fiction story."
- Craig Jones

"Brown's writing is clean and the ideas are highly philosophical, the world-building is extremely well done, and, despite the novel ending on something of a cliffhanger, it is overall a novel that makes the decision to read whatever follows it a sure thing. In short: I'm in. Bring on the beginning of utopia."
- Asher Syed

"David Brown has created a vivid and imaginative world filled with fascinating alien species and advanced technology. It's a well-written and thought-provoking story that explores complex themes in an engaging way. The characters are relatable and the world-building is three-dimensional, making it enjoyable from start to finish. Highly recommended."
- Vincent Dublado

"At first, I actually believed I was reading a screenplay for a marvelous movie as I quickly turned the pages of this near-future, genre-bending tale about how aliens from our own galaxy intervene to address the innate violence they see in humans here on Earth.
A debt of gratitude is owed to this author for opening minds to the possibility of a post-violence way of life in the world. I can't wait to see the movie!"
- Nicky Noxon, Peabody award-winning producer

"As someone who is a regular contributor to Survival International, there was no way I was able to turn away from the ultimate survival story, and one that involves aliens to boot. Brown's pacing is fast and so the story does not have a saggy middle. Entertaining, thoughtful, and very highly recommended."
- Jamie Michele

TREE
HOUSE

IBSN 979-8-9877023-1-4 (paperback)

A Gigantic Leap

Book One:
First Contact

by

David Brown

*For my Family and my
dear late wife, Carolyn,
The First Readers*

And for Peace on Earth

PROLOGUE

On the last day of filming, Stephen Hopkins stood in the shade of a Ceiba tree and watched the interview with a great deal of satisfaction. Ganbigo, the diminutive shaman, was a natural in front of the camera, a smile lighting up his brown wizened face as he explained the controversial funerary rites of the Abigo tribe of northern Peru. Stephen lifted his hat and wiped his brow with his forearm. The documentary would provide a fitting finale to his four-year study of the tribe, but he was eager to leave the heat of the rainforest and go home. He glanced at Gerard playing nearby with two Abigo youths, oblivious of the heat. Penny should see him now. She'd understand why this trip was such a fantastic opportunity for their son.

The clatter of a motor overhead interrupted his thoughts. He walked toward the clearing and watched a sleek black helicopter stir up a small sandstorm as it rocked to a landing. Three men disembarked, ducked their heads against the fierce downdraft, and ran clear of the whirling sand. One man disappeared into the jungle, the other two headed toward Stephen. At a safe distance the two men slowed to a walk. One was tall with a mane of silver hair; the other, short, dark, and rotund. The short man had a mincing walk. Ethan Gorr, a man Stephen tried to avoid on principle. He had named Gorr's company as the major abuser of the Abigo rainforest in a report to the State Department, which created ill will between the two men.

The man with Gorr, the one with the silver mane, was Stephen's father. Televangelists as famous as the Reverend Hopkins hobnobbed regularly with tycoons of industry who wanted to soften the rougher edges of their public image. Even presidents of the United States, past and present, frequently felt the need of the reverend's presence. But Stephen was surprised to see his father in the middle of a Peruvian rainforest.

The *National Geographic* reporter halted the interview with the shaman and trotted toward Reverend Hopkins and Ethan Gorr, the cameraman at his heels. The pair intercepted the new arrivals before they reached Stephen.

"Reverend Hopkins, what are you doing down here?"

"The Abigos, son. They're in great need of salvation, and my church is preparing to send missionaries to spread the word." Even here in the rainforest, the famous voice sounded utterly commanding. "You know Ethan Gorr, CEO of Gorr Resources?"

"Gorr Resources. Logging company, isn't it?"

"Forestry management. The best there is." Gorr talked around the cigar in his mouth.

"And you're here to—"

"Turn off that camera and I'll tell you."

The reporter gave a signal to the cameraman, who lowered his camera.

"We're missing an M15 rifle from our field station up river," Gorr said. "I have to locate it before one of these primitives finds it and thinks it's a toy."

He nodded curtly at Stephen as he passed, then headed for a group of natives a short distance from the hut. The reporter and cameraman hurried after him.

Stephen turned to his father and shook his outstretched hand. "You're the last person I expected to see down here."

"I go where the Lord calls me, son."

"I know. Gerard will be glad to see you."

"Gerard's here? Why in God's name did you bring my grandson down here? Don't you know this is a dangerous place?"

"The Abigo aren't dangerous. They don't even know what violence is, in spite of the media hype about their funerary rites. Which you'd know if you'd read my report."

His father looked worried. "We'd better go find Gerard. With that weapon missing from Ethan's camp—"

A shot rang out, followed quickly by another. Stephen turned in time to see Ganbigo fall. He raced in that direction, feeling as if he were slogging through quicksand, and when he reached the hut, Ganbigo was lying in a pool of blood. Next to the little shaman, so close that their feet were touching, lay the small, still body of his son.

"No!" Stephen cried when he saw his son. He dropped to his knees and pressed two fingers against Gerard's throat. Thankfully, he felt a pulse.

"Is he alive?"

Stephen looked up at the filmmaker and nodded, unable to speak.

"Thank God for that," the filmmaker said. "The little shaman died before he hit the ground. Nothing we can do for him."

Stephen trembled at the sight of his stricken boy. *How could this happen?*

Reverend Hopkins touched Stephen's shoulder. "Ethan has offered to fly him to Lima. Let's get him to the helicopter."

Numb, Stephen picked up Gerard and started toward the clearing. He caught sight of Gorr, cigar in mouth, following a few steps back, along with the third man who had disappeared into the jungle. *Gorr brought the weapon onto the Abigo's land!*

Stephen exploded at his father. "You brought Gorr down here and he shot my son—"

"No, Stephen, they captured the guy with the gun. He's an Abigo."

Stephen's eyes filled with tears as he handed Gerard's limp body up to the pilot.

"Ethan's my friend, Stephen, he's trying to help you…"

#

The jungle receded to a green blur as the helicopter climbed to a cruising altitude for the 45-minute flight to Lima. Gerard lay in the back of the chopper with the reverend's white jacket tied around his waist. The jacket was soaked through with blood, but it had stemmed the flow. The reverend knelt beside Gerard, praying softly. Stephen crouched on the other side and listened to his son's labored breathing, feeling more helpless by the minute. He watched Gerard's skinny chest rise and fall, and for the first time in many years he tried to pray. *Please, God, let him live!* He repeated the silent prayer over and over, but after a few minutes he stopped. Why would God listen to someone who had turned his back on his church?

3

He stretched out beside Gerard and clutched his hand. "Hang on, son, please hang on," he whispered. As he lay there, a haunting melody began to play in his mind, a woman's keening voice from Rachmaninov's *Vocalise*. He often played the piece when Gerard was a baby, especially when he was restless or sick. He had played it to comfort himself but it had seemed to sooth Gerard as well. Now he curled around the small body on the floor of the helicopter and hummed the melody in his son's ear. It felt like a prayer that echoed his anguish.

PART ONE

Six years later...

CHAPTER 1

Chairman Morok gazed out his window at the jagged red peaks of Yxria and listened to the haunting strains of Rachmaninov's *Vocalise*. He rode the sounds like an eagle rides the wind, soaring with joyful abandon, spiraling downward in sadness, soaring, spiraling again and again. When the music ended, he floated back to reality, and grounded himself.

He could not let the Commission go through with its plan. He pressed a button and summoned Counselor Myssa, his most outspoken opponent on the Commission for Emerging Cultures, to his quarters. Soon she would fill his sanctuary with her high, thin voice and her intractable demands.

Outside, his fellow Yxrians were riding the air currents in the red-rimmed canyon. Their wings painted the sky with all the colors of the spectrum. They soared high to clear a sharp peak, then dipped gracefully out of sight into the next gorge. Morok, an eight-foot tall avian species with bright blue plumes, curved black beak, and green-gold eyes, lifted his massive blue-green wings with pride and ruffled them lightly, stirring a slight breeze.

A sharp knock at the door was followed by a piercing female voice. Counselor Myssa burst into the room, "Mr. Chairman, what is the meaning of this order?"

Morok sighed and let his wings droop toward the floor. He turned slowly and regarded the slender chameleon standing in his doorway. She was clad in a diaphanous robe that reflected the iridescent tones of her skin. Between two curved, long-nailed fingers she held a thin metal wafer, with a look of cold fury in her lizard eyes. The wafer bore Morok's personal seal, the sign of a confidential message. Myssa held the wafer far away from her body, almost as if it was poison.

Morok tried to deflect her anger. "Just listen to that music, Counselor. I would give anything to produce sounds like that, wouldn't you?"

Myssa lifted her chin. "Mr. Chairman, the staff voted unanimously for extermination. I cannot believe you are calling for a full hearing of the commission."

Morok issued a command and the music stopped. He locked his eyes on the counselor. "Your staff made a recommendation, Counselor. The commission has chosen to reject it and hold a full hearing."

Myssa blew out a sharp hiss. "*You* have chosen to reject it."

"Does my vote not count?" They both knew that as head of the commission, Morok had full veto power.

"But my staff has studied this tribe for more than two decades! We know the horrors they are capable of—"

"I shall submit new evidence, Counselor, and I fully expect the commission to uphold my position. Now please allow me to—"

"What kind of new evidence?"

"You will learn that at the hearing."

Myssa gave a slow blink. "This is unprecedented! By law, we should have appeared jointly to present *both* our views."

Morok studied her. She was ambitious and competent, but treading on dangerous ground. He sharpened his tone. "The commission studied all the supporting evidence. What could you have added?"

"I could have responded to any new arguments you brought up."

"I brought up no new arguments. I simply asked for another hearing."

Myssa made a derisive sound. "And who will testify at this new hearing?"

"Here is my witness list."

She took the list, glanced at it, gave Morok a slow blink. "It is a very short list."

"It is sufficient to address the concerns we have."

"The concerns *you* have!"

Morok's green-gold eyes reflected his emotions the way crystals reflect sunlight—they sparkled, glowed, flashed, blazed, mirroring the quality and depth of the emotion. Now they glittered as he stared at the counselor.

She persisted. "*I* know how the majority of the commissioners feel."

"Perhaps so, but we *will* hold the hearing." Morok stood and unfolded himself to his full regal height. "Schedule it, Counselor. *Now.*"

Myssa hesitated, then bowed slightly and left the room.

Morok took a deep breath, then pressed another button and gazed out the window taking in the splendor of a Yxrian sunset.

Drakk soon entered the room carrying a small case. He was a Luvash, humanoid in shape, slender and quick on his feet. His skin was a rippled mass of cartilage tinged with blue. His hair formed black ringlets that fit his head like a cap. Like all Luvashites, he was highly telepathic, aided by the two small antennae protruding from the top of his head and the large ear-like spiral in the center of his rippled forehead. Due to their retractable parts and thick cartilage skin, clothing was optional with the Luvash, but Drakk had a closet full of thin, tight bodysuits in an array of colors and fabrics. Today he wore a black suit laced with silver threads that followed the rippled contours of his body.

"Let me see the witnesses you've selected," Morok said.

Drakk extracted a small device from the case. He moved his thumb rapidly over the controls until a three-dimensional image of an alien male specimen appeared in front of them, revolving slowly in the space between the desk and the window.

Morok studied the tight pale skin on the face of the alien, the defenseless body that demanded clothes. The arms were sparsely covered with fine light-colored hair, and the hands were splayed into fragile fingers that had little power of their own.

"Closer," Morok said, and the face of the specimen hung in the air before him. The eyes were the color of the Yxrian sky in the seventh month, and they glowed with an intelligence and compassion that was rare in a species so primitive. "What is the name of the witness?"

"Stephen Hopkins," Drakk said, his antennae quivering slightly. "I have watched him closely for several months. His experience with primitive cultures might convince the commission that the Namuh are worth saving."

7

"But will it convince Myssa?"

Drakk stuttered a laugh. "Probably not. But why does *she* have to be convinced?"

"If we cannot convince one of our own staff, how can we convince a group as diverse as the commission?" Morok motioned toward the hologram. "You said you had two witnesses."

Drakk nodded. "This one is female," he said, moving his thumbs over the control.

CHAPTER 2

Stephen Hopkins read the last page of the bound galleys of his manuscript and scrawled his initials on the title page. The book was finished, finally, seven hundred and fifty-nine pages brimming with passion and fury. He felt as if he'd come home from a tough, dirty war. In a way, he had. For six years, he had struggled to balance objectivity with an obsession to expose corporations whose greed for profits destroyed primitive cultures. He battled daily with his inner demons, which pressed for stronger language and more venomous attacks. He clashed with his publisher on the specificity of his language, on the naming of important names, even on the title of the book, but he'd prevailed in every case because of his reputation and his devotion to meticulous research. That research would show how Gorr Resources funneled political bribes through religious organizations in order to influence votes and favors for logging concessions. In a few months, *Merchants of Evil* would hit the bookstores, and the world would learn just how unscrupulous Ethan Gorr was and how far reaching the effects of his corruption.

Stephen glanced at his watch: five-thirty. He had to hurry or he would be late for his son's sixteenth birthday celebration. He laid the galleys on Nancy's desk so that she could return them to the publisher on Monday, then he shut down his computer. He headed out the door just as his private telephone rang. He picked it up, expecting his wife to reprimand him for being late, but it was a male voice, one laced with full rich tones that made Stephen's chest vibrate.

"Professor Hopkins, you are an anthropologist with expertise in primitive cultures, are you not?" The caller spoke with a stilted rhythm that suggested English was not his native tongue.

"Yes," Stephen said. "Who are you?"

"I represent the Commission for Emerging Cultures," the caller said. "We are holding a hearing on the subject of innate violence in a species. It is the ability to *unlearn* violent behavior in which we are particularly interested. We find your work with primitive tribes quite relevant, and we wish you to testify as an expert witness."

"When?" Stephen asked.

"Now. A black limousine is parked across the street from the south gate of the university. You will leave your office and enter the limousine which will transport you to the hearing."

The caller rang off. Stephen stood for a moment in silence, contemplating the strange call. Then he put on his coat and gloves and wrapped his cashmere muffler around his neck. He walked down the stairs and out the front door of the anthropology building. In November at five-thirty, it was already dark and chilly, but Stephen didn't notice. He walked without thinking, a man on a mission.

He stopped just outside the gate. A black limousine was parked near the bus stop across the street. He waited as a city bus pulled up, discharged two passengers, and pulled away. Then he crossed the street.

As Stephen approached the limousine, the rear passenger door swung open. He climbed in, expecting to greet whoever had opened the door, but found no one there. All he could see was his own reflection in the opaque windows, lit from some hidden interior light.

The air seemed oddly alive, as if there were a breeze inside the car. As he shifted in his seat the breeze grew stronger, eddying around him in a counter-clockwise motion. Then the air swirled faster and faster, sucking him into a vortex. Abruptly, the spin reversed and Stephen felt as if he were dissolving into the air itself.

Particle by particle, he vanished.

CHAPTER 3

Stephen Hopkins regained consciousness on a bus bench across the street from the south gate of Georgetown University. He sat stiffly erect in a gray overcoat like a man unaccustomed to sitting on bus benches. Slowly, he became aware of a man in a dark parka crossing the street, head tucked down against the wind. A yellow Volkswagen screeched to a halt at the traffic light. Abruptly, Stephen snapped to total awareness.

He was sitting on a bus bench with no idea of how he got there.

He pushed his glove back and looked at his watch: 10:04. Saturday. *What happened to Friday night?* His thoughts flew back to the last thing he remembered, leaving his office, walking across campus. Had he sat down on this bench and passed out? *Had he spent the night here?*

He stood up, confused. Ran a hand over his chin and felt stubble. Took a mental inventory of his body. He felt no pain, not even stiffness from the cold. He didn't feel groggy or sleepy, just cold and hungry and confused.

He found his wallet in an inside coat pocket and went through it. American Express card, Visa card, eighty dollars in cash, District of Columbia driver's license. Nothing was missing. He studied the license. The photo showed the same angular face and square chin he'd seen in the mirror when he shaved Friday morning. He recognized his name, his address on Olive Street, his height (6'1"), weight (195), eyes (blue), hair (brown). The license would expire in three years on his forty-fifth birthday. His memory seemed to be intact—except for whatever had happened last night.

What the hell happened?

His heart sank. Yesterday was Gerard's birthday, and Penny had planned a special dinner at home. Did that mean he hadn't gone home? He had no memory of driving home or driving anywhere for that matter—*where was his car?* He looked around; it was nowhere in sight. Maybe it was still in the parking lot. But why couldn't he remember? He had a photographic memory. He could remember minutia like the page number of a particular passage in a book and whether it was on the right-hand or left-hand page. He could remember detailed conversations, even entire speeches if the speaker impressed him enough.

He closed his eyes and tried to focus on the last thing he did yesterday. He finished proofing the galleys of his book, and laid it on Nancy's desk, and then he left his office...
His eyes snapped open. *The black limousine*! It had been parked near the bus stop where he now stood. He remembered crossing the street and climbing into it.

There his memory stopped, as abruptly as if someone had taken scissors and snipped it at that exact point.

Two dark-colored SUVs passed in front of him, going in opposite directions. Across the street, a student with a backpack trudged toward the campus gate. Stephen's office was just beyond that gate. He should simply walk over there, call home, and ask Penny if she knew what had happened.

He started to cross the street, then stopped. A girl sat on her backpack about ten feet away, her head buried in her phone. She looked like a student, in faded jeans, fur-lined boots and a red fleece jacket. He walked toward her.

"Excuse me, young lady, this may seem like an odd question, but do you know how long I've been sitting over there?" He pointed toward the bus bench.

She stared at him appraisingly. "Now, there's a novel pick-up line."

"No, no, no, I'm not hitting on you, I'm married. I'm a professor at Georgetown. I'm not sure what happened but...I don't know how I got here. Did you see me get off the bus or out of somebody's car?"

She gave him an amused smile. "Well, I'd usually notice a handsome guy like you, but no, I didn't see you until just now, when you walked over here. Is something wrong?"

He fumbled in his pockets. "I've misplaced my cell phone. I need to make a call." He turned to leave.

The girl stood and pulled a phone from her coat pocket. "Here, use mine."

"No, I'll just walk over to my office..."

"Stephen!"

A woman in a black leather jacket and gray knit cap trotted toward him. A pale blue muffler was looped around her neck.

"Stephen, are you okay?" She placed her hand on his sleeve. "Where have you been all night? I've been frantic."

Relief flooded him. The blue eyes looking up at him belonged to his wife. He touched a dark curl that peeked from beneath her cap.

"Stephen, answer me! When you didn't come home last night, I drove through the parking lot and saw your car, so I made the security guard let me in your office. I just knew I'd find you slumped over your desk."

"Ma'am, I think the professor has had some sort of memory lapse."

Penny Hopkins glanced at the girl, then at her husband. "Who is she?"

"I... I didn't get her name."

Penny's blue eyes turned frosty. "You don't know her name?"

"Of course not. I just walked over to ask her if she had any idea how long I'd been sitting on that bench over there."

"You slept on a bench all night?"

"I don't know where I slept. I don't remember anything after I left my office yesterday afternoon."

"You can't be serious."

"I'm telling you the truth."

"He is telling you the truth, ma'am," the girl said.

Penny shot her an icy look and took Stephen's arm. "Let's go," she said, tugging him toward the van.

Stephen looked back at the girl. She shrugged and gave him a faint smile.

#

Penny turned the van onto N Street. She had brushed off Stephen's suggestion that he drive his own car home. "We'll get it tomorrow," she snapped. "I don't want you to disappear again."

He could feel anger radiating from her like heat from a furnace. He could see it in the tight thin line of her lips, in the white of her knuckles grasping the steering wheel. But what could he say when he didn't know where he had been or who he had been with? Maybe he had blacked out and slept on the bench. Maybe he'd developed a split personality and cruised Georgetown bars all night. He felt as if he were in the middle of a nightmare.

"How's Gerard?" he asked.

"Crushed that you missed his birthday."

"What did you tell him?"

"I lied. I told him you probably got lost in your research at the library and forgot the time." She stared straight ahead. "Are you going to tell me what happened?"

"I don't remember what happened."

"The man with the photographic memory? Please!"

He hugged his arms to his chest. It was as if sixteen hours had been surgically removed from his mind, leaving the surrounding memories intact. All he could remember of the missing hours was the black limousine, and if he mentioned that without knowing who was in it or where it had taken him—well, that could set off all kinds of alarms in Penny's head.

"Why didn't you at least call me?" she said.

"I didn't have my cell phone."

"Where is it?"

"I don't know where it is. I don't know where I was, I don't know what I did."

He glanced at his wife's profile, saw a muscle in her cheek twitch. He touched her shoulder. "Penny—"

She flinched. "Don't!"

He pulled his arm back and slumped in his seat. They drove the rest of the way home in silence. When she pulled into the garage, she got out of the van and slammed the door so hard Stephen half expected the window to shatter.

He followed her into the kitchen. "Where's Gerard?"

"In his room." She eyed him in suspicion. "Were you attacked? Did someone mug you?"

He shook his head. "I'm okay. Physically."

"But you don't remember anything?"

14

"No."

She held his gaze for a moment. Then she went out to the sunroom and closed the door behind her. A signal that she didn't want him to follow. He tried to imagine how he'd feel if she'd disappeared for a whole night and told him a similar story. He would have a hard time believing it. He headed upstairs to find Gerard.

#

Penny leaned against the sunroom door feeling as if her insides had turned to stone. Had she driven Stephen into another woman's arms with her constant anger and resentment? She had rebuffed him earlier in the week when he wanted to have sex. If she were honest with herself, she had to admit that she almost always rebuffed him, and when she did give in, resentment about the shooting overwhelmed her. How could they ever bridge the gap between them if she couldn't stop blaming him for what happened to Gerard?

The whistling of the birds drew her to the aviary at the far end of the sunroom. Three cockatiels—Noah, Joseph, and Solomon, or Solly as Gerard called him—shared a space the size of a small room. Mesh wire covered the front of the aviary, which was filled with tropical plants and rocks, perches and swings, and a five-foot waterfall at the back.

She opened the door and held out a finger. Noah, her favorite, stepped on to it. He was pure white with a two-inch plume atop his small, round head. The bird looked at her, cocked his head, said, "Love you" in a high, child-like voice.

She studied the bird, wondering, as always, if he knew the meaning of his words. She carried him across the room and sat down on a wicker chaise. Noah walked up her arm and perched on her shoulder. Joseph and Solly flew out of the aviary door and landed in a ficus tree. Solly, mostly brown with a yellow head, whistled an unrecognizable tune while the multi-colored Joseph did his patterned chirping.

She stroked Noah's neck, eliciting a sort of trilling purr, but this time the bird failed to calm her. She had to find out

15

where Stephen had been last night. If he had been with a woman …well, she couldn't bear to think about that.

#

Stephen stood in the doorway to Gerard's room and watched him peck at his computer keyboard. The boy resembled him to an astonishing degree. He had the same blue eyes, same square chin, same tousled hair, Gerard's a few shades lighter and an inch or two longer than Stephen's. His black t-shirt revealed a thick chest and muscular arms that came from lifting himself into and out of a wheelchair every day for the past six years. His legs, wasted and immobile in the chair, looked as if they belonged to another body.

Stephen felt the usual wave of guilt at the sight of them. "I'm sorry I missed your birthday last night," he said. "I'll make it up to you."

Gerard stopped typing. "Mom said you were at the library."

Stephen didn't know how to respond.

The boy hunched his shoulder and leaned forward. "You can tell me the truth, Dad." He grinned slyly. "I'm sixteen now and in some cultures that's the age of manhood."

"You'll think it's weird," Stephen said.

"Well, it must have been important. You wouldn't miss my birthday unless it was important."

Stephen's throat tightened at the total trust in his son's voice. "The problem is, I don't know where I was."

Gerard's eyes widened. "What?"

"Do you mind if I come in?"

Gerard gave a palms-up shrug. "Please."

Stephen sat down in the director's chair, the only other chair in the room, and told his son about getting in the limo on Friday afternoon and waking up this morning on a bus bench. "I have no idea what happened after I got into that limo."

Gerard made an immediate guess. "Seems to me that whoever was in the limo abducted you. Maybe they took you somewhere to interrogate you." He was warming up to his idea.

16

"Maybe it was the FBI and then they drugged you to erase your memory. They can do that, you know. Did they beat you up?"

Stephen smiled at Gerard's active imagination. "I'm quite sure no one beat me up, but the abduction part seems right. I don't want to scare you, but you need to stay alert for anything that seems strange or unusual...cars, people, phone calls. I couldn't bear it if something bad happened to you again."

Gerard's face tightened. "It wasn't your fault, Dad. If I had it to do over, I'd still go with you to Mondogo."

Stephen felt a sudden weariness. All he wanted to do was to lie down and sleep for days. He patted his son's shoulder and wished him a happy birthday again.

As he headed to his bedroom, a swirl of vertigo gripped him and he leaned against the wall to keep from falling. He suddenly remembered that he had felt the same vertigo in the limousine, almost like he was being sucked down a rabbit hole. He continued down the hall as a barrage of images came at him, a luminous gray wall encircled with a black metal strip, odd looking faces that seemed to melt before his eyes, a swirl of blue-green plumes. A thin female voice grated in his mind like chalk on a blackboard, repeating the strange sound "nah-moo."

He stripped off his clothes and got into bed. Had his six-year vendetta against Ethan Gorr finally shredded his mind? But that strange phone call yesterday really happened, and there were sixteen hours he could not remember. Whatever took place after he climbed into the limo was connected with those images and with that nah-moo sound, which echoed like a mantra in his head.

CHAPTER 4

When the door clicked shut, Gerard blew out a deep breath. He hated the way his dad walked around with that dopey guilt-stricken look on his face, and now there was another layer of guilt for missing the stupid birthday dinner. He was just as sick of his mom's coddling. She treated him like a helpless puppy, still asking if he needed help every time she saw him move to and from the chair, and he'd mastered that two months after the frigging accident. But he had lied to his dad just now. He *did* wish he had not gone on that trip to Mondogo, wished he hadn't been shot. He hated that he couldn't walk, and he hated being treated like an invalid.

He turned back to his computer, thinking about his dad. It seemed weird that someone would just snatch him and take him for a joy ride and then dump him back at the same place. Weirder still, his dad didn't remember where he'd been taken.

Impulsively, he spun his chair around, shot to the end of the long room that his parents had created from his old bedroom and the upstairs guest room. They'd installed a wide teak shelf that circled the four walls except for windows and doors. As it went around the room, the shelf widened for a computer desk, narrowed for bookshelves and a sound system, widened again for a long study desk. He had an alcove for a closet, another fitted with a long twin mattress and recessed at one end for a television and bookshelves. The room was his haven. No sharp corners, no narrow passageways, just lots and lots of space.

He wheeled to the computer and logged back on to KASA, using his codename G-Man. Stargunner and Moleman were still online.

stargunner	hey man where'd u go
g-man	my dad just came in
stargunner	u at home i thought ur a college boy
g-man	its my birthday, im home for the weekend
moleman	hey man, happy birthday
stargunner	what r u, about 19
g-man	my dad says he was abducted last night

moleman	no shit
stargunner	what do u mean abducted?
g-man	someone forced him into a limo and took him somewhere brought him back this morning and dumped him on a park bench
stargunner	any clues who did it
g-man	he doesn't remember a thing
moleman	sounds suspicious to me
g-man	whatever i gotta go study
stargunner	hey man its early
g-man	maybe in cali its after ten here see ya
moleman	good luck gman
g-man	ty moley

Gerard logged off. He wondered what Moley meant by *suspicious*. Moley was an intern at the Pentagon and was always telling cloak-and-dagger stories about the military. Didn't he believe someone in ordinary life could be abducted too? If Gunner had said it sounded suspicious, he'd respect that. Gunner was a junior engineer in the space industry on the West Coast, and he was the smartest guy Gerard knew. Someday he'd like to meet him, Moley too.

Then again, maybe not. If he did meet them in person, they'd find out he wasn't a junior at Georgetown like he said. Wasn't a star on the college tennis team. Couldn't, in fact, play tennis or any other sport. He was relieved that they'd agreed early on not to communicate via Zoom, FaceTime, voice, or anything but chat. Because as Joan-of-Right, founder of KASA once wrote, 'We don't care what people look like.' KASA had thousands of members worldwide, but Gerard spent most of his time in a private chat room with Moley and Gunner. The three had connected online a few years ago and remained fast friends.

Gerard rolled to the study desk and spread out his books. Maybe it was better to stay unseen online buddies. Three Musketeers in cyberspace. After all, he didn't have to meet them to solve the mystery of his dad's abduction.

CHAPTER 5

Alone in his New York penthouse overlooking Central Park, Ethan Gorr paced the floor and chewed on a cigar while waiting for a conference call with his brothers on the West Coast. He needed their approval on a logging contract he'd negotiated with the president of Bolivia. And that pissed him off. *He* was CEO of Gorr Resources and the only one of the brothers who actually worked for the company, yet he had to adjust his schedule to accommodate their endless rounds of golf, horse races, ski trips and jaunts to one goddamned island or another. The least they could do was be punctual, but already they were thirty minutes late. Still jerking him around like they had when they were kids.

He stopped at the window and puffed on the cigar. Next to him a telescope was trained on a window across the park. The blonde who lived there had a bedtime ritual he didn't want to miss. He looked at his watch again. Nine o'clock. She wouldn't start for another hour.

He punched a button on the remote and a Salvador Dalí painting slid to one side to reveal a video screen. He punched more buttons, then flopped down on the sofa to review the video presentation his staff had made for his upcoming trip to Bolivia. He paged through his itinerary, a bio of President Barrios, two pages advising him of certain customs he should be aware of: *The President often thrusts his face close to yours in conversation. Don't back away even if he has bad breath...*

Ethan grunted. He didn't need a primer on how to talk to the president of Bolivia.

The phone rang. Ethan clicked to a live image of the building concierge. "I have your brothers on the line, Mr. Gorr."

"Put 'em through," he growled. He took a long pull on his cigar and laid it on the ashtray.

The screen went dark, then split into a Zoom call with J.P. on the left, Doug in the middle, Ritchie on the right. They looked like aging surfers with tanned faces, white teeth, sun-bleached hair.

"You're late," Ethan snapped.

"Hey, runt, not even a 'hello how are you?' J.P. said. Doug and Ritchie laughed.

"This is a colossal waste of time," he said. "A simple logging contract shouldn't need board approval."

"That's how we keep you on the straight and narrow," Doug said.

"It's what Gramps wanted," chimed in Ritchie.

Ethan bit back a retort. The only reason his brothers were in control is because Gramps hadn't changed his will after Ethan's father was killed in a car wreck. The will provided for a three-person board to control the actions of the CEO, and it worked fine as long as Gramps was on the board, but after his death a series of reshufflings put his three brothers in control. The old man would turn over in his grave if he could see how it had turned out.

Ethan outlined the terms of the contract. After the brothers rubberstamped their approval, he said, "I'll present it to Barrios on Thursday."

"You're flying all the way to South America to deliver a contract?" J.P. said.

"I always deliver my contracts in person."

"Seems like a waste of money to me," J.P. said.

"Huge waste of money," said Doug.

"Yeah," said Ritchie.

Ethan tried to keep his tone civil. "I've increased our profits tenfold since Gramps died. You got a problem with that?"

"Touché," J.P. said.

"Keep up the good work, runt," said Doug.

"Yeah, keep it up," echoed Ritchie.

Ethan rang off without saying good-bye and pressed a button to return the Dalí painting to its place. Someday he would tell his brothers how much he hated them, but right now, he needed the legitimacy of Gorr Resources to mask the activities of ERG Holding Company. He had set up the holding company to get around his brothers' control of his salary, a left-over provision of the old man's will, but ERG had turned out to be his own private money machine. For every contract he negotiated for Gorr Resources, he negotiated one or more non-timber deals for ERG, and those profits flowed straight through ERG into a numbered bank account in the Caymans. His grandfather would be pleased that he'd found a way out of the straightjacket imposed by the will.

He looked at his watch. 10:02. He relit the cigar and went to the telescope. He centered the viewfinder, pressed the 1200-millimeter zoom. The blonde across the park came into sharp, voluptuous focus. Gorr smiled. She gazed out the window for a moment. Gorr's eyebrow raised. *This isn't her ritual.* The woman reached down, picked up a giant pair of binoculars, looked Gorr straight in the eyes, and flipped him off with a sneer. Gorr quickly ducked out of sight, as she furiously closed her blinds.

"What is this world coming to?" Gorr mumbled to himself. He pressed another button and all the windows of his penthouse went from clear to dark.

CHAPTER 6

Hands grabbed Stephen, shaking him. Hard. He tried to shrug out of their grasp. He heard someone call his name from far away.

"Stephen. *Stephen!*"

He struggled toward the sound.

"Stephen, you're having a dream, wake up."

He opened his eyes. He was groggy, disoriented.

Penny was sitting up in bed, shaking his shoulder. "What were you dreaming? You were moaning and saying something that sounds like *nah-moo*."

He tried to focus on the dream. He had been walking through smoking rubble with people moaning, calling for help, reaching for his legs as he plodded through thick layers of ashes and dust, stepping over broken shards of glass and concrete. Over it all, like an echo in a canyon, floated a sound. *Nah-moo.*

"Stephen?"

He focused on his wife who was looking at him with concern.

"What is that word—*nah-moo*?"

He had no idea. "It was just a dream, Pen. Go back to sleep."

"Do you want to talk about it?"

"No."

"Are you sure?"

"Go back to sleep."

"Suit yourself." She turned over and burrowed beneath the covers.

He glanced at the clock on the nightstand: 3:35. He knew there was no going back to sleep. He got out of bed, put on his robe, and padded next door to his study. It was his sanctuary in the big house, much as Gerard's room was his son's retreat and the sunroom, Penny's. The walls of the study were lined floor-to-ceiling with books. At the far end of the room, a black leather recliner sat next to a matching sofa and a small coffee table. A large teak desk sat at a right angle to a window overlooking Olive Street. He normally spent most evenings at the desk, working on his book, grading student essays, or researching some knotty problem that dogged his work. Occasionally, he relaxed in the recliner with a novel. Sometimes, when he was restless and fearful of disturbing Penny, he slept on the sofa.

Tonight, as he lay on the sofa, his mind kept returning to the missing hours on Friday night. He thought of the minutes leading up to the phone call at his office. All he could remember was that low melodious voice telling him where the limousine would be parked and to go get in it. He had followed the voice's instructions like an automaton, asking no questions as far as he could remember. And that was not like him.

Did that mean he'd been drugged? But how? Surely, he would remember that. Maybe the voice on the phone hypnotized him in some way. What else could explain his willingness to take instructions from a stranger? He tried to force more images from his memory, but nothing came. The next thing he remembered was waking up on the bus bench.

He could not sit still. He put on Rachmaninov, walked over to the window and looked out at the sky, a dull yellow glow reflecting city lights. It made him wish for the darkness of the rainforest which used to cloak him in blackness so thick it was palpable. He and Penny would sit outside their hut late at night and listen to the night-sounds and talk until dawn. They had been missionaries then, young and in love. That was when they were on the same life path, before he left the church.

The haunting strains of *Vocalise* began, and Stephen was filled with a longing. For what? Communion? Redemption? He felt he'd had no choice but to leave the church, but it had alienated the two people closest to him, his wife and his father, particularly his father. "You're there to save souls," his father had said every time Stephen complained about the missionaries spending money on bibles instead of food and building churches instead of desperately needed hospitals. When he rejected missionary work in favor of anthropology, his father had been hurt and angry, and their estrangement deepened after the shooting in Peru. Now he was as likely to go to his father for solace as he was to go to Ethan Gorr.

He kept coming back to Ethan Gorr. Gorr had a motive: to stop the publication of Stephen's book. But once the book was published the suspects might include other corporations, politicians, and foreign governments.

What if they kidnapped Gerard next time?

Was he again placing his son in harm's way by publishing the book?

CHAPTER 7

Stephen arrived at his office at eight o'clock Monday morning tense with anxiety and groggy from lack of sleep. Dreams of death and destruction continued to haunt him. Last night he'd dreamed about snipers shooting down into the crowds on the National Mall from the top of the Washington Monument. Tourists in brightly colored shorts and t-shirts dropped to the ground, their blood turning the Mall's green grass a dark, vivid red. He had looked up to see a gray-haired man in a window at the top of the Monument, head cocked to one side, eye jammed into the eyepiece of a rifle. As he watched, the man's face grew to the size of a cloud, then morphed into a dozen faces, then a hundred, all peering through viewfinders, all shooting rifles at the colorfully clad tourists on the Mall. And above the roar of the gunfire, he heard a sort of chant: *Nahmoo! Nahmoo! Nahmoo!*

He'd told Gerard about the dream at breakfast and together they had googled different spellings of the 'nahmoo' sound, thinking it might be a mantra the abductors had used to hypnotize him. Google had matched the word with a fictional character, a Korean singer, a makeup brush, a graphics art company, a Canadian exporter, along with dozens of websites written in various oriental languages. None seemed to have any connection with Stephen's abduction.

The sound was the only real clue. The face of the man he'd seen was nondescript, ordinary, like someone's genial uncle. But the sound was distinctive. He thought it might be related to his work. If it had turned up even once in his research, Nancy would remember it. He had called her several times on Sunday, but there had been no answer on her home phone or her cell.

He paced his office, impatient to talk with her. She had not been at her desk when he left on Friday, so she must have left early. But why? He stopped abruptly as his thoughts shaped the unthinkable.

Had she been abducted too?

Maybe she had turned up on a different park bench on Saturday just as confused as he had been. Or maybe she was one of the abductors. He mulled this thought for a moment. Nancy adored Reverend Hopkins, and months before the shooting, his father had brought Ethan Gorr to the university office, where Nancy had been taken in by Gorr's abrasive charm. If either of them was behind this, it was possible she was too.

He gave himself a mental shake. He *was* being paranoid. Nancy was one of the most open, straightforward people he knew. He could not imagine her involved in anything clandestine.

By nine o'clock, she still had not arrived. He called her home and her cell. There was still no answer and no machine picked up. Maybe she was ill. Maybe she was lying unconscious on the floor of her apartment. He lifted the phone to call the police, then replaced it, feeling foolish. There could be a dozen reasons why she was late. He would wait until noon and then he would drive to her apartment to check on her.

At eleven-forty-five, the phone rang. It was Nancy.

"Where are you?" Stephen said. "Are you okay?"

"What?"

"I've been calling you all weekend, your machine doesn't pick up, I couldn't get through on your cell—"

"I forgot to turn on my answering machine and worse, I left my cell phone at home. It's making me crazy to be so out of touch. That's why I called. To see if you need anything."

"You're not at home?" Stephen said, suspicion creeping back into his voice.

"I'm at Williams College for the training session in the new linguistics software. Don't you remember?"

"No."

"You suggested it! You said it might help with the Ponsuelo dialect."

The Ponsuelo were a primitive tribe in Paraguay, the subject of his newest research. If Nancy said he suggested she take the course, he must have done so.

"Dr. Hopkins, are you alright?"

"I'm fine." He hesitated. "Nancy, did you take a phone call for me on Friday about 5 o'clock?"

"No. I left early. I had to do some shopping for the trip and you told me to take the rest of the afternoon off. Don't you remember?"

"What time did you leave?"

"About three-thirty."

He frowned. He suddenly remembered that the call came in on his direct line. The only people who had that number were Nancy, Penny, Gerard, and his contact at the State Department. Oh yes...and his father. He had thought of changing the number after the Abigo shooting, but had never got around to it.

"Dr. Hopkins?"

"Nancy, have you ever heard of a 'nahmoo'?"

"A what?"

"Nah-moo." He exaggerated the syllables.

"You mean, *moo* like a cow?"

He hesitated. He'd never thought of it like that. "I guess the 'moo' part is like a cow—*nah-moo*."

There was a long silence before she spoke. "No, Dr. Hopkins. I don't believe I've ever heard of a namoo."

Stephen thought he could hear suppressed laughter in her voice. He hung up, somewhat annoyed. He was tired of being treated as if Friday night had been some sort of mental aberration. He had disappeared for sixteen hours, he had frightening nightmares, he was walking around with a feeling of dread that he couldn't name, and he was not making the whole thing up.

He had to find out what happened to him, but he hadn't the faintest idea of how to go about it.

CHAPTER 8

Across the Potomac in McLean, Virginia, the Reverend Marshall Hopkins paced the floor, a glass of red wine in one hand, telephone in the other.

Should he call again or not?

Indecisiveness was not his nature, but every few weeks he went through the same ritual. He would call Stephen's number, hoping his grandson would answer. When voice mail picked up, as it usually did, he would hang up. It was futile to leave a message because neither Stephen nor Penny would return his calls. He had not spoken to his son in four years, and it'd been almost two years since he'd talked with Penny.

He set the wine glass on the desk and punched a number into the phone. A woman answered.

He hesitated. "Penny? Is that you?"

After a moment Penny said, "Hello, Reverend."

That's what she used to call him, *Reverend.* "Penny, my dear, how are you?"

"I really shouldn't be talking to you."

He could hear something in her voice, a softening, an opening he might be able to walk through. Instinctively, he switched to The Voice, as his wife used to call it, a voice he had honed on his weekly calls to the altar, a low Southern tone laced with warmth and honey. In the old days, the Voice had filled pews on both sides of the aisle in the small Southern churches where he began his ministry. Later, it had lured millions to his radio and television shows, men and women alike, rich and poor, sinner and saint, and it was the Voice, as much as the message, that charmed the dollars out of their bank accounts and sucked them through the airways like soda through straws.

"You know it's not right for us to be estranged like this, Penny. You're the heart of our family, you can bring us back together again." He picked up his wine glass, took a sip, waited for her response. "Penny? Are you there?"

"I'm here."

"How is Gerard?"

"He's doing fine, Reverend. He's going to a private high school now. He's learning to drive the van."

The reverend's eyes misted. "You know how I feel about that boy. What happened wasn't my fault."

"I know, it's just that Stephen still believes Ethan Gorr was responsible and you were with him down there—"

"Guilt by association?"

"Something like that."

"But my dear, I know Ethan didn't do it, and furthermore, he was never charged with any crime."

"Stephen says Gorr did the dirty work for the Peruvian government, which means they'd hardly indict him. My son is the only one who's had to pay for their crimes."

The reverend took the Voice to a deeper, more intimate level. "What happened to Gerard was a tragedy, Penny. It was one of those awful coincidences that he was there in the first place and in the line of fire. But it wasn't a deliberate act by Gorr or anyone else. Can't we just leave it in God's hands?"

She didn't respond.

He tried again. "Please let me see my grandson."

"I can't do it, Reverend. I'm sorry." She hung up.

He sighed and put down the phone. His long estrangement with his son had begun long before Gerard's accident. It had started with their disagreement on how to spend the church's money. Stephen thought it should be used for food and medical supplies for the poor, especially those in primitive tribes, but the reverend's work was saving souls, pure and simple. That's what God had called him to do. That's why people followed him. His followers were simple, uneducated people for the most part, and they sent money to save their own souls from hellfire and damnation. They wanted the glittering church on the Potomac that he built with their money. Even though many would never set foot inside its doors, it gave them inspiration and hope.

He paused at the desk and refilled his wine glass. When the phone rang, he grabbed it eagerly. Maybe Penny had changed her mind.

"You know anything about the garbage your son is writing?"

The hair on the back of the reverend's neck stood up at the sound of Ethan Gorr's voice. "What do you mean?"

30

"Well, I'm looking at his manuscript and it isn't a pretty picture."

"Manuscript?"

"He's writing a book about his friends, the Abigos, and guess who he's painting as the villain?"

"How did you get a copy of his manuscript?"

"I have my ways."

The Reverend was silent.

"Let me read you a few choice paragraphs," Gorr said.

Gorr Resources is a privately held company that owns concessions to logging and mineral rights in forests and lands belonging to primitive tribes in dozens of third-world countries. The company's modus operandi is to enlist the help of the ruling governments to move the tribes off their lands and onto virtually uninhabitable reservations, after which, Gorr Resources moves in its logging or mining operations. The money that Ethan Gorr uses to bribe officials is a tiny percentage of the profits his company derives from harvesting the trees or stripping the mines.

The question becomes, then; how did an obscure company like Gorr Resources gain such concessions from the governments of foreign countries?

The answer? Through the influence of the government of the United States.

And how did Gorr gain this influence? By lining the pockets of the highest-ranking politicians in the country. Not directly, of course, but by funneling money through religious organizations— organizations that use Political Action Committees (PACs) to spread the wealth to individual politicians and to the Republican and Democratic National Committees.

"It goes on like that for a very long chapter."

The Reverend dropped into a chair, dazed. "Does it name names?"

"Other than mine? Not yet. But if it's published it could wreak havoc with my future relationships with foreign governments, especially those that need a little help from the boys at the State Department. It might dismantle agreements that are already in place. It could even screw me out of awards on domestic issues. Now how do you think that might affect you?"

The Reverend knew exactly how it would affect him. He wouldn't be able to meet his commitments to the dozens of congressmen and senators to whom he'd pledged financial support, support that came indirectly from Gorr's contributions to his ministry. Most of the money stayed in the church, but some of it was used to gain influence and further the mission of his ministry.

It would be bad enough to lose face with them and with the president, but if he were involved in a public scandal, he could lose his credibility as a man of God. He could lose the trust of his followers. He would not let that happen.

"I will do whatever I can to help you," he said, "but nothing immoral or illegal."

"Relax. I just want a meeting with your son. You get me that and I'll take care of the rest."

"He hasn't spoken to me in four years. How can I get him to talk with you when I can't even get him to talk with me?"

Gorr's voice grew cold. "You think about what's at stake. You'll figure out something."

#

Gorr looked down at the green oasis of the park. It didn't seem right to strong-arm a man of God, but protecting the company his grandfather had entrusted to him was his first and only obligation. He would stop at nothing to protect that legacy.

CHAPTER 9

Penny set the phone in its holder. She wanted desperately to tell the reverend about Stephen. His nightmares were getting worse. Last night, he'd had one that troubled her more than all the others. He had sat up in bed, eyes opened wide, and said in a voice filled with sorrow, "You're going to kill us all and there's nothing we can do about it." When she touched his cheek, it was wet. *Are you awake?* she whispered. He didn't answer, just stared at something she couldn't see, a stricken look on his face. He lay down finally and went back to sleep, but she spent the rest of the night wondering who he thought was going to kill them all.

She thought about calling the reverend back. He had always been so easy to talk to. During Stephen's frequent trips to South America, he was always there for her and Gerard. He would take them out to dinner, and after Gerard had gone to bed, they would talk for hours. *How she missed that!* But Stephen had been furious the last time she let his father see Gerard. He considered his father a traitor because of his relationship with Ethan Gorr, but the reverend's friendship with Gorr preceded the shooting, so if her father-in-law was guilty of anything, it was of nothing more than bad judgment. Still, she couldn't talk with him about Stephen until she found out what had happened on Friday night.

She closed her eyes. *Please, God. He couldn't have been with another woman. I'll try to be a better wife. I'll try to forgive him for what happened to Gerard. I promise.*

She paced the room, feeling as if her head would explode. She had to talk with someone. She went upstairs to Gerard's room. She hesitated outside his door, then knocked lightly.

"It's open."

As usual, he was pecking away at his computer, bobbing to some tune streaming through that thing in his ear. She worried about the music he listened to. About the time he spent online chatting with people he didn't know and would never meet. But what could she say? Music and the internet were his life.

"I need to talk to you," she said, raising her voice above whatever he was listening to.

"Sure, Mom." He pulled the earbud out of his ear and laid it on the desk. "What is it?"

"Your dad's having some crazy dreams." She told him about the dream.

"You can't take dreams literally, Mom."

"I know, but I'm worried. Has he talked to you about Friday night?"

"He told me about the limo and the phone call. And about that 'nahmoo' sound. We googled it but didn't seem to have any connection to anything."

Penny blurted out the thought that had been troubling her. "I thought maybe he was seeing someone else—"

Gerard stared at her. "You mean another woman?"

She looked at his trusting young face. She shouldn't have said that.

He laughed. "That's silly. Dad wouldn't do something like that."

She still wasn't sure, but she couldn't say that to her son. She'd said too much already. "Of course, he wouldn't. Maybe it had something to do with the State Department, like he said."

Gerard tilted his head, squinted at her. "I thought maybe he told you what had happened and you were keeping it from me."

She shook her head. "Whatever he remembers about that night, he's keeping it to himself."

"Maybe he should see a shrink."

"Why?"

"I've read about people recovering their memories through hypnosis. Maybe he could get hypnotized and find out what happened."

She thought about it for a moment. They had gone to a couple's therapist a few months after the Abigo shooting. During the second session, she had vented her rage about his taking Gerard on the trip, and he had sat there, guilt-stricken and silent. He had refused to go back. "Your father would never go to a therapist."

"He might. He seems pretty freaked out by this whole thing."

"Maybe if you ask him. He would do almost anything you ask." She wanted to touch her son's cheek, kiss the top of his head, but she knew that would embarrass him. Instead, she said, "Dinner's at six."

He grinned. "Always is."

She went to the sun room and was greeted by shrieking from all three birds. She hadn't paid enough attention to them today. She opened the aviary door and they flew out, Noah in the lead. They circled the room for a few minutes, still shrieking. That was the part she didn't like. In the beginning, she wasn't sure she would like the birds at all. She had bought them for Gerard a few months after the accident, but their care fell on her shoulders, and she very quickly found herself drawn to their intelligence and affectionate nature. She taught Noah to talk and sing and Solly to whistle a dozen tunes. Joseph refused to do either.

She stretched out on the chaise and waited for the birds to calm down. She was spending more time with them since Gerard started private school in September. She had home-schooled him for so many years that when it stopped, she became despondent. She had loved watching his mind leap from subject to subject, then dig deeply into one that caught his interest: dinosaurs, primitive man, U.S. history, astronomy, the last Presidential race, and now space exploration. He had started pressing her two years ago to let him go to a public school, 'like other kids.' You aren't like other kids, she had said, and immediately regretted the words.

Then he and Stephen joined forces and wore her down. She set about researching private high schools in the District. Openings were few. Most parents had enrolled their children when they were in kindergarten, and often before. Emerson Preparatory finally accepted him when they learned about his disability. He had done so well on the placement tests that he'd started the semester as a junior. Now she wondered what she would do when he went away to college. As selfish as it was, she could hardly bear to think about him not needing her any more.

She felt a bird land on top of her head, its claws digging lightly into her hair. She held up a finger and Noah stepped onto it. She held him at eye level. "Hey," she said.

"Hi-de-ho!" Noah replied in his high thin voice.

Solly and Joseph had landed in the ficus tree and grew quiet. She stroked Noah's throat and thought about Stephen. *Was he having an affair?* The thing she had always loved about him was his honesty. Impossible, she thought. She couldn't imagine him being able to conduct a secret affair with all the lies and deception that would involve. But she knew she'd been cold and withdrawn since the accident. Who would put up with that for six years? But if he hadn't taken Gerard on that trip, *if he'd listened to her*, they would have a normal sixteen-year-old who could ride bikes and play ball like other teenagers.

Resentment is like a cancer, Penelope; what you won't forgive will eat you alive.

She could hear her father's voice as clearly as if he were in the room. But when she thought about her son in that god-awful wheelchair, she could not forgive Stephen.

She lay back and closed her eyes. She had to learn how to forgive him for Mondogo and for whatever had happened Friday night. But how can you forgive something when you don't even know what it is?

#

Gerard touched the mouse and the KASA chat screen reappeared. Moley worked at the Pentagon, maybe he'd know whether the State Department would do something as extreme as kidnap a person.

g-man	hey
moleman	welcome back where'd u go
g-man	my mom came in she's worried about my dad
stargunner	he still can't remember who kidnapped him huh
g-man	she thinks he's seeing another woman

moleman	my old man did that once…my mom almost got him thrown out of the pentagon
stargunner	stupid adults
g-man	hey moley u know anything about the state department
moleman	like what
g-man	like, would they ever put out a hit on someone u know tell a guy they'll kill him or his family if he doesn't do what they say.
moleman	sure pentagon does it all the time
g-man	you serious?
moleman	ever heard of covert operations? that's when they do a bunch of stuff in secret and i bet they've killed plenty of people
stargunner	yeah the state department's in cahoots with the cia and the fbi they're all sociopaths you know every last one of em just watch em run for cover when the youth of america takes over the world
moleman	lead the charge gunner
stargunner	im ur man

Gerard pushed back from the desk and stared at the screen. Moleman was just an intern; he wouldn't know what went on in covert operations at the Pentagon. He was just blowing smoke. And Gunner was so radical he'd say anything against the government.

He picked up a forty-pound weight and did some curls with one arm, then switched arms. Whatever had happened on Friday night, his dad had not done anything wrong, and he was going to help him prove it. He returned to the computer, googled the words 'recovering memories from traumatic experience' and pressed Enter.

"Transient global amnesia is a sudden, temporary episode of memory loss that can't be attributed to a more common neurological condition, such as epilepsy or stroke. During an episode of transient global amnesia, your recall of recent events simply vanishes, so you can't remember where you are or how you got there."

Gerard stared at the screen, picked up the weight and resumed curling.

CHAPTER 10

He is climbing through mountains of rubble, following the cries for help. He tugs at great shards of steel, tries to move broken sheets of glass with his bare hands. The cries grow fainter and he stumbles on, blood dripping from his lacerated hands. The stench is unbearable. A wheel pokes through the rubble in front of him. He grabs it, strains to pull it out. He braces his feet and gives one final tug and the wheel pulls free of the rubble. It is attached to an empty chair.

Stephen woke up breathing hard, his heart racing. He tried to grab the image hovering at the edge of memory. There had been some kind of wreckage, but the harder he tried to remember the further the dream receded. It had been like this all week. He would toss and turn for hours, then awake before dawn with vague intimations of death and destruction. Try as he would, he could not wrest a single clear image from the dreams except for the stern visage of a gray-haired man and the haunting sound of *nahmoo.*

He looked at Penny sleeping peacefully beside him, then at the clock on the nightstand. It was 2:21. One week ago at this very moment, he had been in the middle of whatever had happened during his abduction, in the middle of the black hole that now he kept peering into, which refused to yield a glimmer of light. He thought about going to his study to wrestle with his memory, force it to open up, but he was so exhausted he turned over and went back to sleep.

When he awoke again, light was streaming through the window. He dressed and went downstairs. Penny was at the breakfast table reading *The Washington Post.* He had barely glanced at a newspaper all week, too consumed with his own worries to have any interest in the outside world. He sipped his coffee and waited for the caffeine to kick in and energize him to some minimum level of action.

After a while, Penny lowered the paper and laid it beside her plate. She met his eyes.

"You look as tired as I feel," he said.

She said nothing for a minute. "When is this going to stop, Stephen?"

39

He sighed, shook his head.

Gerard rolled up to the table. He glanced at his mom, then handed Stephen a sheaf of papers. "Look at this, Dad."

Stephen looked at the top sheet. It was a copy of an article entitled '*Exploring the Nature of Suppressed Memories.*' He gave his son a quizzical look. "What's this?"

Gerard leaned toward him. "People who've had an amnesiac episode can be hypnotized to recover their memories. That's what you had, wasn't it? An amnesiac episode? According to this article, you can find out what happened to you that night."

"Hypnotic regression is about uncovering past lives. You know I don't believe in that."

"That's not what this is about, Dad. It's about recovering memories from a traumatic event that a person has blocked out of his conscious memory. It says regression therapy's been used in abuse cases where the person remembers years later what happened—"

"Most likely, the memories are planted in the patient's mind by the therapist."

"Dad, look at the writer's credentials. Surely doctors like her don't do that."

"I don't know, son—"

"Would you just read it? I've got to go finish a paper before class."

"You have a class on Saturday?"

"Extra credits for astronomy." Gerard wheeled away from the table.

"We need to leave in thirty minutes," Penny called after him.

"I'll be ready."

Stephen thumbed through the sheets, then read the author's biography. Robin Parker was a psychologist with a doctorate from Stanford and a private practice in the District. He scanned the article. A traumatic event can block a memory from the conscious mind, she had written, but the memory is not erased. If the conscious mind is sufficiently stimulated, it can open a pathway to the memory which is still there. She suggested the analogy of smelling a certain food one had known as a child and unlocking a stream of memories associated with that smell. Like the madeleines of Marcel Proust. The same mechanism causes the flashbacks reported by victims of violence.

That sounded plausible to Stephen, and so did the process described by the author. The therapist regresses a hypnotized patient to the last available memory before the gap, then guides the patient forward in time from that point. It was much like the natural process of finding something that has been lost. He'd tried that with the events on Friday afternoon, but his memory stopped short at entering the limo. *Could hypnosis take him beyond that point?*

Penny watched her husband. Whatever had happened to him Friday night was seeping into his nightmares, and that had her worried. "Could I see the article?" she asked.

He handed it to her.

She scanned it quickly, then handed it back. "I think you should try it. Neither of us is getting any sleep. You toss and turn all night, and I wake up every time you move. I don't know how much longer I can take it."

"Pen, what's the worst experience of your life?"

"What?"

"Gerard being shot, right? Remember how you felt?"

She stared at him, confused. When he called her from the Lima hospital, her world had imploded, and sometimes she still felt as if she were trying to climb out of the ruins. "What's your point?" she asked.

"On the flight to Lima when I was holding his little body I was consumed by fear and dread…fear that he would die before we got to the hospital and dread of what the next few hours, days, months would bring. Now I'm walking around with those same sorts of feelings and I don't know why. When I wake up from a nightmare the feelings are overwhelming that something just as awful, or worse, is going to happen."

Penny felt a flash of anger. To compare whatever had happened to him Friday night with their suffering about Gerard…she took a deep breath and tried to stifle her anger. "Your problem seems to be *not knowing* what happened on Friday night. Doesn't it make sense to try to recover your memories?"

He looked deflated, as if she hadn't said the right words. "So, you think I ought to go see this Dr. Parker?"

"You've got nothing to lose, Stephen."

She watched as he picked up the article and began to read it. She no longer believed that his absence had anything to do with another woman. What it might be instead she couldn't imagine.

CHAPTER 11

Stephen sat in the office of Dr. Robin Parker on the third floor of a mid-rise near DuPont Circle and watched the doctor study his patient form. Her dark blonde hair was pulled back in a ponytail, and a pair of tortoise-shell glasses perched on her nose. He guessed she was several years his junior and felt a sudden flush of embarrassment. How could he possibly tell her he had been abducted?

She looked at him over the rim of her glasses and smiled. "Dr. Hopkins, I notice you didn't answer the question about why you're here. Would you like to tell me?"

"I understand you do regression therapy."

"It's my specialty."

"That's why I'm here." He folded his arms across his chest and crossed his legs.

"You want to be hypnotized?"

"Yes."

"Why?"

Stephen felt decidedly uncomfortable. He stared at the doctor, unable, unwilling, to put his experience into acceptable words.

She laid the patient form on the desk. "Why don't I get a little background to provide a context for the therapy? I see you're a professor at Georgetown. What do you teach?"

"Anthropology. I teach one class each semester. Most of my time is spent on research."

"What's your specialty?"

"Primitive cultures of South America."

"Have you been published? I find it helpful to read anything my patients have written."

"My most interesting article was published six years ago in the *National Journal of Anthropology and Sociology.* It was based on my study of the Abigo tribe in Peru. "

"And the title?"

"The Negative Effect of Modernization on Primitive Cultures."

She scribbled the name on her pad. "I gather from the title you don't approve of modernizing primitive cultures."

He gave a faint smile. "A few enlightened souls in the State Department and the UN share my disapproval, I'm pleased to say."

"Are you involved with the UN and the State Department?"

"They call on me from time to time to evaluate primitive tribes."

"Tell me about one of the tribes."

Stephen felt himself begin to relax. He loved to talk about his work. He told her about the Abigo and about the funerary rites. "The Abigo were a peace-loving tribe that took care of even their lowliest members. They had a crime rate of virtually zero. They did have, however, a controversial funerary rite of ritual cannibalism."

Dr. Parker's eyebrows shot up.

"It wasn't a violent practice," he said quickly. "The tribal shaman took me to the tribe's sacred cave one day and explained it to me. He said the leaders make the choice, and when a leader is ready to make the journey to the Afterland, as he put it—when he's ready to die—he is offered to their god, whom they call Abigondo. They have a special ceremony in which they make a stew of the body, and the young Abigo males eat the stew and the whole tribe celebrates."

Dr. Parker looked somewhat skeptical. "And the purpose is?"

"To transmit to the next generation the attributes of the leader...his bravery, his wisdom, his special knowledge. They believe this helps them grow stronger and wiser each time a leader dies."

Dr. Parker said, "And this tribal shaman, would he be one of the leaders...eaten?

Stephen nodded. "I asked him that, and he said yes, it was the only way for a leader to be sure he would be welcomed in the Afterlife."

"I see."

"I'm not sure you do. The Abigo revere their leaders, and when one passes, the leaders who took part in the ceremony string the deceased leader's teeth in their necklaces. The more teeth displayed in a necklace, the more powerful the leader." He thought of Ganbigo touching the ancestral teeth on his necklace like rosary beads, naming the leaders to whom they had belonged: Ramu, Razulu, Wandigo. Others whose names he couldn't remember.

"This ceremony is confined to tribal leaders?"

"Well, not always."

Her eyebrows shot up again. "And when is it not?"

"I got involved with the Abigos because of publicity about their cannibalism. A missionary had died while he was with the tribe, and I was asked by the State Department to investigate the rumors of cannibalism. It turns out the missionary had a heart attack, and they were honoring his request to take part in the ritual."

Dr. Parker had been scribbling on her pad as he talked. Now she regarded him with a frank stare. "So, they were in fact cannibals."

"Only in the ritualistic sense of the word."

"That's quite fascinating," she said with a faint smile. She glanced at her notes. "Tell me about your wife."

"We met on a missionary expedition in Brazil. We were married during the four years we spent there."

"You were a missionary?"

Stephen nodded. "A long time ago."

"You no longer do mission work?"

Stephen gave a derisive laugh. "Hardly."

"What happened?"

Stephen thought for a minute. How could he put in a few words a complicated transformation that took years? "Let's say I became disenchanted."

"With the natives?"

"No, I loved the native people. I became disenchanted with the crusade to convert them to Christianity."

"Wasn't that what you were there for?"

"That was what the church was there for. I was there to help the people."

"Is your wife still doing mission work?"

"No. She got her master's in special education. Now she's a contributing editor to various journals in her field." He shifted uncomfortably in his chair, glanced out the window. The

45

tip of the Washington Monument peeked through the bare limbs of a Japanese cherry tree. In a few months, the view would be obscured by pale pink blossoms, then by glossy green leaves. Today, traces of the recent snow clung to the bare limbs.

"How's your marriage?"

He jerked his head toward the therapist. "Fine. My marriage is fine."

She jotted a note on her pad.

"My marriage has nothing to do with why I'm here."

"A routine question, Dr. Hopkins. Why don't you tell me about your son?"

Stephen blew out a breath. "Gerard just turned sixteen; he's a real computer nut, serious but funny too, very intelligent. Penny home-schooled him."

"Why was that?"

"Why did my wife home-school our son?"

"Yes."

He crossed his arms over his chest. "I don't think that's relevant."

She held the pen mid-air, looked at him over her glasses. "Everything is relevant in therapy, Dr. Hopkins."

He curbed an impulse to walk out. He did not like this prying into his personal life. "Look, I came here to find out what happened during sixteen hours of my life that went missing. Everything else is irrelevant."

She laid the pen on the desk. "Parents have a reason for home-schooling a child. Sometimes it's because of conflicts within the school or fear of school violence; sometimes it's for religious reasons or to accommodate a child's special needs. Before we talk about your missing hours, it would be helpful to know your reasons for home-schooling your son."

Stephen hesitated, then plunged ahead. "If I tell you my wife thought it'd be easier on Gerard to be home-schooled because he's a paraplegic, then you'll want to know how he became a paraplegic, and if I tell you that, then you'll want to explore the guilt I've carried around for the past six years and—" He stopped abruptly.

Dr. Parker regarded him with calm gray eyes. "And you're not here to talk about all that."

He glared. "I'm here to recover my memories during the abduction." There! He had said it.

"Your abduction?"

He held her gaze. "I was abducted on the night of November 5."

She studied him for a moment. "May I call you Stephen?"

"If I may call you Robin."

The corners of her mouth turned up slightly. "Who abducted you, Dr. Hopkins?"

"If I knew that, I wouldn't be here, would I?"

"All right. Let's start with the day you were abducted. Tell me what happened leading up to the point where your memory stops."

He uncrossed his arms, grasped the chair arms lightly, and told her what he remembered about Friday afternoon and waking up on the bus bench the next morning. He concluded, "I have no memory of where I was or what happened to me during those sixteen hours."

"Do you drink?"

"Occasionally. But I don't have a drinking problem and I didn't have an alcoholic blackout. I was abducted, kidnapped, spirited away...call it what you want."

"Do you have any idea why you were taken?"

He hesitated. *Should he mention his number one suspect?* "It might have something to do with my research."

"Your anthropology research?"

"Yes." He stood. "Do you mind if I stand? I think better on my feet."

"Not at all."

He began to pace in front of the desk. "Six years ago, the Peruvian government moved the Abigo tribe to a reservation nearly a hundred miles away from their homeland. Ostensibly, it was to teach them the *civilized* ways of the world and ease them into the twenty-first century. But shortly afterwards, the Peruvian government awarded logging rights to the Abigo rainforest to a company called Gorr Resources. The Abigo were able to retain rights to about forty percent of their land, presumably so they could return home one day. But Gorr Resources has pretty much depleted the sixty percent they were given, and now they want the rest of it."

Dr. Parker looked puzzled. "So, you think that somebody from this company might have spirited you away to do…what?"

"Ethan Gorr is his name. He wants to coerce me into stopping publication of my book." He told her about the book and why Gorr would not want it published.

She scribbled on her notepad as he talked. When he finished, she looked at him for a long moment. "Tell me again, exactly what happened on Friday afternoon. Start with the last thing you remember."

He paced as he told her about the phone call, walking across campus, getting into the limousine. He paused in front of the desk and looked down at her.

She held his gaze. "So, you got into the limo and you don't know who was in it."

"I know it sounds like a stupid thing to do, but when you work with the State Department, as I frequently do, you don't think twice about covert operations."

The glint of amusement in her gray eyes annoyed him. It was probably a mistake coming here, but he'd had no choice. Penny had insisted.

"You seem agitated, Dr. Hopkins. Why don't you sit down and try to relax? Relaxing may help you remember something."

He shook his head. "I'm an anthropologist, doctor. I'm trained to observe, to remember details. That's always been easy because I have a photographic memory. I remember conversations word for word, as if I've pushed a Play button inside my head. I can close my eyes and describe in detail the inside of the shaman's hut in Mondogo that I haven't seen for six years, but I can't remember a damn thing about what happened to me on Friday night except what I've told you."

"Have you had any unusual dreams since that night?"

He thought of the unrelenting nightmares, the feeling of dread that colored his every waking hour. "There have been dreams."

"Tell me about them."

48

He told her about the war-torn villages and devastated battlefields, about the images of the gray-haired man and the pervasive *nahmoo* sound. "I haven't had a full night's sleep in two weeks."

"What are you feeling right now?"

"What am I feeling?"

"Yes, don't try to *remember* anything, just tell me how you feel."

He felt his energy drain away, as if someone had pulled a plug from the soles of his feet. He sank into the chair and tried to relax. "I have this feeling of doom. I've had it ever since I woke up on that bench two weeks ago. It's like…it's like I'm aware at some level that something very bad happened or is about to happen."

#

Robin Parker studied her patient's face. For the first time since he began talking, she felt she was on solid ground. But she must proceed cautiously. "I can imagine how vulnerable you must feel, Dr. Hopkins. Has your family been supportive?"

"My son has. He's the one who found your article on the internet and suggested I see you. Penny's trying, but she's having a harder time with it. You can imagine how she felt when I didn't come home that night. And how much worse she feels when I can't tell her where I was."

"Does she believe that you don't remember where you were that night?"

"I'm not sure."

Her patient looked noticeably relaxed now, head resting on the back of the chair, legs stretched out in front. "Did you tell her about the gray-haired man?"

"Apparently, I talk in my sleep. She tells me I keep repeating the nahmoo sound." He gave her a faint smile.

"And the gray-haired man, Dr. Hopkins. Does she know about him?"

"What little there is to know."

"How's your sex life?"

"*What?*" Stephen sat up, feet on the floor, ready to pounce. Or run. "What the hell does that have to do with anything?"

She saw a flicker of anger in his eyes, or perhaps it was panic. Either was a realistic emotion of a heterosexual man who'd had a homosexual experience. A truly homophobic man can go into amnesiac shock after an encounter. If that is what it was, it was her duty to bring it to the surface. "Dr. Hopkins, have you ever had erotic feelings for a man?"

Stephen stood abruptly. "*Jesus Christ*! Does everything have to be about sex with you shrinks?" He jerked his coat off the back of the chair and strode toward the door.

She was surprised by his strong reaction. "Please, Dr. Hopkins. I'm trying to help you."

He looked back at her, one hand on the doorknob. "So, what was that? One of your absurd tests? Call the patient a homosexual to see how he reacts?"

"Of course, not."

He crossed the room and leaned over her desk, his face red with anger and frustration. "I don't have time to play games, doctor. I read an article that says you're a respected therapist who specializes in clinical hypnosis. I want you to use that talent to help me uncover the memories that I *know* are there."

She pushed her chair back reflexively. "You're not afraid of what we might discover—"

He cut her off. "I assure you I can handle *anything* we find out—even if it turns out that I fucked a gray-haired old man named Nahmoo!"

CHAPTER 12

Stephen left the doctor's office in a rage. He had expected to get his memories back in one session. Probably could have, if Dr. Parker hadn't insisted on digging around in his past. He retrieved his car and headed toward Georgetown, replaying the session in his mind as he drove. Parker had touched on things he'd just as soon not think about, like the state of his marriage, but that was not the most pressing thing on his mind. Over the past week his dreams had become more vivid and personal. Soldiers murdered women who looked like Penny and bludgeoned children who looked like Gerard. The feeling that something awful was going to happen to him or his family was actually happening every night in his dreams, and those dreams had draped him in a miasma of impending doom.

He headed toward Rock Creek Park. Penny and Gerard would be home, and he was much too agitated to talk to them. He parked the car and started walking. The day was overcast, windy, and bone-chillingly cold. He looped his Burberry muffler twice around his neck, jammed his hands in the pockets of his grey overcoat, and walked head down into the wind. He walked fast to burn off the emotions created by the session. All he wanted was to recover the memories of that Friday night, not to stir up the guilt from his whole wretched past.

He felt embarrassed at his outburst at Dr. Parker. It was not like him to lose his temper, particularly at someone he had just met, someone who was simply trying to do her job. But nothing was *like* him anymore. He was haunted by dreams at night, engulfed in a fog of guilt and impending doom during the day. Dr. Parker had implied he might be repressing memories too awful to examine. He was not so provincial as to think something shameful could not happen to him, but with all his heart, he didn't believe that was it.

"On your left!"

Stephen stepped to the right as two boys whizzed by on skateboards. He stopped and watched as the boy in the lead yelled something over his shoulder to his friend. As they raced on, the sound of their laughter lingered, and the memory of another day in Rock Creek Park came flooding back.

He had taken his son to the park for the first time since the shooting. From the beginning, Gerard had refused to be pushed, insisting from day one on maneuvering the chair himself. On that warm spring day five years ago, Stephen was walking beside him, resisting the urge to put his hand on the back of the chair. They moved along, father and son out for a stroll in the park, the boy turning the wheels of his chair with arms that were growing more muscular every day. Two boys about Gerard's age skateboarded past them single-file, yelling and laughing, and Gerard had stopped and looked after them with a raw longing on his young face that tore at Stephen's heart. Then he pushed ahead of his father, furiously turning his wheels.

Just as Stephen pursed his lips to call out a cautionary 'Be careful,' Gerard shouted, "Hey Dad, look at this" and raised the small front wheels off the ground and spun the chair on its rear wheels. As Stephen looked on with a mixture of fear and awe, his son tipped the chair onto one wheel and then he was spinning around and around, spinning like a dervish on wheels, like a dancer on ice, three full turns at least, before landing on all four wheels facing his dad. He threw out his arms and gave a triumphant "Ta da!"

Stephen had been astonished. When had he learned to do that? What ancestral vein had he tapped for the courage to even try? Certainly not Stephen's. Had he been in the same condition, he would have become bitter and angry, but there was his son, happily spinning in Rock Creek Park on his provisional legs.

Now he watched the two boys disappear beyond the trees, chastened by the memory of his son's courage. Dealing with a few missing hours was nothing compared with what his son had gone through. *Still* went through every day of his young life.

He turned around and headed back to his car. Whatever had happened to him that Friday night had not harmed him physically, and he would not let it continue to consume his mind. He would return to Dr. Parker and recover his memories. Then he would deal with whatever they might reveal.

CHAPTER 13

Stephen returned to Dr. Parker's office the next day. He had requested a two-hour session to accelerate the process, and the doctor readily agreed. She seemed as eager as he to discover what lurked in his memory. Now he watched quietly as she fiddled with the controls on a recorder. Would today's session reveal anything of substance? He felt yesterday had been a waste, but perhaps all that probing had been necessary. All he told Penny and Gerard was that there was nothing yet to tell.

"All right, let's get started." She took a pendulum from her desk and turned on the recorder. "This is Dr. Robin Parker. The patient is Dr. Stephen Hopkins. The date of the session is Tuesday, November 16. Dr. Hopkins, I want you to concentrate on my voice. Relax. Breathe deeply."

He tried to relax, tried to breathe deeply.

She repeated the words, then added "You are getting sleepy, very sleepy."

His eyes drooped closed. Snapped open. He sat up straight. "It's not working, doctor. I was afraid I couldn't be hypnotized."

"Give it a chance. Lean back and close your eyes. Breathe deeply and concentrate on the sound of my voice."

Stephen focused on her soft, rhythmic voice. *Relax, breathe deeply, you are very sleepy*. He let her voice wash over him like an island breeze, and for the first time since the abduction, he felt himself start to relax. *Relax, breathe deeply, you are very sleepy*. He floated on the sound of her voice and let it carry him to another place.

"Tell me what happened on the evening of November 5th."

Stephen described the phone call, the sonorous voice of the caller, the walk across campus to the waiting limo, and the feeling of being sucked into the vortex of space. He fell silent for a long moment.

"Where are you now, Dr. Hopkins?"

"I'm sitting...in a small room."

"Are you alone?"

"Yes."

"Describe the room."

"It's round, no corners, no windows, gray walls, nothing on them. There's a black metal strip near the ceiling, like-like crown molding, but black with tiny holes, like a microphone or a speaker."

"What are you doing?"

"Shhhhh! I hear a voice… it's coming from the black strip." Stephen turned his head from side to side and grasped the arms of the chair.

"What's happening, Dr. Hopkins?"

"The meeting has started." His eyes moved rapidly behind closed lids.

"Dr. Hopkins—"

"It's the voice on the phone. It's Chairman Morok."

The doctor was struck by the change in Stephen's tone as he launched into a speech by someone he called Chairman Morok. His voice changed dramatically. The tone was low and vibrant, the cadence measured and formal.

"Over the past several years," Stephen intoned, "the staff of the Commission for Emerging Cultures has been monitoring a tribe that has been identified as uniquely violent and dangerous. In our long and eventful past, we have occasionally imposed quarantine on a dangerous tribe but rarely have we voted for extermination, as recommended by the staff.

"I understand that to protect ourselves and the world we live in, extermination may prove inevitable, but because of the severity of such a verdict, I have called for this hearing. I believe this tribe possesses inherent qualities which call for a more creative solution. We will hear expert testimony today in that regard and I ask the commissioners to listen with open minds.

Stephen leaned forward, then blurted out in his own voice; "They're talking extermination! My briefing said nothing about extermination!" He moved restlessly in the chair.

"Relax," Dr. Parker said. "Breathe deeply."

Stephen took a deep breath, then another. He resumed speaking in his own voice. "Someone called Counselor Myssa is talking about how sick this tribe is. She says it may be genetically flawed. She says members of the tribe defile their own nests, destroy their own habitats, kill each other in violent conflicts. She pledges to present facts to back up her claims."

Stephen fell silent.

"Go on, Dr. Hopkins. Tell me what you're seeing?"

Stephen moved his head from side to side, murmuring, "No, no, no."

After a few moments, he cleared his throat and began speaking in his normal voice. "Mr. Chairman, Counselor, members of the commission. My name is Stephen Hopkins. I am an anthropologist specializing in the study of primitive cultures. I understand that I am to use my specialized knowledge to testify on behalf of the tribe that is the subject of this hearing.

"Yet I was summoned here only a few hours ago and I've had little time and few resources with which to prepare my testimony. With all due respect, I find it unconscionable that you would seek to judge the ultimate fate of a tribe on the testimony of one person."

He jabbed his palms on the arms of the chair. "Furthermore, I question the intentions of this commission. For all I know, this hearing is a farce and you merely seek to take over the Namuh's lands for your own use. That has been the fate of other tribes I've defended. The more primitive tribe always succumbs to the more advanced. So, let me remind you who I am.

"*I am Namuh*. I am a member of that tribe you wish to remove from the face of the Earth, and I assure you, given sufficient time and resources I can present convincing evidence of the worth and dignity of the Namuh race…if you are indeed who you say you are.

Dr. Parker grew alarmed watching him. He was breathing rapidly, his face was flushed, his hands gripped the arms of the chair so hard his knuckles had turned white. This had happened only once in her practice, and the patient had been psychotic for several weeks afterward. She could not risk that again. She had to bring him out of hypnosis.

He took several deep breaths, as if he were trying to calm himself. His hands relaxed. His breathing returned to normal. She waited another thirty seconds and decided to let him continue…

#

Forty-five minutes later, Dr. Parker brought Stephen out of the trance. "When I count to three, you will be fully awake. You will be calm and relaxed, and you will remember everything."

She watched him closely as he emerged from the trance. He had been under almost sixty minutes, and now he slumped in the chair, eyes closed, arms limp in his lap. She had seen patients who became disoriented or fearful after a regression, as their repressed memories surfaced. Some wailed or cried silently; others became angry. One patient had picked up his chair and hurled it at the window, and she'd had to call security. But Stephen seemed to be processing his memories like a computer. He sat quietly and stared into space, a distant look in his eyes.

She would give him a few minutes. She too needed to collect her thoughts. She had witnessed a brilliant mind at work spinning a spectacular story of condemnation by an all-powerful primal source, complete with threats of retribution and possible redemption. It was a modern display of man's primitive talent for creating stories and myths. She didn't believe for a moment that any of it had actually happened.

She found Stephen looking at her expectantly. "How do you feel?" she asked.

"A bit overwhelmed."

"That's understandable. Do you remember now what happened the night you were abducted?"

"Every detail."

"How do you feel about it?"

He took a deep breath, let it out. "Relieved. Deeply disturbed."

"Relieved?"

"I'm relieved to know there's a basis for what I've been feeling. I know now there's a reason for my nightmares, a reason for these feelings of dread that I have." He gave her a rueful smile. "What do you think about it?"

She chose her words carefully. He seemed to be accepting the memories as reflections of actual events, which was somewhat alarming. "The human mind can create some very bizarre images when it is under stress."

He reacted as if she'd called him a liar. "You think I made it all up?"

"That's not what I meant—"

"You think I'm hearing voices? Seeing people who aren't there?"

"Dr. Hopkins, please. I know it is all very real to you—

"

He stood up, lifted his coat off the back of the chair. "Dr. Parker, you helped me get my memory back, and for that I'm very grateful. But I cannot countenance being called delusional."

"That's not what I'm saying—"

"We're finished, Doctor. If you'll give me the recording of the session, I'll be on my way."

She beseeched him, "We really should have another session or two. There's a lot we need to explore."

"There would be if I were delusional, and the fact that you think I am is insulting. But I got what I came for and I don't want—or need—any long-term therapy." He held out his hand for the recording.

Robin Parker hesitated. She could not in good conscience discharge a patient in Stephen's state of mind. On the other hand, he was no ordinary patient. He was highly educated, a trained scientist who showed no signs of mental disorder. If he chose to believe he'd been abducted by aliens from another planet, well, he wouldn't be the first one. She was reasonably certain he presented no danger to himself or anyone else.

She handed him a thumb drive with the recording, "Good luck, Dr. Hopkins. Please call me if you need to talk again."

Stephen stepped out into the cold gray day and started walking, hands jammed in his pockets, immersed in his memories of what had happened during those sixteen missing hours. He rewound the tape in his mind and watched it all unfold again, solving at last the mystery of the gray-haired man and the *nahmoo* sound. The feeling of dread that had plagued him now had a known source. The memories had been retrieved, but their retrieval created a whole new mystery, one that felt like a ticking bomb strapped to his back that no one on Earth could disarm.

Why had this burden fallen on his shoulders?

He stopped with a jerk when he realized he had walked several blocks past his car. He turned around and headed back. He would tell Penny and Gerard exactly what had happened. But would they believe his story? He didn't doubt that the extraordinary events he remembered under hypnosis had really occurred. They had the absolute ring of truth, and he had to find a way to stop what appeared to be inevitable. And because they rang true, he couldn't waste time asking, *why me?* To do that, he had to locate the one person in the world who might be able to corroborate his experience. A woman he remembered seeing entering the room where he'd been taken that night.

The problem was, he had no idea who she was or where on earth to find her.

CHAPTER 14

When Morok finally got word of the commission's verdict of extermination, he was surprised and dismayed. He immediately issued a veto, only the third of his long career. Did they not remember the tragedy of the Luvash? He could not let another such verdict stand without gathering every possible shred of evidence that the Namuh were salvageable. Now the matter would go before the Supreme Council of Arbiters, and there was much to be done. He summoned Myssa and Drakk to his office.

#

Drakk entered the chairman's office with great excitement. He had never been included in such high-level proceedings. He took the chair next to his colleague, his antennae quivering. Myssa did not look at him. She sat rigidly in her chair, reptilian arms folded tightly across her thin chest.

"I vetoed the commission's verdict of extermination," Morok stated.

"Oh." Drakk breathed out the word. "That means—"

Myssa cut in. "That means we present our case to the Supreme Council."

The Supreme Council! Drakk's antennae bobbed more rapidly.

"Exactly," Morok said. "To prepare, we must reconnoiter a number of different regions on the Namuh planet. Our objective will be to present a balanced view of the species, to show their strengths and virtues, as well as their love of violence. I have decided to send the two of you together."

"Why together?" Myssa looked at Drakk with distaste. "I operate more effectively alone."

Drakk glared at her. He tried to like her, but her cold reptilian stare always made him quiver.

"Sending you together is optimal," Morok said. "Myssa wishes to show Namuh violence in the worst possible light. Drakk wishes to ameliorate it. Somewhere in the middle we shall find the truth."

He handed each a glowing orb. "Here is your first assignment."

The corners of Myssa's mouth turned up slightly as she read it. Drakk appeared crestfallen.

"I strongly suggest you give it your best," Morok said. "The fate of an entire world depends on it."

CHAPTER 15

The Situation Room was President William Wainwright's favorite spot in the presidential mansion because that's where the real power of the presidency is wielded. It is the nerve center of the White House, where the Commander in Chief monitors crises around the world and commands U.S. military forces. Yesterday, from the Situation Room, Wainwright had ordered a preemptive strike on a nuclear facility in North Korea. Today, he hurried to that room for a personal report from the pilot who flew the mission.

Just over six feet tall with a runner's physique, thick gray hair, piercing blue eyes, and a ruddy, unlined complexion, Wainwright looked a decade younger than his sixty-nine years. The power of the presidency sat easily on his shoulders.

The staff seated around the conference table rose to their feet when he walked into the room. Today, eight made up the group, including Secretary of Defense Stuart Weiss and National Security Advisor Kimberly Dyer. Admiral Randy Tate, Chief of Naval Operations, had been video-conferenced from his ship in the Sea of Japan. The president motioned to the staff to sit down as he took his seat at the end of the table beneath the presidential seal.

"We have Commander Philip Spelling on the speaker phone, Mr. President." Kimberly Dyer said. "He's the pilot who led the mission."

"Did you accomplish your mission, Commander?" the president asked.

"Yes sir, Mr. President," the pilot said. "We scored a direct hit. The plant no longer exists."

"Way to go, Commander!" Wainwright punched the air with his fist.

Broad smiles lit the faces of the president's staff as they applauded and broke into excited chatter.

#

In their first joint surveillance, Myssa and Drakk stood in the corner of the Situation Room. An IVS rendered them invisible; telepathic communications made them inaudible.

"No one's asking about casualties," Drakk remarked with surprise.

"The Namuh don't care about casualties," Myssa scoffed. "All they care about is maintaining their supremacy."

#

The pilot's voice interrupted the chatter in the room. "We had a problem with the second missile, Mr. President."

"What kind of problem?"

"It inadvertently hit an apartment complex. According to my report, dozens of North Korean working families lived there. I'm sorry, sir."

"Was it a direct hit?"

"I'm afraid so. There's not much left of the building or anyone in it."

The staff was silent, waiting for the president's reaction. Wainwright stared into the distance. "Serves 'em right," he said at last. "They need to learn that none of 'em are safe as long as that idiot Kyung is in power."

The staff gave a murmur of concurrence.

#

Drakk was shocked into momentary silence. He had been championing the Namuh for decades, and now they were proving to be as violent and corrupt as Myssa said they were. "Hundreds of innocent people were incinerated" he cried, "and the Namuh leader says 'serves them right'! How can he be so callous?"

He glanced at Myssa. Her arguments for extermination were being made for her by the Namuh themselves.

Myssa's reptilian mouth curved into a smirk. "Wait till you see their violence at the religious and personal levels. This pales in comparison."

#

As they waited for Morok in his office, Myssa listened to Drakk drone on about the virtues of the Namuh, championing them still, even after what he'd witnessed in the Namuh's war room. In Myssa's opinion, he was irrationally involved with them, maybe because he was shaped like a Namuh, though he could never pass for one—not with those antennae and that spiral in the middle of his forehead. Myssa had heard rumors that Drakk spent his leisure time shadowing the Namuh, sampling their thoughts and emotions. The fact that his telepathy reached clear across the galaxy was irksome. She had to be standing next to an individual to intercept a thought.

Myssa grew increasingly annoyed as Drakk paced the room and muttered about the Namuh. Each time he reached the wall, he jumped a few inches off the floor and twirled a hundred and eighty degrees, then paced toward the opposite wall, antennae quivering with every step. Finally, she could stand it no longer. "Sit down!" she commanded.

Drakk halted in mid-sentence and looked at her, eyes the color of his jet-black hair. "Why?"

"It is torture watching your little jump-and-twirl. You don't do it in Chairman Morok's presence. I won't stand for you doing it in mine."

"It helps me think."

"Then stop thinking."

Drakk's pale cheeks turned blue with embarrassment, as he took a seat across from Myssa.

Her voice hardened. "We simply must exterminate that violent Namuh species. There is no alternative when violence runs rampant through the entire society. They know no other way to resolve disputes—"

"Not so," Drakk said.

"It *is* so." The iridescent veins in her green lizard skin glowed pink as she became more agitated. "There is violence in every facet of their culture. State to state. Religion to individual. Spouse to spouse. Parent to children. Children to parent. Children to classmates. When have we ever observed such a violent culture?"

"The fate of the Namuh is not up to us. Morok's veto has put it into the hands of the Supreme Council—"

"But—" Myssa's thin voice rose another octave, "we are the ones who present our case, and my argument is irrefutable."

"We'll see." Drakk's antennae quivered rapidly. "I have found that, given the opportunity to examine alternatives, the Namuh will often choose negotiation over violence. Furthermore, in my forays to Planet Earth I have seen a number of primitive tribes in which violence is absent."

Myssa waggled her lizard fingers in exasperation. "Pah! Forays indeed! You spend half your time interceding in Namuh affairs, which you know is forbidden. I should report you to the Commission."

"I am familiar with the Commission's regulations," Drakk said, his face flushing a deep blue. "But I document my intercessions if I think I'm in dangerous territory, and so far, no one has complained. Besides, Morok seems to accept that primitives on Earth are possible proof that the Namuh violence is an environmentally induced condition and not genetic. Quarantine is a much preferable option."

Myssa didn't agree. "Those primitives are but a tiny fraction of the Namuh population. Extermination is our only intelligent choice."

The door opened behind them. Drakk jumped to his feet and twirled toward the door. Myssa rose in a languid motion and waited.

"Sit," Morok commanded as he swept past them, blue-green wings trailing on the floor behind him. He sat down in his pod in front of the window. "Your conversation was quite unprofessional. I would not be surprised if the two of you ended up in Namuh-type violence."

Myssa and Drakk exchanged a glance at Morok's sharp tone.

He rested his elbows on the pod's arms and steepled his golden-ribbed hands. "I am fully aware that you think the Namuh not worth saving, Myssa. And Drakk thinks they can do no wrong, despite the incident described in your report."

Drakk ventured a rebuttal. "I was appalled by what I saw in that war room. But it is merely an aberration of a few individual Namuh."

"Hrmmph," grumbled Myssa. Her iridescent veins glowed pink.

Morok adjusted his wings and settled into the pod. "I have decided to accompany you on the rest of your surveillance. We owe the Namuh an objective assessment of their potential, and after this report, I do not trust that either of you will present your findings in an unbiased manner."

Myssa was unfazed by Morok's criticism. "It is Drakk who biases every report with his implausible emotions."

A dark blue flush crept up Drakk's face. "I do not!"

Myssa pointed a long finger at him. "You are the one who discovered Stephen Hopkins studying that ancient tribe in the jungle and convinced the commission to hear his testimony." She glanced at Morok. "I know you presented the witnesses, but Drakk convinced you that Stephen Hopkins should be on the list. He shadowed him for years—"

Morok's eyes blazed. "Enough! I will remind you that your careers will be on the line at the Supreme Council hearing. I expect your next surveillance schedule on my desk in the morning."

CHAPTER 16

Ethan Gorr handed a fat white envelope to the sharply dressed blue-eyed brunette standing in the doorway of his penthouse. "Count it," he said.

The woman removed her gloves and sat down cross-legged in the hallway and counted out one-hundred-dollar bills into three neat piles on top of the package she was delivering. When she finished, she looked up at Gorr. "Three thousand," she said with a faint smile, scooping up the bills and stuffing them back into the envelope. She stood up and put the envelope inside her jacket and handed the package to Gorr. "Happy reading."

"Tell you what," Gorr said. "I'll sweeten the pie with a bonus."

"A bonus?"

"An extra ten thousand if you can find a way to stop the publication of this book."

The woman gave him an appraising look, eyed the diamond ring on his pinky finger, the cashmere robe on his stubby frame. She looked over his shoulder at the painting in the foyer, a Chagall, maybe an original, and beyond the foyer to the living room with its sleek black and grey décor, the giant flat-screen the size of a wall, the lights of the high-rises across Central Park.

"Well?" he said.

"You overestimate my influence with the publisher, Mr. Gorr, but I'll tell *you* what…the next delivery will cost you a thousand bucks a chapter instead of five hundred."

"I thought we had a deal."

"We do. My rates just went up." She gave him a sly smile and headed for the elevator.

"Greedy bitch," he muttered and closed the door.

He stretched out on the sofa and lit a cigar and began to read. After two chapters, he wondered why he even cared whether or not the book got published, it was so deadly dull. He thumbed through page after page that described deforestation of rainforests, pausing occasionally when something caught his eye:

> Seventy years ago, rainforests covered 15 percent of the Earth's land surface; they now cover less than 6 percent. In

another thirty years, they may disappear entirely, along with them half the world's ten million species of plants, animals, and insects that make their home in the forests. A single tree in Peru, for example, has been found to be home to more than 43 species of ants.

Gorr snorted. Who the hell cares about 43 species of ants? Ants could disappear altogether, along with bugs and spiders and other crawly creatures he had seen in the jungles down there. Still, he knew every species was important in the ecological scheme of things. And that meant more profit. That's why he managed forests the way he did, taking care to disturb as few natural habitats as was feasible.

Another chapter described how the Amazon rainforest, which covers a billion acres in Brazil, Venezuela, Colombia, Ecuador, and Peru, produces 20 percent of the world's oxygen and that 25 percent of Western pharmaceuticals depend on rainforest ingredients, including cancer-fighting drugs like Vincristine.

Now that was interesting.

Gorr could carve himself out a nice little piece of pharmaceutical action for ERG Holding Corp, and his brothers would never see a penny. Maybe he would start with Carlos Barrios in Bolivia. Maybe not. Barrios had hinted about a covert transaction, in addition to the logging contract his brothers had just approved. And there was the clever shipping container proposal he planned to offer Barrios. Perhaps he should wait until he returned to La Paz in the spring. By then, the other deals would be well underway, and Barrios would be ripe for something new. As his grandfather said, never give a man of limited imagination too much to chew on at one time. Meanwhile, he could approach Enrique Serra in Ecuador about the pharmaceuticals. If Serra liked the idea, he might take it to Manuel Rameriz in Peru, a harder sell than Serra but possible nonetheless.

He scanned the rest of the manuscript, then slid it into a desk drawer. No bombshells in these chapters, although he already had reason enough to fear the book's publication. The only way to make sure that never happened was to put pressure directly on Stephen Hopkins, which meant he had to be sure the old man got him the meeting with his son.

#

An hour later, Ethan Gorr headed to the park for his monthly outing with his nephew. Tory was a bright, awkward kid with none of the slick charm of J.P., who had divorced Tory's mother six years ago. Ethan was crazy about the boy and secretly glad that J.P. was no longer in the picture, no longer able to steer Tory toward his own vapid, do-nothing life.

Tory was waiting for him at the south entrance to Central Park. He was a slightly built boy at fourteen, barely taller than Ethan, with the dark hair and dark eyes both had inherited from Ethan Gorr the First. It was part of the reason Gorr was so fond of his nephew.

"Sorry I'm late, boy. Let's head on over to the Tavern on the Green."

"No problem, Uncle E. I know how busy you are."

"Never too busy to miss our lunch, young man. How you doing?"

"My dad made fun of me for wanting to go to music camp next summer."

"What kind of music camp?"

Tory's face brightened. "It's a really cool camp, Uncle E. At Lake Saratoga? Mom had suggested it for my Christmas present. Serious musicians from New York all go there to work together on their music and they bring in really famous guys from all over the world to listen to our music and give us tips. Vincent Midoni will be there!"

"Who's that?"

"Just the top French horn player in the whole world. I'm dying to hear him, maybe get a few pointers. Plus, they put together a small orchestra to learn some advanced stuff with a guest conductor. It's three weeks of nothing but cool music."

Ethan glanced at Tory's animated face. The kid was a sweetheart. "Your dad didn't think it was cool?"

68

"You kidding? He thinks it's girly to play an instrument. Wants me to go to a baseball camp or football camp. Asked me why I was always Frenching a horn. He thinks he is so funny."

"He's a jerk, Tory. He was a jerk to me when I was your age and he's still a jerk. I'm sure your mom will arrange the camp for you. She loves music and she loves to hear you play."

As they approached the water conservatory, Ethan pointed out a tall slender tree. "Tory, take a look at this tree. Doesn't look like much, right?"

"I guess not. What is it?"

"It's a hornbeam tree. Horn means tough. What makes it special is that the wood is very, very hard. One of the hardest in the world. Some people call it ironwood or musclewood because it is so hard and the smooth bark has ripples that look like muscles. The Romans built their chariots of this wood. Today it's used for wooden bowls, furniture and anything that requires really hard wood. It's great for my business because it grows in the understory of much larger trees, and in a dense forest it doesn't branch much. Can you guess why that's good?"

"You can grow a lot of trees in a small space?"

"Right. It's not a fast grower, and it doesn't get very big, but we can sell the wood for big bucks and it's easy to harvest and replant." He smiled at his nephew. "You know what else is special about that tree? It's our tree, yours, and mine. We're hard and tough, you and me, we're worth a lot and we don't give a damn what others think."

Tory looked at him doubtfully.

He had to reach the boy, get him to understand that he had to be tough. "Do you love music, boy?"

"More than anything."

"Is it like a fire in your belly?"

"Well, yeah...maybe."

Ethan wanted to grab him, shake him hard. "Tory, you have to learn to use your daddy's ridicule like wood chips. Throw them on your fire to keep it burning. That's what I did. All my life, I took his taunts and scorn and used them to stoke the fire in my belly. I stoked my fire with his ridicule and with my mother's and Doug's and Ritchie's and all those snot-nosed kids I grew up with, and I turned it all into gold, just like King Midas. I got my revenge." Ethan stopped, breathless.

Tory wore a puzzled look. "I'm not sure I follow you, Uncle E."

Ethan paused. Was it good to motivate a kid with the idea of revenge? The point was to push yourself to succeed, but once you were there, once you had shown everybody, then you should be able to put the fire out and enjoy your success. But the fire had consumed him. Sometimes he thought it had gone nuclear and would keep raging forever. What if that happened to Tory?

"Uncle E, are you okay?"

Gorr took a deep breath. "I'm sorry, boy. I want you to keep that passion for your music, show your dad—show the world—how great you can be." He put his arm around Tory's shoulder. "Let's go in and have ourselves a fine meal."

When he returned home, Ethan wrote a check to Tory's mom for a figure he was certain would cover the music camp. "Fuck you, J.P.," he murmured.

CHAPTER 17

Stephen stood with his back to the fireplace and waited for his wife and son to join him. He could hear Penny moving about in the kitchen, talking with Gerard, preparing tea. *What would they think about the memories he had recovered?* Until now, Dr. Parker was the only person on earth who knew his story, and she thought he was making it all up. Would his family also think he was delusional? He watched snowflakes drift past the window and waited.

A few minutes later Penny came in carrying two mugs. The scent of cinnamon and oranges wafted toward him as she set one mug on the mantle. She took the other to the sofa where she settled under the blue afghan. Gerard pulled his chair next to the end of the sofa and set his soda on the coffee table. They looked at Stephen expectantly.

He took a sip of tea and set the mug back on the mantle. "The regression therapy was successful," he began.

"Cool!" Gerard said. "Do you remember everything?"

"Yes."

"Good. Maybe your nightmares will end now," Penny said.

But new ones may begin, Stephen thought. Instead, he said, "Dr. Parker thinks I had quite a fantastic adventure. She also thinks I imagined the whole thing. I want you to know that. But I also want you to know that everything I'm going to tell you really *did* happen. I don't know why it happened to me; I've been asking myself that question over and over. But the point is, it *did* happen to me, and it's very important that you understand what I'm about to tell you because I'm going to need your help."

Penny's face was inscrutable; Gerard's, open and expectant.

"Okay." He blew out a breath. "I told you about the phone call on Friday afternoon and the limo. I wasn't aware of anyone else in the car, but perhaps I was drugged because the next thing I remember was sitting alone at a table in a small circular room without windows. A black metal strip with tiny holes encircled the room at the ceiling, like crown molding. It turned out to be a speaker system."

"Cool!"

"I didn't question where I was or why I was there, because I *knew*. Don't ask me how, but I knew that this was a critical hearing and that I was there as an expert witness on how to assimilate a primitive tribe into a modern civilization. The issue at hand was whether or not the tribe in question had any redeemable qualities. If it didn't, it would either be quarantined or exterminated because of the danger it posed to others.

"A voice came through the speaker rim introducing someone named Morok who was chairing the proceedings. When Chairman Morok began to speak, I recognized his voice from the phone call the afternoon I was abducted. He spoke a few words of introduction and turned the meeting over to someone he called 'Deputy Director,' who began by saying that the purpose of the commission was to hear a case against a primitive tribe that their staff had been studying for years."

Stephen paused. His son was leaning forward, engaged in the story. Penny was huddled under the afghan staring at the fire. He was suddenly reluctant to continue. He felt as if he were standing on a diving board with no idea how deep the water was or if there was any water in the pool at all.

Gerard smiled at his dad, "This is so great."

Stephen looked at his son and his wife, "Really? Am I making sense?"

"Yes! It's almost like being there," Gerard exclaimed.

Stephen sighed and smiled, "I think I can make the experience even better. When I was with Dr. Parker, she put me into a trance, and I recounted to her exactly what I heard at the hearing. Because of my many years memorizing everything I've witnessed in the field, if I relax enough, I think I can put myself in a similar trance… and run that same tape in my mind for you. It works best when I close my eyes."

Stephen concentrated for a moment, closed his eyes, relaxed… then let the 'tape' run, and began speaking what the Deputy Director said word for word…

"While our esteemed Chairman believes this tribe may possess redeemable qualities—and even believes that we should consider fostering its entry into the Federation—I do not agree with him. I believe the danger it presents is so great that extermination is the only viable solution. That was the staff's initial recommendation. However, the commission has been asked to hear the case to hear new evidence and to consider quarantine. I am speaking, of course, of the Namuh, a violent tribe with a sickness that permeates its entire culture—"

Gerard interrupted. "That's the sound in your dreams—nahmoo!" Stephen continued his recitation as if in a trance...

"...Many think the tribe may be genetically flawed; others believe its sickness is a learned response to a violent culture. Whatever its root, the violence of the tribe is very real, and it presents a threat to the very fabric of our existence. In this hearing, I will present irrefutable evidence of that threat.

Let me start with the Namuh's propensity for violence which exceeds anything we have encountered in our history. Not only do they kill in self-defense, they kill for sport, for pleasure, for money, for revenge. They kill out of greed, out of anger, out of hatred, out of fear. But the Namuh violence manifests itself not just in their wars and crimes but also in their sports and entertainment and their daily lives. Violence is in their blood..."

Stephen opened his eyes and took a sip of tea. "I had wondered why the room was shaped the way it was. When they started their video show, I found out. The light in the room dimmed to total darkness, and images began to appear on the curved walls, moving around the room in slow motion. As the Deputy Director talked about the savagery of the Namuh, war images from our film and television appeared."

He saw a look of disbelief on Penny's face, a look of excitement on Gerard's, as they caught the significance of the reference at the same time. *Our film and television.* He went on. "The soldiers differed only in the way they dressed and the sophistication of their weapons. Warriors in loin cloths with painted faces wielded spears; Romans in tunics brandished swords; blue-clad Yankees slaughtered their grey-clad brothers; fair-skinned soldiers massacred red-skinned tribes. Then came planes with bombs that pitted half the world against the other half.

"The images were three-dimensional, the fighting surrounding me, soldiers falling and bleeding and dying at my feet. At some level I realized I was in the midst of a holographic video, but I felt as if I myself were on the battlefield, immersed in the violence of war since the beginning of time..."

This time, when Stephen closed his eyes, he was again in the room, surrounded by images of war so violent and horrible they defy description, as the Deputy Director spoke...

> "...Over the past several thousand years, such violence has killed nearly one billion Namuh. Imagine that! *One billion!* In the beginning they engaged in hand-to-hand combat using simple weapons like bows and arrows. But that was not efficient enough for them. They created weapons of mass destruction that can incinerate tens of thousands, even hundreds of thousands, of their enemies in one fell swoop."

Stephen opened his eyes and sadly shook his head, remembering the next image. "The room went totally dark for a moment. Then an aerial view of a city appeared, followed by a deafening explosion and a monstrous mushroom-shaped cloud. When the cloud lifted, I saw that the city was leveled and people were crawling from the rubble, moaning, and crying as they streamed toward me, their clothes hanging in shreds—"

"Like your nightmares," Penny said.

Stephen was silent for a long moment, then closed his eyes and ran the tape, seeing everything in his mind as the words of the Deputy Director again flowed from his mouth...

> "...In the past century, more than one hundred forty thousand Namuh were incinerated in two nuclear blasts and many thousands more maimed and poisoned. One would think that such a horrific demonstration of killing power would sicken the killers and end war forever.   One would be wrong.
>
> In the decades following those exhibitions of mass destruction, the Namuh wars continued unabated. Nuclear weapons have not been used again—yet—but during the next decades, two of the largest nations on that tiny planet amassed nuclear arsenals that gave each the power to destroy the other ten times over. Today, even small nations are stockpiling nuclear bombs while others experiment with even more horrific weapons of mass destruction which, with a single deployment, are capable of spreading death and disease over large areas of the planet.
>
> It has been suggested that if we leave them to their own devices, the Namuh will eventually destroy themselves. But we can't take that chance."

Stephen's eyes opened and his hand was shaking as he lifted his teacup to his mouth. The next part of his story was sure to alienate Penny but it could not be omitted. He glanced at her as he began. "The Deputy Director then launched into an attack on religion."

Something in her eyes seemed to close down. She pulled the afghan higher under her chin. He closed his eyes and soldiered on, repeating the words, and reliving the pain...

"...It would seem that the killing of one Namuh by another would be condemned by Namuh religions, and indeed it is. Yet many of their wars have been fought in the name of one god that is worshiped by several Namuh sects, each of which calls the god by a different name.

In the current era, religious groups openly wage war against those whose only crime is a difference of belief. Such groups commit acts of violence against opposing religious sects and against political factions whose dogma or creed does not track their own. They kill medical doctors and plot assassinations of those who oppose their views. Namuh violence is so engrained that some religiously motivated Namuh are willing to sacrifice their own lives in order to kill others in the name of their god. I will show you the most heinous example of religiously motivated Namuh violence..."

Tears filled Stephen's eyes as he opened them again, "What he showed, of course, was videos—holograms—of that awful day in 2001, and I was in the midst of the terrified crowds running through the streets of Manhattan trying to escape the billowing clouds of dust and smoke. I saw the buildings implode—"

He stopped, feeling nauseated.

"It must have been unbearable to feel you were actually there," Penny said quietly.

"Yeah, it was awful enough watching it on TV," Gerard added.

Stephen nodded. "It made me understand what all those people went through that day." After a moment, he continued. "By that point, I was disillusioned with the whole human race. I wondered how it could be possible to paint a more despicable picture of us. But the Deputy Director was just getting started..." Stephen sighed, closed his eyes, and continued...

> "...Then there is violence on the individual level. The Namuh have a rate of non-military violence that is nearly one hundred times the highest recorded crime rate of any other advanced society in our galaxy. Many of their nations and states allow individuals to carry weapons for personal protection. With such easy access to firearms, they regularly kill each other over seemingly trivial issues. A minor difference in appearance, a different choice of lifestyle, a difference of opinion on which driver has the right of way or which sporting team should have won a game can unleash murderous rage.
>
> The Namuh even kill members of their own families: Women kill husbands: men kill wives; parents kill their children. Incredibly, this endemic disease has spread even to the youngest of the tribe. Children as young as six Earth-years have been known to murder their classmates and teachers. Such acts of despicable violence have become almost commonplace at their places of education. This is unimaginable to members of our Federation, but there is no mystery why it happens. Namuh children are raised in a violent culture from the time of birth. They are routinely exposed to violence in their videos, their games, their sports. Figures of violence, both real and fictional, are the stuff of their legends..."

Stephen felt a sudden weariness. He remembered how exhausted he'd been at the end of the hearing. Right now, he wanted nothing more than to go lie down and sleep for about a day.

"You're not finished, are you, Dad?"

Gerard was watching him with rapt attention, absorbing his story like a sponge. Penny looked as if she were close to tears.

"There's more. It's just very tiring to relive all those images."

"Maybe you should stop for a while," Penny said.

"No, this is too important. Where was I?"

"Sports," Gerard said. "You were talking about sports and videos and games."

"Sports, yes," Stephen said, remembering. "They had excavated every imaginable film clip that depicted the violence of our sports. I watched boxers pummel each other until their faces dripped blood; I watched hockey players beat each other senseless with sticks; I watched football players slam into their opponents and leave them unconscious on the field.

"Our violence isn't confined to players either, as I'm sure you remember. I was assaulted with images I'd once seen on the nightly news: a stadium overflowing with soccer fans thrashing one another, a towering basketball player climbing into the stands to pummel a fan, an angry father beating his son's hockey coach to death with his bare hands..."

Stephen's eyes closed, as he recounted what he'd heard and the visuals that pained him again to endure...

"...The fact is, the Namuh worship violent behavior. When children are immersed in a violent culture at a young age, when they grow up in a society permeated with violence, when even their religion espouses or condones violence—is it any wonder that they are the most violent species ever encountered in the galaxy?

Throughout their history, their so-called civilized nations have consistently brutalized the native inhabitants of newly discovered worlds, often slaughtering them en masse. A notable example is the treatment of the indigenous tribes of two continents known as the Americas. By all accounts, these brown-skinned tribes were a peace-loving people who worshiped nature and nurtured the land. The invaders from across the ocean possessed weapons far superior to those of the native inhabitants, and the invaders had fair skin. Given all that I have told you, can you not guess the outcome? The pale-skinned invaders slaughtered the natives, took their land, and banished those who managed to survive to small parcels of inhospitable terrain.

When even minor variations in skin pigment can cause irrational hatred and violence, can there be any doubt how the Namuh would treat *us?*

We have only to look to their portrayal of extraterrestrials in films and video games for the answer. We are overwhelmingly depicted as slimy, villainous, evil creatures that they must destroy in order to survive. Even if we had nothing else to fear from the Namuh, we should fear their innate violence toward beings who are billions of years more advanced, but whose physical differences are as great as a monkey to an eagle."

Stephen paced in front of the fireplace; hands clasped behind his back. "I feel the commission's staff was biased, but I could not find—still cannot find—a single misrepresentation in anything the Deputy Director said. He went on and on, sometimes with visuals, sometimes without. He called us a culture without honor, without even the expectation of honor. He recited some of the most egregious examples of dishonor among our politicians and expressed wonder about our tolerance for such shameful behavior in our leaders when even a minor breach of honor in their worlds precipitates a leader's immediate resignation."

"Why do we tolerate such behavior?" Gerard asked.

He stopped pacing and looked at his son. "That's a good question and I don't have an answer for it. But I do know that acts of dishonor are rampant in our culture. I listened to the Deputy Director excoriate the legal profession for its lack of honor. He pointed out the deceptive practice of lawyers who use untruths and outright lies to win acquittal for a criminal, even when the lawyer knows the person is guilty. But that's just one example. I thought about priests who prey on children, judges who accept bribes, athletes who use drugs to inflate their performance, journalists who invent stories whole-cloth, religious leaders who milk followers of their hard-earned money, and business leaders who deceive shareholders and lie to employees. I know there are honorable people in all professions, but by the time he began his condemnation of our abysmal stewardship of our planet, I was ready to throw in the towel."

A weary Stephen closed his eyes and began to question everything he thought he knew, as he was again in the room and recalled the Deputy Director's words that rang so sadly true:

> "...The Earth sustains the Namuh and other Earth-bound species, just as the planets in the Federation sustain our many species. But while we nurture our planets as fragile sources of life, the Namuh ravage theirs. They pollute the water, poison the air, destroy the rainforests and wetlands. Thousands of Earthly species disappear annually because of the Namuh's blatant disregard for their own planet. What is more astounding, they refuse to change their ways even when it threatens the very existence of their unborn generations. Their lack of stewardship has set into motion climatic changes that could set the Namuh civilization back ten thousand years or perhaps destroy it altogether.

With such disrespect for their planet, is it any wonder that they have failed to protect it from external hazards as well?

The planet Earth orbits a minor sun in a remote solar system of our mutual galaxy. That solar system is a very active one, with hundreds of asteroids and comets continuously invading the Earth's orbit. Asteroids have struck the planet in its past, creating gigantic craters in its crust. Their scientists have correctly deduced that one such impact completely annihilated an entire species—the extraordinary creatures they called dinosaurs—yet they possess such narrow vision and an inflated sense of their own importance that virtually no effort has been made to protect their fragile planet from such external forces.

I will remind you that the Federation is not in the business of planet building, so all of this would be of little concern to us if it were not for certain technological advances the Namuh have made in the past century. Despite their barbaric behavior and their dismal performance in protecting their environment, they are a very clever people. Their scientific and technological progress far exceeds their ability to use either wisely, and three of their technological advancements concern us greatly.

One is telecommunications. The Namuh have been unknowingly broadcasting a cacophony of vile sounds and violent images to the rest of the galaxy for many decades. Many of those images portray violence as the Namuh's preferred method of dispute resolution, and we fear that this might influence some of the less stable societies. Using violence to resolve disputes is an easy first step toward a culture of violence, but it is the antithesis of our methods of dispute resolution. We cannot—I repeat, cannot—allow the Namuh's violent culture to contaminate our galaxy.

I concede that this threat could be considered *indirect* and therefore not critical. I will point out, however, that their advancements in biotechnology and space technology pose a *direct* threat to our civilizations.

As incredible as it may seem, given their age and lack of maturity as a species, Namuh scientists have made great strides in biotechnology. They have already decoded the DNA of their species, and their genetic map is broadcast regularly over what they call the internet. Which means it could be picked up by a rogue planet that wished to breed warriors to cause harm to the Federation. As everyone knows, that has happened before, and even though we have had peace for millions of years, it could happen again.

The Namuh advancement in space technology poses the other direct threat. Granted, their spaceships are as crude as paper airplanes, compared with ours, and only a few Namuh have actually left the planet, those few traveling only as far as their nearby moon. But the Namuh have one extraordinary quality, and that is an ability to apply new technologies rapidly and efficiently. Already they have sent robotic probes to the outer reaches of their solar system, and it is merely a question of when, not if, they will discover how to navigate the wormholes and stringways of the galaxy. Indeed, we believe they could reach many of our planets in fewer than one hundred Earth-years, and that could directly expose our peaceful worlds to the pandemic of Namuh violence.

The question before us is this: is the violence that forms the bedrock of the Namuh species a genetic flaw or a learned response perpetrated by their culture? If it is a learned response, it is possible the Namuh can unlearn their dangerous ways. But if they are genetically programmed for violence, we have but one choice—and that is to exterminate the entire species."

CHAPTER 18

Gerard spoke first, "Dad are you ok? Are you still with us?"

Stephen slowly opened his eyes and looked at his son and his wife, "I sure hope so."

Stephen felt drained. He reached for the mug, but the tea was lukewarm. He put it back on the mantle and sat down in the recliner. Both Penny and Gerard looked stunned, but he could tell his son was processing the data, as he called it. Penny looked as if she were about to explode. She was the next to speak.

"You were abducted by aliens who want to kill us because of our violence." Her voice was flat with disbelief.

He remembered how disturbed he had been when he left Dr. Parker's office, but he'd had several hours to assimilate the information. He tried to reassure her. "It's not quite as bad as it sounds."

"How can anyone contemplate destroying billions of people and still claim to be a peace-loving civilization?"

"You have to look at it from their point of view. Perhaps their civilizations never had violence, or if they did, they've evolved past it to a stage where they have virtually no crime. To them, we're a rogue species with a disease of violence, and they fear we will infect their worlds."

Gerard said, "Infect them? Like with a virus?"

"Think of the bird flu scare a few years back. We didn't exterminate the entire species, but we killed millions of birds around the globe. But we should remember, they did mention an alternative. If they can be convinced that our susceptibility to violence is not genetic, they will impose a quarantine instead of extermination."

Gerard spoke up. "Is there anything we can do to make them opt for quarantine?"

"Yes. That's why I need your help—"

Penny threw the afghan aside and stood up. "Stephen, I'm trying very hard to believe you so that we can put that night behind us and get on with our lives. But this is too much. You sound like one of those crazies who claim they were taken aboard a UFO."

"I know how crazy it sounds, Pen, but I'm telling the truth."

"Those people probably thought they were telling the truth, too! But they were—they *are*—delusional." The word hung in the air as she looked at him sadly. "You need help, Stephen. I think you should go back to Dr. Parker." She picked up her tea and left the room.

After a moment, Stephen could hear her slamming cabinet doors in the kitchen. He looked at Gerard. "Do you think your old man's gone off his rocker?"

Gerard shook his head. "No. I believe you."

"Thank you."

They were quiet for a few moments.

"Why did they call us "namoo, Dad?"

Stephen smiled. It was like his son to focus on the details. "Their early linguists interpreted our texts from right to left. Human was written n-a-m-u-h—"

"Human spelled backward!" Gerard flashed a grin.

"Yes. Morok told me the mistake was eventually corrected, but the appellation remained."

"But they speak English."

"Not really. If I were French, I'm sure they would have spoken French. They probably used a form of automatic verbal translation from their language to ours. Remember, the Federation is hundreds of millions of years more advanced than we are, and we're already capable of automatic translation of the written language, albeit at a somewhat rudimentary level. Verbal translation can't be that far behind."

Gerard was silent for a moment. "They condemned us for an awful lot of things. Did they see anything good?"

Stephen shrugged. "They think we're smart—the way an adult thinks a precocious child is smart. They acknowledge that we're technologically advanced for our age as a civilization and that we're quick to adapt our technology."

"But that's what scares them."

"True. There are other things they like about our culture. Chairman Morok told me they appreciate our art, our poetry, our music—"

"You talked to the chairman himself?"

"Yes. He came to the room."

"What'd he look like?"

"Like one of us. Tall. Grey-haired. A pleasant-looking older gentleman. But he admitted it was a hologram constructed for my benefit."

"I would have asked him what he really looked like!"

"I did. And he asked me if it would make a difference in whether I believed him or not. I had to admit it wouldn't."

"It might have made it more believable to Mom."

"You think she would have been less upset if I could have told her he looked like ET?"

Gerard grinned. "I guess not."

Penny walked through the den without a word and went into the sunroom and closed the door. Stephen glanced at his son and shrugged.

"Dad, what can we do to prevent extermination? Surely there's something!"

Stephen was concerned by the look of grave concern on Gerard's face. There was so much more to tell him, but he was weary to the bone, and all he wanted to do was lie down and sleep a dreamless sleep. "I believe there's something we can do, and I'm going to need your help. But I'm exhausted, son. I'd like to finish my story tomorrow."

"You promise?"

"I promise."

Gerard turned his chair toward the elevator, then looked over his shoulder at his dad. "I know this is serious, but it's pretty exciting too—first contact with an alien intelligence!"

Stephen grinned. "Wow… Yes… Right. I guess I lost sight of that."

Gerard backed his chair into the elevator. He gave his dad a thumbs-up, as the elevator door closed.

Stephen had no idea how much time there was before the aliens' plan for extermination was carried out, but emotional exhaustion is a strong anesthetic. He stretched out on the sofa and was asleep in an instant.

#

The snow was falling rapidly now, surrounding the sunroom with a blur of white. Watching it, Penny felt as if she were in the middle of a snowstorm but without its wetness and chill. The birds too seemed mesmerized by the falling snow, ignoring her as she opened the aviary door. She sat down on the edge of the chaise, taut with apprehension, and tried to pray. *Dear God, you never spoke of aliens. Is there such a thing? I want to believe Stephen. Please help me to understand. I still love him so much. I will always love him. I wish things could be the way they were before...*

Her thoughts would not hold still. It simply couldn't be possible that Stephen had been contacted by an alien civilization. If there were such a thing as aliens, surely astronomers would discover their signals from outer space first. If that ever happened, the president would announce the momentous event from the Oval Office. She wouldn't hear about it from her husband as a tale of abduction.

She felt a rustle in the air as Noah landed on her arm. "Hi," she said.

"Hi-de-ho," Noah replied.

She stroked his neck and watched the snow fall and tried to think about what Stephen might be hiding behind his story of abduction by aliens. Or was he simply sick, delusional, as he said Dr. Parker believed.

"Which is it, Noah?" she whispered. "Is he lying or is he delusional?"

Noah bobbed his small white head, the yellow crest moving back and forth. "Lusional," said the bird in his high thin voice.

Penny made a sound between a laugh and a sob. Noah often picked up phrases instantly if he liked the sound, but she found herself wondering for an absurd moment if maybe the bird knew something she didn't?

CHAPTER 19

The next day Stephen went to Gerard's room after school to tell him the rest of his story. He sat cross-legged on the narrow bed and watched Gerard gulp down a tuna sandwich.

Penny had declined to join them. "If you want to continue to fill his head with that nonsense about aliens, I can't stop you..."

Stephen waited until Gerard had finished the sandwich. "Shall I pick up where I left off?"

"Can I ask a question first?" He rolled closer to the alcove that housed the bed.

"Sure."

"What planet are these guys from?"

"Morok is from a planet called Yxria. He wouldn't tell me the exact location, but he did say it's in our galaxy about a hundred light-years from Earth. It's one of more than 90,000 planets represented by GFED.

"GFED?"

"That's what they call the Federation. And the numbers get even more incredible. He said the Federation planets are inhabited by more than 180 *trillion* intelligent beings which make up almost twenty thousand different intelligent species. Most of their civilizations are hundreds of millions of years old—he said several were more than five *billion* years old—and many have been at peace for more than ten million years."

Gerard stayed quiet for a moment, processing the data. "Why do you think they picked you to testify? I don't mean any disrespect but—"

Stephen laughed. "I've asked myself the same question. Morok said it was because of my work with primitive tribes, especially the nonviolent Abigo. They consider us to be at a very primitive stage of development as a species."

"It sounds funny to think of us as primitive."

"I thought the analogy was fitting at first. They believe our penchant for violence is based on fear and ignorance, the reaction of a primitive people. You may remember that when the Abigo were discovered certain groups feared the tribe would practice its cannibalism on neighboring tribes, so it was proposed to slaughter them or move them to a protected reservation. That's how GFED looks at humans…they're afraid we'll spread our 'disease of violence' to their worlds so they want to slaughter us or confine us to this planet."

Stephen shifted on the bed, noting how intently his son continued to look at him. "Thing is, the analogy breaks down if you examine it closely. The Abigo's cannibalism is a traditional religious rite. They themselves are a gentle, peace-loving people, and they never use violence to resolve disputes. I could hardly make the case that humans are basically gentle or that we use violence as a religious rite, although I have to say that religious fervor accounts for a great deal of our violence and wars. But GFED's primary concern is whether our predisposition toward violence is genetic or a learned behavior."

"So, what'd you say?"

"I assumed they asked me to testify because they respected my work, so I thought that if I aligned myself with the primitive group they feared, they would have to reconsider their judgment. I reminded them that I was human— 'I am Namuh,' I said, 'I'm a member of the very tribe you are judging as unworthy of life.' Then I questioned their motives."

"You challenged them?"

"I guess I did. Everything they'd said about the violence of the human race was true, yet I felt it was the height of arrogance to condemn an entire species out of hand. I suggested that perhaps they were running out of resources for their trillions of inhabitants and that maybe they were planning to take over Earth for their own use. At which point the chairman himself broke in and took me to task."

Gerard grinned. "Cool! Is that when you met him?"

"No, that was later, but I recognized his voice from his introduction of the Deputy Director…"

Stephen closed his eyes and was once again in the room as he recalled Morok's words…

"…Dr. Hopkins, let me remind you of the boundless nature of our universe. It contains more than 100 billion galaxies, and each of those galaxies contains an average of 200 billion stars. Our galaxy—the one you call the Milky Way—has some 400 billion stars, and inhabitable planets, including Earth, orbit a significant percentage of them. If we had imperialistic aims—which we do not—we could choose from millions and millions of planets far superior to yours. So please do not insult us by suggesting we seek to take over your planet for ourselves. The only issue before us today is to decide how to protect our civilizations from the conquer-and-pillage mentality of the Namuh."

Stephen looked at his son, heartened that they were on the same wavelength, "The Chairman's tone was thought-provoking. He sounded like a parent chastising an impertinent child, and it gave me an angle for my testimony."

"You reminded them how young our civilization is, right?"

"Yes. Do you know about Carl Sagan's Cosmic Calendar? If the history of the universe could be reduced to a 365-day year—"

Gerard picked it up. "The last five minutes of the last day of the year would represent the span of recorded history."

Stephen corrected him. "It's even more dramatic than that. The last *ten seconds* of December 31 on such a calendar would represent the last 30,000 years—that's when the earliest-known petroglyphs were carved in some caves in France—and we only learned to write about five thousand years ago, which would be represented on Sagan's calendar by less than 2 seconds, so modern history—the period from the end of the Middle Ages to now—would comprise a little more than one-half of *one second* on this calendar."

"Jeez! We really are babies on the evolutionary scale."

Stephen nodded. "Yes, and I thought I could use that to my advantage. When I continued my testimony, I reminded the commission that they had summoned me to testify about my experience with primitive tribes, and my experience told me that judging the external traits and rituals of a tribe does not necessarily render an accurate appraisal. I asked them to consider the young age of the Namuh civilization..."

This time his eyes remained open as he remembered...

"...As you know, Mr. Chairman, species evolve in response to the demands of their environment, usually changing into a more complex, usually better form. I postulate that to survive in the Earth's early, inhospitable environment, humans evolved into an aggressive species. If you would look deep into your own primitive beginnings, I doubt they would be much different from ours. You've simply had millions, even billions more years in which to evolve. On your time scale, the Namuh civilization is barely out of the cradle. We're still infants, particularly in the sociological realm. For example, practices as abhorrent and primitive as slavery existed in my country less than two hundred years ago and *still* exist in some corners of our planet.

Technologically, however, humans are well on the road to maturity. We recently completed the sequencing of the human genome. I understand that you consider this to be a negative accomplishment, but it may well lead to the understanding and ultimate correction of our violent behavior.

Finally, may I remind you that many groups of humans, specifically the Abigo tribe that I studied, are nonviolent. That should negate the possibility that our propensity for violence is genetically based. If we are given a chance to mature as a species, as a civilization, the characteristics you find so offensive will likely disappear through natural selection over time, just as they have apparently disappeared from your civilizations. On behalf of my fellow Namuh, I ask you to overlook our childlike behavior and help us evolve into mature and honorable citizens of the galaxy."

"Did that convince them?"

"I don't know. But I think it's what brought Chairman Morok to my room after my testimony was over. That's when he told me more about his world and more about why GFED fears a species like us..."

Stephen sighed, closed his eyes, then recounted Morok's powerful yet painful words...

"...My species, Yxrians, reside in ten different solar systems in this galaxy, and we're the principal residents on nearly thirty planets. We are not the oldest intelligent beings in the galaxy by any means, but we have a recorded history of more than a billion years. Despite our advanced ways—*because* of our advanced ways—we fear the Namuh's impact on our civilizations should you ever leave your solar system. We fear it because we have seen what can happen.

Nearly ten million years ago, a renegade species wreaked havoc throughout our part of the galaxy. They killed several million beings in a reckless pursuit of a coveted substance that was purported to extend individual life spans. This species was more advanced than yours, but like the

Namuh they exhibited total disregard for other beings and other planets. Their technology was developing very rapidly, so the Federation voted to eliminate the entire species from the galaxy. As a direct result of that tragic event, we formed the commission on Emerging Species to observe developing species throughout the galaxy. Once a species acquires the capability for space travel, we monitor it on a full-time basis. That is why we are here today—to make sure that history does not repeat itself."

"I asked Morok why he was talking with me if the commission had already condemned the human race. He said his staff had recommended extermination but the hearing was being held to study the matter at the commission level. He studied my work with the primitive cultures and thought my testimony about the absence of violence in the Abigo and other primitive tribes might convince the commission for a verdict of quarantine rather than extermination."

"How would the verdict be carried out?" Gerard asked.

"I asked the same question..." Stephen shook his head and stared into space as he repeated Morok's answer...

"...GFED has placed a probe in orbit around your sun. If the commission's final verdict is quarantine, the probe will be used to stimulate solar flares to interfere with Earth's communications to confine your broadcasts to your own solar system. If the verdict is extermination, the solar probe will be used to shower the Earth with gamma rays in sufficient quantity to eliminate your species. I assure you there would be no pain or suffering. Death would be instant."

Gerard was shocked. "How can they talk about exterminating us like we're a bunch of—cockroaches!"

"I thought pretty much the same thing. Morok seemed to read my thoughts..." Stephen closed his eyes and continued...

"...Don't think I am without emotion, Dr. Hopkins. I care deeply about a species that can produce the kind of music and art and poetry that the Namuh have produced. But in my world, only the wisest, most judicious beings are appointed to hear disputes and render judgments, which gives us complete confidence that any judgment they render is the best possible for a given situation. Any decision can be appealed, but the final authority is the Supreme Council. Few matters are appealed to that level, however."

Stephen stretched his legs out the length of the bed. "I can't tell you how hopeless I felt at that moment," he said. "It was as if a tsunami had appeared twenty feet offshore with no high ground in sight. I asked Morok if anything could be done to save humanity. He looked at me with what appeared to be great sorrow in his eyes and said, 'If the commission votes for extermination, I could veto it and take it to the Supreme Council. Their judgment would be final.' And then he disappeared."

"Just like that? He disappeared?"

"Remember, it was a hologram."

Gerard was silent for a moment. "A gamma ray is just a light ray, right? How can it kill someone?"

"You know that the light spectrum is a continuum, with long, low-energy waves at one end and short, high-energy waves at the other?"

"Yes."

"Gamma rays are at the short end of the spectrum and contain the highest level of energy. They're created when stars collide or explode, and we detect them all over the universe. The sun itself emits gamma rays continuously, but they're deflected by our atmosphere."

"So how could they be used to kill us?"

"I'm not sure, but in my lay opinion, a powerful emission of gamma rays aimed directly at the Earth would slice through the atmosphere like a hot knife through butter."

"Would that vaporize us?"

"No, the rays would destroy our DNA. Instantly."

"Wouldn't that kill every living thing, not just humans?"

"Theoretically, yes. Some scientists speculate that some of the Earth's mass extinctions might have been caused by bursts of gamma rays in our galaxy."

Gerard looked grave, and a little frightened. "So, what you're saying is that we're all going to die soon unless the verdict is quarantine?"

Stephen had a moment of doubt, wondering if he had made a mistake telling his son something so fundamentally frightening. But he needed his help. The world needed *their* help.

"Dad, we can't take a chance on their verdict. We've got to do something!"

That was what Stephen had hoped for. Gerard was rising to the challenge. "That's why I told you all this. I need your help."

"My help?"

"Yes. Most of the commission thinks our violence is hard-coded in our DNA, but if we can convince them that it's not, that humans can change, they may well give us the time we'd need to prove it."

"How can we convince them?"

"Our government could initiate peace talks, negotiate truces between warring nations, declare a unilateral disarmament."

"World peace?" Gerard breathed the words with disbelief, then added. "Won't that take years?"

"Of course, but it wouldn't take long to start moving in that direction. We could take some positive steps to prove to the Federation that our hearts are in the right place. But there's only one person on earth who could initiate a plan like that and make it work."

"Who?"

"Who's the most powerful leader in the world?"

"President Wainwright?"

"If he can't do it, then it can't be done."

"Let's email him."

Stephen smiled. He wished it were that simple. "Do you believe everything I've told you about this?"

"Of course."

"Your mother doesn't believe it. Neither did Dr. Parker, and I don't think the president will either. Not unless my story can be corroborated."

Gerard looked crestfallen. "The only one who could do that is Chairman Morok or someone on the commission. Would they do it?"

"I doubt it." Stephen thought of the woman he had seen at the hearing. "But there may be someone else who could."

"Who?"

"As I was leaving the hearing, I remember seeing a woman entering the room where I'd been. I'm not sure why I felt she was human rather than another hologram, but I did. If we can find her, she might corroborate my story."

"Who was she?"

Stephen swung his legs off the bed, hunched forward, elbows on knees. "That's where I need your help. All I know is what she looked like..."

"And?"

"She was tall, slender, attractive, with long red hair."

"Anything else? Gerard asked.

Stephen thought about it. He could picture the woman standing at the door. She was wearing a dark pant suit with a light-colored blouse. She was about thirty feet away, but he could see her face clearly, could see the way the corners of her mouth turned up slightly, the start of a smile. Then she had pushed the door open and disappeared inside.

"She had a nice smile. But wait a minute...I also know the commission was trying to determine whether our violence is genetic or a learned behavior, so it makes sense they would want to hear testimony about that, probably from someone who has studied children and violence. I was asked my opinion, but I had no basis for comment outside of my work with primitives."

Gerard flashed a grin. "I'll bet my KASA buddies can find her."

Stephen, "Really? That's terrific." His son frequently mentioned his KASA buddies but always dodged questions about them. "But you've never told me what KASA stands for."

For a moment, Gerard looked as if he'd been caught with his hand in the cookie jar. He gave his father a sly smile. "It stands for Koalition Against Stupid Adults."

"But isn't coalition is spelled with a C?" asked Stephen.

Gerard laughed, "Of course it is, Dad. K is for Kids!"

#

Back in his study, Stephen sat down at his computer and googled *Koalition Against Stupid Adults* and there it was at the top of the list: KASA, the Koalition Against Stupid Adults, founded by a blogger who called herself Joan-of-Right. He clicked the link and read a few of her posts. Most appeared to be adolescent rants by a person frustrated with the course of human events. Joan-of-Right declared that adults were involved in a worldwide conspiracy to transform kids into happy little workers to support the lavish retirement lifestyles of the older generations. She was determined to prevent that. Stephen smiled to himself. Instead of staging sit-ins or marching in protests, today's rebellious youth wrote weblogs for nameless, faceless people they would never meet. Stephen wondered if this group of innocuous rebels could really find his mystery woman.

He began thinking about how he would approach her, if and when they did. First, he would ask if she had experienced anything unusual on the night of November 5. If she had, he would draw her out, get her to tell him about it before he told her his story. If it turned out there were blocks of time on that night that she couldn't remember, he would ask her to undergo regression therapy. A psychologist shouldn't have a problem with that, he thought. After all, it was one of the tools of their profession.

After the woman's regression, they would compare memories. If hers tracked his, he would ask his father to set up a meeting with the president. The idea of asking his father for a favor was not appealing, but Penny said he'd called again last week asking to see Gerard. Maybe it was time to let go of his anger and guilt and let his father back into their lives. Asking a favor was one way to begin.

Of course, they had to find the mystery woman first. And if KASA couldn't pull it off, instead of fantasizing his approach, maybe it's time to come up with a plan of his own.

CHAPTER 20

Gerard logged on to KASA and asked Stargunner and Moley to join him in their private chat room. He spent several minutes briefing them on his dad's story about Chairman Morok and the hearing. They responded with sarcasm and alien jokes. Not because they doubted the existence of intelligent life on other planets. They accepted that, just as they accepted the theory of evolution. But no one had ever greeted a chimpanzee cousin at a wedding, and until now, no one they knew had ever come face-to-face with alien beings. And these aliens wanted to kill us.

stargunner	i have a question for you g-man how come your dad just happened to be the first human contacted by aliens
moleman	yeah what's the chance that someone we know is going to be the first contact?
g-man	someone's gotta be first, so why not my dad?
moleman	sounds fishy to me
g-man	look the guy who won the lottery last week is someone's dad and all his friends are probably sitting around saying, how come your dad won it and not mine? the first human contact had to be related to someone so why not my dad?
moleman	it just seems strange
g-man	you think i'm lying
moleman	no no no
stargunner	we believe you everything they said about humans was true we're a sorry race of people
g-man	i don't understand how they can put a satellite around the sun without it melting
stargunner	could be nanotechnology
g-man	what's that

stargunner	technology at the microscopic level it allows you to build a structure from the molecular level up
moleman	how do you know stuff like that?
stargunner	reading, dumbnut you should try it some time
g-man	is nanotechnology something new?
stargunner	nah the idea's been around since mid twentieth century a physicist named Feynman proposed a bottoms up technique for manufacturing you start with molecules as the building blocks and design a product by specifying the properties and placement of each separate atom Feynman didn't call it nanotechnology that word was coined by a guy named Drexler in the 80s he wrote a book predicting that nanotech could eventually produce machines that could replicate themselves
moleman	sounds pretty far out
g-man	do we have any machines like that?
stargunner	not yet but we're getting close a few years back someone managed to join carbon atoms end to end to make a carbon nanotube and then some clever dude figured out how to stretch the tube and then somebody else laid a bunch of them together and discovered they adhered to each other. and voila! they ended up with a microscopically thin sheet of material that was bulletproof stronger than steel, and lighter than goose down
g-man	wow!
moleman	double wow!!
stargunner	that was just the beginning there's a lot more going on in this field now

g-man	you think GFED might have used nanotech to launch a satellite around the sun?
stargunner	could be let's say they took an asteroid and used nanotech to make it convert itself into a probe as it heads toward the sun. when it gets close enough it fires some rockets and places itself in a tight orbit around the sun
g-man	wouldn't it melt that close to the sun?
stargunner	not if it could convert itself into a material harder than a diamond which is denser than any man-made material we have right now Caltech has done studies on material like that they're just not far enough along to get it right
g-man	if they could do all that i guess they could create a solar flare big enough to wipe us out but how would they do it?
stargunner	who knows? but if they could create a really gigantic solar flare it could cause an eruption of gamma rays and a sustained bombardment of gammas could cook us all
g-man	that's what my dad says
moleman	thanks for scaring the shit out of me
g-man	so guys I need your help my dad saw a woman at the hearing and he thinks she can back up his story. he says she's probably a shrink who deals with kids and violence and whether or not violence is genetically driven i told him we could find her on the net
stargunner	ok lets google psychologists and kids and violence and compare notes then we can look for articles and books
g-man	my dad suggested we look for symposiums because they have photos. he says she's a good-looking redhead

stargunner	a pretty woman's all the motivation I need
moleman	i like long dark hair myself, dark velvety eyes
stargunner	nah gimme a California girl with long blonde hair blue eyes

Gerard logged off. Looks were important but *pretty* covered an awful lot of ground...tall or short, dark haired or blonde, blue eyes or brown. Pretty had more to do with a girl's smile and the look in her eyes than with any one physical feature. But if pushed for an opinion, he guessed he'd agree with Moley. Dark haired girls seemed more...accessible. Redheads, you had to worry about their temper and getting freckles in the sun, and blondes seemed so full of themselves, especially the pretty ones, like they expected you to follow behind them about six paces and carry their purse. He wouldn't mind talking about this with Gunner and Moley, if they'd be serious about it, but he felt awkward chatting in quips about something he knew so little about. Would probably *always* know so little about.

He went to Google and began to search for psychology symposiums over the past five years, then narrowed those down to the twenty or so on children and violence. He went back online and compared notes with Gunner and Moley. They'd found the same ones so they expanded their search to origins of violence and tried again. This time they ended up with more than fifty unduplicated symposiums that included women speakers. Most didn't have photographs so they divided up the women's names—thirty-five out of two hundred speakers on the subject— and googled each name for articles.

By midnight, Gerard had a long list of articles from their combined efforts. He began scanning the articles for bios and photographs and ended up with eleven possibilities. All but two had black-and-white photos of the author, and in the two that were in color, one woman was a blonde, the other a brunette. But women changed their hair color all the time. Maybe one of them was now a redhead. He printed hard copies and stacked them in eleven neat piles on his study desk and went to bed. In the morning, his father could review them and if they were lucky, the redhead would be among them.

The hunt was on.

CHAPTER 21

"That domed building is a Shia mosque," Drakk said as he stood with Morok and Myssa in the shade of a building across the street from the mosque. "It is a holy temple of the Muslim religion."

Myssa swung her reptilian eyes toward Drakk. "Are you serious that these people pray five times a day, every day?"

"Yes. They are praying right now in that temple, about a hundred and fifty of them, mostly women and children."

As they watched, a dozen men in dusty green uniforms materialized from the shadows of nearby buildings, each armed with a shoulder-fired missile.

"No!" Drakk screamed as he tuned in to the gunmen's thoughts. "We have to stop them!"

Morok touched his arm. "Do not interfere."

Drakk watched in horror as they fired missiles into the mosque and the building began to crumble. Within minutes the main tower was toppled and the mosque was in flames. Drakk crumpled on the ground as screams of those inside pierced the air.

Myssa was satisfied with this wretched display. "You know that this act of violence has deep roots, don't you?"

"Tell us," Morok said.

Myssa gave a slow blink. "The men who attacked the mosque belong to the same religion as those inside the mosque, they stem from the same roots, they worship the same god, and they knew that at this time of day the worshippers would be mostly women and children."

"They have murdered some of their own," Drakk said in a choked voice.

"Yes. The Shias and the Sunnis are two sects of Islam, and they have been fighting for nearly fifteen hundred years over something so inconsequential it strains credulity. The source of their disagreement is the legitimacy of sainthood for early followers of Mohammed, the founder of the religion." Myssa folded her arms over her chest. "Millions have died over this obscure point."

Morok's wings drooped toward the ground. Christians and Muslims made up over half of the Namuh population, and each religion was as inherently violent as the other. For the first time, he felt the futility of trying to save these creatures.

CHAPTER 22

On Thanksgiving morning, Stephen slept late. He had spent several hours the night before searching for the woman at the hearing and had turned up nothing of interest. He went to Gerard's room when he woke up. "Did you find anything interesting?"

His son grinned and pointed to several stacks of paper on his study desk. "Eleven suspects. All with photos but only two are in color."

"Good work. Let's see if she's in there."

He picked up the first article, glanced at the photo, then the bio, and tossed it aside. He did the same with the next one, and the next, and the next. By the time he scanned the sixth article, he began to get discouraged. What if he never found her? Or what if he found her and she refused to help? He couldn't go to the president without someone to corroborate his story. He would be labeled a UFO nut and Wainwright would laugh him right out of the Oval Office. He continued to scan the articles. One study presented strong evidence that violence was a learned behavior:

> Children learn violent behaviors in primary social groups, such as the family and peer groups, as well as observe it in their neighborhoods and in the community at large. These behaviors are reinforced by what children and adolescents see on television, on the internet and in video games and movies, observe in music videos and hear in their music.

The study, funded by the Brenner Center for Child and Adolescent Health, listed several authors, one of which was female, but the woman in the photograph looked to be of Middle Eastern descent.   Another study presented the case for a genetic predisposition for violence by comparing findings of aggression among chimpanzees with aggression of human youth gangs:

> Both chimpanzees and human street gangs...form male alliances, they defend territories, they conduct "hits" in neighboring territories, and they kill helpless victims.

Another postulated that violence is unlearned, not learned, implying that children are born with a predisposition to violence which has to be unlearned:

> Violent behaviors emerge when the normal process of socialization is disrupted. Violence ultimately signals the failure of normal developmental processes where children learn how to conquer violent impulses.

Both articles had photographs that pictured women much older than the woman he saw at the hearing. He finished the eleven stacks with similar results and turned to Gerard, disappointed.

"She's not there, is she?" Gerard said.

"I'm afraid not."

"We'll keep looking, Dad. We'll comb university faculties and science websites—"

"It's the proverbial needle in a haystack. Not a chance in a million we'll find her."

"I'm not giving up."

Stephen smiled at his son. "Well, if you're not giving up, neither am I. We've got the rest of the Thanksgiving weekend ahead of us. Let's keep digging. Universities are a good idea."

They spent most of Thursday searching the internet for the woman, stopping only for Thanksgiving dinner which Penny prepared with little enthusiasm. She was still somewhat distant and when Gerard mentioned Chairman Morok over dessert, she rolled her eyes.

They continued to search the internet that evening and all the next day, Gerard with his KASA buddies, Stephen alone in his study. They found dozens of articles on the causes of violence, but the ones that appeared promising turned out to be authored by a man or by a woman who looked nothing like the woman he'd seen at the hearing. As he went to bed on Friday night, he believed the search for the mystery woman was hopeless.

CHAPTER 23

"Dad?"

Stephen turned to see Gerard sitting in the doorway of his study, his face bright with excitement.

"You gotta see this, Dad." He rolled into the study and handed Stephen several sheets of paper. "She's on the faculty of a university in California. Look at the photo."

Stephen looked at the black-and-white photograph and caught his breath. A woman was perched on a stool in front of a book-lined wall, arms crossed over her chest. She was looking directly into the camera and the corners of her mouth turned up slightly, almost a smile but not quite, like the one he'd seen on the woman in the hall that night. Her long straight hair reached past her shoulders and was light enough to be a flaming red.

It was her. He was sure of it. He scanned her bio.

> Dr. Heather Eastlake, a child psychologist and professor at the University of California at Santa Barbara, received both her bachelor's degree ('94) and her doctorate ('98) from UCLA. She has worked with hundreds of children with psychological problems and is considered an expert on violent behavior in children. She has written numerous articles on the subject for scholarly journals, as well as popular magazines, and regularly writes chapters for academic textbooks. She is currently writing a book about children's penchant for violence, postulating that it is due to the child's environment and is not likely to be genetically based. The article published here is a chapter from that book.

The article was titled "*When Johnny Gets a Gun: Is it Nature or Nurture?*" He scanned it quickly. Her argument came down in favor of nurture. When he looked up his son was watching him closely. "I think it's her," he said.

Gerard gave a triumphant grin. "So, what do we do next?"

"I'll call her, introduce myself, ask her if she'll meet with me."

"Meet with you?"

"I think it would be a bit sticky to ask her over the phone if she's had any recent memory lapses, don't you?"

"Yeah, I guess."

"She needs to see me face to face, become comfortable with the fact that I'm a professor, like her, and not an internet stalker." He smiled.

"So, when are you going to California?"

"I don't know. It's probably better if I call her at the University which means I'll have to wait until Monday. But if she'll see me, I could fly out as early as Tuesday morning."

Could he really do that? Could he tell Penny he was flying three thousand miles to meet a woman he *thought* he'd seen at a hearing that she didn't really believe had occurred? No, he could not. Which meant he needed a story, and he needed Gerard's help.

He looked at his son's innocent face and plunged ahead. He had no choice. "Gerard, you know how skeptical your mother is about all this. I don't think we should tell her about my trip until I find out if Dr. Eastlake is the woman I saw at the hearing. In fact, I don't think we should mention her at all at the moment. Are you okay with that?"

"Sure, Dad, I can keep a secret. But how can you go without telling Mom something?"

"I've been doing some research for an article with Señor Alvarado. He's the head of an important council in Mexico City. I'll tell her I'm going there to meet with him."

"Okay." He turned to leave.

"Gerard?"

"Yeah?" He looked over his shoulder at Stephen.

"You know I hate to fib to your mother, but I think it's best to wait until I find out if this woman is the one I saw."

"It's okay."

"Thanks for your help. I couldn't have found her without you and your KASA friends."

Gerard looked pleased. "No problem," he said and wheeled out the door and down the hall.

Stephen watched him go. Not only was he deceiving his wife, he was asking his son to lie for him. A new wave of guilt swept over him, embedding itself in his mind.

He tried to go back to work but he couldn't stop thinking about Heather Eastlake. He reread her biography and the article, stared at her photo. *Was she the woman at the hearing?* How could he possibly wait until Monday to call her? He wanted all this to be resolved by Monday. He looked at his watch. Eleven o'clock. Eight on the West Coast. Was that too late to call someone at home whom he'd never met?

He googled her name and found her number. He spent a few minutes thinking about what he was going to say. Then he dialed.

CHAPTER 24

Across the Potomac, the Reverend Marshall Hopkins sat in his kitchen holding a small amber vial. He opened it, tilted it over his hand, tapped it twice. Two small yellow pills dropped into his palm. He stared at them. All he had to do was pop them in his mouth and in less than an hour, he would be lying in a hospital with what appeared to be a heart attack. Surely, that would gain his son's sympathy. Make him feel obligated to do a big favor for his ailing old dad. Surely, he would acquiesce to his father's dying wish and meet with Ethan Gorr. Then life could return to normal.

But were those little yellow pills more dangerous than they looked?

He had thought long and hard about how to meet Gorr's demand for a meeting with Stephen, and he kept coming back to the idea that if he had a life-threatening illness, his son couldn't refuse him. The problem was, at seventy-three, he was as healthy as a forty-year-old and he'd had no idea how to fake an illness that would seem life-threatening enough to require hospitalization. Then an old Army buddy told him about the pills.

They had been on the seventeenth hole at the Army-Navy Country Club and Marshall was winning by two strokes when his buddy mentioned a friend who had faked a heart attack to keep his daughter from moving to Europe.

"He did it with some little yellow pills he got on the internet."

The reverend lined up his putt. "Why didn't he just clutch his chest and fall down?"

"He wanted it to look authentic," his buddy said. "The pills are supposed to simulate a heart attack that appears so authentic even doctors can't tell it from the real thing until they do a whole slew of tests. Then they attribute it to angina or something like that."

The reverend thought about the phone call Stephen would get. *Your father just had a heart attack.* Surely that would bring him around. He putted, and the ball rolled toward the cup, circled the rim, stopped an inch away. "What kind of pills would do that?" he asked.

"They're based on some drug that induces stress, causes the heart to act up."

"Are they legal?"

"I think so. They're made in Canada."

The reverend lost the round. He found it hard to concentrate on a little white ball when all he could think about was little yellow pills. Taking them seemed to be a perfect way to get Stephen's filial attention. He sees his old dad in the hospital recovering from a heart attack, how could he reject any request, especially one as simple as meeting with his father's good friend? Ethan would get his meeting and convince Stephen to stop publication of his book, Gorr's money would continue to flow into the reverend's ministry which would allow him to continue to serve God, and he wouldn't lose face with the president or with his friends on Capitol Hill. There was another benefit as well. If he reconciled with Stephen, he'd be able to see his grandson on a regular basis.

He had researched the pills on the internet and couldn't find them in Canada, but he did find a supplier in Mexico City. The pills had arrived in a plain brown padded envelope. The instructions were written in Spanish with a cryptic English translation: *Take two pills with a glass of water. Call 911. Unlock front door. Sit down to wait.*

He had uttered an incredulous, 'What!' and then read the paragraphs following the instructions which went on to explain what would happen after he placed the call to 911. If paramedics arrived within seven minutes, they would find him complaining of mild chest pains. If it took fifteen minutes, they would find him screaming that his chest was in a vise and being squeezed tighter by the second. If by some unfortunate quirk of fate, it took the paramedics more than 30 minutes to get to him, they might find him unconscious.

In that case, it made perfect sense to unlock the front door.

He had immediately called a pharmacist friend and asked if there was any possibility the pills might be fatal. His friend lectured him about the folly of buying contraband pills over the internet, then assured him the pills had caused no fatalities that he knew of. It was the words *that he knew of* that had given the reverend pause. He didn't want a fake heart attack to turn into a fatal one.

Now, as he dropped the pills back in the vial, another benefit occurred to him. A heart attack could create a goldmine for his next fund-raising event. He had seen it happen with other evangelists. One fellow in Oklahoma had taken in millions after his well-publicized heart attack. More money meant more air time in which to spread God's word to the world, more missions to undeveloped countries whose people were starved for salvation.

He took the vial to the kitchen and set it next to the coffee pot. He had broadcasts scheduled for Sunday and for Monday evening, so he would take the pills Tuesday around noon. That should be a relatively calm period for emergency rooms, and traffic should be light between McLean and the District at that time. He just had to make sure the paramedics took him to Georgetown and not to a hospital in Virginia. He didn't want to give Stephen any excuse not to visit him.

CHAPTER 25

Heather Eastlake picked up the phone on the first ring. The fact that she answered startled Stephen so much that he didn't respond immediately.

"Hello?" she repeated.

"I'm looking for the Heather Eastlake who is a professor of psychology at UCSB," Stephen said. "Would that be you?"

"Yes. Who are you?" Her voice was brisk, impatient.

He identified himself, told her his profession. "I'm calling about an article you wrote on children and violence, the one entitled 'When Johnny Gets a Gun.' I just read it online."

"Ah, that one. I've had many calls about it, but you're the first anthropologist. What's your interest in it?"

"I found your argument against a genetic base for violence quite compelling. It supports a study I did on a primitive tribe in Peru, and I have some important information I'd like to share with you."

"I'm sorry, I'm getting ready to go out—"

"No, no, not this evening. I'll be in Los Angeles Monday on business and I was hoping I might drive up to Santa Barbara to talk with you in person?"

She was silent.

He should have said he found the article in the university library, not online. She might think he was an internet stalker. "Dr. Eastlake," he said quickly, "You can check the Georgetown University website for my credentials, but surely if we meet at your campus office there's no reason to be apprehensive."

"You're right, of course," she said, her voice warming. "I'm free Monday, any time between one and four."

"Excellent," Stephen said. "I should be there by two o'clock."

He hung up feeling greatly relieved. Had she not agreed to see him, the door could have slammed shut on any possibility of overturning the commission's verdict. The door remained open for now, but it could close again if Heather Eastlake wasn't the woman at the hearing. All he could do was walk through it and see what happened.

The next day he told Penny he'd been invited to Mexico City. She was making breakfast. He was sitting at the kitchen counter drinking a cup of coffee. "Señor Alvarado called last night and asked me to meet with him Monday in Mexico City."

She glanced at him, then continued beating eggs as she spoke. "Pretty short notice, isn't it?"

"He's been trying for weeks to find some time for me and apparently something opened up on Monday afternoon." He wondered if his voice sounded different when he lied. Isn't that how you can tell when someone's lying?

"Are you sure it doesn't have something to do with your aliens?"

Her voice dripped with sarcasm. Obviously, she still didn't believe him.

"How can I convince you I'm telling the truth about the GFED hearing?"

She turned and looked at him straight on. "Think about it, Stephen. If there really were intelligent aliens trying to contact us, would they abduct an anthropology professor? Wouldn't they seek out someone like President Wainwright or the Secretary-General of the UN? I don't mean to put you down, but don't you see how implausible it sounds?"

It was implausible, he had to admit that, but her words stung. "Can't you even give me a small benefit of the doubt?"

She did not respond.

He finished his coffee in silence and went upstairs to tell Gerard about the phone call with Heather Eastlake.

CHAPTER 26

When Stephen arrived at Los Angeles International Airport at
eleven o'clock on Monday morning, he felt as if he'd landed in a
different country. The sky was a brilliant blue, the temperature in
the low seventies, the balmy air like summer on his face. Under
different circumstances he would head for the beach and go for a
long walk. Instead, he rented a car and headed north on the 405.
The rental car agent said it would be a ninety-minute drive to
Santa Barbara if the traffic was good. It was not. The 405 was
bumper-to-bumper, but once he turned north onto Highway 101,
traffic loosened up.

North of Ventura, the 101 hugs a narrow strip of
coastline with the blue Pacific on the left, and the Santa Ynez
Mountains rising up next to the freeway on the right. He lowered
the window and tried to enjoy the scenery and the mild weather,
but the gravity of his mission made it impossible. He thought
about the possible outcome of his meeting with Heather
Eastlake. If she was the woman he saw at the hearing and if, like
him, she had been summoned to testify, one of two things would
be true. Either she remembered what happened or she didn't. If
she remembered, she would either be willing to tell or not. If she
didn't remember but did admit to a gap in her memory, she
would either be willing to undergo regression therapy or she
wouldn't. But even if all the positive either-or scenarios
happened and her memories corroborated his, she would still
have to decide whether or not to go public with them. The irony
was, all these possibilities could fall into place like dominoes,
and they still might not be able to prevent extermination if the
president refused to take any action.

It was almost two o'clock when he arrived at the UCSB
campus. He found his way to the psychology building and to
Heather Eastlake's office on the second floor. It was a typical
academic office, books and papers piled high on a nondescript
desk, a book-lined wall behind the desk, and on the other walls
framed posters from the local art museum and something called
the Solstice Parade. In front of the desk was a wooden visitor's
chair sans cushion, and on the corner of the desk, a vase of

purple flowers and a framed quote from the British poet
Christopher Logue:

> Come to the edge.
> We might fall.
> Come to the edge.
> It's too high!
> *Come to the Edge!*
> And they came,
> and he pushed,
> and they flew.

Heather Eastlake stood up and walked around the desk.
She smiled and offered her hand. "I'm pleased to meet you, Dr.
Hopkins."

"It was good of you to see me, Dr. Eastlake," Stephen
said.

She was much taller than she had seemed at the hearing,
maybe five-ten, slender,
small-boned. Other than that, she looked very much like her
photograph, but younger and more vibrant. Her hair hung past
her shoulders in shiny copper waves. Her green eyes were
serious and thoughtful, but she had a ready smile that made
Stephen feel welcome.

"I haven't had lunch yet," she said. "Would you care to
join me? We can go over to the faculty club if you don't mind a
bit of a walk."

Stephen accepted readily. He felt somewhat anxious in
her office, like a grad student with a knotty thesis problem.

They made small talk on the ten-minute walk, as
students in shorts and backpacks rolled by on bikes and
skateboards and electric scooters. At the club, Heather led him to
a table with a view of the Pacific and they ordered lunch-the
pasta special and a glass of wine for her, a Cobb salad, and a
beer for him. They chatted about their families, their academic
backgrounds, the two universities at which they taught. By the
time lunch was served, they were on a first-name basis.

Stephen broached the matter for which he'd come.
"Heather, I mentioned on the phone that I had information to
share with you, but I need to ask a couple of questions. I hope
you won't find them—inappropriate."

She looked at him quizzically. "Go on."

"Has anything unusual happened to you in the past, say, three weeks?"

"Unusual?"

"Yes. Something that didn't conform to your usual day-to-day life. Something that made you stop and think, what was *that* all about?"

She studied him for a moment, then shook her head. "Not really."

He frowned. This was not going to be easy. "Let me be more specific. Was there a time in early November where you can't recall what you did or where you were for one whole evening?"

She drew back, clearly offended. "I beg your pardon?"

"I'm not trying to get personal—"

"Why would you ask a question like that?"

He could see she was taken aback by his invasion of her privacy. He soldiered on. "I know I'm a stranger to you, but I assume you checked me out."

"I did."

"And we're in your faculty club on your campus among your colleagues, right?"

"Right."

"So please trust me for just a few minutes."

She reached for her glass, looked at him over the rim as she sipped the wine.

Stephen decided to tell her the truth. At least part of the truth. "On the night of November 5th, I saw a woman who looked like you, so I went searching for her on the internet. When I saw your picture, I was sure it was you I had seen that night."

"Where exactly did you see me?"

"That's the problem. I don't know."

She stared at him with disbelief. "You don't know?"

"No."

"Did you know my name or my profession?"

"No."

"All you knew was what I looked like?"

"That's right."

"So, what did you do? Google 'tall redheads?'"

He gave her a wry smile. "I made an educated guess that the woman I'd seen was a child psychologist who studied violence in children, so that's who I searched for."

"Why were you looking for a child psychologist who studies violence?"

"I can't tell you that just yet. I can tell you that you were difficult to find."

"Yet you persisted."

"Yes."

"You've gone to a lot of trouble and expense to meet a woman you *thought* you saw one night. It's very, shall we say, suspicious."

"I know. But please believe that it isn't personal, but it's extremely important."

They ate in silence for a few minutes. He was afraid he had lost her, but he couldn't quit now. He pushed his plate aside, rested his arms on the table. "May I venture another question?"

"Would it matter if I said no?"

"Yes." He folded his hands together, as if in prayer. If he thought it would help, he would get on his knees. "But please, don't say no."

"Ask."

"Have you had any nightmares or recurring dreams in the past few weeks? Dreams that left you…disturbed?"

She gave him a quizzical look. "My dreams are often disturbing."

"Has any of them left you feeling frightened or filled with anxiety?"

"Dreams are very personal, Stephen."

He backed off. "I'm sorry, I don't mean to be personal, but something extraordinary and disturbing happened to me on the night of November 5th. I was hoping the woman I saw that night was you and that you might remember what happened so we could talk about it."

She looked decidedly uncomfortable. After a while she said, "Do *you* remember what happened?"

"I didn't at first. But I was plagued by nightmares afterwards, so I finally went to see a therapist who regressed me.

That broke the memory block, and I now remember everything about that night."

"Then why can't you tell me?"

He saw something different in her eyes—a shadow, a guardedness. "Because if you *were* there that night, telling you might influence your ability to recall your memories independently."

She said nothing. She picked at her food, drank some wine. "I wish I could help you, Stephen, but I was home on the night of November 5th. I'm afraid you've wasted your trip."

#

Heather returned to her office feeling as if a piece of a puzzle had suddenly fallen into her lap. There *had* been dreams. They had come on suddenly about three weeks ago, disturbing her sleep, leaving her anxious and depressed. She had awakened in the middle of the night amid images of children wielding knives, slashing each other, laughing like demons. She'd been afraid it was an LSD flashback. She'd experimented with the hallucinogen in college, and the experience had immersed her in such a cauldron of disturbing images that she'd never taken any mind-altering drugs again.

So why hadn't she told Stephen about the dreams?

For a moment, she tried to ignore another memory tugging at her mind. Then she closed her eyes and let it come. She had awakened very late one Saturday morning completely disoriented and had struggled to remember the previous evening. She had gone to a meeting of her professional society, but when she tried to recall what went on at the meeting her mind drew a blank. Just as she was ready to call a friend to ask as discreetly as possible what had happened, the friend had called and asked why she hadn't been at the meeting. That's when she knew she hadn't gone. She made some excuse to her friend, but the truth was, she didn't know where she'd been. All she remembered was going home Friday afternoon to change clothes and then waking up in bed on Saturday morning—with no memory of what had happened in between.

The dreams had started the next night.

Now she pulled out her calendar. She knew this had happened in late October or early November, but she couldn't remember the exact date. She found the notation for the APA meeting on the page for Friday, November 5, at 6 P.M. Next to the notation, she had scribbled the word 'Missed' followed by two big question marks.

Oh god! She must have been wherever Stephen had seen her. But where? Doing what? Maybe something—inappropriate with him or others? Another memory flashed through her mind, this one of an old movie she'd seen on television not long ago. The woman in the film had been drugged and abducted and impregnated with Satan's child. It was nonsense, of course, but what had been done to *her* that Friday night in November? Maybe worse, what had she done?

She picked up the phone and dialed a colleague who used hypnotism in her practice. When the woman answered, she asked for an appointment for the next day.

#

It was almost four when Stephen left the UCSB campus. He had a mid-morning flight on Tuesday, but if he started to Los Angeles at four o'clock, he would hit the peak of rush hour traffic. He took Heather's advice and checked into a small downtown hotel. He spent the next hour walking up and down State Street, trying not to think of the dead end he now faced. If Heather wasn't the mystery woman, he had no idea how to find her. He sat at an outdoor cafe and watched people dressed in tank tops and shorts carrying Christmas shopping bags. In this resort atmosphere, his memories of Morok and the GFED hearing seemed like some bizarre dream. Without someone to corroborate his story, it might as well have been one.

That evening, a small restaurant on State Street beckoned him with thousands of tiny white lights adorning its entrance. He stepped inside and found himself in a veritable Christmas wonderland. Reindeers made of tiny white lights raised and lowered their heads on the balcony encircling the dining room and beside them rotund Santas made of red and white lights turned this way and that. Throughout the room, a

116

dozen Christmas trees twinkled their white lights on and off. Stephen was gripped with a fresh surge of guilt at the lie he'd told his wife. He fled the festive atmosphere and returned to his hotel to order room service.

He put his hands behind his head and stared up at the ceiling. What if he'd been concentrating on the wrong profession? What if the woman he saw was a sociologist or a criminologist or a kindergarten teacher? What if she was one of them—a red-haired hologram from another planet? He pondered these possibilities, but the feeling remained that Heather Eastlake was the woman at the hearing.

But what if he was wrong?

CHAPTER 27

The Reverend woke up with something pulling at his eyelid and a blinding light shining in his eye. His throat felt swollen, and his mouth was so dry his tongue stuck to the roof of his mouth like Velcro. He sensed, rather than saw, a person hovering over him. "Who are you?" he said thickly.

"Good, you're awake," said a female voice.

The light went off and he felt the pressure release on his eyelid. He blinked and saw a shadowy form. He blinked again and a woman in a white coat came into focus. A black stethoscope dangled from her neck. He breathed a sigh of relief. "What day is this?"

"It's Tuesday."

"Where am I?"

"You're in the hospital, Reverend. You've had a heart attack."

"Which hospital?"

"Inova Fairfax."

Hell's bells! He grimaced and closed his eyes tight. He had tried to tell the EMTs to take him to Georgetown University Hospital, but the pain in his chest had been so severe he couldn't get the words out. He remembered saying "Take me to George…" and then a sharp pain hit him. He had tried again but all he got out was "George—" They must have thought he was referring to a person.

"You're going to be fine, but we need to know how PCP got in your bloodstream?"

His eyes flew open. "What do you mean?"

"It's an ingredient used in a new drug to treat sexual dysfunctions. It hasn't been approved yet, but it's being sold in Mexico and all over the internet. Is that what you took?"

He thought quickly. He couldn't let word get out that he was treating a sexual dysfunction. Nor could he let anyone think he'd faked a heart attack. He considered the rock and the hard place and decided on the rock. He let a bashful smile creep onto his still handsome face and summoned the Voice. "Guilty as charged, doctor." His voice came out like silk despite his parched throat, "Could we please keep this between us?"

She gave him a stern look. "Reverend, sexual dysfunction is nothing to be ashamed of. You should have gone to your doctor. You could have killed yourself with those pills." She pulled a pad out of her pocket and wrote something on it.

He glanced at the black nametag pinned to her lab coat. "I know, but in my position, Dr. Ladd—" He gave her a helpless look. "You know how the media and the public would react to news like that."

She was silent for a moment. Her face softened. "I can't keep it off your chart, Reverend, but the official announcement will say you had a stress-related heart attack. How's that?"

"Will the media be able to see my chart?"

"No. That's private."

He rewarded her with a beaming smile. "You're a saintly woman, Dr. Ladd. God bless you."

After the doctor left, he looked at the clock on the wall opposite his bed. It was 2:27. He'd taken the pills over two hours ago. When a nurse came in to check his vitals, he asked her if his son or daughter-in-law had been notified.

"I'm sure we called whoever was listed as your emergency contact," she said.

He touched the tube hanging out of his nostrils. "Can I get rid this thing?"

She glanced at the machine behind the bed, then reached down and pulled the tube out of his nose. "Can you breathe, okay?"

He took a couple of breaths and nodded. She draped the tube on a hook behind the bed. He tried to flirt with her but she was all business. He glanced at her nametag. *Stephanie Trahos, RN.* That explained it. RNs were usually impervious to his charm. As she turned to leave, he asked her to get his cell phone from his coat pocket. "It's in that little closet," he said, pointing to a narrow door across from the bed.

Nurse Trahos looked annoyed, but she opened the door to the patient closet.

"It should be in my left coat pocket," he said helpfully.

She retrieved the cell phone and handed it to him.

He gave her his best smile. "Thank you, Nurse Trahos. God will bless you for this," he called as she left the room. He thought he saw her roll her eyes as she closed the door. He looked at the clock again. 2:47. It was going to be a long day.

He pondered what Dr. Ladd said. *You could have killed yourself with those pills.* Granted, it hadn't gone as smoothly as planned. He had followed the instructions to the letter, unlocking the front door, lying down on the sofa in the living room to wait for the paramedics. The chest pains had started almost immediately and he worried that maybe his heart hadn't been as healthy as he'd thought. He had trouble breathing and had broken out in a cold sweat. By the time the paramedics arrived— fourteen minutes after he'd placed the call—he was lying on the living room floor feeling as if an 800-pound gorilla was sitting on his chest.

Still, all's well that ends well. All he had to do now was wait for Stephen to show up or call.

When his cell phone rang, he grabbed it.

"How you doing, Reverend? I heard you got hammered by your heart."

The reverend swallowed his disappointment. It was only Ethan Gorr. "How'd you know about it?"

"CNN just gave you 15 seconds."

"What'd they say?"

"Said you'd suffered a mild heart attack."

"Is that all?"

"What'd you expect? You're not the goddamned Pope."

The reverend smiled. Dr. Ladd had kept her word.

"So, when are you going to get me that meeting with your son?"

"That's why I'm in the hospital, Ethan."

There was a brief silence, then, "You faked a heart attack to get your son to meet with me?"

The reverend was silent.

Gorr barked a laugh. "I had no idea you were so goddamned clever," and hung up.

The reverend sighed. "Desperate men..." he said to the empty room.

CHAPTER 28

When Penny heard the word *hospital* her first thought was '*Something has happened to Gerard!*' She gripped the telephone with both hands. "This is Mrs. Hopkins," she said in a high, strained voice.

"Are you related to Reverend Marshall Hopkins?"

"He's my father-in-law." She felt a brief surge of relief.

"Ma'am, we admitted him this afternoon. He appears to have had a mild heart attack."

She remembered the phone call last week when she hung up on him. "Is he going to be okay?"

"He's resting now. Would you like his room number?"

She wrote down the number and thanked the woman for calling, then sank into a chair at the breakfast table clutching the phone. She had wanted to say yes when he asked to see Gerard last week. Instead, she'd hung up on him. *What if he dies without seeing his grandson?* She would be guilty of denying a man of God his last wish.

She wandered through the house trying to decide what to do. She would go to the hospital, of course, but she needed to talk to Stephen first. What was it, three hours earlier in Mexico City? She dialed his cell and got his voice mail. She left a message for him to call her, then began looking for the name of the hotel he had mentioned. She had jotted it on a yellow post-it, but where had she put it? She finally found it on her nightstand in the bedroom. She went to her computer and looked up the number on the internet and dialed it. The desk clerk told her in heavily accented English that Stephen Hopkins was not registered.

"Please see if he has checked out."

After a moment, the clerk said the hotel had never had a guest by that name.

Penny tried to summon her faded college Spanish. "*¿Es usted seguro? Intento otra vez, por favor.*" Are you sure? Try again, please.

The clerk rattled off a spate of words.

Penny had no idea what she was saying. "*Olvidese!*" she said. Forget it!

She found another hotel in Mexico City where she and Stephen had once stayed. She dialed the number, but this clerk's English was even worse. She slammed the phone down. Stephen would just have to wait until he got home to find out his father had had a heart attack.

#

Three hours later, she was on I-66 heading toward the Inova Fairfax Hospital in Falls Church, Virginia. She drove within the speed limit, eager to get there but reluctant as well. Stephen should be with her. After all, the estrangement was his fault, not hers. She had never approved of his severing ties with his father, but it had been easier to go along than to fight with him. She merged onto the 495, and saw the sign for her exit two miles ahead. She thought about the reverend lying alone and frightened in the hospital room. She and Stephen were the only family he had.

She exited and circled right on Gallows Road, found the hospital entrance, and parked the van. Inside, she bought a red Amaryllis at the gift shop. When she walked into the reverend's room, he appeared to be sleeping. An IV tube ran from the back of his hand to an inverted plastic bag dangling above his head. She felt a tightening in her throat. *He looked so frail!* She set the Amaryllis on a table and removed her coat and gloves and draped them over a chair. When she looked up, he was watching her.

He held out his arms. "Penny," he whispered, with a weak smile.

She burst into tears and leaned down to embrace him.

"It's all right," he said in the silken voice she remembered so well. "It's God's way of reminding me I'm just His vessel."

"I'm so sorry, Reverend."

"All is forgiven?"

She nodded, unable to speak.

He patted her hand until she regained her composure. She asked about his heart attack, how it had happened, what the prognosis was. He brushed away her concern as if a heart attack was an everyday occurrence. "Tell me about Gerard."

They talked for an hour, stopping only when a nurse came in to check on him. She told him about the years of home-schooling Gerard, about his recent switch to high school and how much she missed their time together. She told him how bright his grandson was and about his interest in primitive tribes and how she hoped he might become a missionary someday. "He can still be a missionary in a wheelchair, can't he?"

The reverend assured her he could.

"The problem is, Reverend, he stays in his room most of the time chatting on the computer with his internet buddies. There are so many harmful, impure things that he could get involved in. I worry about him ever finding God. He seems to have picked up Stephen's disrespect—I should say *contempt*—for the church."

"You bring him to see me, my dear, I'll nudge him in God's direction. Now tell me about Stephen. What has my son been up to?"

The reverend watched his daughter-in-law's face change at the mention of Stephen's name. Her lips tightened; her eyes became guarded. She said he was due back from Mexico City that evening. Then she grew silent. It was as if the words and emotions that had flown so freely for the past two hours had to be reined in and stuffed back into a protective shell. Things must not be good between her and Stephen. But he was back in her good graces now. He could help her, maybe learn a thing or two about Stephen and his book in the process.   "Penny, would you like to pray with me?"

"Oh, Reverend, you don't know how much I need that," she said, tears spilling down her cheeks.

He smiled and took her hand in both of his and began to pray.

#

Gerard sat in front of the school and waited for his mother. She was late, probably because of the snow but he didn't mind. Snow reminded him of good times: snowball fights with his friends, building snowmen with his dad, making snow angels with his mom. He took off his glasses and turned his face up and let the snow fall on it. The beep of a horn brought him back to the present. He wiped his glasses and put them on and started toward the van.

Penny lowered the window. "You need any help?"

"No, Mom."

He hoisted himself into the passenger seat and reached down for his chair. He folded it and slid it behind the seat while his mother threw plaintive looks at him. In the beginning, she had insisted on lifting the chair into the van herself. One day, he refused to move until she got back into the driver's seat. He knew it was hard for her to sit quietly and not even offer advice, but he had to prove he could get in and out by himself before she would agree to install the hand controls he'd been asking for since September. He was wearing her down though, he could see it.

She told him about his grandfather's heart attack as she pulled away from the curb.

"Will he be all right?"

"He's going to be fine."

He remembered Papa Marsh, as he used to call him, taking him to the circus and to baseball games in Baltimore when his dad was on one of his many trips, but after the accident, he stopped coming around. Gerard kept asking when he was coming back, until he saw how it upset both his parents. One night he overheard one of their arguments and realized his father held his grandfather responsible for the shooting. But that was stupid. The fact that he was there when it happened didn't make him responsible for it.

"He wants to see you."

Gerard looked at his mother with surprise. "You'd allow that?"

"Of course."

"He's been asking to see me for the past two years. Why are you saying yes now?"

His mother shot him a look. "How did you know he's been asking to see you?"

"The answering machine, Mom. He left messages."
Geez! She must think he was oblivious to what went on in their house.

"Baby, I'm sorry, it was wrong of us to keep him away, and I want to mend that fence."

"Why? Because he's had a heart attack and you're afraid he might die?"

His mother was silent for a moment. He could feel her disapproval.

"Gerard, sometimes it takes something like this to remind us how precious family is. That's why he'll be staying with us for a while. I'm checking him out of the hospital in the morning if he's well enough to come home."

"He's coming to our house?"

"We can't let the poor thing stay in that big house in McLean all by himself."

"What's Dad going to think?"

"I'm sure he'll be fine with it. I tried to call him to tell him about Papa Marsh's heart attack, but his cell phone wasn't on. I tried a couple of hotels in Mexico City, but he wasn't registered. Do you know where he's staying?"

Gerard thought fast. "He's already in the air, Mom. His plane lands in three hours."

He watched the snow fall past the window. His dad would get his mom's message on his cell, but he didn't know about the calls to the hotels. Gerard would have to warn him so he would have time to think up a cover story.

He watched the snow fall past the window. What would have happened if she'd found Alvarado's number and called him? She'd have learned his dad had lied about the trip. Weird! You never knew what would trip you up when you told a lie. Would his lies to Moley and Gunner come back to haunt him some day?

CHAPTER 29

It was snowing hard by the time Stephen's plane landed at Dulles International Airport two hours late. He pulled his carry-on from the overhead bin and joined the queue of passengers leaving the plane, still thinking about his meeting with Heather Eastlake. He had replayed their conversation over and over, looking for clues he might have missed, clues that might indicate she had been the woman at the hearing, but her words kept echoing in his head: *I'm afraid you've wasted your trip.*

By the time he made it to the parking lot through the covered pedestrian walkway, his car was layered with snow. He threw his carry-on in the back seat and scraped the snow off the windows, then joined the queue headed for the parking kiosk. He turned on his cell phone and was greeted by a sharp ping and a text message reading "2 missed calls."

He called his voice mail and heard Penny's voice: "Where *are* you? Call me." The second message was from Gerard: "Dad, you have to call me on my cell before you talk to mom. It's urgent."

He paid the parking attendant and pulled into the line of traffic exiting the airport. It was snowing hard and the traffic inched forward. He punched Gerard's number into the speaker phone. "What's the problem?" he asked, when Gerard answered.

"Papa Marsh had a heart attack."

Stephen's heart sank. "How bad is it?"

"Not so bad, I guess. They're discharging him tomorrow."

"That's good." He felt relief, then a wave of guilt at their long estrangement.

"Mom's bringing him here to recuperate."

"She's bringing him to our house?"

"Yes."

He maneuvered the car onto the 267 and turned on the windshield wipers. It was starting to snow hard.

"Dad, are you okay with that?"

He thought for a moment. *Was he okay with it?* He hadn't seen his father in more than four years, hadn't really wanted to see him. But how would he feel now if the heart attack

126

had killed him and he could never talk to his father again? The undercurrent of guilt he'd felt for years would consume him, that's how he'd feel. Now here was a chance for reconciliation, not just for him but for the whole family.

For a moment, Stephen's attention was caught by a car ahead of him in the left lane. It spun a three-sixty, then continued on as if nothing had happened.

"Dad?"

"Sorry. It's snowing like crazy. I'm glad your grandfather's coming to our house."

"Dad, there's something else."

"What?" He saw his exit ahead and began to slow down. The wipers were impotent against the snow, which now swirled fiercely into the windshield.

"Mom tried to call you to tell you about Papa Marsh."

"I know. She left a message on my cell to call her."

"Well, here's the thing. She tried to reach you at a hotel in Mexico City and she asked me if I knew where you were staying, but it was five o'clock by then and I just said you were already in the air."

Brake lights flashed red through the curtain of snow and he tapped his brakes, then pushed the pedal hard as the car ahead of him stopped. His tires skidded slightly, then gripped the ice. The red lights dimmed and the cars began to move slowly. He gripped the wheel, eased the car forward. "Thanks, son. I'll square it with her," he said, hoping fervently that he could.

"Did Dr. Eastlake turn out to be the woman you saw?"

"No. Looks like I flew to California for nothing."

"Sorry, Dad."

"Tell your mom I'll be home in a few minutes."

He turned off the speaker phone. Not only had the trip been a waste of time, lying about it to Penny may have created a serious problem. Now he would have to deal with that and with his father. And he had no idea what to do next about the threat from GFED.

CHAPTER 30

The next afternoon, Stephen drove the van to Fairfax to pick up his father. The sky was a brilliant blue and snow was piled like meringue on bare limbs of trees and bushes and lay in deep drifts against the sides of buildings. He was oblivious to the beauty of the day, his mind on Penny and the lie he'd told her about his trip. She had been asleep when he got home from the airport, and this morning she had been busy preparing the guest room for his father's arrival and hadn't mentioned her phone calls to Mexico City. He would have to tell her the truth tonight.

His father was sitting in a wheelchair when Stephen walked in. "Son," he said, his eyes welling with tears, "It has been so long."

"Hello, Dad." He felt a stinging at the back of his eyes as he crossed the room. He stuck out his hand but his father opened both arms and Stephen leaned down and gave him a brief hug, then pulled away. "Do you have a bag or anything?"

"Just that lovely flower Penny brought me. I didn't really have time to pack."

Stephen gave a short laugh and handed the potted amaryllis to his father. "Tell me how it happened."

"I called 911 when I started having chest pains, but by the time they arrived I felt like my chest was going to crack open."

Stephen listened as his father talked about his short hospital stay, but once in the car, they fell silent. He concentrated on the still icy road while his father held the plant in his lap and hummed some vaguely familiar hymn. It was an old habit that Stephen used to find soothing.

After a few minutes, he stopped humming. "We really should talk, you know, clear the air."

Stephen was silent. This was the part he'd been dreading.

"I've forgiven you for leaving the church. Did that a long time ago. So, we can put that to rest, can't we?"

Stephen bristled. He didn't need his father's forgiveness. He had every right to pursue the career he wanted. He caught himself before he blurted out words that sounded even to him like adolescent resentment. "I'm happy with the work I'm doing."

"Well, that's what's important. Now, as to that shooting in Mondogo—"

"No!" Stephen shot a look at his father. "We don't have to talk about that. I *won't* talk about it. It happened. It's over. Gerard is doing amazingly well despite his useless legs—"

The reverend slapped his hand on the dashboard. "I know you blame me but I had nothing to do with it! As God is my witness, I had nothing to do with it."

Stephen gripped the wheel, took a deep breath. "Of course you didn't. Now let's drop the subject. You've got a long recuperation ahead of you."

#

The reverend grasped the potted flower with both hands and stared out at the white landscape. The reconciliation wasn't going quite as well as he'd hoped, but at least it was underway. He would be at Stephen's for a while, a long while if he had any say in it. There was plenty of time. He leaned back in the seat and resumed humming.

#

Dinner was a festive affair that evening. Penny had prepared poached salmon, steamed vegetables, and brown rice, while setting the table with the family's special occasion Limoges china, fresh flowers, and candles. As they gathered around the table, she lit the candles and poured sparkling water for Gerard and the Reverend, and champagne for Stephen and herself. When they were seated, she lifted her glass and said "Welcome home, Reverend."

"Welcome home, Papa Marsh."

"Welcome to our house, Dad." Stephen touched his glass to his father's.

The reverend beamed. "You have no idea what this means to me." He gave each of them a long slow look. "To our family," he said.

Penny smiled. "Of course next time, I'll pour you champagne and I know that you prefer a standing rib roast with Yorkshire pudding, but we've got to be careful with your heart."

The Reverend returned her smile. "Of course, my dear. So very thoughtful of you," silently wishing he was enjoying a celebratory glass of champagne and his favorite Yorkshire pudding instead of brown rice.

During dinner, he regaled them with stories about his early missionary work. Penny and Gerard listened raptly, but Stephen felt as if he could hardly breathe. His father seemed to suck up all the oxygen in the room.

As soon as dessert was over—fresh fruit instead of the usual bread pudding with rum sauce, another of the reverend's favorites—Stephen excused himself and went to his study. He tried to read, but he kept reading the same paragraph over and over. Finally, he gave up and turned on the music. He leaned back in his chair and put his feet on his desk and lost himself in the sounds of Rachmaninov's *Second Piano Concerto*. When his cell phone rang, he looked at the Caller ID. An 805 number. Heather Eastlake. He had not expected to hear from her again, and his pulse quickened at the sound of her voice.

"I'm a little embarrassed to call you," she said.

"Why?"

"Because I lied to you."

"About what?"

"The very thing you came to see me about."

Stephen held his breath and waited.

"I *have* had recurring dreams, horrible nightmares about children killing other children."

"But no missing hours?"

"That's the second lie." She told him about missing her APA meeting and waking up late on Saturday with no memory of what she'd done or where she'd been the night before.

Stephen was elated. "Why didn't you tell me when I was there?"

"I was embarrassed. I was afraid something inappropriate had happened that night and that you must have known about it or been involved in it."

"Inappropriate?"

"You know...that maybe I'd been drugged." She was silent for a moment. "It almost drove me crazy not knowing what I'd done or what had been done to me. But I'd almost put it out of my mind when you showed up. Then you told me you'd seen me somewhere and you were so mysterious about it...it just freaked me out. I had absolutely no idea what you'd seen me doing or with whom."

"I'm sorry. I never meant to imply—"

"It's okay. I'm glad you found me because it forced me to confront my lack of memory about that evening. After you left, I called a friend at the Miller Memory Lab here at UCSB and asked for her help."

Stephen felt as if he'd just seen a glimmer of light after being stranded in a deep dark cave. "Have you done it yet?"

"This morning. I remember *everything* that happened that night. It is literally unbelievable."

She had been there! The glimmer of light became a floodlight. Even without hearing the details, he was certain her memories would match his own. "I want to hear everything, Heather, but please don't tell me about it yet."

"Don't tell you?" She sounded puzzled. "You flew all the way out here to find me and now you don't want to know?"

"I *do* want to know. But if your memories are what I think they'll be, it's critical that they be absolutely independent of mine. We each need to write what we remember about that night before we talk about it."

"Why?"

"In case we need to prove to others that we didn't corroborate on a hoax."

She was silent for a moment. "All right. But I want to talk about it in person. I can come there on Friday."

More delay! He thought about suggesting they exchange emails now and have a preliminary phone conversation. Then decided against it. He understood her need for a face-to-face meeting. "Can I make a hotel reservation for you?"

"I'll take care of it. I always stay at the Hay-Adams."

"Good. We can have lunch there Saturday."

"Couldn't we get together Friday night? I'm about to go crazy with this in my mind."

He thought of the elaborate dinner Penny was planning to celebrate his father's birthday on Friday. "That would be difficult for me."

"Saturday then. Lunch at the Lafayette Room."

"I'll see you there."

"Stephen?"

"Yes?" He could hear her take a tremulous breath.

"It really happened, didn't it?"

He felt as if she had just stepped up and lifted an enormous boulder off his shoulders. He was no longer in this alone. "Yes, Heather. It really happened."

CHAPTER 31

The next day, Penny set about her weekly task of cleaning Stephen's office. She sang as she cleaned, feeling a lightness not just in her spirits but in the house. The air seemed warmer, lighter. It was almost as if a different family had taken up residence in their home.

She was dusting his desk when she noticed a ticket confirmation from United Airlines. She glanced at it without thinking; then for some reason she looked closer. IAD to LAX, LAX to IAD. Dulles Airport to Los Angeles, Los Angeles to Dulles. She looked at the date. Departure: Monday, November 29. Return: Tuesday, November 30. There was no flight to Mexico City.

She stood still for a long moment remembering how she'd tried to reach him about his father's heart attack. A coldness spread out from the center of her stomach and ran through her veins like an icy current. She folded the confirmation and tucked it into the pocket of her sweat suit.

That evening, she confronted Stephen in the bedroom. He was sitting in his chair reading a book, glasses perched on the end of his nose.

She pulled the ticket confirmation out of her pocket and thrust it at him. "I found this when I was cleaning your office." She folded her arms across her chest and leaned against the bedpost.

He grimaced when he saw what it was. He laid the book on the table next to the chair and removed his glasses. "I didn't go to Mexico City."

"Obviously."

"I went to California to meet the professor I saw when I was abducted."

She was silent, waiting.

"When I told you and Gerard about the memories I recovered during regression, you walked out and said you didn't want to hear any more. But there was more to the story. As I left the hearing, I saw a woman entering the room I'd just left."

"That was the professor you went to see?"

"Yes. I thought that maybe she'd been a witness at the hearing, like me, and if so, she might be able to corroborate my story. Gerard helped me find her on the internet, so I called her and asked her to meet with me."

"You involved our son in this?" Her eyebrows went up like flags.

"Penny, the woman was my chance to prove that what happened to me that night really happened. She was my only chance."

"So, was she abducted by aliens, too?" She looked at him coldly.

He ignored her sarcasm. "She wouldn't even admit she'd had any missing time, maybe because I was a stranger, but after I left, she underwent hypnosis. I think her memories are going to match mine—"

"What do you mean, you *think*?"

"We haven't actually talked about them yet. We're meeting Saturday to compare stories and decide what to do."

"You're going back to LA?"

"No." He stood up, took a step toward her. "She's coming here. Tomorrow night."

Her hand flew to her throat. "When were you going to tell me?"

He said nothing.

"You've been lying about her since the beginning!"

"Pen, I'm sorry I lied about the trip. But it's about GFED, not about the woman—"

"Stop it! I'm sick of hearing about GFED and aliens from outer space. Why don't you just admit you're having an affair?"

"Because I'm *not* having an affair."

She was silent. Two bright pink spots had appeared on her cheeks.

"Penny, you have to believe me. I am *not* having an affair."

She closed her eyes, blew out a breath, opened her eyes. She looked angry and bewildered. "I don't know what to believe any more."

She went into the bathroom and closed the door. He heard the lock turn, then the sound of water running in the bathtub. It was a signal he had learned to recognize over the years, a signal that she wanted to be alone, probably for the whole night. He picked up his tea and book and padded down the hall to his study. He could hear the low thrum of music from Gerard's room at the end of the hall. He hoped it had drowned out the sound of their argument. And he prayed that the reverend had slept through it.

He closed the study door and stretched out on the couch. He had been wrong not to tell her about Heather, but she hadn't wanted to hear any more about the hearing. She had walked out of the room, and she'd refused to listen to the rest of the story the next day. If he had told her he was going to Los Angeles to meet a woman he'd seen at those hearings, she would have thought just what she thought now: that he was having an affair. She simply would not believe that extraterrestrials existed, so how could she believe he had met with them? Maybe she couldn't believe it because they had chosen to make contact with *him*. Sometimes that was too much for him to accept as well. He struggled with it every morning. For a moment or two before he awakened fully, his mind was blessedly blank, and then the memories of that night would pour in and he would have to slog through layers of his own disbelief. Sometimes he almost convinced himself he'd had an elaborate dream and then he would listen to the recording of the session and when he heard his voice recounting the words of Morok and the Deputy Director, it was as if he were hearing *their* voices, and the experience would come back in full living color and he would know that it had been real.

Now there was hope that something could be done about the commission's verdict. Heather would corroborate his story, he was sure of that, and they would be able to go to the president for help. What happened after that was out of his control.

CHAPTER 32

As he crossed the opulent lobby of the Hay-Adams Hotel, Stephen wondered how Heather could afford to stay at such an expensive hotel on a professor's salary. Of course, if she saw the brownstone in Georgetown that he'd bought with his mother's money she might have similar thoughts. In the Lafayette Room, he spotted Heather at a table for two near a window. She wore a sweater slightly darker than her copper hair, which was pulled back in a ponytail. Beneath the table, he could see jeans-clad legs and tan boots. A tan leather jacket was draped over the back of her chair. She was staring out the window.

He started toward her table when the maître d' intercepted him. "I'm meeting the lady at that table," he said, motioning with his head.

Heather turned at the sound of his voice and waved. The maître d' nodded and backed away.

Stephen made his way to the table. They shook hands and exchanged hellos. He glanced at the white envelope lying on the table in front of her. The transcription of her memories no doubt. His was in his briefcase. He sat down opposite her and placed his briefcase beside his chair.

"Is that it?" he said, gesturing at the envelope.

She nodded and smiled. "It's about to burn a hole in the table."

He noticed a waiter on a trajectory to their table. "Shall we order before we start reading?"

"Can you get something to drink first? I can't eat until we read these things."

"Fine with me. I'll have the same wine as the lady," he said to the waiter. "We'd like to wait a few minutes before we order lunch."

"Are you ready?" she said, as the waiter walked away. Her lips curled in a hint of a smile. Her green eyes were serious.

"More than ready."

They exchanged their transcripts and read in silence. Stephen finished first. He was jubilant. She had provided fewer details, but her experience tracked his in almost every way. She remembered the same round windowless room with voices

136

emanating from the black rim that encircled the ceiling. She heard the same introduction from Chairman Morok, the same condemnation of the Namuh, saw the same violent holographic images. There were minor differences in their experiences. A limousine had not picked her up. She had been at home getting ready for her meeting and was apparently taken from and delivered back to her bedroom. She had received no holographic visit by Morok at the hearing, and there was no mention of how the quarantine or extermination would be implemented.

He sipped his wine and watched her as she read. Her face wore a look of despair, and he remembered how desperate he had felt when he realized the full impact of what he'd experienced. She must be going through that now, realizing with every word she read that the experience had not been a dream. He felt a flush of guilt at his jubilation.

#

Heather finished reading and placed the transcript carefully on the table. She did not want to look at Stephen, as if by not meeting his eyes she could postpone the fearful reality that was crowding in on her. Finally, she looked up. He was watching her with great compassion in his eyes.

"I feel as if I've just stepped off a cliff," she said.

"That's pretty much how I felt when I left the therapist's office."

"Do you suppose it could have been some sort of weird shared dream?"

"It happened, Heather. I am absolutely convinced of that."

She was quiet for a moment. "Do you know if the commission's final verdict was quarantine or extermination?"

"No. Morok said he had done what he could, whatever that meant, and that our fate was up to the commission."

"This is surreal."

"To say the least."

"Who have you told about it?'

"The therapist, of course, and my wife and son."

"Did they believe you?"

"My son did. My wife and the therapist think I'm nuts, that I'm imagining the whole thing. What about you? Have you told anyone?"

"Just my friend who did the regression."

"What did she say?"

"She was so excited she couldn't stop talking, but I didn't put much credence in her response. She's one of the top memory researchers at the lab but also a UFO nut." Heather gave a subdued laugh. "Listen to me! That's what people are going to call us, UFO nuts."

"We didn't see UFOs."

"No, we talked to the aliens that fly them."

They stared at each other for a moment, then burst out laughing. The laughter died quickly as they pondered the gravity of their situation. They drank some wine.

"I liked the way they called us Namuh," she said, her hand curved around the stem of her glass. "It helped me look at us objectively."

"I agree. I find myself thinking of us as Namuh."

She leaned forward. "Everything they said about us was based on our actual behavior, Stephen. But violence is not genetic, it's learned. Some learn it from their families; others from television and movies and video games; kids who grow up in ghettos sometimes turn to violence for survival. But it's all around us. All you really have to do is turn on the news. But the human race is *not* predestined for violent behavior by our DNA. I believe that with all my heart."

"Do you think we can change? As a race?"

She thought about it. Violence wasn't prescribed by DNA, but it was deeply ingrained in the culture. How could it possibly be eradicated? "I have to believe that we can change, given enough time and effort. But how are we going to convince GFED of that?"

"They need to see evidence that we're working to change our violent behavior, governments and individuals alike."

"How can we do that on a scale they would even notice in time to prevent extermination?"

"Someone with a worldwide presence has to convince the world that the threat is real."

"Who could do that? The UN?"

"If the UN had any real power, it would be ideal, but it doesn't."

"Who then?"

"The President."

She raised her eyebrows. "Wainwright?"

He nodded.

"You've kidding! He's in bed with the NRA, he believes in capital punishment, he's pouring money into the military—"

"But he's the most powerful leader in the world and he's smart. If we can convince him the threat is real, I think he'll do something about it. Anyway, he's our only hope."

She looked at him skeptically. "How will we get to him? I have no political connections. Do you?"

"My father knows the president."

"Really?"

"Somewhere in my mother's family tree there were Wainwrights. I think she's a second cousin to the president. But my father's connection has more to with his financial support of the party than with family ties."

"What does your father do?"

"He's a minister, an evangelist, actually."

"Ah! Marshall Hopkins is your father?" Heather's eyes widened as she said the name.

"Yes."

"I would never have guessed."

He sensed disappointment in her voice. "Hey, we don't choose our parents. He and I have been at odds for years because of religion. But he's a golfing buddy of the president. He could get us a meeting."

"But if you're estranged..."

"I guess you could say the estrangement is over. He had a mild heart attack while I was in California, and Penny insisted he recuperate in our guest room."

"Where's your mother?"

"She died seven years ago."

"I'm sorry."

"She had cancer," Stephen said by way of explanation.

They were silent for a few minutes, sipping their wine.

139

"Why us, Stephen? There are hundreds of child psychologists and cultural anthropologists in the world. Why did GFED choose us?"

"I've asked myself the same question."

"I can't stop asking it. I'm very good at what I do and I'm sure you are too, but others in our fields are just as capable, so why us?"

"Maybe it was fate or more likely, blind chance. There are a limited number of child psychologists and cultural anthropologists who had the precise knowledge and experience they wanted, so it had to be somebody in that small universe. In my case, it was probably my work with the Abigo and their nonviolent nature. In your case, you're the best in your field."

"But of course," she said, with a smile.

"The point is, they tapped us and now we both know what happened that night and what could happen to the human race. We can't sit on that knowledge and do nothing."

"You know we'll be putting our professional reputations on the line. Once this becomes public, we'll be labeled UFO freaks, just like I labeled my friend."

He rested his elbows on the table, clasped his hands beneath his chin. "Meeting with the president doesn't have to mean we're going public. I'm sure he would keep a lid on something like this as long as possible. But even if it means going public, how can we do nothing?"

"We can't be the only witnesses GFED called. Surely there are others."

He could see the doubt in her eyes, the desire to ignore the gauntlet that had been thrown at their feet. He'd had similar thoughts. *This does not belong to me. Let someone else do it.* He put his hand over hers. "Did you see anyone else when you were at the hearing?"

"No."

"So, if there are others, how do we find them? No one is going to come forward without someone to corroborate their story. It's up to us." He became aware of his hand on hers and withdrew it quickly. "We have a chance—no, we have the *responsibility*—to try to save the human race."

She gave him a half-smile.

"I know how absurd that sounds, but it's true. We have to convince the president that the Federation is real and that the threat is imminent. After that, it's up to him. But we have to take it at least that far." He leaned back in his chair and waited.

She said nothing for a few moments. Finally, she raised her wine glass toward him. "I am Namuh."

He looked at her solemnly and raised his glass. "I am Namuh," he replied.

As they touched glasses, he thought of the path that lay before them and he felt as if the world had just tilted on its axis.

CHAPTER 33

Marshall Hopkins was watching a golf tournament in the den when Stephen returned from his lunch with Heather. He was stretched out on the sofa, the blue afghan pulled up to his chin, a glass of red wine in his hand.

"Where are Penny and Gerard?" Stephen asked.

"Gerard's in his room, Penny's in the sunroom. She doesn't look very happy today, is something wrong?"

"I need to talk to you, Dad."

He reached for the remote control.

"Let's go to my study. I don't want Penny to walk in on us."

"Can it wait till after the tournament?"

"No, it can't."

The reverend cast a lingering look at Jon Rahm who was lining up a putt. He heaved a great sigh, took the afghan and wine glass, and followed Stephen upstairs. He made himself comfortable on the sofa and listened as his son told a preposterous story about being abducted by aliens. The longer Stephen talked, the more bizarre the story became. Now he was saying the aliens had threatened to wipe out the whole human race with gamma rays from the sun. *Such nonsense!* He was obviously suffering from some kind of hallucination. Hopkins held his tongue. He could not afford to alienate his son. Finally, Stephen told him about finding a psychologist who supposedly corroborated the fantastic tale.

"Sounds pretty serious, son."

"*Pretty* serious? I guess extermination of the human race could be considered pretty serious."

He rushed to amend his words. "That was certainly an understatement. In fact, I find your story fascinating. And alarming."

Stephen challenged him with a look. "Do you believe me?"

Marshall Hopkins projected a lifetime of evangelistic sincerity into his voice. "Yes, son, I believe you. How can I help?"

"You're the key, Dad. We need you to set up a meeting for us with President Wainwright. We have to tell him about the threat."

The reverend was quiet for a moment. He could get Stephen the meeting he wanted, but did he really think the president would lead a peace movement? How could a son of his be that naïve? If there really were such a threat, Wainwright would more likely launch an attack against the aliens. "What would you expect from the president?" he asked.

"Action of some kind to convince the Federation that we're willing to change our violent behavior. But this is a threat to the whole world, not just the United States. The President would have to get other world leaders involved—"

"Do you know what those leaders would do if they learned of a worldwide threat? They'd join the president in a preemptive strike against the common enemy."

"That would be exactly the wrong response, can't you see that? It would support GFED's view of us as a violent species."

"I see," the reverend said, though he didn't, really.

"A worldwide peace movement would give us some credibility. It could forestall the extermination process. Maybe prevent it altogether."

"A worldwide peace movement."

"Yes."

Stephen crossed his arms over his chest. "Maybe you could promote a peace movement through your millions of followers. Convince other religious leaders to do the same. Help it take hold at the grass roots level."

The reverend sipped his wine. Funny how things turn out. He had orchestrated a heart attack— risked his life in fact— to get back in Stephen's good graces so he could ask *him* for a favor, and now this extraordinary door had opened, as if nudged by the finger of God. If he set up this meeting with the president, Stephen would be under a moral obligation to return the favor by meeting with Ethan Gorr. *The Lord surely did work in mysterious ways.*

"Well?" Stephen was looking at him expectantly.

He hesitated before he spoke. When Wainwright learned the true nature of Stephen's visit, he would brand him a UFO crackpot, and his own friendship with the president would suffer. But if he refused to set up the meeting, worse things would happen. Stephen wouldn't agree to meet with Ethan Gorr, and that book of his would be published with all of its consequences. That would severely damage if not end his relationship with Wainwright, and it would greatly hamper his work in the church. He was not at all sure that everything Gorr did was legitimate, but like it or not, his ministry required a great deal of financial support and Gorr was a key contributor of that support.

The reverend chose the lesser of two evils. "Wainwright owes me a favor or two. I'll give him a call. Now," he said, slipping unconsciously into the Voice, "I have a favor to ask of you."

#

Later that afternoon, Reverend Hopkins made two phone calls from the guest bedroom. First, he dialed the private residence at the White House. That was one of the perks of his financial support, easy access to the President of the United States.

The president was cordial, as always. He asked about Hopkins' heart attack and they made small talk for a few minutes, then the reverend got to the business of the call. "Mr. President, I have a great favor to ask of you if I may."

"Of course, Reverend."

"Would you meet with my son Stephen and his colleague about a matter that relates to national security?"

"What do you mean, national security?" There was an immediate shift in Wainwright's tone, a pulling back, a reservation.

Hopkins had no intention of mentioning extraterrestrials to the president of the United States. "He wouldn't elaborate on the details, in light of my recent heart attack. Just said it was extremely important and it could affect national security."

There was silence on the other end of the line.

The reverend remembered something Stephen had said. "He asked if you would have your science advisor in the meeting so maybe it has something to do with those tribes he studies. Maybe one of them has a virus that threatens the country."

"I don't know, Marshall..."

"Mr. President, you know Stephen's reputation. He has worked with the State Department many times and he wouldn't ask for a frivolous favor." He refrained from adding, *just an outlandish one that will make him look like a fool.*

"Okay, Reverend. Call Halloran Monday morning and tell him I said to work Stephen in as soon as possible."

"Thank you, Mr. President."

Hopkins hung up, feeling somewhat diminished. He was used to granting favors, not asking for them. Granting favors made him feel noble and magnanimous. Asking made him feel like a supplicant, and he didn't like being in beggar's shoes. He shook off the feeling and dialed Ethan Gorr's number. His machine answered. He left a terse message: "My son agreed to meet with you. Call me so we can work out a time."

He hung up feeling even more diminished than after the call with Wainwright. What had happened to that noble feeling he got from granting favors? Ah, there was the rub. Gorr hadn't asked for a favor, he'd *demanded* that Hopkins set up a meeting with Stephen or else. The implied threat had galvanized him into the desperate act of faking a heart attack to keep Stephen's book from being published. He had to protect his image and the integrity of his ministry, and that, unfortunately, depended on money from Ethan Gorr and others like him.

Money! It really was the root of all evil. If it weren't for the money, he wouldn't give that sleazy little toad the time of day.

CHAPTER 34

Twenty-two thousand feet above the Caribbean, a happy little toad sat in the salon of his corporate jet and puffed on a Trinidad Fund adores. He had first tasted the cigar six months ago in the office of the Undersecretary of Defense, Duane Barber. Barber had waxed poetic about the cigar's exquisite taste with its subtle hints of chocolate and coffee and how it used to be produced exclusively for Fidel Castro. *Pretentious bastard!* Who cares about a two-bit dead dictator like Fidel Castro? And how the hell can you taste coffee and chocolate in a goddamned cigar? Still, a case of rare Cuban cigars makes an impressive gift, which was why he was carrying a case to Bolivia for the newly elected President Carlos Barrios.

Two hours later, puffing on another Fundadore, he landed at El Alto International Airport in La Paz. A limousine sent by Barrios whisked him directly to the presidential palace, and an aide escorted him to the president's office. It was much grander than the Oval Office, where he had once attended a private reception. The antique furnishings were dark, some heavily gilded, and the domed ceiling was at least fifteen feet high with religious-looking frescos painted on the bowl of the dome. *What did they think this was, the goddamned Sistine Chapel?*

President Barrios stepped forward to greet him. He was a small slender man with classic Latin features and exquisite grooming. Gorr was immediately cheered by the fact that Barrios didn't tower over him like the lanky U.S. President. He could handle the couple of inches that Barrios had on him.

He handed Barrios a box of Trinidad Fundadores. "You know, these were once produced exclusively for Fidel Castro."

Barrios thanked him effusively. "Fidel gave me a case of Fundadores many years ago, but they are long gone. I'm delighted to have the opportunity to savor them again."

Goddamn it! He should have brought something American, like a case of Jack Daniels. He stifled his annoyance as Barrios launched into a story about Castro. He preferred to get down to business but he knew from experience and from the admonitions of his staff that was not going to happen, not in

146

Latin America. There would be a sumptuous multi-course meal with a different wine for every course, followed by brandy and cigars, and only then, sated with food and drink, would they begin to talk business.

President Barrios, however, surprised him. He ushered Gorr out the Palace's rear entrance where three black limousines waited, surrounded by half a dozen men who looked like the Latin version of secret service agents. Gorr and Barrios climbed into the middle limo and sat opposite each other, and the three cars set off on a tour of the countryside. As the entourage circled the palace and headed north toward Lake Titicaca, Barrios pointed out the snow-capped Illimani Mountain. "*Magnifico, no?*"

"Yeah, magnifico."

Barrios gave Gorr a sly look. "I'm sure you couldn't care less about sightseeing."

Gorr started to protest, but Barrios stopped him. "This is not a sight-seeing tour, Señor Gorr. It is simply safer to speak in the privacy of this automobile than in my office. We search the office every week for listening devices—'bugs' I think you call them...but somehow my political opponents manage to hide them again by the time of the next search. The automobiles we guard continuously and still search them twice a day."

"I understand." Gorr was in favor of anything that would prevent their conversations from being recorded.

"You know that we recently gained access to the Pacific through a corridor in the Atacama Desert?"

Gorr nodded. He had read that the passageway had been granted to Bolivia by Chile's last president who had been ousted a year ago. The new Chilean president might well want it back.

"We need to protect that access," Barrios said.

In earlier conversations Barrios had dropped veiled hints about importing contraband material into his country. Gorr had been sure it was weapons he wanted, and he had structured a deal with his contacts on the military weapons black market. He took the cue. "I can get you what you need to protect it, Mr. President. I have ways of delivering advanced weapons—the best the U.S. has to offer—without any trace of their source or ultimate destination."

"What kind of weapons are we talking about, exactly?"

"You name it, I can get it."

"M16s?"

"Yes."

"Shoulder-fired missiles?"

"Absolutely."

Barrios nodded approvingly. "How will you implement all this?"

"Warehouses are the key. You will need warehouses for your local storage; my company will need warehouses to store our logging equipment. I propose we share the warehouses. When I ship my logging equipment, your weapons will be hidden inside."

Barrios' eyes lit up. "Your equipment is large enough to handle hundreds, even thousands of weapons?"

"Hell, my semis and trailers are big enough to supply weapons for a small war! Plus, we can hide them in our loaders and skidders and bulldozers—"

Barrios laughed. "I get the picture."

Gorr gave a sly grin. "When we unload the weapons, you can lock them in a warehouse and paint 'Logging Chemicals. Danger!' on the side. No one would ever think of looking there."

Barrios chuckled appreciatively. "*Perfecto!*"

He readily agreed to contract with Gorr Resources to build the warehouses, then they talked about possible locations. Finally, they shook hands to seal the agreement. There would be nothing in writing that could be traced to either man.

Gorr offered Barrios a cigar as they headed back to the palace. It was time to talk about the little surprise he had saved for last. He pulled out his lighter and lit Barrios' cigar, then his own. "Do you have any need to ship certain, shall we say, *sensitive* goods out of your country?"

"I beg your pardon?" Barrios looked wary.

"My company will be shipping a steady stream of mahogany logs to U.S. ports, right?"   "Of course."

"We could use a few of the logs as covert shipping containers."

"Covert shipping containers?"

Gorr leaned forward. "Logs are usually cut into twelve to fourteen-foot lengths. A few logs in each shipment could be hollowed out to create secret compartments. Whatever is placed inside these compartments would be hidden deep within the log and shipped to the same destination."

"What kind of sensitive goods are we talking about?"

"That's strictly up to you, but I can guarantee you that U.S. customs agents aren't going to be pushing around three-thousand-pound logs looking for suspicious materials."

"And how would you be paid for the products shipped in such containers?"

Gorr smiled benevolently. "I'm sure we can negotiate a fee that's appropriate to the products being shipped."

#

The President of Bolivia looked with increased respect at the short round man across from him. It was not often that he underestimated people, but he may have let Gorr's appearance cloud his usually acute judgment. "What about your people? Would they know what was in these covert containers?"

"No," Gorr said. "Here's how it would work. I'll supply you with containers marked 'Wood Preservatives,' in which your, uh, manufacturers can pack their goods and deliver them to our warehouses. They'll pay me a shipment fee which I'll split with your country. When the shipment reaches its destination, the buyers of your goods can pick up the containers, and after they remove the goods, they can ship the containers back to you for reuse."

Barrios smiled. The idea was quite ingenious. It would give Bolivian coca growers a way to ship certain coca-based products to virtually any destination in the world at very little risk. But it would be political suicide if his opponents ever found out about it. He would have to make sure nothing could be traced back to him. "I'm curious, Mr. Gorr. How will you explain the hollowed-out sections to your customers that buy the mahogany logs?"

Gorr laughed out loud. "You'd be surprised at what you can sell to certain Americans. All I have to do is tell my smaller customers some cockamamie story about how the logs were harvested in an environmentally sensitive way and offer them a discounted price. They'll line up to buy them."

Barrios smiled. This was an interesting fellow indeed. "Mr. Gorr, you are an innovative thinker and a true friend to my country. Keep us in mind if you have any other revolutionary ideas." He winked when he uttered *revolutionary*.

#

Ethan Gorr watched the city of La Paz recede beneath him until it was obscured by a thin layer of clouds. He clipped off the end of a cigar. He had finally presented the logging contract to Barrios after a five-course lunch, but Barrios was much more pleased with the weapons deal and the covert containers. Actually, so was he. Profits from those two agreements would be twenty times that of the logging contract and would go directly to ERG Holding Company. Which meant he would make twenty times what his brothers made from the logging contract.

He smiled to himself and put his feet on the opposite seat and lit the cigar. He took a deep draw, held the smoke in his mouth. He blinked in surprise. By God! It *did* taste a little like chocolate. And coffee. And maybe a hint of caramel?

CHAPTER 35

Stephen parked at the Hay-Adams Hotel where Heather was waiting for him for the short walk to the White House. A young woman ushered them down a thickly carpeted hall into a small conference room in the West Wing. In the middle of the room was an oval conference table surrounded by eight low-backed chairs.

"You may wait here for the others," the woman said.

"Will the president be joining us?" Stephen asked.

The woman glanced at her notebook. "I have Kevin Halloran, Kimberly Dyer and Calvin Williams on my list."

"But not the president?"

"No. But he's been known to pop into a meeting unexpectedly." She smiled and closed the door. They took seats facing the interior windows.

Stephen frowned. "You'd think he would be interested enough to show up for a national security matter."

"Maybe he sends his staff to check things out first," Heather said. "Kimberly Dyer is the National Security Advisor, Halloran's his Chief of Staff. That's pretty high level. Do you know who Calvin Williams is?"

"The only Calvin Williams I know used to play for the Lakers. I doubt it's the same person."

As if on cue, Calvin Williams entered the room. He was a six-foot-six African-American who moved with the fluid grace of a dancer. He wore a dark blue suit, white shirt with French cuffs threaded with gold cufflinks, and a pale-yellow tie. His head was shaved as if to show off its elegant shape, and a tiny gold hoop graced his left earlobe. On his left ring finger was an NBA championship ring.

Stephen and Heather stood when he walked in.

"You must be Dr. Hopkins and Dr. Eastlake," Williams said, offering his hand first to Heather, then to Stephen. "I'm Calvin Williams, the White House science advisor."

Stephen tilted his head back and met Williams' eyes with a smile. "It's a pleasure to meet you. I used to watch you play for the Lakers. You were formidable."

Williams laughed, a deep mellow laugh. "In a former life."

"When did you join the president's staff?"

"About a year ago. After I retired from basketball, I completed my Ph.D. in quantum physics, then spent a dozen years in academia and private industry. Now I'm co-chair of PCAST, the President's Council of Advisors on Science and Technology." He blew out his breath and grinned. "I wake up every day wondering how *that* happened."

They laughed.

"Here comes Ms. Dyer," Williams said, glancing at the window.

Kimberly Dyer was talking over her shoulder to an assistant who was trotting to keep up. Her blonde hair was cut short except for a long shock on top that tended to fall forward when she lowered her head. She dressed exclusively in crisply tailored black or white suits with moderately short skirts and a splash of color at the neck. Today she wore black with a splash of emerald green. She leaned toward the assistant and said something inaudible, then tossed her hair back and opened the door. The assistant scurried away.

"Hello, Calvin," Dyer said as she walked in. She glanced at Stephen, then at Heather, who had both risen to their feet. "You must be the professors with the national security issue."

"I'm Stephen Hopkins and—"

"Halloran briefed us." She waved them back to their chairs and sat down at the head of the table. "He's late as usual. Can we get started? I have exactly twenty minutes before I have to meet with the Secretary of State."

"We expect the president to join us, ma'am," Stephen said.

Dyer fixed him with an icy stare. "Do we?" Her voice, which tended toward shrill, rose on the first word, along with her eyebrows.

"We do," he said with a confidence he didn't feel.

"Well," she said, glancing at the window. "Here comes the boy who would know."

Kevin Halloran walked in looking hassled in blue shirt with rolled-up sleeves and a red tie knotted loosely at his neck.

He was in his late thirties, medium height with a biker's build, clean-shaven, slicked-back hair the color of wet sand, and the eyes of a predator. When he spoke, he fired the words like bullets from an Uzi.

"I see we're all here. Have the professors been introduced? Stephen here..." he jerked his head toward Stephen, "is an anthropology professor at Georgetown University and son of the Reverend Marshall Hopkins...I'm sure you know who he is, pastor to Presidents and all that." He turned toward Heather, "...and Heather is a psychologist from the University of California in Santa Barbara. Back in my days, UCSB was the hottest party school in the country."

Heather returned his smirk with a cold smile.

Dyer said, "Can we get on with the meeting?"

"By all means, Kimberly." He sat down at the other end of the table. "Okay, professors, let's hear it. You said this had something to do with national security."

Stephen refused to be intimidated. "We requested a meeting with the president. Will he be joining us?"

"Mr. Hopkins—"

"*Dr.* Hopkins," Heather said.

Halloran snapped a look at her. "What?"

"It's *Dr.* Stephen Hopkins," she said, holding his gaze. "Not mister."

Stephen groaned silently. They were not getting off to a good start.

"Right. *Dr.* Hopkins, as Chief of Staff my job is to vet all meetings of this nature and decide whether or not the president needs to get involved. Right now, you've got the attention of the top security person in the country, a first-rate scientist, and the eyes and ears of the president. That's me. So, let's get started."

Stephen shifted his attention to the others at the table. If he got through to anyone, it would not be Halloran. "Dr. Eastlake and I have learned about a grave threat to the security of America—actually, to the security of the world." He hesitated, then took a deep breath and dived into the void. "The threat is from a federation of civilizations from elsewhere in our galaxy."

He saw the incredulous expression on Kimberly Dyer's face and he could almost feel Halloran roll his eyes. Only Calvin Williams held his gaze. Stephen continued. "I understand that mentioning an alien civilization makes anything we say immediately suspect but I beg you to take us seriously. We are not amateur astronomers and we did not have an encounter with a UFO. We are respected scientists in our fields, and before this experience—which Dr. Eastlake and I had separately—we did not know each other. We are laying our reputations on the line by coming here. We are doing so because making the president aware of this threat is absolutely critical for the safety of the world."

He paused. All three were staring at him intently. He hurried on before anyone could make a comment. "Every scientist I know believes that intelligent life exists outside our small remote planet. Many of them believe there are advanced civilizations out there, and that contact with one of them will happen sooner or later. It has happened sooner than any of us expected.

"Six weeks ago, on the night of November 5th, Dr. Eastlake and I came into direct contact with an entity that calls itself the Galactic Federation which represents thousands of advanced civilizations in our galaxy, far advanced of any civilization on Earth."

Dyer interrupted. "I thought you said your experiences were separate."

"They were. We met each other three weeks later, but it turned out that everything happened on that same night."

Dyer raised her eyebrows. "I see."

Stephen continued. "The Federation—they call it GFED—considers humans to be a primitive tribe with a proclivity toward violence that makes us unfit for association with their civilized worlds. They fear we'll spread our violence—our exaltation of violence—to the rest of the galaxy."

"Now how would we do that?" Halloran asked.

"We already broadcast our violent culture to the universe every minute through the airwaves, and now that we've decoded the human DNA, they fear we'll broadcast that as well. Plus, we may soon possess the means of sending manned spacecraft beyond our solar system, and that has made them fear that we may physically contaminate their peaceful civilizations with our violent natures. The hearing at which Dr. Eastlake and I appeared was convened to determine what action was to be taken against the human race—"

Dyer interrupted again. "With all due respect, Dr. Hopkins, why were the two of you selected as the first contacts by an alien intelligence?"

"I don't know that we were the *first*, Ms. Dyer, but I believe they selected me for my experience with primitive tribes. It would, presumably, give them some insight into the primitive tribe they call the Namuh. That's their word for the human race."

"Why the hell would they call us nahmoo?" Halloran looked as if he had swallowed something unpleasant.

Stephen explained the origin of the word.

Dyer turned to Heather. "And why did they choose you, Dr. Eastlake?"

"The Federation is interested in human's propensity for violence and whether it is genetic or a learned behavior. I've published widely in this field as it pertains to children. I assume that's why they chose me."

"Out of all the scientists in the world these aliens picked the two of you," Halloran said.

Stephen said, "They may have called other witnesses, but we have no direct knowledge of that. The point is, they consider humans a threat to the other peaceful civilizations in the galaxy. To protect themselves from contamination by our violence, they are considering a preemptive strike, to put it in terms you can relate to."

"A preemptive strike." Kimberly Dyer stared at him.

Stephen rested his arms on the table and leaned forward. "Ms. Dyer, if we can't convince them that humans can change our violent ways, they will annihilate every human being on Earth."

They all stared at him. For a long moment, no one spoke.

"Where was this hearing held?" Dyer asked.

"We don't know. Neither of us has any memory of how we got to or from the meeting place."

Halloran smirked. "They probably beamed them up to an orbiting space station."

"The military knows every fragment of steel that is orbiting this planet," Dyer said. "If there were an alien space station out there, we would know about it."

Calvin Williams spoke up. "If the professors were teleported to a space station, it wouldn't have to be orbiting the Earth."

Dyer and Halloran looked at him as if surprised he was still in the room.

He shrugged. "Theoretically, teleportation is instantaneous travel through duplication of the original object— or person—in another place. If the professors were indeed teleported to a space station, it could have been orbiting Alpha Centauri as easily as Earth."

Dyer said, "This is all a little too sci-fi for me."

"So you're going to ignore it?" Williams asked.

Dyer gave him a stony look.

"C'mon, Kimberly. We raise the terror alert anytime the CIA monitors a slight increase in cell phone activity. And now Dr. Hopkins has suggested that we may be *annihilated* by an alien civilization and you're going to do nothing?"

"It's the word 'alien' that makes me somewhat skeptical, Calvin."

"With all due respect, you need to think outside the Beltway. Contact with an alien civilization is *not* so far-fetched. Ask any scientist. You shouldn't dismiss the subject out of hand."

Halloran turned to Stephen. "Did these aliens tell you *how* they're going to zap us?"

"Precisely that way, Mr. Halloran," Stephen snapped. "They plan to zap us with gamma rays from a probe they've placed in orbit around the sun. The good news is, it will be quick and painless."

Halloran looked as if he were torn between a wisecrack and a sober question, but Dyer spoke first. "I think the president should hear this directly from the professors," she said to Halloran. "How quickly can you get him here?"

#

President Wainwright walked into the conference room fifteen minutes later.

A murmur of "Mr. President" went around the table as everyone stood.

He leaned over the table and shook hands with Stephen. "Good to see you, Stephen. I trust your father is recovering from his heart attack?"

"Yes, Mr. President. He's doing very well."

"Glad to hear it. He's a tough old bird."

Stephen smiled. "That he is, sir."

Wainwright offered his hand to Heather. "You must be Dr. Eastlake."

"It's a pleasure to meet you, Mr. President."

"Please take your seats." He turned to Stephen. "Tell me about this national security threat."

Stephen summarized his meeting with GFED and described their fears about the human race and their verdict of either quarantine or extermination. Heather corroborated his story.

The president looked increasingly perturbed as they talked. "This group fears we'll contaminate their worlds with our violence, is that the essence of it?"

"Yes, sir. They fear us like we fear a new strain of virus. When we were threatened by Covid, we took steps to eradicate it to keep it from spreading. That's what they say they will do to the human race if they determine that our violent behavior is genetic."

"They would kill eight billion humans as if we were a virus." Wainwright's voice was flat.

"That seemed to be their message, sir."

"And if they determine our violence is behavioral rather than genetic?"

"They would initiate a quarantine to prevent us or our broadcasts from escaping our solar system. The fact that we might be broadcasting the human DNA concerns them greatly."

"And you don't know which verdict has been rendered?"

"No, sir."

157

Wainwright turned to his National Security Advisor. "What the hell do you make of this, Kimberly?"

"With all due respect to the professors, sir, we've had no sign of a threat from space. How can we respond to a peril we can't identify?"

Halloran broke in. "Quite frankly, sir, I think it's a crock."

Stephen glanced at Heather who was looking at Halloran with obvious distaste.

Wainwright ignored his Chief of Staff and turned to Dyer. "Has our military spotted any UFOs?"

"No, sir."

"What about our observatories? Have they picked up anything orbiting the sun?"

She shook her head. "A satellite orbiting the sun would very likely melt, and besides, it would be impossible to use a man-made satellite to control the sun's gamma rays."

"We're not talking *man-made* here."

The president looked at Calvin Williams.

Williams said, "Sir, scientists have been expecting contact with an alien civilization for decades, and if this is it, we would be very foolish to judge their technology by ours. It's feasible that an advanced civilization could have materials that wouldn't melt close to the sun, and it's not that difficult to postulate how they might control the sun's energy."

"I hear what you're saying, Cal, but what we have is a vague threat by something *purported* to be an alien civilization. How can we possibly react to that?"

"I'm just saying, we shouldn't dismiss it out of hand."

"Mr. President, I believe there's something we can do. Something *you* can do," Stephen interjected.

"And that is?"

"Make a dramatic move toward peace. Announce a unilateral withdrawal of troops from, say, Iraq, or wherever else we have them right now."

"Do you have any idea what you're asking?"

"It would be a show of good faith from the most powerful leader in the world. I think that could convince GFED to table any immediate plans for extermination."

"But you're not sure."

Stephen hesitated. "No, I guess I'm not sure."

Halloran interrupted. "Sir, I think you should be aware that both professors have a history of pacifism. Dr. Eastlake was arrested a few years back for lying in the street to protest the Iraqi war. Not that there were any tanks rumbling down the streets of Santa Barbara, but you get the point."

Heather spoke up. "This is not just about military violence, Mr. President. GFED is also concerned about individual violence. But changing our culture of violence will take a very long time whereas you can initiate an immediate and dramatic halt of military violence."

Stephen added, "This is a threat to all of humankind, sir, not just to America. To convince GFED that we are serious, a peace movement must be worldwide. You would need to get the UN involved."

The President gave him a steely look. "You want me to go to the UN and say aliens are threatening to blow up the world and we should all lay down our arms."

Stephen had to admit that sounded a bit naïve, but it was exactly what he wanted him to do. "It might work."

The President stood up, and everyone rose. "I have a great deal of respect for your father, Stephen, and I know you and Dr. Eastlake are highly respected in your fields, but what you are suggesting simply isn't feasible. I am not going to make a fool of myself in front of the United Nations."

"Sir, we wouldn't have come to you if the threat were not real—"

"I'm sure you believe that, but you may be victims of a hoax designed to play on your pacifist sensibilities."

Stephen could not believe he was going to do nothing. "Mr. President, please—"

The President stopped him with a gesture. "I dislike war and violence as much as anyone, Stephen, but we live in a very complex world and unless I have some kind of proof that this threat actually exists, there is nothing I can do."

CHAPTER 36

Heather swirled her wine and watched it form legs which ran slowly down the inside of the glass. The meeting had been a disaster. Calvin Williams had murmured a polite good-bye, but Dyer and Halloran had followed the president out of the room without so much as a parting glance. The same woman who had ushered them into the conference room ushered them out, and Heather suggested they go to the Hay-Adams for a drink. At ten past eleven, it was a bit early to drink, but it wasn't every day one got slapped in the face for trying to save the world.

She glanced at Stephen who was staring dejectedly at his drink. "We did everything we could, Stephen."

"They treated us like UFO freaks."

"I should have told you about my anti-war activities. Halloran's linking us with peaceniks, as he so quaintly put it, didn't help."

"It wouldn't have mattered. The FBI has a file on me too."

"Really? Why?"

"You have to have high security clearance to work with the State Department."

"You worked for the State Department?"

"They've called on me occasionally to report on a primitive tribe. But that's not the only reason for the FBI's interest. I've written articles advocating gun control, and there are probably a few diatribes in my file protesting the Iraq war."

"I'm glad to know you're a kindred spirit."

He looked up, met her eyes. "Not so kindred."

"What do you mean?"

He was silent for a minute. "I once plotted to murder someone."

She stared at him with disbelief. "I don't believe it."

He took a long swallow of his drink. "What are we going to do about GFED?"

"Wait! You can't say you plotted a murder and leave me guessing!"

"You don't really want to know the details."

"Yes, I do. You brought it up, so tell me."

He blew out a breath, drank some scotch, said nothing for a moment. "I've told you my son can't walk because of a spinal cord injury."

"Yes."

"I plotted to murder the man who was responsible."

"Who was that?"

"Ethan Gorr." He told her about Gorr and about the shooting of Ganbigo and Gerard.

"But your son was shot accidentally, wasn't he?"

"Yes. But Ganbigo was deliberately murdered at the behest of Ethan Gorr and he didn't give a damn who got in the way. It happened to be my ten-year-old son."

"You're sure this man did it?"

"He didn't pull the trigger but he caused it to be pulled. I'm sure of that."

"Was he convicted of the murder?"

Stephen gave a soft grunt. "He wasn't even indicted. I talked to the State Department and the Peruvian government. I tried to file civil charges. Nothing worked. I had no proof that he hired the gunman and the slimy little toad walked."

Heather wasn't sure she wanted to hear the rest. She sat through a long moment of silence. "So, you plotted to kill him."

Stephen looked at her defiantly. "Damn right I did. I had to watch my son struggle every day to learn how to live without his legs—" His throat tightened. After a moment, he went on. "I bought a gun...did you know you can buy handguns on the internet?"

She shook her head, trying to picture Stephen buying a gun with the intention of killing someone.

He drank some Scotch. "I bought a Smith & Wesson for five hundred bucks, had it sent to my Georgetown office, took shooting lessons from a local gun club. All the while I was researching Ethan Gorr. Found out he lived in Manhattan on Central Park West. As soon as I became proficient with the gun, I drove to New York one Friday and stalked him for the entire weekend. At one point I was standing about ten feet away as he got into a taxi. I had the gun in my pocket, finger on the trigger."

"Jesus!" Heather whispered. When he said he had plotted a murder, she had imagined him making elaborate plans

161

in his head. She had not imagined him standing getting ready to pull the trigger.

He looked up. "I couldn't do it."

She held his eyes for a moment, then looked away. The thought that he came that close to murdering someone made her nauseous.

"Worse than you imagined?" he asked.

She searched for a response. "I can understand your rage, Stephen, I really can. But..." She shrugged. "It's a lot to absorb. Did you ever tell your wife?"

"No."

They sat in silence while Heather struggled to process this new image of Stephen. He had seemed troubled, haunted even, when she met him, but she attributed it to the burden imposed by the GFED meeting. She felt a sudden wave of sympathy. He'd had to live with enormous guilt. He didn't need her condemnation as well. She flashed him a friendly smile. "The important thing is, you didn't pull the trigger."

He said nothing.

She tried again. "That's what makes us human, Stephen, the ability to reject a murderous impulse."

"No, that's what makes us the *Namuh* that GFED fears: this impulse toward revenge and violence. We meet violence with violence, and that's exactly what I planned to do. The fact that I didn't actually murder him is irrelevant."

"And you feel guilty about it."

"It's right up there with my guilt for putting my son in harm's way."

Heather could tell he was drowning in guilt. She tried for a professional response. "I understand that you violated your own precepts of what is right and wrong, but you have to forgive yourself. We can't put our children in protective bubbles all their lives. You can't continue to beat yourself up about taking Gerard with you."

He blew out a breath. "I think Morok knew about my aborted attempt to kill Gorr."

"How could he have known?"

"He told me that GFED's greatest deterrent to crime is the ability to scan the images in a person's brain. The images of a crime render the criminal's own conviction."

"You think they performed a scan on you?"

"I don't know, but if Morok knew that someone like me—a congenial anthropologist, a former missionary—could pursue a violent impulse almost to completion...well, it would lend a lot of weight to the idea that Namuh violence was genetic."

"Stephen, please. Surely Morok is too rational to condemn an entire race because someone thinks about killing another person. We have a propensity for violence to be sure, because we're exposed to it almost from birth. But it's a learned response, not a genetic one. That's what I told GFED in my testimony, and that's what I believe."

He gave a rueful smile. "But it does give credence to their belief that humans are irreparably prone to violence. Besides, there were other avenues I could have pursued—"

"You did, remember? You tried to get Ethan Gorr indicted."

"I could have done something else. I could have simply written a book to expose him—which of course, I did. I should've been content with that and not taken it any further."

"Stephen, I swear, you seem to grasp at reasons to feel guilty."

He shrugged.

She took a sip of wine. She wanted desperately to get past this. "Morok told you he had the power to veto the extermination. So, it's not over as long as we have him on our side."

"The arbiters can override his veto."

"Still, he seems to have taken a personal interest in the Namuh. Maybe he can convince GFED to fire a warning shot of some kind. Something that will get the president's attention and convince him the threat is real."

"Let's hope it doesn't come too late."

She wanted to stay and talk longer but she had a plane to catch. "I have to go pack, Stephen, but we can't walk away from this. We have to try to come up with some alternatives."

They stood. She held out her hand. "Call me next week. We'll compare notes. And Stephen," she smiled wryly, "please try to let go of some of that guilt."

#

That night at dinner, Stephen recapped the meeting for his family. When he finished, Penny said, "It was probably unrealistic to think the president would just say, okay, we'll shut down the military."

"I think he was stupid and irresponsible for not listening to you," Gerard said.

"Son, he's not stupid. We had a very difficult task."

The reverend put on a sympathetic face. "You tried, Stephen. You gave it your best shot. That's all anyone can ask."

Stephen pushed away from the table, despondent. The human race was sitting on death row and the last appeal for clemency had just been rejected.

"You okay, Dad?"

"I'm fine." In truth, he was anything but fine.

"Where are you going?" Penny asked.

"To bed."

"But it's only eight-thirty."

"It feels like midnight."

His father followed him to the stairs. "You remember your meeting tomorrow, don't you? Two o'clock at Gorr's office?"

Stephen leaned against the railing. Ethan Gorr was the last person on earth he wanted to see. "I need to cancel. I don't think I can stomach that man right now—"

"A deal's a deal, son. I promised you a meeting with Wainwright and you got it. The fact that it wasn't successful doesn't alter the fact that I kept my promise. I expect you to keep yours."

He spoke in a tone that once could shame Stephen into doing anything his father wanted done, a tone he hadn't heard since he was a child, but he was too tired to argue. He mumbled "Okay" and continued up the stairs.

"So, you'll be there?" his father called after him. "Two o'clock sharp?"

"I'll keep my promise, Dad," he said grimly. But he couldn't promise it would be a successful meeting.

He went into his study and closed the door and stretched out on the sofa. He punched a button on the remote and Rachmaninoff's *Second Piano Concerto* filled the room. The piece always uplifted him, filled him with strength and resolve, but tonight as the music washed over him, he felt as if he were drowning in waves of despair. He had taken his mission seriously. He had traveled across the country and lied to his wife to locate the only person who could corroborate his story. He had managed to get an audience with the president of the United States and he'd told him about the dire threat to all humankind. And he'd been dismissed like some gullible UFO fanatic. There was nothing left to do except sit back and watch the world drift toward its ultimate demise.

CHAPTER 37

"Do not be alarmed."

The voice was deep, melodious; the articulation, precise, somewhat stilted, as if English were not the speaker's primary language. Stephen recognized it at once. He sat up and laid his book face-down on the sofa. He lowered the volume on the remote and looked around the room. He saw nothing. Then came a slight rustling of the air, and Morok materialized in the recliner next to the sofa, a gray-haired man with a pleasant face and piercing green eyes. He was dressed as he had been on that night in November, in a gray suit, white shirt, red tie.

Stephen felt no more alarmed than if his father had walked in and sat down in the chair. Surely it was unnatural to be so calm in the presence of an extraterrestrial. But he looked so normal, so *human*. "Chairman Morok," he said. "I didn't expect to see you again."

Morok smiled. "You seem troubled, Dr. Hopkins."

"I've had a difficult day."

"I know. I came to tell you about the commission's verdict."

"I've thought of little else these past few weeks."

"They voted for extermination."

The words seemed to echo in the room. Despite everything, he had not believed that would be the verdict. He had failed utterly.

Morok continued. "I thought the decision was too extreme, so I exercised my veto."

Stephen felt as if he had just been pulled back from the edge of an abyss. "You vetoed extermination?"

"Yes."

"What happens now?"

"The case goes to the Council of Supreme Arbiters. They can sustain my veto or override it. Either way, their decision will be binding. Meanwhile, we will continue to implement the quarantine."

"I cannot tell you how relieved I am, Mr. Chairman, but why did you veto the verdict?"

166

"I have learned something startling about the Namuh memory. The commissioners were positive they had removed your ability to recall anything you heard or saw the night of the hearing. That both you and Dr. Eastlake managed to recall everything is quite an anomaly."

Stephen leaned forward. "You erased our memories?"

"Not exactly. We simply deleted the continuity of thought storage so that those particular memories could not be accessed. It is similar to the way your computers erase the index to a file name when you delete a file. What we did not realize were the capabilities of the Namuh memory. We are not sure whether your mind establishes alternate connections to specific memories or whether it has a redundant storage mechanism or both. But you were able to recover your memories under hypnosis, so obviously they were intact. We have not seen anything like that in other species, and we are quite anxious to learn more about it. It could have great ramifications to our justice system."

"Mr. Chairman, where did the limousine take me that night? Where was the hearing held?"

Morok made a strange trilling sound that sounded something like laughter. "After you entered the limousine, you were teleported to a space station."

Stephen remembered Calvin Williams' comment about teleportation. "So, you disassembled my molecules in the limousine and reassembled them in your space station."

"Not exactly. A better analogy is that we copied your molecules and reassembled them in our space station."

"And you reversed the process and deposited me on the bus bench the next morning?"

"Let me just say we returned you there. Compared to yours, our technology is so advanced I cannot begin to describe it in terms a Namuh could understand, but that is how we travel the galaxy."

"I see," Stephen said, though he didn't really. There was so much he wanted to know about Morok's civilization, but the most important thing was to learn how they had developed a nonviolent culture. Maybe that would help him think of a new way to approach the president.

"The bedrock of any society is its method of resolving disputes," Morok said, as if he'd read Stephen's thoughts. "The Namuh's method is violence, which feeds on the fact that every aspect of your civilization is polarized: schools, churches, sports, families, villages, countries. That polarization is intensified by leaders who choose to defile rather than debate their opponents, by clergy who demonize rather than respect other religions, by a media which inflames rather than informs their audience. A polarized society can never settle its differences peacefully. If a dispute is personal, you resort to fisticuffs at one end of the spectrum and murder at the other. If the dispute is communal, you resort to war and terror.

"I'm oversimplifying, of course, but compare that with the way Yxrians and other GFED members resolve disputes. Arbiters are assembled to hear both sides of an argument and render a judgment. Our arbiters are trained in the law and operate at various levels of society. But they all begin at the local level where they resolve domestic and personal issues. If they do well at that level, they move on to resolving business and property disputes. Then they move up to what you might call the state level, then on to what corresponds to your regional and national levels, and finally to the planetary and galactic level. At the higher levels, the arbiter becomes a member of a council that settles major issues between countries and planets. The important thing is, each move to a higher level is based strictly on merit—not on political affiliation or financial interests or personal ideology.

"How do you judge their merits?"

"The more decisions that are accepted without appeal to a higher-level council, the greater the merit of the arbiter. And that merit is reinforced if a case is appealed to a higher council and the arbiter's decision is upheld. Our judicial system is more complex than that, of course, but it ultimately is based completely on merit. In comparison, Namuh judges are often elected or appointed without any regard for merit, and your system lacks a way to systematically reward good judges and remove bad ones."

Stephen had to agree. Too many judgeships were filled by the political process. Even at the highest level, a politically elected president nominated justices to the Supreme Court and a politically elected congress confirmed them.

Morok continued. "Our highest authority—our court of last resort, if you will—is the Supreme Council of Arbiters, which would be something like a World Court, if the Namuh had one. The Supreme Council is made up of the highest level of arbiters from across the galaxy. By the time an arbiter has risen to this level, he or she is deemed a wise and judicious being. That is why we can accept as fair and final the council's judgment.

"But you didn't accept the commission's judgment," Stephen protested. "You vetoed the decision to exterminate the Namuh."

"That was a verdict of a lower-level commission, one made up of scientists from various parts of the galaxy. I can veto their decision, as I have done with the Namuh, but no one has veto power over the Supreme Council. Its decision will be final."

Stephen embraced the hope of reprieve by the Supreme Council. That was all he had. "Is this method of dispute resolution the reason for your nonviolent culture?"

"It eliminates one of the reasons for violence, but it's just one strand in the intricate tapestry that is our culture. An essential strand of the tapestry is a complete lack of poverty, and that is an outgrowth of our economic system."

"You have no poverty?"

"None. It is difficult to understand the poverty we see on your planet, even in the richest countries like your own. In GFED, member planets provide for each citizen's basic needs at a comfortable level—food, shelter, clothing, education, and health care—so they do not have to worry about the necessities of life.

"Some countries have tried that here," Stephen said, thinking of the former Soviet Union. "It didn't work."

"I know about those experiments. But their leaders were often corrupt and they stifled individual initiative. Moreover, their process was poorly articulated."

Stephen thought of the primitive tribes he had studied. Most had lived under a communal ethic that varied from tribe to tribe. A social hierarchy was usually involved, but the basic needs of tribal members were met through the joint efforts of the entire tribe. But the tribes he studied had numbered only a few hundred members. Morok was talking about two hundred trillion. He said this to Morok and added, "Your taxes must be exorbitant to sustain a system like that."

"On the contrary. In our world, what you call *taxes* is probably less per capita than in your country. When the basic needs of a citizenry are met, there is little cause for violence, which means we need only a minimal level of security. We simply spend that currency differently for the basic needs of the citizens. We have several levels, each targeted for one need and one need only. One currency is for food, others for shelter, clothing, education, health care. Each citizen is given a sufficient amount of these basic currencies to enjoy a reasonably comfortable lifestyle."

Stephen said, "We have a form of targeted currency called food stamps, which can be used only for food, but they carry a social stigma. Anyone who uses them is considered to be on welfare, which is looked down upon in this country."

"Ah, it wasn't that long ago that paper money replaced gold nuggets as the standard currency in your country. No doubt, paper money carried a stigma at that time, but it is highly respected now, is it not?"

"That's true, but what happens to the work ethic with your kind of system? Doesn't it create a stagnant welfare society?"

"Some, of course, choose not to work, although they can be assigned societal work when needed. They are content to have their basic needs provided, but they don't have the luxuries of life or the satisfaction and honor that comes with creative and fulfilling work."

"And those who do work, what do they do?"

"They join professions or what you call companies, they invent products and services, they start businesses or volunteer for nonprofit entities. They succeed or fail, based on market conditions—very much like your capitalistic system. The difference is, if they fail, they won't go hungry and they won't be without shelter or healthcare or education."

"Doesn't this kind of system stifle creativity?"

"On the contrary! It *nourishes* creativity. Think about it, Dr. Hopkins. Your artists and performers often struggle in demeaning jobs to provide for the necessities of life; many never get a chance to pursue a career in their art. But GFED citizens who wish to do so can devote all their energies to their art because their basic needs are met. It is a very free and rewarding way of life."

Stephen was intrigued. "What kinds of arts do you have?"

Morok smiled. "Our visual arts and literature are quite extraordinary, but I believe we have nothing that equals the Namuh music. The piece you were listening to when I arrived stirs such wondrous emotions within me…first I want to weep, then I find my spirit soaring. And *Vocalise,* by the same composer—that piece embodies tragedy in a way that is haunting and comforting at the same time."

Haunting and comforting! Stephen remembered those same feelings as he hummed that piece to his injured son as the helicopter carried them to a hospital in Lima. "I'm glad to know something in our culture pleases you."

"Namuh music is played across the galaxy. It is one of the reasons I was reluctant to side with my fellow commissioners, even before we learned of your extraordinary memory. I prefer your classical compositions, but others find your jazz intriguing, and some of our younger citizens enjoy your early rock-and-roll, as you call it."

Stephen allowed himself a bit of sarcasm. "Maybe your commission planned to confiscate our music before they exterminated us."

Morok stiffened. "We do not confiscate creative works. They are cherished and protected by the entire Federation."

"But you don't compensate our artists for their work."

"Quite the opposite. GFED's intellectual property rights are far more generous than yours. Our artists retain the rights to their creations forever, and in some societies the creative rights pass to the artist's heirs after his or her death. These rights extend even to artists outside the Federation. So, each time we reproduce the Namuh art or music or literature, what you would call a royalty is recorded in an account in the name of the original artist."

Morok trilled a laugh. "The heirs of your Beatles would find themselves very wealthy indeed should Earth ever join the Federation. Even Rachmaninov's descendants would be quite well off."

"I find it odd that you would pay royalties to beings you consider primitive and violent."

"It's called *honor*, Dr. Hopkins. Something your species once had when a Namuh's word or handshake created an unbreakable bond. We pay royalties to honor the creative ability to produce such music. Honor is another thread in the tapestry that I mentioned. It works hand in glove with our economic policies and our method of dispute resolution to create a climate of nonviolence."

As he listened, Stephen felt a wave of his earlier despair. To even begin to create a world of nonviolence, humans would not only have to change their judicial and economic systems, they would have to somehow reclaim the trust and honor and decency of another age. He could not imagine how it could be done.

#

"Dr. Hopkins, the ultimate decision is up to our Supreme Council, as I told you earlier, but a dramatic change in the Namuh attitude toward violence might convince them that you can change. I am not talking merely about the violence of nations against nations. To convince the Council that a change could take root and permanently alter the Namuh's violent behavior, they would have to see substantial evidence of a change in the attitudes and actions of individuals, as well as nations."

"Millions of humans long for peace," Stephen said, "but we're steeped in fear of each other. Any deep and lasting change will be slow to manifest. What I'd like to know is this: if we take steps to overcome our fear and start moving toward peace and nonviolence, will that be sufficient to convince your Supreme Council?"

Morok stood. "Perhaps. If we can discern some progress at both the global and individual levels. The solar probe is in place, however, and the quarantine will proceed as planned."

Stephen stood up and stuck out his hand. "That is all we can ask."

Morok looked at the thin pale skin of the outstretched hand, the soft vulnerable flesh, and felt a sudden rush of admiration for the species. He had always viewed the Namuh in the context of their violence. Now that he was looking at one face to face, he realized that violence might have been the only way such exposed creatures had managed to survive, indeed thrive, throughout their short turbulent history. Maybe all they needed to repudiate violence was to be shown that it was not the only or best method of survival.

"I may appear substantial enough for a handshake, but if I extend my hand there would be nothing there for you to grab but air," Morok smiled. "Thank you for the kind gesture."

The chairman's face began to glow, as if lit from within. Then he vanished, and where he had stood there appeared a feathery sunburst of blues and greens surrounding two glittering green-gold eyes above a curved black beak-like nose. The image hung in the air like the grin of the Cheshire Cat, and then it was gone. Although it lasted only a second, Stephen was quite sure he'd just caught a glimpse of the real Morok.

CHAPTER 38

The sky was low with thick gray clouds as Stephen drove down Pennsylvania Avenue to Ethan Gorr's office. He kept his mind off of Gorr by thinking about Morok's visit the night before. When he told Heather all about it, she agreed, the chairman's message had been clear enough. Extermination was tabled temporarily, but the human race must prove that it could change from a violent society to a peaceful one. How was that supposed to happen? They had failed with their message to the president, and now he felt as if he were holding a ticking bomb with no way to get at the timing mechanism.

Gorr Resources occupied part of the second floor of a three-story red brick building on G Avenue near the Capitol. A small brass plate mounted on the wall next to the polished oak door was the only identification. Stephen opened the door and stepped into a large room furnished in sleek tones of gray and silver. The only splash of color in the room was exotic pink and purple floral arrangement on a low table in front of a gray leather sofa. Behind the vacant reception desk was a glass-walled conference room, and beyond that, a window framed a view of the Capitol.

He stood for a moment uncertain where to go. Then he heard muffled footsteps on the thick gray carpet, and Ethan Gorr rounded the corner, a dark rotund man with short thin legs, wearing a suit the color of the sofa, a white shirt and solid red tie. The last time Stephen had seen him was five years ago, entering the taxi in front of his condominium on Central Park West. The big difference was, Stephen did not have a gun in his pocket this time.

"Dr. Hopkins," Gorr said, crossing the room with an outstretched hand. "Good to see you."

Stephen looked down at the little man and forced himself to shake Gorr's hand.
"I'm here at my father's request," he said. He resisted the urge to wipe his palm on his jeans.

"Lucky man, your father. A lot of men his age wouldn't have survived a heart attack."

Stephen tried to control the old feelings of rage that crowded his mind. "My father said you had some new information about the Abigo. Could we talk about that? I don't have much time."

"Of course."

Gorr led the way into the conference room which was furnished with a highly polished ebony table surrounded by eight high-backed grey chairs. In the middle of the table were three silver trays. One held white china cups and stemmed crystal glasses. Another held two silver pitchers with steam escaping through the spout of one and droplets of water collecting on the sides of the other. The third tray held an assortment of sweet rolls and a bowl of large strawberries arranged in concentric circles. It looked like an advertisement for a conference at a posh hotel.

"May I offer you coffee? Water?" Gorr asked.

"No thanks."

Stephen took a chair facing the view of the Capitol. Gorr sat at the end of the table to Stephen's left.

"How about a sweet roll? They're from a little bakery down the street, best in the District."

Stephen resisted the urge to cram a sweet roll down Gorr's fat throat. "Let's get on with the meeting."

Gorr rested his arms on the table, clasped his hands, leaned forward. "I know you were against our obtaining the forestry management of the Abigo land. But we're doing good work down there, and my company wants to make what you might call reparations to the tribe. We're under no obligation to do so, of course, but we feel a certain gratitude for their willingness to let us harvest their timber. So, here's what we'd like to do. We would like to set up a fund for the education of the Abigo children, help them make the transition to the civilized world." Gorr's tone was smooth as oil, conciliatory, confident.

Stephen thought of Ganbigo's body lying on the ground a few feet from Gerard's. His rage reached a low simmer. "The Abigo are a hell of a lot more civilized than we are in many ways. Did you ever consider they might not want to join our civilized world?"

"We all have to move forward, Dr. Hopkins."

Stephen took a deep breath, let it out slowly. "The Peruvian government has control of the tribe. You'll have to go through their channels if you want to set up an education fund."

"We've already taken steps to do that. But I thought you might like to announce it to the tribal leaders since you've been so close to them."

Stephen stood up, flexed his fingers to keep them from balling into a fist. He looked down at Gorr. "That was before their shaman was killed. After that, the other leaders didn't want anything to do with me. You see, they thought Ganbigo's death was tied to my bringing white men like you into their tribe."

Gorr remained seated. He glanced at Stephen's right hand, which was hanging low by his side, the thumb moving rapidly against the fingers in a silent snapping motion. He should have offered Stephen the biggest carrot first, the one he was sure would bring him around. He leaned back in his chair. "Dr. Hopkins, your son has my very deepest sympathy for the injury he sustained in Mondogo. The reverend says he has turned out to be a very bright, capable young man, and I would like to see him go as far in life as someone in his condition can go. That's why I want to make you an extraordinary offer."

He gave Stephen the kindly smile of a generous benefactor. "I want to pay for your son's education…four years, six years, whatever he wants, at any university in the country. Not only that, when a cure is found for spinal cord injury, I'll see that he is the first in line for the treatment."

"In return for what, Mr. Gorr?" With great effort Stephen managed to get the words out in a civil tone.

Ethan Gorr felt like laughing. Every man had his price if you knew how to find it. His smile broadened. "All I want from you is your friendship…" He hesitated at the look on Stephen's face, and amended his words. "And if not your friendship, then your respect. And should you ever find yourself writing about the events in Mondogo, I would appreciate a generous attitude to Gorr Resources. That's all it will take to give your son the best education and assure him of the quickest medical breakthroughs money can buy."

"That's all?"

"Yes." Gorr folded his hands over his stomach and smiled benevolently.

Stephen's rage bubbled to the surface. He leaned on the table and thrust his face within inches of Gorr's. "You money-grubbing little toad! If you think I would take one cent of your bloody money, you're dumber than you look."

Gorr pushed back from the table, grasped the arms of his chair. "I'm making this offer only once, Hopkins. If you're smart, you'll take it." The oily tone was gone, so was the obsequious smile. "Otherwise, I'll use my power to make sure your son is the last in line for any cure that's found."

For a moment, Stephen was speechless. His rage exploded, triggered by Gorr's cruel words. He grabbed his lapels and lifted the little man out of his chair and shook him like a piece of dirty linen. He wanted to bash his head against the wall until the fat greedy eyes spewed blood.

Suddenly, he realized what he was doing and shoved Gorr away and headed blindly for the door.

Gorr lay crumpled against the wall. "You'll pay for this, Hopkins," he yelled at Stephen's back. "You'll pay big time for this!"

#

That night, Gorr paced the floor of his Manhattan penthouse barely able to contain his fury. The man had thrown him against the wall! His feet had literally left the floor. He had not felt such humiliation since grade school when his brothers used to pick him up and toss him back and forth like a goddamn human Frisbee. He always ended up crumpled on the ground or the floor of the gym, howling with pain and humiliation.

But he was not that kid anymore. He was rich and powerful. Heads of states asked him for favors, even the goddamned President of the United States shook his hand at receptions and called him by name. And this arrogant nobody had the nerve to attack him! He could ruin the son-of-a-bitch.

The vase of red tulips on the coffee table caught his eye. He grabbed it and hurled it against the wall. He looked at the tulips lying amid the shattered glass on the floor. He walked over, gave them a savage kick, and kicked them again.

CHAPTER 39

Myssa stepped out of the airfoil shuttle and blinked slowly. In front of her a crowd of Yxrians and other creatures milled around a fountain that shot plumes of water a hundred feet in the air and created a fine mist. She could feel the slight spray that cooled the air around the fountain. She scanned the crowd with her lizard eyes, but did not see Morok and Drakk. Morok had said to meet them at the entrance to the theater but she saw nothing that looked like a theater, just an impenetrable thicket of giant conifers. Then she realized that the crowd was ambling toward the thicket and disappearing into its depths. She fell in behind a black-feathered family of four whose red-tipped wings trailed behind them like a train.

She gave a start when Morok and Drakk appeared at her side without warning. She had never mastered the ability of personal teleportation, and she resented those who could. "There must be a theater in here somewhere," Myssa said by way of greeting.

"In all your years on Yxria, you've never been to our legendary amphitheater?" Morok said.

"I came to study the Namuh, not to sample your performing arts."

"I think tonight's program might clarify your thoughts about the Namuh."

Myssa bristled. So that is why he invited her, to sway her opinion about his precious Namuh.

"It's one of our classics," Drakk said, "the Luvash-Xeth Tragedy." He was walking backward, facing them. His antennae glowed blue in the night air.

"Ah, that one," Myssa said. She looked at Morok. "Is it a modern adaptation?"

"No," Morok said. "It's set at the time of the tragedy, a million and a half years ago, and all the action takes place on planet Luvash, just as it did in the historical event."

"But Mr. Chairman, you said the play will ameliorate my thoughts about the Namuh. Yet they are very like the Xeth, with the same propensity toward violence, the same impetuous, uncivilized behavior. I believe the Xeth got what they deserved, so why would I change my mind about the Namuh?"

"You will see, Counselor," Morok said.

The forest gave way to a view of the amphitheater, and Myssa caught her breath. In front of her was a three-thousand-foot red rock cliff, and protruding from it a few hundred feet from the bottom was the amphitheater stage, from which stairs descended to a long lower stage that split the viewing area down the center. Flanking the stage were rows of conifers, taller than any that Myssa had ever seen on Yxria or Earth or her home planet Imazhi.

"Quite impressive, Mr. Chairman."

Morok led them to a viewing space above the tip of the lower stage. "The actors will speak in our local avian dialect, which can be somewhat difficult." He handed them each an earpod. "These will translate everything."

Before Myssa could attach the earpod, thousands of brightly colored avian creatures burst forth from openings in the red cliff and began flying above the stage in an intricately choreographed aerial dance. Their songs that filled the air sounded strange and ethereal to Myssa's lizard ears. Then the avians formed a circle, hovering above the stage, listening intently as a news-bird interviewed a Luvash scientist who described the nano-drug that would become a legend.

Myssa's mind fast-forwarded to the present. That nano-drug was the forerunner of the NB-2000, which was now available to most species throughout the Federation. Even the lowly Snedlians could use it to self-repair their bodies and triple their lifespan. Except the Reptilia. Her species. She stiffened as her attention returned to the stage, which was filled with celebratory dances and songs depicting the reception of the original NB-1 throughout the early days of the Federation.

"Watch this!" Drakk whispered in her ear as the sound changed abruptly to a pounding cacophony and the giant Xethans took over the stage.

Myssa had never before seen the legendary creatures portrayed in a live production, but here on that red-rock stage they came to life in all their malevolent fury, waving their four arms, shaking their oversized fur-covered heads, stomping around the stage like the angry giants they had been. As every young GFED-er knew, the Xethans had been accepted into the Federation amid great controversy, and their membership had come with provisions. They were given one hundred years in which to become a more transparent society and to abolish the slavery of semi-sentient creatures, which was rumored to be rampant on certain continents of Xeth. Myssa was not surprised that the Xethans were among the shortest-lived beings in GFED. Of course, they would covet the new nano-drug.

The furious dance of the Xethans subsided as the Xethan Trade Minster Ixor strode onto the stage. He was a giant among giants, an imposing fourteen feet tall, and his voice shook the very air as he made a case to the Luvash scientific trade board for the Xethans' right to NB-1. When questioned about the rumored slavery, he refused to answer, and he refused to allow a Luvash delegation to visit Xeth for the purpose of customizing NB-1 for Xethans. He wanted the actual nano-drug formulas. When his request was rejected, a massive air attack force leveled the Luvash facility, killing everyone inside, including Ixor whose booming voice could be heard from the smoldering ruins. "Death to all Luvash! Death to all Luvash!"

Momentary darkness cloaked the amphitheater, and then, powered by nanobot mist, the air glowed white, signaling intermission.

Myssa did not wait for Morok to speak, as tradition required. The second the light-mist appeared, she burst out. "Don't you see! The Namuh will react exactly the same when they get the power to travel to our planets, and that is not going to be long. We have to deal with them just like the Federation dealt with the Xethan."

"No, Myssa," Drakk said. "There are far too many disparities between the Namuh and the Xethan to draw such parallels."

Myssa gave him a slow blink. "The similarities are too dangerous to ignore."

"Mr. Chairman, please tell her," Drakk implored.

"Be patient," Morok said. "The play will say all that needs saying."

When the light-mist dimmed, the ruling chairman of
Xeth took the spotlight in a moving soliloquy that revealed his
anguish at the attack on Luvash.

> I would tear out my heart if that act could restore life
> to those who were killed by my kin.
> I would blind my own eyes if that act would undo
> the suffering of their families and friends.
> It matters not that it was the heinous act of a single Xethan, it
> was an attack by a citizen of Xeth and that makes it mine.
> And yet I understand the fury that was in his heart.
>
> His only child was wasting away, her organs deteriorating at an
> alarming rate, and NB-1 would have saved her.
> Would not I have done the same had it been my Ooletitia?
> But I must set aside my feelings of kinship,
> I must go to Yxria to appeal the Luvash decision.
> I must invite them into our midst and offer reparations.
> I must be the leader of the Xeth.

As the spotlight dimmed and the actor withdrew from the
stage, Myssa took a tremulous breath. Why was *she* touched by
such as he? She heard little of the act that followed. She knew it
all from the history kinders: The Xeth leader went to Yxria and
made his plea, but it failed to move the members of the GFED
Commission. The Luvash believed that the attack on the Luvash
Trade Center was a direct order from the Xeth leader himself and
not an emotional response by an errant commander. By a vote of
eleven to four, the Commission refused to order the Luvash to
sell NB-1 to the Xeth. Within days, the Xeth retaliated with a
massive biological attack on planet Luvash. Within three months,
more than 200 million Luvash died of incurable diseases, and the
Luvash did not recover their scientific and intellectual
preeminence for more than four thousand years.

At the second intermission, Myssa said to Morok, "I
cannot conceive that any commissioner would fail to vote for
Namuh extinction. They don't have to see this play to draw a
parallel between the Namuh and this savagery of the Xeth." She
gave him a slow blink. "Is that what I am supposed to take away
from this evening?"

Morok's green-gold eyes glittered as he spoke. "I fear,
Myssa, that you are obsessing on the observed violence of the

Namuh. If you would take a broader view, you would see their compassion, their extraordinary creativity. Tonight, we've heard Yxrian music at its best, yet it pales in comparison to Namuh music. I do not believe such traits can coexist with genes of violence."

"To what, then, do you attribute their violence?"

"Any number of things. Inappropriate distribution of life's necessities. Food, health care, education, housing, clothing—"

"Rightly. They're like rats scrambling for a bite of cheese."

"But that is an economic mistake," Morok continued. "It reflects a lack of ingenuity among Namuh governments. It is not a fatal flaw."

Myssa blinked. "So, there is something else I should expect from this performance? Something that will change my mind about exterminating the vermin?"

Morok was silent for a moment. When he spoke, his voice was filled with sorrow. "Exterminating a species is not without its own perils."

As the final act of the pageant unfolded, the Xcthan giants danced under the Xethan sun as they celebrated the deaths of two hundred million Luvash. On Yxria, the GFED commission contemplated the revelry of the Xeth amid the suffering of the Luvash, and the commissioners came to a unanimous verdict. Xeth must pay.

As the Xethans danced, their sun began to grow. It doubled in size before they noticed the increased heat. "It's an illusion," cried Xethan leaders, but within days the oceans on Xeth began to boil and the sun kept growing, incinerating all life on planet Xeth.

Darkness descended in the theater, and Myssa prepared to leave. The pageant had been interesting, but she had learned nothing she had not already known.

Morok touched her arm. "It's not over."

"But that's how it ended," Myssa said.

"The history kinders didn't reveal everything," Morok said. "Watch."

The lights came back on and the air above the stage was filled once more with thousands of Yxrians, but they were not soaring in celebration of the end of Xeth. They were moaning and keening and plucking feathers from their heads. One by one they dove into the ground, taking their own lives, until the stage was piled high with feathered bodies and the silence of death fell over the crowd.

A lone voice came out of the silence. "After the destruction of planet Xeth, more than 20,000 fellow Yxrians took their own lives, six of them GFED commissioners who ordered the extermination. We must remember that technology is a two-edged laser. It enables us to extend the lives of suns and manage the climates of beleaguered planets. And now, in a single act, we have obliterated ten billion sentient beings."

"And," the voice intoned, "we have paid."

#

As Morok flew to his home in the Yxrian red cliffs, he thought of Stephen Hopkins. The way the Namuh had accepted the burden of trying to save his people stirred Morok in much the same way as Rachmaninov's music. This particular Namuh was a kindred spirit. *Surely there were others like him.*

Morok pondered the thought. Maybe the cure for violence was in the seed of violence itself. After all, this Namuh had battled his own violent impulses and had won at least part of that battle. If the tribe could learn to nurture the cure rather than the seed, perhaps it could become worthy of admittance to the Federation.

As he soared through the night skies, a plan began to take shape in his mind.

PART TWO

CHAPTER 40

One week into the New Year, a blackout struck Washington D.C. Stephen Hopkins was in his study reviewing the final proofs of his book, but his mind was elsewhere. His outburst against Gorr was wrong and it had filled him with anger and shame. When his father learned what had happened at the meeting, he was so displeased he moved back to McLean and refused Penny's pleas to spend Christmas with them. Penny accused Stephen of having destroyed their family again and had barely spoken to him since then. Even Gerard's sunny disposition had dimmed since his grandfather left. And the GFED threat lurked like a dark shadow at the back of his mind.

The house went dark at the same instant his computer blinked off. That was nothing new. For the past several weeks, the city had endured sporadic power outages, each lasting only a few minutes. Stephen got up and felt his way to the window and looked out into total blackness. Apparently, the whole neighborhood was without power. He found a flashlight in a desk drawer and stepped into the hall.

"Stephen?"

He pointed the light in the direction of the bedroom and illumined Penny standing in the doorway in her robe. "Looks like the whole neighborhood is blacked out."

"I've got candles," called Gerard from the other end of the hall.

Stephen saw a faint glow from his son's open door. He held out his hand to Penny. "C'mon."

She took his hand and followed him down the hall. Gerard was fiddling with the dials on a battery-powered radio. All they could hear was static.

"Keep trying," Stephen said. "I'm going to check the neighborhood."

Outside, flashlights bobbed in the darkness as neighbors clustered in groups up and down the street. Stephen joined the closest group. "Anyone hear any news?" he asked.

"Not yet, but it looks like it got the whole city."

"Yeah, there's no glow from M Street," offered another.

"I haven't seen a night this dark since the blackout of '03."

"That one got the whole East Coast."

"Look at the sky...you can actually see the stars."

Stephen walked a few steps away from the group and turned off his flashlight. He tilted his head back and looked at the patch of sky directly overhead. The stars popped out of the blackness like millions of tiny spotlights. The pale swath of the Milky Way stretched across the sky and a waning moon peeked through the treetops. He gazed into the star-studded blackness and thought of what Morok had said: *Tens of thousands of inhabited planets, trillions of intelligent beings in this very galaxy.* It was too much for the mind to grasp.

He said goodnight to his neighbors and went back inside. Gerard was still hovering over the radio. "There's nothing but static.

"I'm going to bed," Penny said. "Can I have the flashlight?"

"I'll come with you."

They left Gerard fiddling with the radio, trying to find a station that had not been silenced by the blackout. Stephen stopped at the bedroom door and took Penny's arm. She looked up at him questioningly. He turned off the flashlight and darkness fell over them like a blanket.

"Stephen! Turn on the light."

"Pen, it's so dark outside you'd think we were in the rainforest. Let's go for a walk."

"It was warm in the rainforest, remember? It's freezing here."

"We can bundle up."

"You bundle up, I'm going to bed."

He hesitated.

"Stephen! The light?"

He turned on the flashlight and followed her into the bedroom and waited until she lit a candle. Then he slipped on a fleece-lined jacket and gloves, pulled a black knit ski cap over his ears, and headed back downstairs. Outside, he turned off the

186

flashlight and put it in his pocket and began to walk. The darkness was almost palpable. Except for the cold, it reminded him of the dark nights of the Peruvian rainforest. He stopped for a moment and listened. A dog barked in the next block, the distant freeway gave off a faint buzz, a burble of voices floated toward him from a darkened porch. Peaceful civilized sounds. Nothing like the screams and cries and clatter that made the rainforest seem like a living, breathing creature.

He resumed walking. If he'd brought his phone, he could call Heather, but it probably wouldn't work in a blackout. Cell phones hadn't been reliable since before Christmas. Nor had anything that depended on satellite communication: television broadcasts, internet reception, airline communications, GPS guidance systems. Reception was intermittent, signals were dropped, background static was ever-present. It was as if wireless communication had been set back thirty years. Official blame was placed on increased magnetic turbulence on the sun, but as satellite communications worsened, he wondered if perhaps GFED had implemented its quarantine.

He felt the cold seep down the collar and up the sleeves of his coat and through the denim of his jeans. He turned around and headed home through the darkness.

#

The blackout was unprecedented in scope, as Stephen learned when he logged on to his computer Saturday morning. Headlines vied for attention: "Power Outage Plunges Western Hemisphere into Darkness," "Half the Globe Loses Power in Freak Blackout," "Power Outage Creates Havoc in Two Continents," "Were Terrorists Behind the Massive Blackouts?"

He clicked a headline and began to read.

> A blackout hit the entire Western Hemisphere last night at 10:07 Eastern Time, plunging millions of people on two continents into darkness. From Halifax to San Diego, from Anchorage to Santiago, blackouts stopped elevators and subways and commuter trains. Across North and South America televisions shut down, computers crashed, cell phones went silent.

By mid-day, he learned that the official blame was placed on an extraordinarily powerful solar flare rated a category X50+. According to one article…

> …the plus sign indicates that the intensity of the flare was 'off the scale' of the Angstrom band, the device used to measure solar flares. The flare was several times greater than the powerful flare in November 2003 estimated as an X20. In fact, Friday night's flare was so powerful that some monitoring satellites were blinded by the scale of the event.
>
> Astronomers say the sun is in the last year of its eleven-year cycle of solar activity, so we should expect increased solar flare activity. Evidence that this has already begun is found in the increase in X-rays bombarding the Earth over the past few weeks which have caused major disruptions in satellite communications devices. Such a barrage of x-rays normally precedes a solar flare, so scientists tell us that while the flare was expected, its magnitude was not, and they warn of the probability of another flare very soon. The next one is predicted to be relatively weak, much like an aftershock that follows a major earthquake.

The more Stephen read, the more he felt in his gut that the scientists were wrong. Morok had said a solar satellite would be used to implement the quarantine, and if necessary, the extermination. Based on the quality of satellite communications, the quarantine had already begun. But did the massive flare that blacked out half the globe indicate that GFED was just warming up for the real thing?

#

The second flare struck on Sunday, causing blackouts across Europe, Asia, Africa, and Australia. Far from the minor aftershock predicted by scientists, the magnitude of the second flare was estimated as a category X60, had the Angstrom scale reached that high.

Dubbed *solar tsunamis* by one excited newscaster, the powerful back-to-back flares created a breeding ground for apocalyptic theories. Some postulated that the flares were harbingers of the death of the sun, despite the fact that scientists declared the sun would burn for several billion years more. Eschatologists insisted the flares were a divine signal that the Rapture was imminent, and some of the more rabid believers began gathering in remote locations for the anticipated liftoff. A third theory suggested the blackouts weren't caused by solar flares at all but by the concerted efforts of worldwide terrorists. When the lack of massive casualties was pointed out, the response from this group was: wait till the next one.

Sunday's flare removed any lingering doubt in Stephen's mind about GFED's involvement. "Two flares are no coincidence," he said to Heather when he called her Sunday night. "It has to be GFED."

"Do you think it's a warning shot to get our attention, or a practice shot for the *coup d'état?*"

"My guess is a warning shot. Morok said he had vetoed extermination."

"But the GFED commission can override his veto."

"Yes, but—" Stephen paused… "you may think I'm nuts, but I think he would contact me again if that happens."

"Should we try to reach the president?"

Stephen thought of the arrogant look on Kevin Halloran's face when they left the White House after the meeting in December. They would have to go through him to get to the president. Halloran would brush them off like lint from his lapel. "I doubt we could get past the Chief of Staff."

"You're probably right. But we just can't sit here and do nothing."

"I think we have to wait it out. Somebody on the president's staff is bound to connect the solar flares with what we told them, and when they do, they'll call us."

CHAPTER 41

"That's it," said Ethan Gorr, pointing toward the red brick building as he pulled into a parking spot across the street from Emerson School.

Sly Wicker said nothing.

"The kid's got blond hair, wears glasses," said Gorr.

"Don't you think the damned chair's enough to identify him?" Wicker said.

"Could be other cripples in the school," Gorr snapped. He drummed his fingers on the steering wheel and watched the entrance to Emerson School.

Sly Wicker was silent. He had done Gorr's dirty work for years. He was the man who pulled the trigger on the shaman in the Peruvian rainforest so many years ago, not the Abigo who was framed. And it was his bullet that put Gerard in the wheelchair. But that was ancient history, those tracks were covered up years ago. Now Sly had other worries on his mind, "Lots of risk in kidnapping that boy."

"You've done worse."

"But no one knows who I am. This kid's grandfather is a celebrity. If things go wrong, I could go to prison for life."

Gorr snarled, "This is non-negotiable, Wicker. You waver one nanosecond and I'll make sure the Feds know who you are and everything you've done."

Wicker cut his eyes toward Gorr. "Yeah?"

"Yeah."

"I'll tell them you hired me."

"No, I didn't. And there's no way you can prove it. I made sure of that."

"You turn me in, who'd do your dirty work?"

Gorr shrugged. "There's always somebody who'll work for good money."

Wicker didn't respond.

"There he is," Gorr said as a boy wheeled his way toward the entrance gate. He lifted the binoculars to his eyes, lowered them. "Hell, that's not him."

They continued to watch as children and teenagers streamed out of the school and spilled into the street, some heading toward cars, others toward waiting school buses. Finally, another wheelchair appeared, manned by a young boy with fair hair and steel-rimmed glasses. Gorr peered through the binoculars, handed them to Wicker. "That's him."

Wicker watched Gerard through the glasses as he wheeled toward a green van parked on the street in a handicap zone. He watched the boy lift himself into the driver's seat, then collapse the chair and haul it into the space behind the seat.

"You'll follow him down 24th to Washington. He turns left there and goes past the construction site near 18th. That's where you'll put up your roadblock so he'll have to turn on 19th. You'll grab him near the alley in the middle of that block." He glanced at Wicker who was still peering through the glasses. "You got that?"

"What if he takes a different route?"

"I've been watching him. He never varies."

Wicker grunted, handed the binoculars back to Gorr. "Cripples make me nervous. Makes me want to put them out of their misery."

Gorr didn't want to hear that. "Damn it, Wicker. You better not harm a hair on that kid's head!"

Wicker gave a hint of a smile. "What if they don't meet your demands? You just going to let him go?"

"Hopkins isn't going to let anything happen to his kid. I'm a thousand percent sure of that."

Wicker wasn't so sure, but he didn't say anything.

"So we're set?" Gorr said.

Wicker gave Gorr a long steady look. Tomorrow, four o'clock."

CHAPTER 42

At 10 o'clock on Monday, Gregory Milhone, head of the National Aeronautics and Space Administration (NASA), was handed a report stating that the Vulcanoid satellite had recorded an unidentified object inside the orbit of Mercury. He read it carefully. Then he placed an urgent call to the National Security Advisor. He had met Kimberly Dyer briefly when she visited the NASA headquarters two years ago just after her appointment as National Security Advisor. He had found her sharp and attentive and, in a high-powered predatory way, very sexy.

He cut right to the chase. "I have a report in my hand that might explain the blackouts this weekend."

"I'm listening."

"Are you aware of the Vulcanoid Belt?"

"What is this, Greg? A Star Trek trivia quiz?"

Milhone laughed politely. "No. It's background for what I need to tell you. Vulcanoids are fragments of asteroids or comets that orbit the sun inside Mercury's orbit. Their presence was speculated for years, but until 2008, no one had actually seen one because of solar glare. But now we know they're there, thousands of them, in a gravitationally stable orbit about seven to fifteen million miles from the sun.

"Now here's the problem. The satellite that studies the Vulcanoids has detected an unidentified object inside the Vulcanoid orbit—"

"What the hell does that mean—unidentifiable?"

"The object has not been identified. It's not a Vulcanoid—it's several times larger than that and about a million miles closer to the sun."

"Maybe it's a wandering comet."

"We don't think so. We're getting reports that it's generating unusual emissions."

"And the emissions indicate what?"

"That it's not a natural object. We put our best analysts on it, but they had difficulty interpreting the data. After the second flare on Sunday, we began scrutinizing the data more closely and one of our guys noticed an unusual anomaly: The object appears to change orbit."

"What do you mean?"

"The orbit decreased to about three million miles and then the object appeared to discharge a burst of high energy particles and then—instead of falling into the sun as we would expect—it returned to its original six-million-mile orbit."

"That's six million miles from the sun?"

"Between six and seven. The sun doesn't really have a surface, you know, so we measure distances from the corona, the outer region."

"How does it relate to Mercury's orbit?"

"Mercury is about thirty-six million miles from the sun. But the point is, this anomalous change in orbit happened *twice* within a 48-hour period—once would have been extremely bizarre behavior. Twice is beyond the pale."

"So, what do you make of it?"

"I'm not sure..." The NASA chief paused. "The changes in orbit and the high-energy emissions appear to coincide with the solar flares that caused the blackouts. The first blackout occurred on Saturday at 12:57 GMT, which was 9:47 pm *Friday* night Eastern Time. So, the CME from the first flare—"

"Speak English, Greg."

"Sorry. CME stands for 'coronal mass ejection.' That's a stream of energized particles released by a solar flare. It's the CME—not the flare itself—that creates havoc with electrical grids and causes blackouts.

"Anyway, the CME from the first flare left the sun fifteen hours before the blackout hit the Western Hemisphere, which means the solar flare *occurred* fifteen hours before the blackout. That's corroborated by the Keti Observatory and others. Moments before the flare erupted on the sun, the satellite changed orbit."

"Are you saying the object *caused* the flare?"

"There's more. The same thing happened at the time of the second solar flare which occurred fifteen hours before the blackout hit the Eastern Hemisphere on Sunday at 12:33 GMT. The object changed orbit and emitted the sharp bursts of energy moments before the CME blast left the sun."

"How long has this thing been in orbit?"

"We don't know. Frankly, Kimberly, we would never have known about it if it wasn't for the new Vulcanoid satellite."

Kimberly was silent. Surely, he wasn't saying what she thought he was saying. "Greg, are you absolutely sure this thing is not one of our satellites? Didn't we send one to Mercury?"

"Yes, but that one is where it's supposed to be. I'm positive this one's not ours. Anything we could put out there would melt before it got that close to the sun."

"Then you think this object caused the solar flares and the blackouts."

"Not officially."

"Okay, unofficially."

"We can't be one hundred percent certain, Ms. Dyer, but there appears to be a definite connection."

Dyer was silent, absorbing the information. There was only one conclusion to be drawn from Milhone's message: Some other country had passed the U.S. in the technology race. "Consider this top secret until we find out who launched the goddamned thing," she said to Milhone. Then she placed a call to President Wainwright's direct line.

#

An hour later, Kimberly Dyer took the elevator to the Situation Room in the basement of the White House. She greeted the president and took the seat to his left. She nodded at the others gathered around the conference table: Secretary of Defense Stuart Weiss on her left and across the table, Chief of Staff Kevin Halloran, Chairman of the Joint Chiefs General Harrison Gethers, and Calvin Williams, the president's science advisor.

She opened her briefcase to remove her notes, her sleek blonde hair sliding over her forehead. She flicked her hair back in place and briefed the group on her conversation with the NASA chief.

The president turned to General Gethers. "If we didn't put it there, General, who the hell did? China? North Korea?"

The general sat stiffly erect before his Commander in Chief, holding his cap loosely in his lap. He wore a dark olive uniform festooned with ribbons and medals on the left with four

194

silver stars marching across each shoulder. The military look was completed by his closely cropped grey hair, chiseled face, square chin, and steely gaze.

He shook his head. "If America can't do it, no one can. A satellite that close to the sun would melt like a Popsicle. Plus, you'd have to be able to operate it at that range, which is beyond our capability. And we sure as hell can't manipulate the sun. I can't even imagine the kind of technology that would take."

Secretary Weiss said, "Maybe the sun pulled BepiColumbo into orbit…" He paused at the blank look on Wainwright's face. Weiss was an ex-astronaut who looked as if he'd been placed in the room by a Hollywood casting director. He was clean-cut, close-shaven with short graying hair and a faraway look in his eyes that said he had been places, seen things few others had seen. He followed the space program closely and found it hard to believe the president didn't keep up with it. "A joint venture of European Space Agency and Japan it launched in 2018."

"That was NASA's first guess," Dyer said. "But BepiColumbo completed several flybys of Mercury, and it's right where it's supposed to be. Besides, like the General said, if it were the BepiColumbo it'd be burnt to a crisp that close to the sun."

The president said, "Is NASA sure this thing's not an asteroid or a comet?"

"Milhone ruled that out."

"How can they be sure, Kimberly? Maybe a moon broke loose from Mercury's orbit and got caught by the sun—"

"Mercury doesn't have any moons," Weiss said.

Kevin Halloran spoke up. "So maybe a passing comet got pulled into orbit."

Dyer gave him an exasperated look. "Explain to me, Kevin, how a natural object can oscillate in its orbit. Explain why it's emitting something NASA can't interpret. Explain how it is that the sun can't melt it. It's not a goddamned asteroid or comet." She glanced at the president. "Sorry, sir."

"Why are we ignoring the elephant in the room?"

They all turned to look at the president's science advisor.

Calvin Williams had pushed his chair away from the table so that he was slightly apart from the others, a maneuver he often used to observe group dynamics. He was impeccably dressed in a grey Armani suit, white shirt, and yellow tie, but he looked as relaxed as if he were on the beach, one arm draped over the back of the chair, both long legs stretched out in front. He cocked his dark, smooth-shaven head at them. The gold hoop on his left earlobe gleamed.

"If this thing is not an asteroid or comet, then it has to be a satellite," he said. "And if we didn't put it there—if China or North Korea or some other country didn't put it there—then some other intelligent beings did." He held the president's gaze. "It could be a solar probe from the Galactic Federation."

The president raised both eyebrows. "The Galactic Federation?"

Williams nodded. "The professors referred to it as GFED at our meeting in December."

No one spoke for a long moment.

Wainwright leaned across the table. "What you're saying, Cal, is that the damn thing was put there by aliens to destroy the Earth."

Williams shrugged. "It could very well be the object described by Dr. Hopkins."

The group broke into an excited buzz, trying to recall the details from the meeting in December with Stephen Hopkins and Heather Eastlake.

The president interrupted their chatter. "Cal, I want you to talk to your scientific colleagues and find out what they think this thing is. Make sure it stays confidential. And I want all of you back here in two hours." He stood up. "We better hope to hell the media doesn't get wind of this before we figure it out."

#

At 1:00 p.m. the group reconvened to hear Calvin Williams' report. He had managed to reach six fellow members of the President's Council of Advisors on Science and Technology— two physicists, a chemist, an astrophysicist, a microbiologist, and a space engineer.

"Mr. President, they were unanimous in their conclusions: No material made on Earth could withstand the heat of the sun at a distance of three million miles, and the idea of a technology that could control solar flares was so farfetched no one could even speculate on how it might be done."

"Do they think the thing is from outer space?" Wainwright asked.

"They do." He looked around the table. "Most scientists in this field have been expecting contact with another planet for decades. They're excited but not surprised."

The group fell silent. The president turned to his Chief of Staff. "Find out where those two professors are and get them in here."

CHAPTER 43

Sly Wicker leaned against a building in the alley between 19th and 20th, watching the street for the two gang members he hired. They were the last piece of the plan. So far everything had fallen into place. The construction barricade would go up at 3:15. When the Hopkins kid left school at 4:15, his van would be directed onto 19th Street, and the two thugs would divert it into this alley, where he would pretend to save the kid from a carjacking. The abduction would take less than five minutes. Easy.

Sly lit a cigarette, glanced at his watch. Where are the little rats?

They rounded the corner into the alley. He moved his cigarette in a small arc to catch their eye, and they ambled toward him. The taller of the two made a mock salute. "You Sly Wicker?"

They were in their late teens. Tight, sullen faces. Baggy jeans. Nikes the size of boats. Dark jackets loose enough to hide a weapon. They came highly recommended. "Are you Bo?"

"Yeah, and that's my buddy Weeds," Bo said, jerking his thumb at the other boy. "Mr. B said you had a job for us. You wanna tell us what it's about?"

"I need a little help with a guy who owes me money," Wicker lied. They didn't have to know about the kidnapping. All he needed was for them to fake a car-jacking. They would stop the van, try to pull Gerard out, at which point Wicker, like a good Samaritan would rush in to offer his help. The two thugs would take off down the alley, and Wicker would quickly knock him out with a little chloroform, tie him up and stuff him into the trunk of Wicker's car, and take him away to the holding place.

He explained this to Bo and Weeds, except for the part where he doped Gerard and stuffed him into the trunk. "You understand what you're to do?"

Bo nodded, a smirk on his young face. "We got it. You wanna play super-hero. Make the kid think you're saving his ass."

"What I want is for you to do your job," Wicker growled. He thrust two hundred-dollar bills at the boy. "You do good, you'll get the rest from Mr. B."

#

"Here he comes, here he comes," Weeds whispered, bouncing on his heels.

"Let's go," Bo said.

They ran out into the street waving their arms at the driver of the green van, motioning to him. Gerard slowed and turned the van into the alley. He hit the brakes hard when Weeds stepped in front of the van. The black teenager fell to the ground, and Gerard jerked the gear shift into park. "Jesus, I hit him!"

At that moment, Bo yanked the driver's door open. Weeds scrambled to his feet, and they both grabbed Gerard's arm and tried to pull him out of the car. Resisting with all his might, Gerard flexed his left arm and stuck his elbow into Weeds' face. Then he launched a punch at Bo's face that sent him staggering backward. He drew back for a shot at Weeds when suddenly everything stopped. He sat motionless, fist drawn back, eyes staring into the darkness, mind gone blank.

Sly Wicker watched the struggle from behind his car parked near the alley. When Bo took a punch, Wicker started toward the van, then stopped abruptly. "What the hell!"

He watched, mouth agape as Bo and Weeds rose several feet off the ground and were hurtled down the alley airborne, arms and legs flailing. At the end of the alley, they collapsed to the ground on top of each other. They scrambled to their feet and looked around, their eyes wide with terror, then sprinted around the corner and disappeared.

#

Drakk stood on the rooftop of a nearby building and chuckled, his antennae quivering. *That had been fun!* As soon as he dealt with Sly Wicker, he would release Gerard from his mild trance. All the boy would remember would be two thugs trying to pull him out of the car. He wouldn't recall how he'd got away from them.

"What exactly are you doing?"

Drakk spun around at the sound of Myssa's high, thin voice. "I was helping to avoid a catastrophe," he said, peevishly.

"When will you learn to let these things play out in their own time and space?"

A bright blue flush crept up Drakk's neck and cheeks. "You don't have to tell Morok. What would that accomplish?"

"It might help to keep you in line," Myssa said. She studied him with cold reptilian eyes, then said with the barest hint of a smile. "If you insist on interfering with these creatures, at least do it with a little flair."

Drakk's antennae quivered frantically when Myssa vanished from his side and reappeared in front of Sly Wicker.

Wicker took a step back when a creature resembling a green lizard appeared out of nowhere. It was over five feet tall and standing upright. It looked him directly in the eyes and said, "If you do not want to face attempted kidnapping charges, Mr. Wicker, you really should leave the country now."

Wicker tried to make sense out of what was happening. The kids levitating down the alley, a guy in a lizard suit. Could Gorr have planned all this as a practical joke? He scrapped that thought. Gorr was devoid of a sense of humor. So how did this lizard-guy know his name?

"Maybe this will convince you to get the hell out of Dodge," Myssa said just before she morphed into a likeness of Ganbigo.

A thin wail escaped Wicker's lips at the sight of the diminutive shaman he had murdered six years ago. He turned and stumbled to his car. He sat for a moment gasping for breath, his heart racing. Then he headed straight for the airport.

Before his plane to São Paulo took off, Sly Wicker texted a message to Ethan Gorr. "Goddamned job aborted. See you in Hell."

Stephen looked up when Gerard tapped on his door. Something in his face alarmed Stephen. "What's wrong, son?"

Gerard rolled in and said quietly, "Promise you won't tell Mom?"

Stephen frowned. "You know I can't promise that."

Gerard blew out a breath. "There was a roadblock on 20th, and when I took the detour, a couple of guys waved me down and motioned me into an alley. Then one of them fell down on the street right in front of the van. I thought I'd hit him, so I stopped and then they were both at the door, pulling at my arm, trying to drag me out of the car. I elbowed one of them and punched the other one in the face—"

"Did they pull you out? Did they hurt you?" Stephen was horrified at the thought of Gerard being dragged out of the car.

"Dad, it was weird. One minute I'm getting ready to throw a punch, the next I'm just sitting there and the guys are gone."

"What did you do?"

Gerard shrugged. "I backed out of the alley and came home."

"You didn't see where they went?"

"Nope. It was almost like I dreamed it."

Stephen said a silent prayer of gratitude that his son was safe. "So you weren't dragged out of the van?"

"No. I still had my arm drawn back to throw the punch, and nobody was there. Do you think it really happened?"

Stephen had no idea what had really happened, but the last thing he wanted was for his son to doubt his own eyes. "Something probably spooked them. Maybe they saw a police car drive by. The important thing is, you're okay."

Gerard said, "Do we have to tell Mom?"

Stephen gave a rueful smile. Gerard had been driving just since Christmas, and Penny would not hesitate to take away the privilege if she learned about this. "It's not good to keep secrets, but you're okay, and I don't see what would be gained by upsetting her."

Gerard flashed a grin. "Thanks, Dad. That's the only thing I was afraid of, that she'd say I couldn't drive anymore."

#

After his son left, Stephen slumped in his chair as the fear of what could have happened settled over him. The image of Gerard being dragged out of the car was more than he could bear, and without conscious thought, Ethan Gorr's face surfaced. If Gorr found himself facing prison or financial ruin because of Stephen's book, he would stop at nothing to extract revenge.

Which meant that Stephen no longer had a choice. Although the book might decrease the pillage of rain forests and ameliorate the injustice wreaked on primitive tribes, it could end his son's life, and he could not take that chance. He would call the publisher and put an end to the whole damned thing. It just wasn't worth it. Especially with the fate of the entire world still on his shoulders.

CHAPTER 44

Calvin Williams' survey of his fellow PCAST members had created a flurry of emails among the scientific community. Before Williams had rejoined the White House staff for the one o'clock meeting, the story had found its way onto the airwaves. The unidentified solar object was quickly dubbed a USO—a take on the acronym UFO—and radio and television talk shows began batting the story around with any expert they could corral on short notice. Even UFO fanatics were being asked their opinion with a modicum of newfound respect.

Reverend Marshall Hopkins received a phone call from CNN at 9:30 AM. They were airing a special edition of *Walter Anderson* that evening with a panel of scientists to talk about the unidentified solar object. Would the reverend be interested in joining the panel to represent traditional religious views?

Hopkins had not been listening to the news and was not aware of the object orbiting the sun. The subject didn't really matter, though. In the past when he appeared on Walter's show, the television audience for his Sunday morning sermons had jumped noticeably. He readily accepted but declined the producer's offer to patch him in by satellite from CNN'S Washington studios. Satellite communication had been unreliable for several weeks. He didn't want to take a chance that a loss of signal would cut him off in mid-sentence.

He listened to CNN while he threw some clothes and shaving gear into a small carry-on bag. Two young anchors were speculating about the possible origin of the solar object.

The female anchor said, "UFOs always turn out to be some super-secret aircraft being tested by the military, so this USO thing is probably a spy satellite. The question is, is it spying on us or on our enemies?" She gave her male co-anchor a toothy smile.

"Scientists are saying it can't possibly be manmade, Sheila."

"Scientists don't know everything, Roger."

"Why is it so hard to believe that an alien civilization put it there?" Roger said. "There are billions of stars out there, probably millions of planets, any one of which could be more advanced than we are."

Hopkins paused in the middle of folding a shirt. Stephen had told him he'd testified at a hearing held by an alien civilization. It had seemed like a fantastic tale at the time, but he'd said the aliens were going to put an object in orbit around the sun, and now, there was indeed an object spinning around the sun which scientists said could not have been made by humans.

He tried to remember what Stephen had told him about the object. Something about it playing havoc with satellite communications as part of a quarantine? Well, communications had indeed been on the fritz for the past few weeks. And the other thing? Ah, yes. The other thing was that the solar object could be used to exterminate the entire human race.

If all this was true, how could he reconcile it with the Word of God?

He finished packing, deep in thought. In a few hours, he would be expected to explain how all contact with an alien civilization impacted religious belief. And he had no idea what he was going to say.

#

At three o'clock that afternoon, Stephen called Heather from his Georgetown office. They chatted for a few minutes about the solar object.

"Hold on a moment," Heather said. "My assistant's making frantic motions in the doorway."

He could hear her talking in a muffled voice with someone, then he heard a loud "*What!*"

She returned to the phone. "You are not going to believe this. There are two FBI agents here who want to talk to me. I'll call you back when I find out what's going on."

He still had the phone in his hand when Nancy stepped into his office and closed the door. She looked at him with wide eyes.

"Dr. Hopkins? There are two men in my office who say they're FBI agents. They have a cop with them and they want to talk with you."

Stephen considered the FBI's simultaneous appearance in two professors' offices on opposite coasts. It could not possibly be a coincidence. The President had connected the dots.

CHAPTER 45

Marshall Hopkins sipped a glass of red wine in the first-class cabin of an Airbus 319, finishing off a conversation with his friend Jason, a fellow member of the clergy, just before takeoff.

"So, what are you going to say on *Walter Anderson*?"

"I'm not sure, Jason. But if there *are* aliens out there, maybe they're the Antichrist. The Bible doesn't say what form the Antichrist will take, so why not an alien civilization?"

"That's nonsense, Marshall. Antichrist just means false prophet or someone who corrupts the Christian faith. Paul of Tarsus himself was considered by some to be the antichrist. So were Peter the Great, John Calvin, Martin Luther, and half the popes in the Middle Ages."

"So how do you explain the existence of intelligent aliens if it turns out they launched that USO?"

"Look at it this way. Why would God limit himself to one little planet? Why wouldn't He use the whole universe as His canvas? Why not populate a second planet? Why not dozens or hundreds? Why not thousands?"

A flight attendant stepped to the front of the plane and asked everyone to fasten their seat belts and turn off their cell phones in preparation for takeoff.

The reverend later mused on Jason's comments as he enjoyed a sumptuous lunch and watched the clouds float by his window. Maybe this was just another challenge he'd have to square with the Bible. He had met the challenge of the Big Bang theory by quoting Genesis and saying, "When God said, 'Let there be light,' that 'light' was the Big Bang!" He met the challenge of DNA by telling his flock that it was simply God's blueprint for creating every living thing, and evolution was just an alternative theory to Intelligent Design, although the latter was rapidly losing ground. Such things weren't spelled out in the Bible for good reason. How could God have explained cosmology or microbiology or nanotechnology to simple, uneducated shepherds?

As the plane flew on toward New York, he began to shape his next sermon in his head. He would draw parallels from the thirteenth century to fit the twenty-first. In the Middle Ages, men of God had to deal with the discovery that the Earth wasn't flat, that it revolved around the sun instead of the other way around, and that there was a great land mass beyond the sea inhabited by a race of strange people with dark skin. Christianity had survived it all, had in fact thrived in that land beyond the sea, and Christianity would survive this latest challenge. He would comb the Bible for some hint of the existence of other worlds. The Great Book, after all, has many layers of meaning; he simply had to interpret God's words in light of this new information.

High over the Eastern Seaboard, the perfect opening for the sermon coalesced in his mind. He could imagine his words flowing through the airwaves in the full rich tones of his Voice:

Jesus said it all in John 14:2: "In my Father's house are many mansions: if it were not so, I would have told you." Our Father's house, my friends, is our great and glorious universe; the many mansions are the millions of planets that populate the Universe; and the souls who inhabit those planets are God's people, just like you and I, and like you and I, they are hungering for salvation.

He pulled a note pad and pen out of his briefcase and began to write.

CHAPTER 46

At the FBI headquarters in Washington, D.C., a young female agent ushered Stephen Hopkins into a small rectangular room furnished with a table and two chairs. The agent removed the handcuffs and left the room. Stephen rubbed his wrists, remembering the surreal quality of his arrest. The cop had recited his Miranda rights, handcuffed him, and led him out the door while Nancy watched, a frozen look of disbelief on her face. A few students had clustered in front of the building and they stared with mouths agape as the cop put him in the back seat of a police cruiser, pressing down on the top of his head just as he'd seen in countless television dramas. The FBI agents slid into a black sedan parked behind the squad car and trailed them off the campus.

"Why have I been arrested?" Stephen had asked the officer.

"You have the right to remain silent, you have the right—"

"Forget it," he'd said, and caught the officer's sly grin in the rear-view mirror.

Now, left alone in the small room, he sat down in the chair facing the door. He wished he could call Penny but the female agent had confiscated his cell phone, along with his wallet and keys. He could only hope that Nancy had had the presence of mind to call her. He looked around the room. The walls were bare and windowless, except for a clerestory window that ran the width of the wall at the far end of the room. He could see nothing through the glass, but he assumed people on the other side were watching him.

Was Heather experiencing the same thing at the FBI headquarters in Santa Barbara, or more likely, LA? Their simultaneous arrests surely had to do with their conversation with the president in December. They had told him that GFED would put a satellite in orbit around the sun, and now there was something orbiting the sun that no one could identify. Plus, two massive solar flares had darkened the entire planet. No doubt the president was looking for answers. But why *arrest* them?

The door opened, and the younger of the two arresting agents came in and sat down at the table. He introduced himself as Special Agent Jacob Reed. Reed had short-cropped hair so blonde it looked almost white and a cherubic face that belied the gravity of his profession. He smiled a friendly smile at Stephen.

"Dr. Hopkins, our country is facing a possible national emergency so in the interest of time I'll dispense with the usual review of your personal history. We know who you are and we know a great deal about your background."

"I want to call my attorney."

"If you'd like to play lawyers with us, go right ahead. Call your attorney and see what he suggests. This is a matter of national security that protects all of us."

Special Agent Reed broadened his smile and leaned forward. "You have the right to remain silent, professor, but I can tell you that would be unwise. We are simply requesting your help."

Stephen considered remaining silent, but if he refused to answer their questions, he would look guilty of *something*. Besides, he had nothing to hide. If this was about GFED, he had already told the president and his staff everything he knew. He nodded at the agent. "Ask your questions."

"Good decision." Special Agent Reed loosened his tie and leaned back in his chair. He looked as if he were settling in for a long siege. "What do you know about the blackouts that occurred this past weekend?"

When Stephen testified at the hearing on the Abigo shooting, his lawyer had cautioned him to answer questions directly but not to elaborate. That seemed like wise advice here. "I know they occurred."

"Do you know who or what may have triggered them?"

"The consensus of the scientific community is that solar flares caused both blackouts."

"Do you agree with them?"

"Yes."

"What do you think caused back-to-back solar flares bigger than anything ever before recorded?"

"I've read that this is a peak year for solar activity."

Special Agent Reed sighed. He wore a look of troubled impatience, as if he were questioning a recalcitrant child about taking a friend's toy when he had actually seen the kid take the toy. "Let's cut the crap, professor. We know there's an object orbiting the sun and we know you told the president back in December that this would happen. Do you think this satellite had anything to do with the blackouts?"

"If you're asking me what I *think*, the answer is yes."

"Who put that satellite in orbit?"

"I don't know."

"Who do you *think* put it there?"

"I think it was placed there by GFED."

"And what is GFED?"

"It stands for Galactic Federation."

"And that is?"

"I was told it is the governing body for a large group of planets in our galaxy."

"Who told you this?"

"Chairman Morok."

"Is Earth one of the planets in this so-called Galactic Federation?"

"Not yet."

The agent smiled at him. "Okay, professor. Now, tell me everything you know about this GFED putting a satellite in orbit around our sun."

Stephen said, "I was abducted on November 5th of last year and taken to a special hearing of the GFED commission. The chairman of that commission, Chairman Morok, advised me that the Earth was being placed under quarantine and that a satellite would be placed in orbit around the sun to interfere with our global communications."

"And why would they want to interfere with our communications?"

"So that we could not continue to broadcast our violent ways—and perhaps our DNA code—to the galaxy."

Stephen was irritated at the skeptical look on the agent's cherubic face. *Arrogant little punk.* "I reported all of this directly to President Wainwright and his staff in December. I didn't know about the blackouts then, but they might be a by-product of the quarantine."

Agent Reed was quiet for a minute. "You haven't told me anything I don't already know, professor. I've listened to a recording of your meeting with the president, and you know what? I don't think you're telling us everything you know."

"You're wrong, Agent Reed. I'm telling you everything I know." Stephen could see the young agent bristle at his words.

"Maybe you don't know how serious this is. Those blackouts affected the entire world. If they had lasted any longer, or if there had been a third or a fourth, it could have shut down the worldwide economy and caused mayhem all over this globe. So, I need to know who this GFED really is. I need to know who Chairman Morok is and I need to know about your involvement with them. Is that clear?"

"I wish it were only that simple."

The agent's eyes narrowed. "Pardon?"

"Agent Reed, I told President Wainwright everything I know about GFED and Chairman Morok, which isn't much. All I learned at that hearing was that they might put a satellite into orbit around the sun to interfere with our communications. I assume the satellite does not belong to any nation on Earth. Is that true?"

"I will ask the questions here."

Stephen said nothing.

"Have you heard from this GFED chairman since your meeting with the president in December?"

Stephen hesitated. If he told the agent that Morok had come to his study after the December meeting, he would appear delusional. It was one thing to say he had talked to aliens at a hearing, which Heather could corroborate. It was another thing entirely to say the alien had dropped by his study for a chat. He decided to lie. "No, not since the GFED hearing."

Special Agent Reed crossed his arms over his chest and stared at him. It seemed that several minutes went by. Stephen forced himself not to fill the silence.

Finally, the agent spoke. "The FBI knows of no such organization as GFED. We know of no such person as Morok.

Believe me, professor, if they existed, we or our sister agencies would be aware of them."

He uncrossed his arms, pulled his chair closer to the table, put his forearms on the desk and clasped his hands in front of him. "Now let me tell you something else we know. We know about your history of supporting pacifist initiatives. We know about your involvement with extremists like Heather Eastlake. We know that some pacifist groups have adopted terrorist methods and have declared themselves to be enemies of America. We believe you may have been unwittingly duped by such groups that want to bring down this country. Or maybe—" he thrust his head at Stephen, "maybe you're a willing participant."

He paused to let that sink in. "I personally do not believe you want to harm this country, Dr. Hopkins, so you need to stop spinning your little tales of outer space and help us identify the terrorists who are causing these problems."

Stephen placed his hands flat on the table and leaned toward the agent. "I am *not* involved with terrorists."

The two men glared at each other over the table.

Stephen blinked first. He leaned back in his chair. "Is it possible I was duped about the meeting with GFED? I don't think so. I am a trained scientist with years of experience dealing with bizarre primitives. I have unraveled incredible myths perpetrated by various shaman upon their tribes. But I am convinced—scientifically convinced—that GFED *does* exist and that Chairman Morok is indeed who he says he is."

"What makes you scientifically convinced?"

"The fact that two different regression therapists could elicit independently—from two people who had never met— identical memories of what happened on the evening of November 5th, when neither of us originally remembered anything about that evening."

The door flew open and the older, heavier agent who had arrested him came in and slammed the door behind him. He leaned against the door, hands behind his back, and stared at Stephen. He had a florid complexion and a look of disgust on his face, and the jacket he had worn when he made the arrest was gone, and the sleeves of his white shirt were rolled up, exposing hairy forearms.

Agent Reed stood up. "Meet my partner Special Agent Clive Bartels," he said, a sly smile on his cherubic face. "He'll take over the questioning from here."

Agent Bartels walked over to Stephen and looked down at him. "I've heard about all of your crap I can stand. Two of our agents were making a drug sting during Friday's blackout, and guess what? They were killed because they couldn't see two inches in front of their faces." He leaned down, thrust his face close to Stephen's. "One of those agents was my best friend, and I'll do whatever it takes to get the truth out of you. You got that, asshole?"

CHAPTER 47

Reverend Marshall Hopkins arrived at La Guardia, barely an hour before the Walter Anderson broadcast began. A limousine picked him up and whisked him to the CNN studios with just enough time for a quick once-over by the make-up crew. A thin woman with a long braid down her back escorted him to the cavernous studio where Walter Anderson sat with his guests waiting for the director's countdown. Walter greeted him warmly just as the producer called, "Let's go, people."

The reverend took the empty seat on the left. Walter leaned toward the camera as the producer began the countdown. When the red light came on, he began. "Tonight, two burning questions trouble the world: What is that strange object orbiting our sun? And is it related to the back-to-back blackouts that struck our planet this past weekend? The answers to those questions may illuminate a history-making event that will affect all of mankind."

"On our panel tonight, we have Dr. Andrew Coulter, one of the most celebrated astronomers of our time; Dr. Kedan Imarada, a distinguished astrophysicist at the Jet Propulsion Laboratory; Dr. Janice Baker, an astrobiologist, chemist, and author currently on the staff of the London think tank Futurist Planning; and my good friend and world-renowned evangelist, the Reverend Marshall Hopkins. "Andrew, let's begin with you. What is that thing orbiting the sun?"

DR. ANDREW COULTER
No one really knows, Walter. It's remarkable, given its extraordinarily tight orbit, but so far, we can't explain it by any conventional means.
WALTER ANDERSON
Could it be responsible for the blackouts last weekend?
DR. ANDREW COULTER
As an astronomer, I observe phenomena in the sky, I don't like to speculate on their effect on the planet.
WALTER ANDERSON
Dr. Imarada, would you care to speculate?

DR. KEDAN IMARADA

From what we have learned, it seems that the orbital anomalies appear to be close to the timing of the blackouts, but that could be a coincidence or a chicken-or-egg problem.

WALTER ANDERSON

You mean, which came first, the blackouts or the satellite's orbital anomalies?

DR. KEDAN IMARADA

Exactly. From our vantage point, it would appear that the orbital anomalies came first but we can't be certain.

WALTER ANDERSON

So, what's all the furor about?

DR. KEDAN IMARADA

The facts are difficult to rationalize, Walter. Based on scientific knowledge, we would expect a steady and rapid decay of orbit from an inert object like this one, but it's maintaining a stable orbit. Moreover, the apparent increase, then decrease, in orbit contradicts the expected behavior of a natural object. Then there are the mysterious emissions.

DR. ANDREW COULTER

Both the emissions and the orbital anomalies could be explained by an asteroid breaking up as it neared the sun. Or they could be explained by outgassing.

WALTER ANDERSON

What is outgassing?

DR. ANDREW COULTER

Near the sun, liquids, and gases in an asteroid or comet would be heated and then vaporized by the extreme temperatures. The resulting pressure could cause the vaporized material to explode outward through the surface of the asteroid or comet. Think volcano.

WALTER ANDERSON

Some are suggesting this thing is an alien space station or possibly some kind of a satellite put into orbit by terrorists or a rogue nation. Janice, you want to respond to that?

DR. JANICE BAKER

I don't believe it could have been created by any technology known on Earth, based on its observed characteristics. Nor does any other scientist I know. So that pretty much rules out a terrorist group or rogue nation. As far as aliens go, who knows what their capabilities might be? Anything is potentially possible, but we have no evidence that it was placed there by aliens—

WALTER ANDERSON

But you just said that scientists agree it could *not* have been created by any technology on Earth. Doesn't that lead to the conclusion that a technology *not on earth*—an alien technology—created it?

DR. ANDREW BAKER

Possibly. But it seems highly unlikely that any non-terrestrial intelligence would go to such lengths just to create a couple of blackouts.

WALTER ANDERSON

Reverend Hopkins, there's a lot of talk going around today about the end of the world and the coming of the antichrist. What will it mean to religion if it turns out there are extraterrestrials with advanced technology? Aliens who are smarter than us?

REVEREND HOPKINS

Walter, I've been giving this a good deal of thought, and I've come to the conclusion that we have to stop thinking of God in such small terms. When Moses led his people out of Egypt, God was the Yahweh of the Israelites, the Jews. Then he became the God of Christianity and the Allah of the Muslim world. And then the world itself expanded until God encompassed the entire globe. Why is it so difficult to think that God could encompass the whole universe, creating people and nations on hundreds, or millions of planets? We may feel somewhat diminished by these kinds of thoughts, but it doesn't diminish God. It enhances him.

WALTER ANDERSON

How does that square with the Bible? People will say that if there were other species on distant planets, the Bible would have mentioned it.

REVEREND HOPKINS

The Bible is written in metaphors and parables, Walter. Take the verse in John that says, 'In my Father's house are many mansions.' Metaphorically, that could refer to the universe that is filled with planets. Jesus knew about the planets, of course, and if they are inhabited, he knew about that, but how could he

216

convey such a concept to the simple fishermen in that simpler time? He could not, so he spoke in parables, assuming that one day we would become advanced enough to understand and welcome the concept.

WALTER ANDERSON

So, you welcome the possibility of alien civilizations more advanced than we are?

REVEREND HOPKINS

Absolutely. God created the universe and he has every right to populate it as he sees fit.

WALTER ANDERSON

Dr. Coulter, what do you say to the reverend's theory?

DR. ANDREW COULTER

I applaud his ecumenical vision. But there have been rumors of UFO landings and alien invasions for years, and no one has ever proven the existence of a UFO and no one has ever introduced us to an alien from outer space. So, despite its strange behavior, I think a reasonable scientific explanation will soon be found for the solar object—and probably a very prosaic one.

WALTER ANDERSON

Janice, do you believe there is alien intelligence out there somewhere?

DR. JANICE BAKER

In my field, we believe that the odds heavily favor the evolution of life on other planets. But some of us also believe that the odds of such life having reached our level of intelligence or any level of space travel are quite small. If you—

DR. ANDREW COULTER

How provincial can you be, Janice? It is the height of arrogance to think that we humans are the most advanced species in a universe that contains untold billions of stars. In our galaxy alone we estimate more than 400 billion stars—

DR. JANICE BAKER

I don't need a lecture on the size of the universe, Andrew. But *if* intelligent life had developed on another planet and *if* it had ventured into space, it is quite likely that we would have already heard from them, especially based on the very numbers you just cited.

DR. ANDREW COULTER

Why? Why would we have already heard from them? It's highly unlikely that Earth—a little planet in the far corner of a minor galaxy—would even be on the radar of a more advanced civilization.

DR. JANICE BAKER

The SETI program has been listening to the universe for decades, and there has not been a single instance of an intelligent signal—

WALTER ANDERSON

What is SETI?

DR. JANICE BAKER

The acronym stands for the search for extraterrestrial intelligence. SETI uses radio telescopes or optical arrays to search the universe for signals that *might be* from other civilizations. If someone wanted to contact us that is probably how they would do it.

WALTER ANDERSON

Why would someone want to contact us?

DR. JANICE BAKER

It stands to reason that one advanced civilization would want to contact other advanced civilizations, just as we want to. Such contact might or might not be designed to reach *us,* but intercepting any kind of galactic communications would let us know that other intelligent beings are out there and vice versa. Keep in mind, Walter, we ventured into space more than 50 years ago—

DR. ANDREW COULTER

Fifty years ago! What makes you think 50 years of space travel makes us advanced? There could be hundreds of civilizations millions of years more advanced than we are. They could be so advanced that, to them, we would seem as primitive as aborigines.

REVEREND HOPKINS

Shame on you, doctor! We are not aborigines, we're all God's people. If this object is from another planet, it is still God's planet and the people on that planet are still God's people, just like us, even if they happen to be more advanced.

WALTER ANDERSON

Because this is such an important issue. I'm going to break protocol and take a few calls from our viewers. Boise, Idaho is on the phone.

VIEWER FROM BOISE

Thank you, Walter. My question is for Dr. Coulter. How do you know this USO hasn't been there all along? Why do you think it's new?

WALTER ANDERSON

Good question. Andrew?

DR. ANDREW COULTER

The object is large enough that it surely would have been reported by numerous observatories had it been there all along. Let me say that we've had reports over the past year from amateur observers that an object was on a trajectory toward a close approach to the sun, most likely a comet or an asteroid, but those reports have not been absolutely confirmed.

WALTER ANDERSON

Here's another call, this one from Fairview, Arkansas.

VIEWER FROM FAIRVIEW

My question's for Reverend Hopkins. Sir, do you really believe all that crap you're spewing?

REVEREND HOPKINS

I beg your pardon!

WALTER ANDERSON

Sorry, Reverend, that one slipped past us. We'll take more of your calls when we come back.

#

Penny turned off the television. She was too sick with worry about Stephen to listen to Walter Anderson even if the reverend was on the panel. Nancy had been close to hysterics when she called to say that Stephen had been led away in handcuffs by the FBI, and Penny knew immediately that it had something to do with that thing orbiting the sun. But why *arrest* him? He'd tried to warn the president about it a month ago and he hadn't believed him.

And neither had she.

The thought stopped her short. She had never believed a word Stephen said about his encounter with an alien civilization, not really. Not even after Heather Eastlake had corroborated his story. Now it looked as if he might have been telling the truth—a truth that apparently concerned the government enough to send the FBI after him.

She went upstairs to Gerard's room, tapped on the door, pushed it open. She watched him pecking furiously at his computer and wished for a moment that she could slip up behind him to see what he was writing. She stood at the door. "Your grandfather was on Walter Anderson tonight."

He stopped typing and pivoted toward her: "No way!"

"Way," she said with a smile. "He was on a panel discussing that solar object."

"What'd he have to say about it?"

"Oh, he said that God paints on a larger canvass than we give him credit for, meaning the whole universe instead of just Planet Earth, and that the Bible is a book of metaphors and parables. It was quite beautiful, actually."

"What'd dad say about it?"

She hesitated, not knowing quite how to tell him. "Your dad's not here."

"Is he still at work?"

"No." She told him what Nancy had told her.

"Why would the FBI want to talk with him?"

"I'm sure it's related to his meeting with the president when he told him about that...alien federation. What'd he call it?"

"GFED. Galactic Federation."

She felt tears crowd the back of her eyes. Here they were talking seriously about alien beings. Things were changing in ways she had never dreamed possible. "I never believed anything your father said about his abduction, and now it looks like it might all be true."

"Mom, don't worry. It was a lot to believe."

"But you believed him from the start."

Gerard shrugged. "I had an occasional doubt. But then we found Dr. Eastlake and she'd had the same experience. It all made sense."

Not to me, Penny thought. She hadn't believed Stephen even then; she'd thought he might be having an affair with Heather Eastlake. She gave her son a wry smile. "I don't think anything will ever make sense to me again."

She left Gerard's room and went down to the sunroom. The birds began to shriek when she walked in. She closed the door and opened the aviary. The birds flew out, Noah in the lead. He circled the room once, then settled on her shoulder. Solly and Joseph landed in the ficus tree and continued to shriek.

"What's going on?" she said to Noah as he walked down her arm and settled on her wrist.

"Lollapalooza," he said in his high thin voice.

She laughed. It was one of the first words she'd taught him simply because she liked the sound of the word and she wanted to see if he could say one with multi-syllables. He rarely said it, but when he did, he wouldn't stop. Now he said it over and over like a chant: "Lollapalooza, lollapalooza, lollapalooza."

She stretched out on the chaise and thought about what the reverend had said on Walter Anderson. Maybe life did evolve on other planets, just as it had evolved here. She knew that planets with the necessary ingredients to support life had been discovered, so why couldn't life have evolved more rapidly somewhere else than it had here? Or maybe those planets in GFED were simply a lot older than Earth. Either way, would the life forms be human-like or would they have evolved in a totally different direction? She knew very little about the science of such things; all she had to go on were science fiction films where aliens were depicted as ghostlike forms with big almond-shaped eyes or humanoids with pointed ears or wizened lizard-like skin or, so often, as ubiquitous slimy menacing monsters. Of course, those were all imaginary creations, but what form would evolution on another planet really take?

She sighed in frustration. Whatever their form, the idea that they'd singled out Stephen as an emissary for their message was hard to accept. *Why him, dear God? Why did you place this awful burden on him, on our family?* There was no good answer, not one she could think of anyway.

She came out of her reverie and realized that Noah was sitting quietly on her wrist. "What's up, Noah?"

"Lollapalooza," said the bird.

CHAPTER 48

Ethan Gorr was watching *Walter Anderson*, lying on his king-size bed amid a small mountain of pillows. When the old man started talking about God painting on a larger canvass, he muttered, "Idiot," and clicked the off button. Reverend Hopkins had called him in December wanting to know the outcome of his meeting with Stephen. "It was a goddamned disaster," Gorr had said. "Well, I got you your meeting," Hopkins said. "I'm sorry it wasn't successful."

The pious prick! And now, there he was on television spouting off about God and aliens. Ever since the damn thing was discovered, that's all anyone talked about, speculating on what it was, how it got there, whether it was really from outer space. Who the hell cared? He had more important things to think about, namely Hopkins and revenge. He'd made him a generous offer in December. But the bastard had thrown it back in his face, grabbing him—*him, Ethan Gorr*—and shoving him to the floor.

Ok, so the kidnapping plan went south, but it did stop the publication of that goddamned book. And of course, the whole world had changed since then…but Gorr still wanted revenge.

Gorr lay awake in the darkness and let his thoughts flow freely until they coalesced into a plan. Then he turned over and went into a deep sound sleep.

CHAPTER 49

Special Agent Carla Korinski shoved a photograph across the table. "Which one is you?"

Heather recognized the photograph. It had been taken eight years earlier during the second Iraqi war: A hundred or more demonstrators lay on their backs in the middle of State Street in Santa Barbara. She lay near the edge of the group, front and center to the angle of the camera. The photographer caught her just as she looked directly at him. She pointed to her image. "That's me."

"And they let traitors like you teach our kids!" Korinski hissed.

"I protest all acts of war, whoever initiates them."

Korinski glared at her and pulled the photograph away and pushed another toward her. "Point yourself out."

She was standing in the front row of a crowd waving placards. Hers said "Bring our Troops Home NOW!" She pointed at herself.

She'd marched in dozens of peace rallies during college and afterward, and Korinski seemed to have photos of them all. The agent held up several photographs and asked her to identify herself and to admit that she was protesting the legitimate actions of the United States of America.

Heather pointed to her image in each photograph and repeated that she was protesting all acts of war. She wished Agent Hart would return. He was the one who had escorted her from the UCSB University to the Santa Barbara airport and sat next to her on the flight to Washington. He had been kind enough to remove the handcuffs once they were airborne, and he'd played the "good cop" at the beginning of the interrogation. But he had left the small stuffy room hours ago and left her to the tender mercies of Special Agent Carla Korinski. Now Heather wanted nothing more than to punch Korinski in her smug little face and lay down and go to sleep.

Korinski shoved another photograph at her, and Heather caught her breath. It was a black-and-white shot of a man and a woman sitting on a park bench holding hands and smiling at each other. The man looked to be of Middle Eastern descent.

"Who is Jamal Alshahri?" Korinski asked.

Heather hesitated. She had met Jamal on a trip to Boston in July 2001. She had been at the Ritz Carlton for a conference on children and violence; he was there on business. They had met in the hotel elevator and before they reached her floor, he had invited her for a drink and she'd agreed, and they had gone back downstairs to the bar. There was an intensity about Jamal that she found attractive, a hint of mystery in his dark intelligent eyes. They had spent the week together and there was talk of his coming to Santa Barbara or her going to Phoenix where he lived. But the next time she saw him was on television shortly after the attack on the World Trade Center and the Pentagon. There he was amid the suspected terrorists, staring into the camera, his intelligent eyes hot and defiant. He had been arrested in a terrorist cell in Arizona.

"I want a lawyer," Heather said. "I have a right to have a lawyer present."

Korinski "Of course you do. But if you're telling us the truth, you don't need one."

#

On another floor in the same building, Stephen was expressing the same sentiment to Special Agent Clive Bartels. "I want to call my lawyer."

Bartels shoved Stephen's chair with his foot and nearly tipped it backward. Stephen grabbed at the table for support.

"Well, professor, you can call your lawyer whenever you like. But if you simply tell us the truth now, the easier it will be on you—and on your family."

Bartels glanced at Reed who was leaning against the wall, one foot pressed flat against it. "By the way, partner, did we pick up his family yet? Or his red-haired whore from Santa Barbara?"

Reed said, "We have the redhead. Two agents are on their way to the professor's house now."

Bartels looked at Stephen. "We just might have to take the wheelchair away from that kid of yours and see how far he can crawl."

225

Stephen caught his breath. Then he came out of the chair and lunged at Bartels. Agent Reed grabbed him from behind before he could touch the other man and pushed him back into the chair.

Bartels looked pleased with himself. "You just attacked a Special Agent, professor. That's a federal offense, you know that? You could go to prison or better yet—" he leaned toward Stephen, "you've just given me license to do anything I want to your sorry self."

Stephen struggled to control his temper. Attacking a federal officer was in fact a crime. He took a deep breath.

Agent Reed said, "Clive, why don't you let me finish the interview. I think the professor will be more cooperative now."

"Hell no! I'm just getting to the good part." He moved behind Stephen, leaned down, put his mouth close to Stephen's ear. "Now you listen close, asshole. Either you give me the answers I need or I go down the hall and tighten the vise on the redhead's thumb. And if that doesn't work, I'll do the same to your pretty little wife. And if that doesn't work, I can think of some brand-new measures we can try out on that boy of yours."

Stephen felt his insides go soft. They couldn't be serious. The FBI didn't torture private citizens, not in America. He forced himself to think rationally. This was the kind of violent behavior GFED was condemning. And he had just done it himself. Blinded by rage, he had lunged for Bartels, and if Reed hadn't stopped him, he would have attacked him. Just as he had attacked Ethan Gorr.

His thoughts pushed their way into words. "This is exactly why GFED has condemned us. Violence is how we solve our problems, it's all we know. Maybe they should just annihilate the whole human race."

Bartels was still standing behind his chair. "Hear that, Reed? Now he's threatening to annihilate the human race." He grabbed Stephen and pulled his head back against the chair. "I'll show you violence, you candy-assed professor. Your family won't recognize you when I finish."

"Clive."

Stephen could feel Agent Reed hovering above him. "*Clive!*"

Clive Bartels let go of Stephen and shoved his head forward. He walked around the chair and looked down at him. "Okay, spaceman, this is your last chance to cooperate. Who the fuck is this Morok character?"

A sharp pain zagged up the back of his neck when the agent released him. "I've already told you."

Bartels started for the door. "Your turn, Reed. I'll be back with a few tools to convince the professor how serious we really are."

Reed sat down in the chair opposite Stephen. "We try to control my partner, but he has a mean streak and he likes his job. He really likes it, and he'll push it as far as the law allows, sometimes farther, if you want to know the truth. The point is, you can spare yourself another go-round with him if you'll just cooperate with me."

Stephen guessed they were deliberately provoking him, trying to get him to lose his temper so they'd have a real reason to hold him. He knew they had Heather in custody, but he thought they were bluffing about Penny and Gerard. But what if they weren't? He looked at Special Agent Reed. He seemed like a sane person, a nice guy with a baby face—the Good Cop—Stephen thought suddenly, against Bad Cop Bartels. Was all this just a little exercise from the FBI rule book? He decided to try again.

"I don't know how to convince you that I've been telling you the truth, Agent Reed, but let me review what happened to me on November 5th of last year." He spent the next thirty minutes going over the details of his abduction, his appearance at the hearing, tracking down and finding Heather Eastlake, meeting with the president in December. "I have spent the past two months trying to understand all this. You have to believe that I'm telling you everything I know."

The door opened and a man Stephen hadn't seen before brought in several items and laid them on the table. Stephen looked at them closely. The only things he recognized were a syringe and something that looked like a vise, with a long screw that could be used for tightening. It was then that he felt the first prickling of fear.

He looked at the agent. "Does the president know this is going on?"

Reed didn't answer.

Stephen tried again. "I have reviewed my experience from every angle. Heather Eastlake and I have crosschecked each and every detail, and we always come back to the same conclusion. We were contacted by beings from another planet, and as incredible as it may sound, I am convinced that they put that satellite into orbit and that if we don't do the right thing, they will very likely destroy us."

Agent Reed stared at the wall for a few minutes, then turned back to Stephen. "Let's assume this Morok character is not a terrorist from another country on this planet."

"Morok is not a terrorist, period."

The agent sighed. "Where is he from? What is his last name?"

"I don't know."

"Describe him for me."

Stephen described Morok as he had appeared at the hearing.

The agent stared at him. "You're telling me this alien is a kindly-looking grey haired old man?"

"I'm sure he used that demeanor for my sake. I don't know what he really looks like."

Reed went on for another hour. Stephen found it hard to concentrate. He wanted to put his head down on the table and go to sleep. Finally, Reed left and a female agent came in and led him down the hall to a room with a narrow cot and told him he could sleep, but when he lay down, he found he was too keyed up to go to sleep. He worried about Penny and Gerard. He wondered how Heather was faring. He kept going over the agents' questions, reviewing his answers. Had he said the right things? Had he done everything he could?

He must have dozed off because he came to with a start at the sound of a voice. It was the female agent who had entered the room. She handed him his wallet, watch and cell phone. "President Wainwright wants to see you," she said.

He looked at his watch. It was 8 o'clock, almost sixteen hours since he was arrested in his university office. He called

Penny and told her he was all right and should be home by noon. Then he talked to Gerard who told him that news of the solar object had been all over the internet and television news, even the thing about its anomalous orbit and strange emissions.

Stephen was too tired to care. He splashed some water on his face. The nightmare was finally over.

CHAPTER 50

Two hours later, Stephen was driven to the White House and escorted to a small waiting room in the West Wing. A secretary brought him a cup of coffee and he took it gratefully. He was exhausted but still wired from the interrogation. He wondered if Heather fared any better.

He sipped the coffee and waited for the caffeine to kick in. There was some logic to the FBI treating him like a criminal. To them, the massive blackouts had been caused by terrorists, *alien* terrorists perhaps, but terrorists nonetheless, and he was associated with them; ergo, he was a prime suspect. But his emotional core rebelled. He had wanted to smash his fist into Agent Bartels' face, meeting violence with violence. He wondered again if this proclivity toward violence was written in the human genes.

The door to the waiting room opened and Heather walked in. She looked as if she had not had any sleep either. Her emerald suit was uncharacteristically rumpled, and her auburn hair, always coiffed to perfection, was pulled back in a careless ponytail. Her face showed signs of strain, but her green eyes were blazing. "I have *never* been treated so shabbily in my entire life!" she hissed in a low voice.

"When did you get here?"

"They flew me here on an FBI plane last night, then spent the past ten hours interrogating me like a criminal!"

"I was hoping they would be more respectful with you."

"Hardly! They led me out of my office in handcuffs. *Handcuffs!*" She paused. "Do you suppose we could sue them for false arrest?"

"You don't mean that, do you?"

"At this moment? Absolutely!" She took a deep breath and blew it upward. "Did you get any sleep?"

"A couple of hours on a stone sofa. How about you?"

She shook her head. "They just finished with me an hour ago. I think they would have kept going if the president hadn't sent for us."

A secretary poked her head in the door. "The President will see you now."

They followed her through a series of hallways and across a plushly carpeted waiting room. She opened a massive oak door and motioned them into the Oval Office.

Wainwright moved from behind his desk and walked toward them. He offered his hand, first to Heather, then to Stephen. He gave them his warmest politician's smile. "Dr. Eastlake, Dr. Hopkins, I owe you an apology—two apologies in fact. I apologize for not taking you seriously in December and I apologize again for putting you through an FBI interrogation."

In unison they murmured, "Thank you, Mr. President."

He motioned toward the facing sofas where Kimberly Dyer sat. She was dressed in a black suit with a splash of magenta at the neckline. She stood and flicked her blonde hair off her forehead as they exchanged greetings. The president took the Chippendale chair at the end of the sofas. Stephen and Heather sat on the sofa opposite Dyer.

Wainwright crossed his legs, looked from Stephen to Heather, back to Stephen. "I'll get right to the point. You're here because of what we've learned about this object orbiting the sun. As you might expect, every solar observatory in the world has been studying the thing, and it has exhibited some very strange behavior. Kimberly, tell them what we've found out."

Dyer repeated what she'd learned from NASA. She told them about the satellite's tight orbit, the signals it was emitting, and its erratic behavior at the time of the solar flares, all of which had puzzled the scientists. Most of them thought the emissions might be due to outgassing and that the solar flare could have caused the change in orbit, rather than the other way around.

"But the scientists don't have all the information," Dyer said, directing her comments at Stephen. "They don't know what you told us in December, that this—Galactic Federation, as you called it—had talked about putting a solar probe in orbit to either quarantine or exterminate the human race. If they had that little morsel of information, it might solidify their views."

Wainwright steepled his fingers and fixed an imperative stare on Stephen. "Do you think this satellite is the solar probe they mentioned?"

"Yes, sir. I thought it was a GFED satellite the minute I learned about it. And that was before I knew about its unusual behavior. I have no doubt it was put there by the Federation."

"Have either of you had any further contact with them?" His eyes flicked toward Heather.

"No, sir."

"Have you?" He fixed his gaze on Stephen.

Stephen hesitated. He hadn't told the FBI he'd seen Morok in his study after the December meeting because he feared it would make him look delusional. How could he now tell the president? "I have not," he said with a twinge of guilt.

Wainwright was silent for several moments. "Whoever it belongs to, it's playing havoc with our telecommunications satellites. That fits with the quarantine you mentioned."

Stephen nodded. "It does."

"Could it be a first step to extermination?" Dyer asked.

Stephen shrugged. "I don't know. The Chairman said he could veto a verdict of extermination, but the GFED commission can override his veto, just as Congress can override the president's."

Wainwright looked worried. "If they go for extermination, they'll use solar flares to blast a stream of gamma rays directly at the Earth, right?"

Stephen recalled Morok's words, *Death would be instantaneous and without pain.* "Yes."

Heather spoke up. "Mr. President, it seems to me that GFED has simply given us a warning shot— two warning shots in fact— in the form of the blackouts. Maybe they want us to be aware of their power so we'll do what they want."

"Which is?" prompted Dyer.

"Demonstrate that we're not an irredeemably violent species."

"And how would we do that?"

"We said this in December. Make a spectacular move toward peace. Something big, like unilateral disarmament."

Dyer shook her head but remained silent...

The president leaned forward, elbows on knees, hands clasped. "What do you think, Stephen?"

"Heather's right, sir. If Chairman Morok *did* veto extermination, the commission would have less reason to override the veto if they could see that we're serious about becoming less violent. I suspect that all they want at this point is evidence of our willingness to *try*."

"What do you think, Kimberly?"

She flicked her hair off her forehead for dramatic effect. "Mr. President, if I learned of a threat from an unknown enemy, my first step would be to gather as much information as possible to assess the enemy's strengths and uncover its weaknesses. Then I would look for ways to defend against the strengths and exploit the weaknesses. If the enemy was not a terrorist group, I would suggest a face-to-face meeting to search for common ground.

"In this case, that approach isn't possible. We're forced to rely on the guidance of two people who say they have met with these…extraterrestrials. But we must retain some healthy skepticism, sir. Dr. Eastlake is a well-known anti-war activist, and here she is, advising us to take an unprecedented action like unilateral disarmament. With all due respect, it sounds like she has her own agenda."

Stephen watched a flush rise on Heather's cheeks. He glanced at Wainwright. Did the man have the courage to do what needed to be done? He took a deep breath, plunged in. "Dr. Eastlake's agenda is the same as mine, Mr. President, and that is to do whatever is necessary to prevent extermination of the human race. Maybe we're naïve to think unilateral disarmament is possible, but the IRA did it a few years ago. Shouldn't you at least let other world leaders know about GFED?"

"You're asking me to tell the world that a group of aliens has threatened us with annihilation and we should lay down our arms?"

"Yes!" Heather locked on to his eyes. "That's exactly what you need to do, Mr. President. Lead! The world has followed us into war, why not ask them to follow us into peace?"

Dyer glanced at Stephen and murmured, "It's more likely they'll smell weakness and follow us to our graves."

"Ms. Dyer," Stephen said. "I called my sixteen-year-old son this morning and he told me all about the solar object—the emissions, the tight orbit, even the orbital anomalies—everything your scientists told you. The public knows about it! They believe that it somehow caused the blackouts and they're pretty sure it's not under the control of this planet."

He turned back to Wainwright. "The word is out there, Mr. President. It's on the airwaves and the internet and on the lips of people around the world. And I suspect the world is waiting for your guidance."

The president stood up, and the others did the same. "Thank you both for your help. I will meet with my advisors and we'll decide on the next step."

As the two professors left the room, Kevin Halloran entered through a side door. He monitored all meetings in the Oval Office at Wainwright's request

Dyer was talking. "I think we need to step back and take a deep breath and reassess the situation. We're being naïve if we accept at face value everything these two people have said."

"Kimberly's right, sir," Halloran said. "These people do *not* represent the best interests of our country. Nothing would make them happier than to see our military shed their uniforms and frolic in the streets with flowers in their hair."

"May I remind you both that our own scientists believe the satellite is from an alien planet."

Dyer said, "I'm just saying, we shouldn't be in a rush to take this public."

"Yeah," Halloran said. "We could end up looking like Tweedledee and Tweedledum."

Dyer gave him an exasperated look.

Wainwright ignored him. "Kimberly, call a meeting of the National Security Council. Kevin, then set up individual meetings after that with Baker, Sanchez, and O'Malley," he said, naming the vice president, the Speaker, and the majority leader.

Dyer looked alarmed. "Do you intend to recommend unilateral disarmament?"

"I don't know yet. Just schedule the meetings, Kevin."

After they left, Wainwright paced the floor behind his desk. He was damned if he did and damned if he didn't. If he went public and called for disarmament and the professors were wrong, he would be a laughingstock and his political career would be over. Worse, if he called for disarmament and the satellite turned out to be made in China or North Korea, he would be seen as a failed leader, the Neville Chamberlain of the twenty-first century, and his career would definitely be over.

But what if he didn't act? What if this thing did turn out to be an alien satellite and he did nothing? What then?

In all his political life, he had never been so plagued with doubts, but he could not do nothing. He would have to proceed in stages. After he met with his advisors and the leaders of Congress, he would videoconference with the G-8 leaders. Maybe then he'd go public. Maybe not. He was sure of only one thing: Once it was revealed that Earth was targeted by an alien planet, all hell was going to break loose.

#

Heather lowered her seatback as far as it would go and idly rubbed her wrists as Stephen turned onto the 267 toward Dulles airport. She could still feel the way the handcuffs had pressed into her skin whenever she moved during the ride from Santa Barbara to LA. Had it really been less than twenty-four hours ago? She looked out at the thick gray clouds and thought of the sunny skies of California. Somehow it seemed wrong to be going home, but they had done everything they could. It was up to the president now.

She glanced at Stephen, who looked deep in thought. "How far to the airport?"

"Ten minutes," he said. "Are you okay?"

"Just exhausted."

"I feel like I should apologize for getting you involved in all this. Are you sorry I did?"

She thought about it. Her brother had been the only man she had been able to talk to since her divorce, and his death four years ago had left an empty hole in her life. Then she met Stephen, and he became the brother she no longer had. She would not trade anything for that.

He glanced at her. She smiled and shook her head. "I'm not sorry. For lots of reasons."

"Like what?"

"For one thing, I like knowing what's going on behind the scenes. If you hadn't found me, I would be learning about the solar satellite through the media, like the rest of the world. Instead, I'm privy to top-level secrets, and that's quite a kick!"

He smiled. "What else?"

She paused, trying to put into a coherent statement the vague thoughts she'd had for weeks. "I've always wanted my life to mean something—in the greater scheme of things, you know? That's why I marched against all those wars; that's why I work with disturbed children. These things offer me a chance to move beyond my own boundaries and make a difference in the world, however small it might be. And now...now you and I are going to be part of history!"

"Assuming we all survive."

"Well, there is that."

"If our roles in this become public, you know we'll be fodder for the tabloids. I can see it all now—professors nabbed by little green men." He smiled as he said this.

"I know, but that's transitory. Once history sorts through it all, we'll be seen in a very special light because we will have been the first humans contacted by an alien race. And if we ever do find our way toward world peace—if Earth becomes part of the Galactic Federation—we'll become legends."

"Legends in our own time, huh?"

She gave a short laugh, acknowledging the hyperbole. "It may not happen in our own time, but it will happen eventually. That means our lives will have made a difference. I've had to pinch myself in the last few days to believe that all this is real. But it really *is* happening, isn't it?"

"Yes, but there's a long way to go. We don't know what the president is going to do. He might not do anything."

They rode in silence for a while. When she saw the exit signs to Dulles Airport, she broke the silence. "There's another reason I'm not sorry you found me. I think the memories of that night at the hearing would have surfaced eventually, and I would have been alone with them. I can't imagine how I would have come out of that with my sanity intact."

"I know what you mean. If I couldn't share this with you, I don't know how I would cope." He held out his hand. "We make a good team."

She took his hand and squeezed it. "All we can do now is wait and see what the president does."

CHAPTER 51

The media descended on Olive Street the next morning. Stephen was eating a late breakfast when the telephone rang. Penny answered it and handed him the phone with a puzzled look. "It's a reporter."

He took the phone warily. "Hello?"

"Dr. Hopkins? I'm Carrie Winters with Channel 4. We've received information that you've had personal contact with the aliens who are responsible for launching the solar object. Would you care to step outside and give us a brief statement on camera?"

"Where did you hear that?"

"I'm not at liberty to say."

"I have no comment," Stephen snapped and hung up.

"What'd she want?"

"She wanted me to 'step outside' and comment on my meeting with the aliens."

"You're kidding."

He shook his head grimly and went to the front door and looked out the window. A slender blonde in a red suit stood in front of his house, microphone in hand. She was facing a cameraman whose shoulder-mounted camera was pointed at Stephen's front door. A blue van with WRC-TV painted on its side was parked across the street.

"Goddamn it," he said.

"How did she know about the aliens?"

"Someone apparently leaked it."

"But who?"

"The only ones who know about it besides us and Heather are the president and his staff."

"Would they leak something as sensitive as this?"

On impulse, Stephen opened the door and stuck his head out. "I want you to get the hell out of my yard. Now!"

The reporter turned around. "Dr. Hopkins—"

He slammed the door and turned back to Penny. "I probably shouldn't have done that."

"Let's turn on the TV."

"Channel 4." He followed her into the den.

The blonde reporter in the red suit appeared on the television screen. Her eyes sparkled with excitement.

"We're interrupting our regular programming for breaking news. Rumors have been rampant that the satellite orbiting the sun was placed there by intelligent beings from somewhere in space. No one has been able to confirm this, but Channel 4 has just learned that a professor at Georgetown University has actually been in contact with the aliens. According to our sources, Dr. Stephen Hopkins, professor of anthropology, met with the aliens two months ago at a secret location.

I'm standing outside the Hopkins' residence in Georgetown. Dr. Hopkins did say a few words although we can't air his entire statement..."

Stephen groaned when he saw the next image. His face looked like a thundercloud, as he stuck his head out the door to yell at the reporter. They had bleeped the four-letter word but it was obvious what he had said. The camera returned to a close-up of Carrie Winters.

"That was the extent of Dr. Hopkins' statement, so we are left with many questions. Did he really meet with aliens from outer space? Did they place the object in solar orbit? If so, why? Do they mean us harm? Is the government aware of any of this? And perhaps most mysterious of all, what is Professor Hopkins' role in all this? We at Channel 4 will not rest until we have answers to these questions.

I'm Carrie Winters for WRC-TV, reporting live from Georgetown in our nation's capital."

"Christ!" Stephen said.

Penny turned the television off. "What do we do now?"

"Call Gerard and warn him not to talk to any reporters. By the time school's out, they'll be so thick out there he won't be able to drive down the street."

#

From his office on K Street, Ethan Gorr smiled as he watched the WRC-TV story about the professor and the aliens. He had considered leaking it to CNN but felt that a local station would be more likely to act quickly on an anonymous tip. He had found Carrie Winters' name on the station's website, and now there she was, delivering a tantalizing story he couldn't have scripted better. Hopkins' irate appearance at the door was priceless, and his refusal to comment only fanned the media flames. By noon, television crews would be parked in his driveway and tabloid reporters would be hiding in bushes.

Gorr clicked off the television with satisfaction. Revenge was sweet, and it was only going to get sweeter.

CHAPTER 52

Gerard nudged the van through television crews and reporters and cameramen lining both sides of Olive Street in front of his house. As he turned into his driveway, a swarm of reporters descended on the van. He pressed the garage door opener and eased the van into the garage. Several reporters followed him as far as the garage door; Carrie Winters strode into the garage, her cameraman close behind. She stood at the driver's door, microphone in hand.

Gerard lowered his window.

Carrie Winters shoved the microphone at him. "Are you Stephen Hopkins' son? Did you see the aliens too?"

"You're trespassing, ma'am. If you don't get out of my garage, I'm calling the police."

He punched 911 on his cell without taking his eyes off the reporter. She kept tossing questions at him. Only when he started to talk to the emergency dispatcher did she stop. He held the phone away from his ear. "Are you leaving or shall I give them my address?"

"Okay, okay," Winters said and walked back toward the street with her cameraman in tow.

Gerard waited until they had cleared the garage door, then pressed the button to close it. *Jeez! Now he knew why rock stars sometimes punched out photographers.*

When he told his mom and dad what had happened, Penny called the headmaster at Emerson Prep and told him Gerard would be staying home the rest of the week. "He thinks it's an excellent idea under the circumstances," she said when she hung up.

Gerard rewarded her with a big grin. He went to his room and logged on to KASA and saw Gunner and Moley chatting about the media siege at a professor's house in Georgetown.

Bet that's G-MAN's old man, Gunner had just written.

Gerard hesitated. *What if they saw a photo of the professor's son in a wheelchair?* They'd know he wasn't the twenty-year old college student or the tennis champ he'd claimed

241

to be. Of course, he could always say it was his brother, but that would just be another lie.

He logged off before they noticed his presence online. At least he didn't have to run the gauntlet of reporters twice a day. Less chance of being caught on camera. Maybe they'd all be gone by the time he went back to school.

CHAPTER 53

Stephen looked out his window and watched the media milling about on the street below. A few minutes earlier, he had stepped out in the back yard for a breath of fresh air, then stormed back inside when he heard a reporter call to him from behind the shrubs. He should be strolling across campus, enjoying this mild winter day, but now he was a virtual prisoner in his own home

He logged on to check his email and found a note from the Dean granting his request for a leave of absence until the media frenzy blew over. There was a message from his publisher commenting on Carrie Winters' broadcast, which had apparently made national news. In light of recent events, the plight of humans versus aliens was infinitely more intriguing than another book on primitive tribes. They were now thrilled he'd decided to scrap the Abigo book and suggested he hurry up and write about his contact with the aliens.

He logged off without replying. His life was turning into a circus and he didn't know what the hell to do about it. It had been two days since his meeting at the White House and he'd heard nothing, not even a hint that the government was willing to acknowledge the alien nature of the satellite. How much longer could they continue to ignore it?

Suddenly, he felt another presence in the room. He turned around to see Morok sitting in the recliner, dressed as always in a gray suit, white shirt, red tie. Did this mean good news or bad? He swiveled his chair to face him. "Hello, Mr. Chairman. It is good to see you again."

"Likewise, Dr. Hopkins," Morok said in his sonorous voice. "That is quite a crowd in front of your house."

"Someone tipped off the media that I'd met with the aliens—" He caught himself. "Sorry, Mr. Chairman, that's their word, not mine."

"And you do not want to talk to them?"

"Not until there's proof that you exist. Right now, I look like a crackpot."

"The blackouts seemed to have caused a lot of concern among your people."

"Yes. And now the world's in a tailspin about this object orbiting the sun."

Morok smiled. "Then my proposal should be quite timely."

"Your proposal?"

Morok settled back in the chair and clasped his hands in his lap. "Our scientists take great pride in their advancements in memory research over the past several hundred millennia, and the fact that two individual Namuh have emerged from an encounter with functional memories of the episode both puzzles and intrigues them. The commission has been deluged with their requests for permission to study the Namuh memory."

"Why is there so much interest in memory?"

"Memory research has contributed enormously to our study of emerging species. Our scientists are able to interact with individual members of a species and then alter the individuals' memories so that they have no recollection of the encounter. This is done of course to protect the mental health of the individual.

"Before our encounter with the Namuh, GFED scientists had rarely experienced a failure. Now they are acutely aware that two Namuh individuals have retained precise and detailed memories of the GFED hearing. It is alarming to them that your memories survived their alterations."

"Because it means their techniques failed?"

"Exactly." Morok paused for a moment, as if gathering his thoughts. "I told you about our ability to solve crimes quickly and efficiently by tapping into a suspect's own memories?"

"Yes. You said it has reduced your crime rate to almost zero."

"It has accomplished something else equally important. It has created a pattern of honor among our citizens, and that affects every layer of our society."

That made no sense to Stephen. "How would reading a person's memories create honor?"

"Honor is an indirect benefit. You see, we have had this technology for several hundreds of thousands of years, and our citizens know we can discern the truth in a matter of minutes. So, if they commit a crime, it is virtually certain it will be revealed by their own memories. As a result, *not lying* has become ingrained in their consciousness. Our citizens rarely lie about anything."

"How is that connected to humans' memory capability?"

"Finding a species with a redundant memory pattern brings our whole scientific process into question. Since we failed to eradicate all pathways to your and Dr. Eastlake's memories of the GFED hearing, we want to learn from our failure. To bridge this gap in our technology, we want to study the Namuh brain and memory storage patterns."

Stephen became alarmed. He pictured humans being dissected by alien scientists in a futuristic laboratory somewhere in space. It smacked of the too-common UFO abduction story. "How do you intend to do that?" he asked.

"Shortly after we talked in December, I presented a proposal to our Supreme Council of Arbiters for a formal study of the Namuh. It is a way to satisfy our scientists who want to study your memory structure and to satisfy those of us who believe in the potential of the Namuh to mature into responsible members of the galaxy. There was opposition at first. One arbiter pointed out, correctly, that nothing has changed about the Namuh's endemic violence. But in the end the council accepted my proposal."

Stephen's spirits began to lift as he realized the implications of Morok's words. "So why did you activate the solar probe? Why did you cause the blackouts?"

"The council thought it prudent to proceed with quarantine. They refuse to allow the Namuh to continue to pollute the galaxy with broadcasts of violence and possibly DNA patterns. Nor were they willing to gamble on your space technology remaining at its current level. Once your scientists discover how to navigate space, it will be too late to stop you. The satellite is there to control these things—and to remind your fellow Namuh of the more drastic alternative should we need it."

"The sword of Damocles."

Morok's eyes moved rapidly, searching his memory banks for the reference. "Ah! 'An ever-present peril hanging over one's head.' Yes, you could say that. But I doubt you would have gained the attention of your president if the satellite had not been in orbit."

"That's true." Without the blackouts and the solar satellite, no one would believe there was an extraterrestrial force at work, and Wainwright would remain skeptical and complacent and unwilling to take any action at all. "Tell me about your proposal."

The contours of Morok's face glowed as he spoke. "I propose to recruit Namuh volunteers to live on various GFED planets for the next twenty years. Our scientists wish to put these volunteers through psychological, intelligence and physical tests with close monitoring. In return, the volunteers would be taught about the scientific, economic, and political advancements of our civilizations. If the Namuh on Earth live up to their part of the agreement, the volunteers will return home in twenty years to educate your race and to put GFED-type policies and practices into place."

Stephen was stunned. *Humans could gain thousands of years of knowledge in the span of one generation.* "What is our part of the agreement?" he asked.

"The Namuh must fulfill two important conditions. First, all nations on Earth must agree to complete and total disarmament and must remain disarmed and peaceful during the twenty years the volunteers are gone."

"That is not going to be easy."

"It will be easier than the second condition. Namuh citizens must also renounce violent behavior on a personal level. Violence is not just a problem of your institutions. They simply reflect the mindset of the citizens, and your mindset is toward violence. It permeates the Namuh culture on a global scale and has since the beginning of your civilization. Until violence is eradicated at the personal level, it will remain in your institutions."

"I agree, but how do we even start such a massive transformation?"

"It can start with your religious, academic, entertainment, and political leaders. They can begin the process at the top by changing laws, setting examples, using their national forums to cajole and inspire. But leaders cannot impose peaceful behavior and nonviolence on the people. The change in attitude has to come from the people themselves.

"This movement will not succeed until the majority of individual Namuh have assimilated an abhorrence of violence into their very beings. Then your institutions will reflect the non-violent mindset of its citizens."

Stephen tried to imagine such a world. "What you're describing is a sort of 'trickle-down/trickle-up' eradication of violence."

"Exactly." Morok gave him a benevolent smile, as if a student had just grasped an exceedingly difficult concept.

Stephen felt almost paralyzed by the enormity of what lay ahead but the opportunity was incredible. "It won't happen overnight, Mr. Chairman. I find it difficult to believe it will happen in a mere twenty years."

"We understand that. We would be looking for signs of establishing minimum living standards for Namuh worldwide, which we believe would go a long way toward reducing violence. We would also look for signs that you are trying to implement a reliable system of dispute resolution. A sufficient change of attitude in these two areas would convince us that you are indeed on a path toward a nonviolent culture."

"And if we make progress, you'll send our volunteers back to Earth?"

"They will return to teach you what they've learned about the Federation's science and technology. If your progress toward nonviolence is sufficient, it is possible Earth might be invited to join the Galactic Federation."

"And if we fail?"

"I strongly suggest you not consider the possibility of failure."

Stephen knew what could happen if they failed. Extermination of the human race. "What if there are rogue nations who won't disarm?" he asked.

"We look at the Namuh civilization as one organic entity. It is up to your leaders to bring any rogue nations into alignment, which of course needs to happen without violence."

"What kind of volunteers are you looking for?"

"We want minds that are open and eager to learn and not set in the ways of the Earth. That means, for the most part, men and women below the age of twenty. We also wish to watch the development of small children, which means we will accept their parents as well."

Morok paused. "There will also be a few slots open for specialized professions," he said. "Maybe an anthropologist and a child psychologist?"

It took Stephen a moment to realize Morok was inviting him and Heather to accompany the group. It was too much to absorb at one sitting. He uttered the first thought that came into his head. "I couldn't leave my family."

"Bring them with you."

He thought of Penny's likely reaction to the invitation. "I—Chairman Morok, I am honored, but—I just don't know."

Morok gave a sort of shrug. "You don't have to decide at this time. However, I need your help in presenting my plan to your people."

"Of course." He thought of the flash of blues and greens he had seen at the end of his meeting with the chairman in December, the black beak, the round, golden eyes. He had been sure he had seen a glimpse of the authentic Morok. Shouldn't the volunteers see at least that...or more?

"Mr. Chairman, at the GFED hearing, your counselor talked about how negatively the Namuh would react if they should come face-to-face with a being from one of your planets. That implies that you look very different in reality than you do right now."

"That is true."

"Whenever I study a primitive culture, I learn everything I can about their tribal customs before I visit the tribe so that I'm not taken by surprise by any unorthodox ritual. I propose that you reveal your true appearance to the volunteers before they leave for your planet."

The chairman made what sounded like a laugh, "Are you calling us a primitive culture?"

"No, but it is a similar situation in the reverse."

Morok smiled. "I was attempting a teasing remark as you would call it. But you are right. We are sufficiently different from the Namuh that an orientation would be practical, although I think you would find Yxrians—my species—spectacularly beautiful in our differences. But beauty is in the eye of the beholder, is it not?"

"That it is."

Morok continued. "Yxrians are just one of the thousands of species represented by GFED. Many are quite different from us *and* from the Namuh. Your volunteers will not meet them all, but before they leave planet Earth, I will allow them to see me as I appear in my world."

He stood. "I must leave now. You will find my proposal in your email."

Stephen stood also. "How can you send emails?"

Morok looked amused. "Surely you are not still asking *how*."

Stephen remembered a quote from some writer: *Sufficiently advanced technology is indistinguishable from magic*. When he showed Ganbigo his digital camera years ago, the little shaman couldn't fathom how such a thing could work. That gap between their two cultures was a few thousand years. The gap between Yxrians and twenty-first century humans spanned a billion years.

"I will be in touch," Morok said.

The contours of his face brightened, and Stephen found himself looking into the round green-gold eyes above a beak-like ebony nose, just as he had at the end of their meeting in December. And then, just as before, there was a feathery swirl of blues and greens before he vanished.

249

CHAPTER 54

Morok's strange image lingered in Stephen's mind, the way a shape will linger on the retina when the eye is exposed to a bright light. He thought about Morok's invitation to join the volunteers and wondered if it was really possible, he might go. *Did he actually want to go?* Part of him did, another part didn't. He couldn't figure out which part was the truer voice.

He checked his email. The proposal was there, looking like an ordinary email, except it was from 'Chairman Morok, Galactic Federation' and it bore no return email address. He couldn't imagine casually exchanging emails with an extraterrestrial. GFED's email technology would probably look like magic to him. He printed a copy of the proposal and began to read.

The first section repeated what Morok had just told him about the interest of GFED scientists in studying the memory storage function of the Namuh brain. The section concluded with the statement:

> The Federation proposes that a group of Namuh volunteers spend twenty years on GFED planets to learn about GFED's economic, social, political, and technological innovations that have led to the development of the peaceful Federation. After twenty years, the volunteers will return to Earth to teach the Namuh what they have learned.

The next section described the changes in the Namuh's culture of violence that must take place during that twenty-year period in order for the volunteers to return to Earth with GFED's advanced technologies. Last came the part describing how the Namuh volunteers would be selected. Stephen read it carefully, jotting down salient points:

- A maximum of twelve hundred Namuh volunteers would be selected.
- Six hundred slots would be reserved for candidates aged sixteen to twenty-two; up to 100 slots would be filled by children between the ages of one month and fifteen years, with two parents or guardians allowed to accompany each child. The remaining 300 or so slots

would be reserved for certain professions in which the GFED was particularly interested.

- Volunteers would be selected to represent the diversity of the Namuh culture.
- The deadline for applications was January 25, two weeks from the current date.
- Each finalist would be interviewed by the Namuh leader and then by Chairman Morok. If a finalist were rejected by the Chairman, the runner-up would take his or her place, assuming they qualified as well.
- The group would depart Earth on March 12, two months from the current date. During the sojourn, annual holographic visits would be allowed with families on Earth.
- The volunteers would return to Earth in twenty years *if* the Namuh met the conditions specified in this proposal.

Stephen read the proposal again, looking for some mention of what would happen if Earth didn't meet the conditions outlined in the proposal. He found nothing. No mention of the quarantine, not a word about extermination should Earth fail to make sufficient progress on the path to peace.

Why hadn't Morok spelled out the threat? Perhaps he thought the solar flares had sufficiently demonstrated GFED's power. He was, after all, looking for volunteers for a twenty-year sojourn to a planet in the galaxy a hundred light years away. Maybe he feared it might dampen enthusiasm for the sojourn if he came across as a heavy-handed villain.

One item had especially intrigued him: A Namuh would be appointed to lead the sojourn. *Would it be him?* And would that mean he would have to go?

He could think about that later. He had to get the proposal in front of President Wainwright. He called the White House and got Kevin Halloran.

"That's quite a little media storm you've created, Dr. Hopkins. How does it feel to have reporters camped on your doorstep."

"I didn't create it."

"Who else would leak the fact that you've had personal contact with the aliens?"

"I don't know, Mr. Halloran. Perhaps someone on your staff?"

"We do not have leaks in this White House."

"Fine. Chairman Morok has asked me to deliver a proposal to the president."

"He's not available until next week."

"This won't wait until next week. If one of those television reporters outside my door happens to get wind of this before the president sees it...well, I don't think he would be too happy."

Stephen immediately regretted the veiled threat, but Halloran's arrogance rubbed him the wrong way.

The Chief of Staff was silent for a moment. "You can't come to the White House and that's final. If the press corps learns that the man who met with the aliens is meeting with the president, all hell will break loose."

"A phone call then. The earlier the better."

"Seven o'clock in the morning," Halloran snapped. "That early enough for you?" He hung up before Stephen could reply.

#

At dinner, Stephen told Gerard and Penny about Morok's proposal. He wanted them to hear it from him before it became public.

Penny looked skeptical. "Who in God's name would volunteer to go to another planet for twenty years? It's ridiculous."

"I imagine young people will be lining up to go," Stephen said.

Gerard peppered his dad with questions, then grew uncharacteristically quiet. He refused dessert and asked to be excused early.

That worried Stephen. He could tell his son was intrigued with Morok's proposal. *What if he wanted to apply?* Would GFED take someone with special needs like Gerard's?

252

He hoped fervently that they wouldn't and immediately felt ashamed at the thought.

He glanced at Penny's worried face. Could he ever talk her into going? He wasn't sure, but if Gerard applied for the sojourn, he would have to consider it. He couldn't face losing his son for twenty years, and he knew Penny would never get over it.

#

After dinner, Stephen called Heather from his study. She answered on the first ring.

"I was just going to call you," she said. "Did you know you made the network news this evening?"

"That's not surprising. There must be thirty reporters outside my door."

"CNN keeps showing that shot of you glowering at that reporter. Have you seen it?"

"I try not to watch. What are they saying?"

"Just a lot of inane speculation about 'the professor and the aliens.' How'd they get your name?"

"I wish I knew."

"You won't give them mine; I hope."

"Of course not. Listen, I called to tell you about something else. Morok appeared in my study this afternoon." He told her about Morok's proposal, emailing it to her as he spoke.

"That's incredible! Have you told the president?"

"I have a phone call with him at seven in the morning. Halloran won't let me in the White House with this media craze going on."

"What do you think he'll say?"

"Who knows."

"He can't continue to ignore this, Stephen."

He toyed with the idea of telling her about the glimpse of Morok he'd seen at the end of the meeting, then decided not to. There really wasn't enough to go on. "Morok invited both of us to go on the sojourn."

"He invited us personally?"

"He said there would be a few slots open for specialized professions, then rather pointedly mentioned that one slot would be reserved for a cultural anthropologist—another for a child psychologist."

"My God!"

The line went quiet for a moment. "Are you there?" he asked.

"Will you go?"

"I don't know."

"I will."

He laughed. "You can make a split-second decision on something like that?"

"How can you not? Talk about something that will make your life meaningful."

He felt somewhat put down. "I have Penny and Gerard to think about."

"I'm sorry. That was a thoughtless comment."

"It's okay. If I were unencumbered, I would jump at the chance."

Even as he said the words, he wondered if he really would? He had traveled to the most exotic jungles on Earth, immersed himself into a primitive, cannibalistic culture without a thought for his own safety. So, he wasn't without courage or curiosity or a sense of adventure. *But a journey to the stars?* The very thought gave him vertigo.

CHAPTER 55

At six o'clock the next morning, Stephen received a call from Kevin Halloran. "Email me the proposal so the president can read it before your call."

"You'll have it in twenty seconds," Stephen said, and wrote down Halloran's email address.

At seven o'clock, Halloran called back. "I'm putting you on a speaker phone with the president and Kimberly Dyer."

Stephen heard a click, then Wainwright's voice.

"I don't even know how to begin to respond to this proposal," he said. "First, you say the aliens are going to exterminate us, then they're putting us under quarantine, now they want us to sacrifice hundreds of our children."

"With all due respect, Mr. President, GFED is offering us a chance to take a gigantic leap into the next millennium in just twenty years. These children will learn science and medicine and technology that are millions of years more advanced than ours, and in twenty years they'll bring that knowledge back to Earth. How can we not accept that?"

"Assuming, of course, there are people who want to go."

Kimberly Dyer spoke. "It sounds to me like they want to put the volunteers under a microscope and study them like laboratory rats. If they like what they see, how do we know they won't keep them and exterminate the rest of us?"

"I guess we don't know that for sure, but Chairman Morok believes the human race is worth saving. He wants to help us make the move to the Galactic level. That's the only reason we have this proposal."

"How do we know GFED is for real, Dr. Hopkins?" Dyer said. "And if it is, how do we know this Morok character is authorized to make such a proposal? I don't mean to malign your integrity, but how do we know you're not trying to perpetrate an elaborate hoax on the world?"

"I didn't make up the solar satellite, did I?"

There was silence on the other end.

"Mr. President, do you have any doubt I'm telling the truth?"

"Put yourself in my shoes, Stephen. The only real evidence we have of contact by an alien planet is the appearance of that object orbiting the sun, which may or may not have caused the power outages. Granted, we have eyewitness reports from you and Dr. Eastlake, but I could fill the White House with people who claim to have had encounters with extraterrestrials."

Stephen could not think of a response to that.

Wainwright continued. "The G-8 leaders have seen the same scientific reports I have about the satellite, but there's no consensus that it's from an alien planet. Most of them think I'm delusional because I had the audacity to suggest we consider unilateral disarmament. And now, you want me to tell them we're going to send hundreds of children to some planet in outer space." He sighed. 'It does strain credulity."

"If it's direct proof you need, sir, you may well get it— in the form of a gamma ray bombardment."

Stephen felt a flush of embarrassment. He had just chastised the President of the United States.

"Stephen, I am the leader of the most powerful nation on this planet. Surely your Chairman Morok will grant me the courtesy of a face-to-face meeting."

"I agree that he should, sir, but I don't know how to contact him. He just…appears."

"How does he know where to find you? Does he have your phone tapped? Is he monitoring you by satellite?"

"I don't know. I've told you everything I know about him and about GFED. If they do monitor me, perhaps they are aware of your desire to meet with him. Maybe he'll pop into the Oval Office for a visit."

He immediately regretted his flippancy, but he had to make the president understand. "With all due respect, sir, I don't believe this is a negotiation between equals. I don't think the two of you are going to sit down and negotiate the future of the world. They have made an offer which we can accept or reject. It seems to me we should accept it."

There was another silence. Then the president spoke, "Let me be crystal clear, Stephen. I will not send our youth to another planet for twenty years unless I know with whom and with what I'm dealing. I cannot continue to act through an

256

intermediary. Until I can meet directly with this Chairman Morok, this matter is closed."

There was a click, then silence.

Stephen placed the phone back on its holder. There was nothing else he could do. He could only hope that Morok *was* monitoring the situation and would take whatever action was needed to get the president's attention.

CHAPTER 56

By Friday night, most of the media had gone. Only the Channel 4 group remained, camped in a van in front of the Hopkins' house. Carrie Winters had knocked on the door several times, calling to Stephen to please give her a statement. He had refused to open the door. Tonight, sitting at his computer, he found it difficult to concentrate with the muted sounds of rock music coming from the media van. No doubt it would elicit complaints from his neighbors. He turned off the computer and stretched out on the sofa with a book. He couldn't concentrate on that either. He turned off the reading light and watched the play of moonlight on the trees outside the window. He must have dozed off because a voice awoke him with a start.

"Prepare yourself."

Stephen sat up abruptly. Morok had appeared just two days ago. Why was he returning so soon? As he watched, an image began to coalesce in the bright-moonlit room.

The gold-green eyes appeared first, the black beak-like nose, the feathery blue-green swirl around the face. Then came the rest.

Stephen caught his breath and stared at the creature illuminated by moonlight. He stood more than eight feet tall with a crest of blue-green plumes that brushed the ceiling. A feathery beard of blue-green iridescence covered his cheeks and neck and merged into a cloak or cape of the same texture and color, and beneath that, there appeared to be matching trousers or leggings of some sort. Were these clothes or was Morok some kind of avian being, a gigantic blue-green humanoid eagle?

"The latter," Morok said in the familiar lilting voice.

Stephen stood up. He took a deep tremulous breath. "I am honored to meet you, Chairman Morok."

Morok stepped forward, offered his hand.

Surprised, Stephen clasped it. He looked down. In the moonlight, Morok's hand appeared golden and embossed, as if he were wearing textured leather gloves.

Morok stepped back, folded his hands beneath his cloak. "Your president wants a meeting with me, so I must reveal myself to him. I wanted you to see me first."

"I am greatly honored."

"Let us sit, shall we?"

Morok lifted his iridescent cloak and lowered himself onto the recliner which all but disappeared under his huge frame. His blue-green plumes stretched toward the ceiling; his feathery cloak pooled on the floor on either side of the chair.

Stephen noticed that his feet appeared to be clad in ribbed golden boots, much like his hands. He willed his gaze back to Morok's face, which glowed blue-green in the moonlight. "You know about the president's demand to meet with you. Were you somehow in the room?"

Morok trilled a laugh. "It is difficult to describe our monitoring technology. In a sense, we isolate and intercept the thought waves of subjects we wish to monitor."

"You read our minds?"

"Nothing as simplistic as that, I assure you, but I cannot reveal our technology. When the time is right, perhaps, but not now."

Stephen could not take his eyes off the exotic creature opposite him. He wished he could see him in daylight, touch his feathery blue-green cloak. "You said you are going to reveal your real self to the president."

"I fear I must, although it is unprecedented for someone of my standing to take such a step. Some of my colleagues are calling it appeasement. They say we should simply take the Namuh subjects we wish to study, the way we took you and Dr. Eastlake."

Stephen was aghast. "You cannot do that!"

"Technically, we could. We will not, of course. Our ethics would not allow it, my colleagues notwithstanding." He leaned toward Stephen. "Our scientists are eager to study your memory function, but our interest in the Namuh is much greater than a mere research project. I have convinced the arbiters that the Namuh could make a contribution to the galaxy once your species matures. Our primary goal is to help you mature as a civilization. That is the purpose of my proposal. That is why I must take the extraordinary step of meeting with your leaders."

Morok stood. The moonlight reflected on the iridescent blues and greens of his cloak. "I have no more time tonight."

Stephen felt the air in the room move, as if a small breeze had somehow entered through the closed window, and he watched in awe as Morok lifted his arms and spread his great blue-green wings from wall to wall. He stood immobile for a moment and then vanished.

CHAPTER 57

Stephen found Penny in bed reading. "I'm glad you're still up," he said. "I need to talk to you."

She gave him a quizzical look and laid the book on the nightstand. "You look…strange."

He sat down on the side of the bed. "I just saw Morok."

"Again?"

"No, I saw the *real* Morok—the extraterrestrial, the alien being."

Penny's eyes widened. "Here? In our house?"

He nodded. 'He's going to meet with the president and he wanted me to be the first to see him as he really is."

"What does he look like?"

"He's…" Stephen hesitated. "He's magnificent. He's very tall, close to nine feet with his plumes."

"His plumes?"

"He's avian."

Penny's hand went to her throat. "Are you saying he's bird?"

"Bird-like." Stephen told her about the green-gold eyes, the black beak, the blue-green iridescent feathers, the golden ribbed hands, and feet. "Just before he left, he spread his wings—"

"Wings!"

"Yes. They spanned the length of my study."

"My God!"

They were silent for a moment, Stephen remembering the creature he'd seen, Penny imagining it.

"It's not such a stretch to think that sentient beings could evolve from bird-like creatures," Stephen said. "We evolved from simians."

"Yes, but the size of the brain had something to do with it, didn't it? And opposing thumbs?"

"Morok's hands seemed to be shaped like ours, so somewhere along the evolutionary path on Yxria, at least one species of birds developed opposing thumbs. As for brain size, you told me yourself that some birds have large brains for their body weight."

"Ravens and blue jays and crows."

"Right. And didn't you tell me about a crow that used a sort of tool?"

"There are stories of wild crows using twigs to get at food, and I read about one crow in captivity that bent a wire to get food out of a pipe."

"He actually made a tool, then."

"Yes. And I didn't tell you about the bird that played a jazz duet with a musician!" Penny's eyes were shining.

"Really?"

"I read an article written by the musician in my birding magazine. He said that many of the qualities that define human music are in the songs of birds: rhythm, structure, pattern, repetition, and variation, and I know that's true because of Joseph. He has about three different tunes that he chirps and they have a definite structure and pattern and rhythm. He'll repeat one over and over for a while, then switch to another."

"What about the bird that accompanied the musician?"

"You can listen to it, it's on the musician's website. The musician is playing a clarinet and the bird—a white-crested laughing thrush—sings along as if he knows when to come in and when to solo. And the guy also recorded the song of a forest bird called a veery. What's really amazing is when you play the recording at a slow speed, it sounds just like an intricate jazz riff."

Stephen nodded slowly. "And some birds have the capacity for speech."

Penny smiled. "Noah talks to me all the time. Sometimes I think he knows what he's saying."

"So, over billions of years, some bird species on Morok's planet evolved the mental and physical attributes needed to fashion tools, create art, build cities."

"I wonder what cities look like where the inhabitants fly instead of walking! He can fly, can't he?" Penny's eyes brightened.

"I'm sure he can. Otherwise, the wings would have atrophied. Morok's were alarmingly large."

They fell silent.

After a while, Penny reached for Stephen's hand. "Hold me," she whispered.

He took her in his arms. Tonight, changed everything. For the first time in a long time, the love lost between the two of them was finally rekindled. And the entire world was about to change in ways that had yet to be imagined.

CHAPTER 58

The timing was a challenge. The world's eight major industrial democracies spanned the globe, from the US to Europe to Russia to Japan, and it was the leaders of these countries—the Group of 8, or G-8, as they were called—whom Morok had chosen to address personally. Since it was virtually impossible to find a point in time when all of the leaders were alone, he had to resort to telepathy to contrive temporary absences of two spouses and two associates.

The historic meetings took place concurrently at 15:57 GMT on January 15, a day that would be indelibly etched on the minds of the seven men and one woman who were the G-8 leaders on that day.

In Washington, D.C., at 10:57 on Saturday morning, President William Wainwright sipped a cup of coffee as he finished a late breakfast alone in the private dining room on the third floor of the White House, the First Lady having been called away unexpectedly to a meeting with her staff. Five hundred miles to the north in her Ottawa office, Prime Minister Anne Bouchard reviewed an itinerary for her upcoming trip to Australia.

On the other side of the Atlantic, where it was 3:57 in the afternoon at No. 10 Downing Street, Prime Minister Charles Bartlett reached for a crumpet as he prepared to enjoy his afternoon tea. At the Presidential Palace in Paris where it was an hour later, President André Cèline concentrated on placing the orange No. 5 ball in the far-right corner pocket of the billiard table. His associate had just received an urgent phone call from his wife asking him to hurry home, so Cèline was finishing the game by himself.

In Berlin, Chancellor Hans Brandt lay on the sofa in his den watching a televised soccer game of the Germans versus the Australians. His brother had just excused himself for an urgent call from Mother Nature. In Italy, Prime Minister Luigi Agnello was in his red Maserati singing an aria from Puccini's *Tosca* at the top of his lungs as he roared northward on the Autostrada del Sole on his way to Florence to see his long-time mistress.

In Moscow, where it was 6:57 in the evening, President Leo Serganev sipped an icy vodka while he waited for his wife, who was uncharacteristically late, to join him for a reception for the Chinese Minister of Foreign Affairs. It was just almost one a.m. in Tokyo where President Takeshi Eto, curled in a fetal position in his private bedroom, was sawing logs.

At that moment, 15:57 GMT, a tall, kindly looking gray-haired man in a grey suit, white shirt, and red tie appeared in eight different places around the globe...

...In Washington, William Wainwright spilled his coffee when the man appeared beside the breakfast table. "What the hell!" He pushed his chair back and stood up. *How had this man got past the Secret Service?*

"You said you wanted a face-to-face meeting with me, Mr. President," Morok said. "Here I am."

Wainwright felt his knees go weak. He reached for the chair.

...In Ottawa, Anne Bouchard looked up from her desk. "I'm not taking any meetings until after lunch. Please see my secretary."

...Charles Bartlett held the crumpet in mid-air and raised his eyebrows at the man who had suddenly appeared out of nowhere. "Who the bloody hell are you?"

...André Cèline looked wildly around the room, then held his cue stick at the ready and waited for the gray-haired apparition to speak.

...Hans Brandt glanced at the man sitting in the chair across the room and growled, "The fucking Aussies are whipping our ass." He did a double-take. "You're not Helmet," he said, frowning.

...Luigi Agnello swerved and almost clipped a passing car, then wet his pants. "Perhaps you should pull into that roadside park," said his gray-haired passenger.

...Leo Serganev got to his feet when the gray-haired man appeared in the drawing room. "Would you care for a drink?"

...Takeshi Eto opened one eye and saw a gray-haired man sitting at the foot of his bed, then threw an arm across his forehead and tried to go back to sleep. He was getting quite tired of these relentless nightmares.

"I am Chairman Morok from the Galactic Federation," Morok said to each of the G-8 leaders in his low, lilting voice. "I have come so that you might know I am for real."

One by one, each acknowledged Morok's presence... Wainwright grasped the arms of the chair with both hands and forced himself not to call the Secret Service agent stationed outside his door... Anne Bouchard laid her pen on the desk and regarded the man warily... Charles Bartlett laid the crumpet on his plate and stared... Andre Cèline closed his mouth and slowly lowered the cue stick... Hans Brandt sat up and focused his attention on the man across the room... Luigi Agnello pulled the Maserati into the roadside park and turned off the engine. He pushed back against the driver's window, grasped the steering wheel with one trembling hand, the seatback with the other to steady his trembling hands, and stared at his passenger... Leo Serganev said, "Would you care to sit while we talk about this?"... Takeshi Eto sat up and rubbed his eyes and peered at the man at the foot of his bed. He remembered an earlier conversation with the American president, something about a message from an alien planet. Suddenly, he came fully and completely awake.

Morok began to speak. He explained who he was and where he came from. He acknowledged that the solar satellite was placed in orbit by the Galactic Federation and that its purpose at this time was quarantine. He described the extent to which GFED civilizations surpassed the youthful civilization of the Namuh and explained why they feared contamination from the human race. He said the majority of GFED representatives had voted for the extermination, but he, Morok, believed that humans were worth saving. That was why he was making his proposal.

He explained the terms of the proposal. He stressed that the volunteers would be returned to Earth in twenty years, but only if the human race had made great strides toward the rejection of its culture of violence. He repeated that GFED could not, *would not*, accept into the Federation a civilization that tolerated, even worshiped, violence, as the Namuh did.

Each of the G-8 leaders attempted to negotiate. That was how their worlds worked.

President Wainwright said, "Chairman Morok, the United States will not be dictated to. Why don't you come to my office on Monday and we can begin discussions?" The Canadian Prime Minister insisted that Morok negotiate with the Prime Minister of Great Britain; Charles Bartlett asked if he might arrange a meeting with the King. The European leaders passed the buck among themselves, each vowing silently to support the idea of electing a president of the European Union to whom they could hand over decisions such as this. Leo Serganev offered to form an alliance with GFED and bring the others in line with their joint demands. Takeshi Eto did the same.

"I am not here to negotiate," Morok told them. "I have come to deliver my proposal in person so that you will know it is authentic and will present it in good faith to your people."

"How do I know you're really from another planet?" the American president said. "You could be a practical joker or even a terrorist disguised as a mild-mannered old man."

Wainwright's question was echoed in one form or another by the other leaders who were hearing Morok's speech at the same moment.

Morok stood. "Rise," he commanded.

Wainwright stood up. So did Bouchard, Bartlett, Cèline, Brandt, Serganev, and Eto. Luigi Agnello opened the door of the Maserati and climbed out and faced Morok in the brightly lit roadside park.

The transformation of the mild-mannered gray-haired man into Morok, the Yxrian extraterrestrial, took less than ten seconds. First the eyes changed into glittering golden-green orbs above a black beak of a nose, and as the leaders watched in stunned silence, the blue-green feathers materialized and the avian Morok stood before them, towering above the tallest of them, his crested plumes reaching skyward.

The G-8 leaders were shocked into silence.

Morok spoke from his great height: "If this doesn't convince you I'm not one of you, look for another sign very soon."

As the most powerful leaders on Earth watched in frozen silence, he spread his great wings and vanished.

Wainwright stumbled to the door and jerked it open. The agent looked up.

"Did anyone enter this room just now?"

"No, sir."

"Did anyone leave?"

"The First Lady left about an hour ago."

"No one else?"

"No one else, sir."

"You're absolutely sure?"

"Yes, Mr. President. Is anything wrong, sir?"

"No."

He closed the door and picked up the telephone and called his Chief of Staff. "Get the G-8 on a videoconference."

"On Saturday?"

"Now! I'm on my way down."

"But it's after midnight in Tokyo."

"Get them now!"

He slammed down the phone and headed for the elevator, two secret service agents in his wake. When he arrived in the Oval Office, Halloran looked grim.

"The power's out, sir," he said "Apparently the whole city is in another blackout."

Wainwright thought of Morok's parting words: *Look for another sign very soon.* He was still trembling from the sight of the avian creature towering above him. He didn't need another sign.

CHAPTER 59

This time, the blackout was worldwide and lasted twenty-four hours, long enough to create chaos in towns and cities around the globe and convince the most skeptical that something otherworldly was indeed at work. It was also long enough to produce perfect accord among the G-8 leaders who knew exactly what had caused the blackout and why.

After power was restored on Sunday morning, President Wainwright met with the G-8 leaders in a videoconference. The first few minutes were chaotic with everyone talking at the same time about the exotic creature they had seen. When they finally realized that Morok had appeared simultaneously in eight different locations around the globe, speaking to each of them in their own language, they fell silent.

President Wainwright said, "We're dealing with an unprecedented power."

"No shit," said Leo Serganev.

"Chairman Morok is not of this world," Anne Bouchard said.

"I don't believe in extraterrestrials," Hans Brandt said.

"You probably think the moon landing was a Hollywood stunt," Luigi Agnello said.

"Who's to say this visitation wasn't?" retorted Brandt.

Charles Bartlett said, "Gentlemen, please! Let's discuss the Galactic Sojourn."

"Galactic Sojourn," mused Andre Cèline. "It has a certain ring to it."

They reviewed the terms of proposal.

"Finding volunteers will be easy as long as we don't tell them they'll never return to earth," Takeshi Eto said.

"But they will return in twenty years," said Bouchard.

"*If* we can learn to live together peacefully," Agnello said.

Eto snorted. "Do you honestly believe we're all going to disarm and leave our countries defenseless?"

"We have no choice," Bartlett said.

The leaders fell silent. In the end, ignoring the vast differences in time zones, they agreed to address their nations that evening in simultaneous broadcasts.

"We will be delivering a message that will change the world forever," President Wainwright said. "The shock will be lessened if we present a united front."

That afternoon, broadcast and internet media around the world carried announcements of the upcoming simultaneous broadcasts by the G-8 leaders. At 12:00 GMT, families around the globe gathered anxiously in front of their televisions; commuters watched on their cell phones; people in bars fell silent and gazed at TV screens mounted high above the bar; drivers on freeways and city streets turned up the volume on their radios. On Monday, January 17, the world's leaders began their synchronous broadcasts.

#

President Wainwright paused for a moment in the doorway that led into the House chamber of the Capitol and listened to the loud rumblings of the crowd. He had asked for an emergency joint session of Congress instead of broadcasting the speech from the Oval Office, feeling that would convey a stronger symbol of strength and leadership than speaking from behind his desk. Calling for an emergency session at seven a.m. had set the rumor mills buzzing, but he'd had no choice. The G-8 leaders' message had to be broadcast concurrently, or the uproar from an early leak would obfuscate the message. The sergeant at arms announced his arrival, and he started down the aisle toward the front of the chamber, greeting members of Congress on both sides of the aisle, ignoring the puzzled looks on their faces.

He stepped onto the podium and reached up to shake hands with Speaker of the House Duke Sanchez, and Vice President Nelson Baker, but did not hand them a copy of his speech, as was traditional, and he had a fleeting moment of pleasure at the perplexed looks on their faces. He didn't particularly care for either man, possibly because Baker was one heartbeat away from the Presidency, Sanchez, two, and the heart that had to stop beating for either to succeed him was his own.

The Speaker introduced him again to another standing ovation, and he smiled and nodded as he waited for the applause to subside. Looking out over the House chamber, he spotted friends and a few enemies. The justices of the Supreme Court sat in the front row; behind them were General Harrison Gethers, General Abner Moore, and the other joint chiefs. Kimberly Dyer was there, along with Stuart Weiss and other cabinet members. A few rows back, the senator from New York who had been his vociferous opponent in the recent presidential race was clapping perfunctorily.

The president held up his hands, motioning for quiet. When it came, he looked out over the audience and tried to project a confidence he didn't really feel. He had declined to use the teleprompters and now, with his stomach fluttering like a trapped butterfly, he hoped he could get through the speech without stumbling.

He gave the traditional greetings and then launched into a detailed description of the solar satellite, its tight orbit, its emissions, and its orbital anomalies, all of which the crowd was aware. Then he told them the thing that some suspected but no one had really believed.

> "The conclusion of the world's top scientists is that the satellite was launched by intelligent beings from outside our solar system. Those beings used the satellite to generate the solar flare that caused yesterday's worldwide power outage, as well as the back-to-back blackouts earlier this month."

Wainwright paused as the murmur that swept through the audience grew to a rumble. *You ain't heard nothing yet,* he thought, as he waited for the Speaker to intercede. When Sanchez gave the gavel three loud raps, the audience grew quiet and the president continued.

> "I urge you not to jump to any conclusions, but to listen carefully to what I have to say. These beings appear to be a peaceful and peace-loving race, and one of them has personally contacted me and the heads of states of

Britain, France, Germany, Italy, Canada, Russia, and Japan. As I speak to you tonight, those leaders are addressing their nations about our contact with this extraterrestrial being.

"We met with Chairman Morok who is from a planet called Yxria which is about one hundred light years from Earth in our Milky Way Galaxy. Yxria is part of a Galactic Federation. According to the chairman, the Federation—which they call GFED—is made up of more than 90,000 planets with civilizations that are hundreds of millions of years old, and in a few cases, billions of years old. There are almost twenty thousand intelligent species on these planets, and more than 180 *trillion* intelligent beings.

"To put this into perspective, the human race numbers about eight billion and has existed as a species for about two hundred thousand years. As a civilization, we've been around for less than ten thousand years. It should be obvious, then, that GFED civilizations are many millions of years more developed than ours. The satellite orbiting our sun is a small testament to their advanced technology.

"The good news is that these civilizations are peaceful and nonviolent. They have managed in their millions of years of existence to completely eradicate war and all forms of violence. So, we have nothing to fear from them if we are willing to learn from them.

"In that regard, Chairman Morok has presented the G-8 leaders with a proposal for a Galactic Sojourn, which may be the most extraordinary and potentially beneficial expedition in Earth's history."

He paused again to let the murmur of the crowd rise and subside. The Speaker rapped his gavel, and Wainwright continued.

"GFED will offer a limited number of our citizens the opportunity to travel to Yxria and other GFED planets. This sojourn will last for twenty years, and during this time the contingent of volunteers will learn about advances in science, medicine and technology that are not yet dreamed of here on Earth. They will study the social, legal, and political advancements that provide the framework for a peaceful civilization. In twenty years, they will return to teach us what they have learned and to prepare Earth for entry into the Galactic Federation.

"In exchange, the Federation has only one requirement but it is monumental and far-reaching: We must transform the human race into a non-violent civilization. If we fail to do this, one of two things will happen to the human race, and both are bad.

"If we do not become a peaceful society, our planet will either be quarantined or the human race will be exterminated."

He held up his hands for quiet before the crowd could react.

"Quarantine means that the Federation will take measures to isolate the Earth from the rest of the galaxy and we will be left to wallow in our violent ways. This is the lesser of the two evils, and it will happen if we don't change and if their studies reveal that our violence is a learned behavior.

"If we don't change and human's endemic violence is revealed to be a genetic flaw, the Federation will eradicate the human race from the face of the Earth in order to prevent the spread of violence to the rest of the galaxy."

This time, the murmur rose to a roar. Sanchez pounded the gavel. "Quiet, please! Quiet, please!"

Wainwright raised his voice above the continuing murmur of the crowd.

"Make no mistake. The Galactic Federation is serious about protecting its worlds from the propagation of human violence. Its members will not admit a violent, warring planet like Earth into the Federation, nor will they allow it to undermine their peaceful way of life.

And they have the power to implement their decisions. The recent blackouts which were caused by their solar satellite should convince you of that.

"So, let us look at this as an unprecedented opportunity for world peace. As a first step on this road to peace, I and other world leaders will be meeting at the United Nations over the next few weeks to put into place a plan for worldwide disarmament. Other measures designed to wean our societies away from violence will be introduced over the next several months. This will not be an easy task, and it will take months to make significant inroads, years to see substantial changes. But we must begin.

"During the coming days and weeks, I urge you to resist the temptation to panic or to make drastic changes in your life. Go about your life as usual, and give us, your leaders, a chance to take these first baby steps toward worldwide peace.

"I urge you to spend some time contemplating the opportunity before us. Imagine a future filled with worldwide peace and prosperity. Dream of the miracles in science and technology that await us if we have the courage to take this giant leap into the future. Then think about what you can do personally, as a family, as a community, to move forward in the direction of peace.

"I urge the media to do the same. I urge every journalist and reporter and newscaster to resist the urge to sensationalize these events, though sensational they may be; I urge you to resist the impulse to politicize them. Instead, think seriously about what has happened and speculate seriously about what we can make happen.

"We cannot move far down the path of peace without the help and determination of all Earth's people. A true transformation into a peaceful civilization must take place at the grassroots level. The desire for peace and the repudiation of violence must germinate in the hearts and minds of all citizens and take root in the farms and villages and towns and cities of our great country and in the countries around the world.

"I know how incredible all this must sound to you, but scientists around the world and many, many ordinary people have long accepted the idea of the existence of intelligent life outside our solar system. This moment of first contact was bound to happen. That it happened on my watch I consider both fortunate and challenging.

"Today, my fellow Americans, we stand at the edge of a new world vision, one that stretches far beyond our current earthly boundaries. I ask that you open your minds and imagination to the limitless possibilities that now lie before us. I ask you to step forward with me in the direction of that new exciting world.

Thank you. Good night and God bless Planet Earth."

For fifteen long seconds, the president faced the audience in silence, and then someone in the front row began to clap and the applause, tentative at first, grew into a thunderous ovation, this one, seemingly heartfelt.

CHAPTER 60

Stephen turned off the television before the ovation ended. He couldn't bear to listen to the news pundits trivialize the gravity of the moment. He glanced at his wife and son, both of whom looked stunned-and they had known what was coming. He wondered how the rest of the world was taking the news.

Gerard spoke first. "Notice how he said 'God Bless Planet Earth' instead of 'God Bless America' like he usually does."

Stephen nodded. "It's the beginning of a paradigm shift."

"What's that?"

"It's a change from one way of thinking to another to incorporate something new and far reaching. It happened in 1957 with the Sputnik launch."

"The beginning of the space age?"

"The space age actually began around 1950 when a fellow named Wernher von Braun began developing rockets for the Army, but the general public didn't pay much attention to it until the Soviet Union launched the Sputnik satellite. That caused an immediate paradigm shift as world thought began to seriously consider the possibility of space travel."

"Won't this be just a new twist in the space age paradigm?" Penny asked.

"In a way, yes, but contact with extraterrestrials is so monumental, it will change the way we think about almost everything. Our politics will change, philosophy will change, religion will change—"

"You mean Christianity?"

"I mean religion in general. Most religions, including Christianity, are sect-oriented. They focus on their particular interests and beliefs, but this paradigm shift will force them to expand their view of humanity and of the world."

"How can Christianity change without destroying itself? It's the very essence of our being." She gave Stephen a wry look. "At least, it's the essence of *my* being."

Stephen could hear the sadness in her voice. "Look at it this way, Pen. Christians can cling to the literal interpretation of the Bible and continue to believe that God created Earth and that humans descended from Adam and Eve as the only intelligent species. In which case the omniscient, omnipotent God of Christianity will become a local god, confined to his limited domain of Earth. The same holds true for other religions that focus on a single story, a specific book."

"What's the alternative?"

"The alternative is to expand the idea of God to one that encompasses the whole universe. Religion can learn to embrace such theories as evolution and DNA and consider them God's tools, rather than turning them into threats against religious tenets. If religion can do this, it will have taken a giant step toward discarding its reliance on magic and myths."

He watched his wife contemplating what he'd said. He knew such a paradigm shift would be difficult for her.

She shook her head as if to clear her thoughts. "Do you think world peace is really going to happen?"

"I don't know. I'm sure it won't happen overnight, but I'm hoping the world can move in that direction. You heard what the president said about the need for peace to take hold at the personal level. Religion can and should play a major role in facilitating the path to peace."

She studied him for a moment and for the first time in months expressed admiration. "It looks like you and Dr. Eastlake were successful after all."

Stephen shrugged. "It was Morok's visit to the president that did it. Wainwright wasn't going to budge until he had met him personally."

He glanced at his son who was looking off into space. He could almost see his mind working, sifting through the president's words, matching them with what Stephen had told him earlier about the sojourn. "What do you think, Gerard?"

"What does Morok look like?"

He hesitated. If Gerard applied for the sojourn and was accepted, he would see Morok for himself, and Stephen didn't want him to have any preconceived image from an inadequate description. He exchanged a quick glance with Penny. "Let's just say, he's awesome, in the original sense of that word."

"Please tell me…"

"I don't want to ruin your first impression when you actually see him."

"Will I see him?"

"I have a feeling everyone is going to see him before all this is over."

Stephen felt a curious sense of detachment as they continued to talk about the president's speech and the sojourn. For weeks after his abduction last November, he had had a feeling of dread, not knowing what was going to happen but certain it would be disastrous. When he found Heather, he had grown hopeful that they could do something to avert the disaster, but after their meeting with the president in December, hope had given way to despair. Now Morok's sojourn had opened a gateway to the galaxy, and the future stretched before them all the way to the stars. Such a gateway would create a sea change in the attitude toward world peace, and when the sojourners returned there would be a prodigious leap forward in science and technology and in all the world's social institutions. It was exhilarating to contemplate.

He thought about his own future. If he accepted Morok's invitation, he could join the first wave of Earth's galactic pioneers, maybe even become a key player on the galactic stage. Or he could stay behind and be an observer of history. The choice was obvious: who wouldn't rather be a player than an observer?

But if the decision were that simple, why hadn't he told Penny and Gerard about the invitation? Gerard was probably already making plans to go, and even though Penny would probably reject the idea out of hand, he thought he could bring her around. They were not the reason for his silence. It was his own ambivalence about the sojourn. He had gone back and forth in his mind about the possibility of traveling to the stars until he felt like Hamlet contemplating Yorick's skull. But Hamlet had merely to consider existence over non-existence, the turmoil of life over the annihilation offered by death. He, Stephen, must think about the turmoil of life on two different levels: one, a comfortable and familiar existence, though dull at times and tragically flawed; the other, mysterious, and unknown, but truly an "enterprise of great pith and moment."

He felt as if he were riding a wave of inevitability. Events were marching forward now on their own volition, one event setting another into motion. He would have to make a decision soon, or events would march forward without him.

CHAPTER 61

On Monday, the initial reaction to the landmark speeches was surprisingly mild around the world. Markets in London and Tokyo posted gains, followed by an increase of 50 points in the Dow. But by noon, the Dow started to slide. When it dropped 900 points in one hour, the U.S. markets were forced to close three hours early, and reports of the impending chaos began to drift in. People were lining up for blocks at ATMs and gas stations. The sale of guns and survival equipment were surging in discount stores and sporting goods outlets, and by the end of the day, grocery stores were virtually emptied of food and water.

The chaos continued the next day. There were random stories of people leaping from high buildings in cities around the world. In Montana, a group of survivalists declared an alien-free zone that they would defend to their deaths. In Kansas City, an amateur videographer filmed a street preacher pulling an Uzi from beneath his coat and opening fire on his listeners and passers-by and killing more than a dozen people. In Los Angeles and Detroit, Oklahoma City and Miami, there were riots and random murders.

On Tuesday evening, the president and other world leaders took to the airwaves again to calm the people. At the end of his speech, Wainwright chastised the American people. "The aliens are calling for peace, and we're showing them the most violent, ugly side of human nature. For God's sake, let's get it together."

The next day a mood of uneasy calm settled over the world, only to be shattered on Wednesday when the *New York Times* reprinted a sketch of Chairman Morok that had appeared in *Der Spiegel*. The German magazine attributed the details of the blue-green feathered image to an anonymous source who claimed to have had personal contact with the extraterrestrial. The reporters who had camped outside the Hopkins' residence a week ago descended upon Olive Street again, and when Stephen refused to talk with them, they found a steady stream of people who were more than happy to talk about their own abductions, but everyone agreed that their alien looked nothing like blue-green birdman in the *Times* sketch. This galvanized religious leaders who had access to cable or television networks. Many of them filled the airwaves with interpretations of the Book of Revelation, describing in great detail how the Antichrist would arrive, the forms he could take, the havoc he could cause.

The havoc was, in fact, real, and it continued as the world struggled for equilibrium amid its first contact with alien beings.

#

In New York, Ethan Gorr flipped through television channels with disgust. Everywhere he turned there was nothing but talk of aliens and antichrists. *Had the world gone completely mad?* Yesterday Carlos Barrios had phoned him to make sure the shipment of arms would not cease. "I'm being pressured by the United Nations to disarm," he said, "but Bolivia is landlocked by its age-old enemies and if we give up our arms and our neighbors don't, we'll be as defenseless as children." Gorr assured him the shipments would continue.

He paced the floor of his penthouse and thought about the fear he'd heard in Barrios' voice. His country was surrounded by Peru and Chile in the west, Argentina and Paraguay in the south, and the behemoth Brazil, which hugged the country in the north and east like a jealous lover. Barrios' fear was understandable, but if he was reluctant to give up his arms, perhaps his neighbors would be as well.

Gorr stopped before the window and looked out at the lights of the city. He had made millions exploiting the greed of world leaders. Maybe it was time to examine the possibilities of exploiting that other great human motivator, fear. And if somehow Stephen Hopkins suffers in the process, all the better.

CHAPTER 62

Gerard replayed the opening scene of his favorite sci-fi film. His dad had bought him the DVD when he was recuperating from the Abigo shooting, and he had watched it countless times over the years. Amid a cacophony of sounds, the camera focused on a satellite view of the East Coast. The camera pulled back to capture a complete view of the continent, the Western Hemisphere, the blue oceans, the sounds lessening as the view broadened, and it kept pulling back until the noise lessened to a muted roar as the whole planet became visible, a blue-and-white globe suspended in black space. Then the moon rushed into camera view, shadowing the Earth, and the noise grew fainter as Mars hurtled by, trailed by a flurry of asteroids, the massive Jupiter, Saturn with its rings, the ice-blue globes of Uranus and Neptune, and the dwarf planets. The noise grew fainter still as the Earth shrank to a pale blue dot and then a point of light.

And then only silence.

Fluffy clouds of nebula floated by, a rush of stars coalesced into a huge galaxy spinning slowly in space, its long arms reaching out like a spider. There was no sound at all as galaxies slowly spun like giant pinwheels through a black void.

Gerard stopped the DVD. He wished he were looking out the window of a real spaceship on his way to the stars. On his way to Yxria. The intensity of his desire to be part of the Galactic Sojourn alarmed him. *Would they take someone like him?* What if they had a rule that you had to be of sound body to make the trip? What if they were prejudiced against people with disabilities like his?

But that wasn't logical. GFED's technology was millions of years more advanced than Earth's, so it stood to reason their medicine was equally advanced. They might be able to wave some sort of magic wand and make his legs good as new. He knew that was wishful thinking, but he still wanted to go. He had the application in his hand. He had printed it from the UN website and completed all the relevant information, but he couldn't submit it without his parents' signature. At sixteen, he was old enough to go without his parents, but he still had to have their permission.

He wheeled down the hall to his father's study and paused at the open door. "Dad, I need to talk to you."

Stephen looked up from his computer. "What's on your mind?"

Gerard wheeled over to his desk and handed him the application. "I want to apply for the sojourn, and I need your signature."

A peculiar frown passed briefly over his father's face. He took the application, and as he read it, he rubbed his thumb against his fingers in a silent snapping motion. It was an unconscious habit that meant his dad was upset. When he finished reading, he sat and stared for a long time out the window.

Gerard stood the silence as long as he could. "Dad, this is the most important thing in the world to me. *I have to go.*"

Stephen met his eyes. "It's not a summer jaunt across Europe. You'd be gone for twenty years to a planet a hundred light-years away."

"I know." He felt a sudden jolt of guilt, as if by wanting to go he was rejecting his family. "I would miss you and Mom, but there'll be communication. They said we'd have holographic visits at least once a year, so it's not like we'd be totally cut off from each other."

"Tell me why you want to go," Stephen said wearily.

Gerard rolled his chair closer, leaned toward his dad. "It's like a chance to leap a million years into the future, to find out what's out there. Just that possibility makes staying here on Earth seem like—I don't know—like slogging around in the mud."

"Why do you want to speed up the future?"

"No one has to speed up the future, it's here. GFED *is* the future."

"Gerard, you'd be thirty-six years old when we see you again. Or more likely, we'd *never* see you again. Your mother and I will probably be dead for thousands of years by the time you return."

"No—"

"That's what Einstein believed. I'm no physicist, but I think he postulated that traveling through space and traveling through time are inversely proportional. Let's say you travel to Yxria at the speed of light, you'll age very slowly in Earth-years while you're there, but when you return to Earth, everything on the planet will have aged thousands of years."

Now his dad was trying to frighten him, trying to make him feel guilty. He was not going to bite. "Stargunner says that Einstein's theory wouldn't hold if space travel is instantaneous, like it could be with teleportation. Besides," he added, "wouldn't Morok have mentioned it if this aging thing was a problem?"

The snapping motion of Stephen's hand had stopped. "You're probably right. Morok didn't mention time relativity as a problem. It is still just a theory, after all."

"I *know* we'll see each other again, Dad, and things will be so different with what we can learn and bring back to Earth. Please help me convince Mom, please."

"You know it's possible you won't be accepted because of—"

"—because of my legs," he finished. "I know, but I still want to apply."

#

Stephen studied his son's hopeful face. He knew, of course, that he would leave home one day, but he had always thought it would happen in stages: first college, then a job, then marriage and perhaps a move to another city, maybe even another country—but never to another planet. Still, how could he tell him he couldn't go? If he were Gerard's age, he knew he would be dreaming of nothing else. He himself had spent the past three days toying with the idea of accepting Morok's offer to accompany the group. If he did, Gerard wouldn't have to go through the application process with its possibility of rejection. Maybe Penny would go if she knew it was the only way she could stay close to Gerard.

But another thought had been tugging at his mind, too. In order for the volunteers to return with GFED's advanced technologies and knowledge, those remaining on Earth must lay the peaceful foundation on which the returning sojourners could build a new future. To achieve that goal, it would take people who truly believed in the quest for peace. Maybe his role was to stay behind and help Earth find its way. But the thought of losing Gerard was almost more than he could bear.

He tried again. "Life on Yxria will be unimaginably strange, you know. The landscape, the people, the language, the customs—"

"But that's part of why I want to go!"

"What if you can never come home? If humans can't make the profound transformation toward peace that is required, you won't be allowed to come back. Have you thought about that?"

Gerard jerked upright in his chair. "Dad, if we can't learn to live in peace, I'm not sure I want to come back."

That answer startled Stephen. And it convinced him his son had thought about all the possibilities. "Okay," he said.

"Okay?"

He smiled at Gerard. "I think I should talk to your mother first, let her get used to the idea that you want to go. Then we can talk to her together."

Gerard beamed. "Thanks, Dad."

"If we can get your mother's approval, I'll put in a good word for you the next time I see Chairman Morok."

Gerard let out a whoop of joy!

As Stephen watched Gerard wheel out the door, he felt the enormity of what was transpiring. His son might actually journey to the stars.

History would be forever divided into BG and AG— Before GFED and After GFED—or who knows, maybe historians would dub it Old World versus New Worlds, like Europe and America after 1492. Whatever the terminology, the world he knew, the world he grew up in, spent his first forty-two years in, would become outdated, antiquated, made irrelevant by the new worlds that lay beyond the sun.

But he didn't have to stay behind. He could accept Morok's offer of a free pass on the sojourn. He could have one last great adventure and travel to the stars. The question was: Would he? Should he? Could he?

CHAPTER 63

Heather Eastlake had applied for the Galactic Sojourn the day after it was announced, despite Stephen's assurance that Morok had reserved a place for them. If there really was a spot reserved for a child psychologist, she wanted to make sure her name was on the list. Now she sat at her kitchen table making a list of things to do if she were selected. "How do you pack for a twenty-year absence?" she muttered to herself.

She reread the brief that she'd printed from the UN website. It stated that everything the sojourners needed would be provided once they arrived on Yxria, but she wanted her own clothes, her own shoes, her own cosmetics. She shook her head impatiently. What was she fretting about? She hadn't even been accepted yet.

"You have been accepted."

Heather gave a startled yelp and turned around. Standing behind her was a gray-haired man with a kindly face dressed in a grey suit, white shirt, red tie. She recognized him from Stephen's description. "Chairman Morok?" she said in a tremulous voice.

He nodded. "I wanted to tell you personally that your application to the sojourn has been accepted."

She was astonished that he would bring the news in person. "Thank you, Mr. Chairman."

"I have a proposal for you, Dr. Eastlake. We must have a leader to act as liaison between the Namuh volunteers and GFED—more specifically, between the Namuh volunteers and me. I had thought to offer a joint leadership to you and Dr. Hopkins, but I fear he may not be joining us, so I am offering it to you. Are you prepared to accept it?"

She opened her mouth but no words came out. She cleared her throat. "I'm honored, Mr. Chairman, and surprised…overwhelmed, really." She was embarrassed that her voice cracked, as if she were frightened. Which she was not, even though her heart was racing.

"You impressed me with your intelligence and objectivity when you appeared at the hearing, and it is quite important to have a Namuh psychologist on the sojourn, especially one experienced in dealing with children. As you know, most of the volunteers will be children or young adults."

She nodded encouragingly, not trusting her voice.

"I will also need your help before we leave. You will be the official spokesperson for GFED, which means you will handle all media inquiries and any public appearances you think necessary to maintain public awareness and interest in the sojourn. You must also assemble a staff to interview the candidates and select the finalists."

"Select the finalists?"

"Yes. It has been less than a week since the announcement of the sojourn, and I believe there are already half a million applications. These must be winnowed to a number that can be interviewed by you and your staff. I will have the final say on who is ultimately accepted, but you must select the twelve hundred finalists, after which I will meet with them personally. It is important that I observe their reactions to me and other aspects of the Federation.

"Their reactions to you?" She was unable to take her eyes off his face which seemed to be glowing as if lit by an inner light.

"My species is nothing like the Namuh. Do you not think it wise that the sojourners see what we look like before they leave their home planet?"

"Of course." She hesitated, realizing the implication of what Morok had just said. "Will I have the same privilege?"

The Chairman smiled. "My dear, you are going to be my official liaison for the next twenty years. We will work as closely as your president and his chief of staff, so you must become comfortable with our differences."

She nodded.

"Prepare yourself.

As his metamorphosis began, Heather put her hand to her throat, and when he stood before her in all his avian splendor, she was flooded with a mixture of terror and awe. He was magnificent—but could she really live in a world inhabited by creatures like him? And he had mentioned thousands of other species. Would they be even more different? *What was she getting herself into?*

"I can see you are somewhat disturbed by my appearance, but you must understand there are thousands of extraordinary species in our galaxy, Dr. Eastlake, many of them quite different from the Namuh."

She noticed that his mouth, obscured by feathers, did not move when he spoke. Was he communicating with her telepathically?

"Yes, I am," he said, answering her unspoken question.

She felt suddenly disoriented. She looked around the room as if for escape.

"Dr. Eastlake, please relax. I am not reading your mind in the way that you think. Only thoughts that have direct application to the subject at hand are open to my mental tracking. If you find that uncomfortable, I can disengage that function while I am in your presence."

She shook her head slowly from side to side. He waited while she collected herself. Finally, she spoke, her breath rushing out with her words. "You are magnificent!"

Morok inclined his head, accepting the accolade.

"But Mr. Chairman, I'm afraid I've failed an important test. If your appearance disorients me this much, how will the children react?"

"Do not worry about the children. Adult Namuh find it difficult to accept that a being who looks like me can think and speak, much less do magical things like read thoughts. To adults, it is as if an eagle has swooped down to chat about the state of the world."

He gave a sort of trill. Heather wondered if it was his way of laughing.

"But Namuh children are much more open," he continued. "Their minds have not yet become calcified by the expected norms of your world. I expect most of them will accept me and others who look even more different with barely a ripple of concern. Nevertheless, if there is any initial shock, it should diminish before they depart for Yxria. That is why I must interview them myself."

"What happens if some of them sail through the interviews and then discover, once they're on Yxria, that they can't take it?" Heather fervently hoped she would not be one of them.

"There will be an orientation during which the sojourners will be introduced to basic life conditions on Yxria. Anyone who is uncomfortable with that will be returned to Earth."

"Will that be the only opportunity for a volunteer to return before the end of the sojourn?"

"Yes." He paused. "Do you still want to go?"

Heather took a quick inventory of her feelings. Already she was growing accustomed to talking with this spectacular blue-green avian. Her heart had slowed considerably, and she was no longer dry-mouthed, no longer speechless, no longer filled with fear. "Yes," she said, her voice now clear and strong. "I want to go more than ever."

Morok's eyes glittered. "I believe you will be a great asset, Dr. Eastlake, to me and to your sojourners. I will be in touch before the time for my interviews."

"How will you contact me?" she asked quickly.

There was no answer. He spread his great blue-green wings and, with a slight rustle of feathers, vanished.

"*Holy mother of God!*" she breathed.

#

That afternoon, she received a call from the Secretary-General of the United Nations.

"I have been advised that I should announce your appointment as Director of the Galactic Sojourn."

"Thank you, sir," Heather said, and wondered how it had happened so fast.

"Don't thank me. Thank Chairman Morok. He said you were his personal choice."

"The chairman came to see you?"

"Yes. A pleasant looking gentleman, not at all what I expected. He said I should simply announce the appointment and that you would know what to do. I confirmed with President Wainwright that you were indeed one of Chairman Morok's original contacts, so I assume the appointment is legitimate."

"Yes, sir. The chairman met with me this morning."

"This morning? He does not waste time, does he?"

"No, sir."

"I will make the announcement on Monday. We must stay in close contact over the next few weeks to see that all goes smoothly, do you agree?"

"Yes, I do. This is all very new for me as well. I trust I can count on you or your office to assist me with protocol and procedures?"

"Of course."

There was a pause at the other end of the line. Heather wasn't sure whether or not the conversation had ended.

"Tell me, Dr. Eastlake, does Chairman Morok really look like one of us?"

Heather smiled. "I think he chooses a benign form when he first appears, so as not to unduly alarm us."

"So, he looks quite different?"

"Yes, sir. He is quite spectacular looking."

"I see. Well, good luck, Dr. Eastlake."

Heather watched the stream of students passing her window. Three months ago, her life had familiar, well-defined boundaries. She was a respected professor at a good university. She lived in a jewel-like city she loved, among friends she adored. And now, everything was in flux. Sometimes it felt as if she had fallen down a rabbit hole and nothing was as it seemed.

One thing was for sure. However much her life had changed up to this point, it would change another 180 degrees after the Secretary-General made his announcement on Monday.

CHAPTER 64

Gerard could hear them shouting at each other through his closed door. He wheeled over to the door and opened it.

"I will *never* let him go!"

His mother's voice carried through their closed bedroom door and down the hall; his father's voice was muffled. He heard his mother sobbing. Then she cried, "Get out! Leave me alone!" and he quickly closed his door. He heard his dad's footsteps in the hallway, then on the stairs. He heard the front door open, then close sharply.

Part of him wanted to race down the hall and tell his mother he didn't want to leave her, but he knew it was his guilt talking. He wanted to go on the sojourn so desperately it scared him. He didn't know what he would do if she didn't sign his application. Or if it was rejected.

He logged on to KASA. Now that the media were no longer hovering outside his house, he had admitted to Gunner and Moleman that the professor in the alien story was indeed his dad. "I knew it," Gunner had said, and that was the end of that.

He watched their back-and-forth chatter about the sojourn. They had both applied, but why not? They were over twenty-one, so they could do what they pleased. He felt a surge of resentment against his parents, against his *mother*. She was the one holding him back. She always wanted to hold him back. *It wasn't fair.* Gunner finally noticed he was online.

stargunner	you submit your application gman?
g-man	im working on it
stargunner	better hurry deadline's next Friday
moleman	think we'll make the cut?
stargunner	sure who wouldn't want three cool dudes like us
moleman	im not sure I want to live with you for the next 20 years gunner
stargunner	we shouldn't be talking about this online even if it is encrypted everything is supposed to be kept confidential until the official announcement.

Gerard fell silent as Gunner and Moley chatted about other things. What if they all got to go? On one hand, it would be great to be around them all the time. On the other hand, they'd find out he'd been lying to them for the past two years about being a tennis star and a senior at Georgetown. They'd see him for what he was: a teenage cripple.

Get a grip! There was nothing he hated more than a sorry-ass whiner, and he would not become one. He would find some way to get his mother to sign the application, and he'd deal with Gunner and Moley when he met them.

#

Down the hall, Penny picked up the phone and dialed a number. After three rings, Marshall Hopkins picked up. When she heard his voice, she began to cry.

"Penny, is that you?"

"Yes," she managed through her sobs.

"What's wrong? Is it Stephen? Gerard?"

"No."

Her chest tightened and she gasped for air. She laid the phone down and tried to breathe through her nose, pinching first one nostril and then the other. She could hear the reverend's frantic voice on the phone. Finally, she picked up the phone. "I'm sorry, I couldn't catch my breath—"

"Tell me what's wrong."

"Stephen wants me to sign Gerard's application for that awful sojourn. I won't do it, Reverend, I won't. This whole thing is crazy. Life on other planets...how could that be? How could God allow it?" She started to sob again.

"I've been struggling with that question, too, Penny," he said comfortingly, "and I think we have to broaden our concept of God. We have to look at the whole universe as God's creation, because it is, you know. He is limitless. He can encompass whatever we might find in the stars."

"You don't think the aliens are the Antichrist?"

292

"No, my dear. The aliens are the ones who live in a world of peace. It seems to me we should be welcoming them with open arms so we can learn how to do that here on Earth."

Penny was struck by that remark, struck by how it rang true. She would certainly believe her father-in-law over those who were fanning the flames of fear. But the idea of sending her son to another planet was unthinkable. "Gerard thinks this sojourn is the greatest possible adventure, but how can I give him up for twenty years?"

"Maybe it will turn out to be an adventure in which he finds God."

He began to repeat the message he had delivered on his Sunday morning broadcast, about the whole universe was God's canvas, not just one small planet in a single galaxy that was home to the human race.

Penny listened to his soothing voice, his comforting words. Could this faraway planet where Gerard wanted to go really be under God's aegis? And if it was, should she let him go? She thought about what Stephen had said about the possibility that GFED's advanced technology could heal Gerard's legs. When he returned in twenty years, he would be a grown man, yes, but maybe one with legs that worked. How could she deny him that?

#

Late in the afternoon, she went to Gerard's room. His door was open. He was lying on the bed, legs tucked under a green throw, hands clasped behind his head.

She tapped on the door. "Can I come in?"

"Sure," he said.

She pulled the director's chair next to the bed and sat down, glancing at the bony shape of his legs under the throw. When their eyes met, his lips tightened and a pink flush crawled up his neck. She knew he was ashamed of his legs; despite everything she and Stephen had done to try to make him feel accepted and whole.

"You really want to go on that sojourn?"

He nodded. "More than anything."

293

She searched his face. "So much can happen in twenty years, Gerard."

He grasped the metal rings above his bed and pulled himself upright, careful to keep his legs covered. He reached for his mother's hand, covered it with both of his. "Mom, you know how much I love science fiction?"

Penny nodded, unable to speak. Her hand felt lost in his.

"Well, it's not fiction anymore. Everything those writers could have imagined…and more, has happened, and I have a chance to see it. Not just to see it, but to be part of it, and to bring all that knowledge back to Earth. I can help change our world!"

Penny watched his face as he talked. It was animated and glowing. She felt something break loose inside her chest, and she found herself nodding in agreement, even as tears spilled down her cheeks.

"Mom, are you saying yes?" His voice rose with excitement.

She kept nodding, the tears kept flowing.

"Yes!" he shouted, and he pulled his mother out of her chair, pulled her toward the bed, and wrapped his arms around her. "You won't regret this, Mom. I promise you won't regret it."

CHAPTER 65

On Wednesday, February 16, Heather checked into the Hay-Adams Hotel in Washington, D.C. She and her staff of six had spent the past two weeks traveling the globe to interview the eighteen hundred semi-finalists for the Galactic Sojourn, and she was weary to the bone. She kicked off her shoes and lay down on the bed. She wanted more than anything to order room service and go to bed early, but she'd agreed to have dinner with Stephen and his wife, which presented her with mixed feelings. Stephen had become her safe haven over the past few weeks, the one person with whom she could be herself instead of Director of the Galactic Sojourn. Now, instead of relaxing over a quiet dinner, she would have to put on her social face for a woman she'd never met.

Oh well! She turned on the television and found a news channel. There was an announcement of another peace treaty, this one between Israel and Palestine, and the signing of the UN's worldwide disarmament agreement by the last hold-out of the 191 member nations. The two newscasters were as casual as if they were discussing the latest bill passed by Congress. The paradigm shift Stephen had described had taken place.

She turned up the sound when she saw herself on the screen, emerging from the terminal at Dulles airport. She was surrounded by the four secret service agents loaned to her by the president. As they walked down the roped-off corridor to a waiting limousine, she had seen the placards being waved by people on either side of the ropes with their slogans: *Red-haired she-devil!... The Antichrist and the Redhead!... Death to the Alien and the Redhead!* She hadn't seen the small, wiry man who'd ducked under the ropes because the agents had closed around her and shoved her into the limo, but now, as she watched the scene on television, she saw that the man had something small and dark in his hand and a wild look in his eyes, and then one of the male agents shoved him to the ground. The newscaster said the man had not yet been identified.

Heather turned off the TV and closed her eyes and remembered the rush of fear she'd felt as the agents pushed her into the limo. She'd thought the dangerous part of her job would be the actual spaceflight, not walking through an airport terminal, and the thought that someone actually wanted to harm her was hard to accept.

After a while, she showered and dressed for dinner in a black silk pant suit with a Mandarin collar. She put on a pair of jade hoop earrings and slipped on a pair of black heels and headed to the elevator feeling uncharacteristically nervous. She spotted Stephen across the lobby with a woman in a burgundy suit with a long skirt and matching boots. Stephen smiled when he saw her and they headed her way.

"Hello, Stephen," Heather said, offering her hand. They usually gave each other a quick hug, but that didn't seem appropriate at the moment.

Stephen introduced his wife. She was petite and very pretty with short dark curly hair and a warm smile.

"I've heard so much about you," Heather said, feeling like an Amazon in her three-inch heels.

"And I've heard a lot about you," Penny said, "but mostly from the media. You'll have to tell me what's true and what's hype."

Penny smiled up at her and Heather started to relax. As much as she liked Stephen, how could she not like his wife?

They made small talk over drinks. Stephen was clearly uncomfortable, but he began to relax when he saw that the two women were getting along. By the time dinner was served, the conversation had moved to the Galactic Sojourn.

"You're interviewing Gerard tomorrow, aren't you?" Penny asked.

Heather nodded. "It's just a formality. If anyone has a free pass, it's your son."

Stephen said, "Is that what Morok said?"

"Yes. He would like you to go, of course, but if he can't have you, he's predisposed to take your son—" She stopped when she saw Penny's expression.

Penny looked at her husband. "What does she mean, 'he wants you to go'? You never said that."

Stephen frowned, pursed his lips. "The Chairman mentioned there was a place on the sojourn for an anthropologist. I suppose he meant me."

Heather remained silent. She wished she'd chosen her words more carefully.

Penny glanced from Stephen to Heather, back to Stephen. "Do you *want* to go?"

He stared at his plate. "At first, I did. Then the more I thought about it..." He met his wife's eyes. "I think I can help more by staying here, doing what I can to see that we keep our part in this bargain so there'll be an Earth for Gerard to come back to."

So there'll be an Earth to come back to.

The words set off little explosions of introspection, and they were silent for a long moment as each peered into the uncertain future. Whether they journeyed to the stars or remained on Earth, their lives would never be the same. Absorbed in her high-profile life of the past few weeks, Heather had lost sight of that.

Stephen broke the silence. "So, Heather, if you hear things aren't going well down here, just ask the chairman to beam us up!"

They laughed and the conversation lightened. By the end of dinner, they were chatting like new best friends. As the two women said good-bye, Penny leaned in close and whispered, "Take care of my little boy." She squeezed Heather's hand and turned abruptly and started across the lobby.

"Will she be okay?" Heather asked.

"She'll be fine," Stephen said. "My father has convinced her that Yxria is under God's dominion, same as Earth, so she's trying to believe that God can watch over Gerard there just as easily as here, but she still cries every time she looks at him."

"It must be difficult."

He gave her a quick peck on the cheek. "Good luck, tomorrow. Call me when your interviews are over."

Heather watched him cross the lobby to Penny, who was waiting by the door. He put his arm around her shoulders as they walked outside. Heather felt suddenly disoriented, as if the events of the past weeks had swept away all her moorings. Maybe it was Stephen's comment about having an Earth to come back to. She had been so focused on leaving that she hadn't given two thoughts about what would be happening on Earth while she was gone.

She went to the bar and ordered a brandy. When it came, she inhaled the aroma, took a sip, and closed her eyes as the warmth of the amber liquid rose in her head. Would there be brandy or wine on Yxria? What would the food be like? Where would she live? What would she wear? Would she have a car? On a planet where the ruling race had wings, would there even be cars? She took another sip of brandy. *What had she gotten herself into?*

CHAPTER 66

The next morning, Heather prepared for her last three sojourner interviews, each intriguing in a different way. She felt sure all three would make the cut and had left three slots open on her short list. She picked up the phone and dialed the receptionist. The Hay-Adams had been pleased to let her use their corporate conference room for the interviews and had offered the assistance of their staff. "Send in Abigail Moore, please."

She glanced over Abigail's application, which was printed in block letters in purple ink. She was fifteen, a straight-A student at Emerson Preparatory School, the only daughter of General Abner Moore, whose profession she'd given as 'Head of the Army' with a home address in Arlington, Virginia. In the space for the mother's name, she had written 'Gone to Heaven.' For skills, she'd listed 'Internet Whiz Kid, Culinary Genius (I know 101 ways to make tofu delicious), Tennis Champ (I could beat the skirt off Angelina Wong if I just had more time to practice).' Angelina Wong was the Michelle Wie of the tennis world, having won the previous US Open at age fourteen. Under interests, Abigail wrote 'Surfing the Net, Writing Science Fiction Stories, Reading, Shopping, Dancing.' It was her reason for wanting to go on the sojourn that had most intrigued Heather and made her smile. Abigail had written:

> *All my life people have told me I'm extraordinary: in looks, brains, sports, dancing, cooking, you name it. Everything has come to me so easily that I'm afraid it is all an illusion created by a father who adores me. I want a challenge big enough to require the whole of my being to rise up to meet it. A trip to the stars might just do the trick.*

Her video essay had shown a tall, willowy girl with long dark hair and dark luminous eyes dressed in tight faded jeans and a bulky white sweater. At the end of the video, the camera had moved in for a close-up and the girl had leaned toward the camera, lowered her eyes to half-mast and said in a throaty whisper: "You *need* someone like me on this voyage, and since there *is* nobody else like me on this planet, you simply must take *me*."

Heather had been amused by her provocative manner and wondered if she had thought the video would be reviewed by a man. Now she was curious how Abigail would present herself to a female interviewer. She looked up to see the girl in the video standing in the doorway of the conference room.

Abigail Moore wore an elegant navy pantsuit and high-heeled navy pumps. A white cotton blouse with a large crisp collar framed her face and followed the lapels of her jacket into a modest V. Her dark hair was glossy, her make-up subdued, her nails conservatively manicured with white French tips. Except for the coquettish twinkle in her eyes, she looked as if she were posing for a church magazine for teens.

"Dr. Eastlake, first, let me say that I have read everything I could get my hands on about you and I think you're just about the most fabulous role model for young girls and whether I am chosen to go on this sojourn or not I hope to be able to follow in your footsteps one day and make my mark on the world the way you have." She finished breathlessly and strode over to Heather and stuck out her hand. "I am honored to meet you, ma'am."

Heather gave a wry smile as they shook hands. "Do you really think you can flatter your way into the sojourn, Miss Moore?"

Abigail's pert little face fell. "Ohmygod, have I blown it? Please call me Abby and please, please, please tell me I haven't blown it."

By the end of the interview, Abigail had convinced Heather that she had what it would take to thrive on a journey to the stars: she was intelligent, independent, unconventional, with a large dash of adventure in her soul. Heather told her she was accepted as a finalist, assuming her father would let her go.

Abby grinned impishly and wiggled her little finger. "See this, Dr. E? My daddy's wrapped around it so tight he can hardly move. He'll let me go."

Heather smiled. "I've no doubt you're right, but I will confirm it with General Moore tomorrow."

After Abby left, Heather looked at her watch. Almost three-thirty. Just enough time to freshen up before her interview with Gerard Hopkins.

She went to the bathroom adjacent to the conference room, washed her hands and splashed water on her face, then patted it dry with a towel. She stared at herself in the mirror. She looked tired. She *was* tired. But Gerard was the next-to-last interview. She would have no more official duties until the 24th when she would introduce the sojourners at a special ceremony at the United Nations. There was plenty of time to rest before that.

She returned to the conference room and moved the chairs away from the table and pushed them up against the far wall. She opened the door and nudged a rubber doorstop under it. She sat down and glanced at Gerard's application. He had listed one of his interests as Primitive Cultures. In his video essay, he'd talked about his trip to Mondogo when he was ten, describing how gentle the Abigo were and how much he had loved them, especially the shaman named Ganbigo. "They were just like me," he said, "even the adults. They were all like children." He had not mentioned the shooting.

She picked up the phone and asked the receptionist to send him in. As she waited, she remembered what he'd said at the end of his video essay:

> *"Think of it this way: All the time and effort and energy other kids have put into riding bikes and dancing and playing sports, I've put into the upper half of my body, namely my brain. I can out-think anybody my age and half the people twice my age. And that's not all*—he gave the camera a sly look and stretched his muscular arms toward the camera, palms up— *See these arms? They can bench press two hundred thirty pounds. And that's what I have to offer: brains and brawn. Both of which might come in handy on a trip to the stars."*

He had turned and flexed his arms in a body-building pose, and as the camera moved in for a close-up he winked. Heather had been charmed. Now she heard his wheels on the hardwood floor and waited expectantly.

Gerard paused in the doorway, glanced at the chairs lined up against the wall across the room, looked at Heather and gave her a broad grin. He glided over to where she was sitting. He wore blue jeans and a black t-shirt stretched tight across his chest. A puffy-looking tan jacket lay in his lap across his legs. "Hello, Dr. Eastlake, I'm Gerard Hopkins."

She shook his hand, a man's hand engulfing hers just as Stephen's did. "Hello, Gerard, I am so pleased to meet you at last."

"Me too. I'm the one who found you on the internet." A rosy blush crept up his cheeks. He rolled backward to a comfortable distance.

"And thank heavens for that," Heather said with a laugh.

He looked up and laughed with her.

She found him as charming in person as he was in the video. He was open, natural, *authentic*. "I was impressed with your application, Gerard, and with your video. Did you realize you omitted your 'reason for going'?"

"I found it sort of hard to put down on paper."

"Can you tell me why you want to go?"

He was quiet for a moment. She could almost see him organizing his thoughts. When he spoke, he looked directly at her, "You know how the world now seems to accept the fact that we've been contacted by aliens who are superior to us?"

Heather nodded. She wasn't sure there was widespread acceptance that the aliens were *superior*, just more technologically advanced.

"My dad called this a paradigm shift. You know what that is?"

"Yes."

"Well, everything here on Earth belongs to the old paradigm. Our latest medical discoveries are antiquated compared to theirs. Our spaceships are clunky and cumbersome, our technology is old-fashioned. Now when I look at my iPhone or Xbox they seem like old toys I discarded when I was six. I feel like my future here has already been lived. That's why I want to go on the sojourn. It can give me back my future." He stopped. "That sounded pretty lame, didn't it? And selfish."

Heather was startled by what he had said. She had had remarkably similar thoughts.

"You've voiced your feelings most eloquently, Gerard. I would be quite pleased if I could do as well." She paused. "If you go on this sojourn, you'll be thirty-six when you return to

302

Earth. How do you feel about leaving Earth as a teenager and returning as a fully mature adult?"

"It could be worse than that. My dad thinks there's a possibility the Earth will age thousands of years while I'm gone twenty."

Heather smiled. "Morok assured me that won't happen. Einstein's theory of relativity doesn't apply to instantaneous travel."

He blew out a breath. "That's what I told my dad."

"Still, twenty years is a long time."

"I know, but I've given it a lot of thought. I know I'll miss them, especially my dad, but the paper said there would be holographic visits. That's not the same thing as seeing them in person, I know, but it's better than phone calls or email."

He was silent for a moment. "It's my future, Dr. Eastlake," he said finally. "It could be theirs too. Just because my mom's afraid to make the leap doesn't mean I have to stick around and hold her hand." He stopped, stared at the jacket in his lap. "I didn't mean to criticize my mom. She isn't really holding dad back; he feels like he's needed here."

"Gerard, look at me."

He looked up.

"That is the best answer you could have given me. You acknowledge the pull of your family but you also realize that they are responsible for their own destiny, just as you are for yours. It shows that you know your own mind. But they do support you in this, don't they?"

He nodded. "Yeah, I guess they do."

Heather stood up and stuck out her hand. "Congratulations. You made the cut."

He let out a whoop and grabbed her hand in both of his and pumped it. "Is the interview over then? I've got to go tell my dad."

Heather nodded.

He spun his chair around and wheeled toward the door, then stopped and looked over his shoulder at her. "You won't be sorry, Dr. Eastlake, I guarantee you," and then he was out the door and Heather heard a loud 'Yes!' as he rolled down the hallway.

She smiled and picked up the last application. It was the interview she had been most eagerly anticipating. But this one would not be held in the Hay-Adams conference room. She would meet the candidate for drinks and dinner in the Lafayette Room. She put the applications and notepad in her briefcase and went to her room to change clothes.

#

Thirty minutes later, she was seated at a table in the Lafayette Room, the same table she had shared with Stephen at their first meeting almost three months ago. Through the window, she could see the silhouettes of armed guards patrolling the roof of the White House in the gathering dusk. Apparently, the president's house must still be guarded as the world marched steadily toward peace. She sipped a glass of red wine and watched them while she waited for the last Sojourn candidate.

"Good afternoon, Dr. Eastlake."

She looked up into the dark handsome face of Calvin Williams. The gold hoop on his left earlobe gleamed in the candlelight. She smiled and offered her hand. "It's good to see you again, Dr. Williams."

"Please call me Cal."

"And you should call me Heather," she said, as he lowered his long body into the chair opposite her. Even sitting down, he gave the impression of unusual height, accented perhaps by his perfectly shaped shaven head.

She sneaked glances at him as they looked at the menus. During the meetings with the president, she had been impressed with his intelligence and sensitivity, but she was surprised when she saw his Sojourn application. She'd scanned it with interest. He was forty-seven, divorced for ten years, no children. The former pro-basketball star had received his doctorate in quantum physics twelve years ago and was appointed to the president's staff shortly after Wainwright took office. On his application, he'd written 'the world and everything beyond' as his interests, and his reason for going on the sojourn had echoed Gerard Hopkins' reason and resonated deeply with her own.

Every scientific discovery in the past century has paled in the harsh light of the discovery of advanced civilizations beyond our planet. It's as if you were the smartest, most handsome kid in school and then someone held up a mirror and you could see just how ignorant and ill-shaped and peculiar you really were. We now know that scientific knowledge in another part of the galaxy has progressed millions of years beyond our own. We now know how immature, how infantile, we appear to advanced civilizations. All the scientific achievements we have made over the past two millennia—and there have been many—are just baby steps. It will take us millions of centuries to reach the level of the GFED civilizations—if indeed we don't destroy ourselves first. The Galactic Sojourn gives us an opportunity to accept the mentoring of a mature, advanced species and to make a truly gigantic leap forward for all humankind. I want to accept their mentoring, so that I may become one of the mentors of a new and better Earth.

Calvin Williams looked up from his menu and smiled a dazzling smile. Heather mentally added his name to her short list of finalists.

CHAPTER 67

Standing at his window overlooking Central Park, Ethan Gorr thought the world had gone nuts. Yesterday, President Wainwright had announced the dismantling of all nuclear warheads in the United States, and now he was being hailed as the statesman of the century, the man who would lead the world toward peace. *What bullshit!* The government had been exploiting fear for decades, and now suddenly we're suddenly going to make nice with our neighbors? Yet countries were falling all over themselves to follow Wainwright's lead, even Iran and North Korea. It was like watching a flock of sheep follow their leader over a cliff.

The ringing of the telephone interrupted his thoughts. He answered it and felt a small flicker of shock, as the caller identified himself and the country he represented.

"I understand you're the go-to man for covert weapons operations," the man said.

Gorr hesitated. He had made agreements with a few renegade leaders to reassemble and hide the weapons they were dismantling in extravagant public ceremonies, and he had agreements in place to purchase inventories from weapons manufacturers who were facing possible bankruptcy. That did make him the king of covert weapons operations. Still, he would never have expected a phone call from this man.

"You know that you're calling on an unsecured line?" Gorr said.

"It's encrypted from this end. I assure you it's safe."

"That's not good enough. If you want to deal with me, I'll need to see you in person with proper identification."

The caller was silent, thinking perhaps about how he could manage that. "All right. I will meet you in Central Park tomorrow at 3 pm sharp."

"It's a big park, General."

"Pick a landmark I can find."

Gorr thought for a moment. "The Strawberry Fields Memorial." He gave the General directions and added, "Come alone."

"You think I want anyone to know about this?" There was a click and the line went dead.

Gorr stood for a moment, holding the phone in his hand. "I'll be damned," he said.

CHAPTER 68

The next day, Stephen received an email from Heather's office stating that Gerard had been accepted as a finalist in the Galactic Sojourn. He found Penny lying on the chaise in the aviary staring up at the ceiling. Gerard had told her the night before that he'd made Heather's short list, and she took the news with a smile, but after they went to bed, she had been inconsolable. It was obvious she still hadn't recovered. She gave him a long sad look when he walked in.

"It's official. He goes to New York on Saturday for his interview with Morok." He handed her the email.

She refused to take it. "It's moving too fast."

"I know."

"Read it to me."

Stephen read it. "I'm pleased to notify you that Gerard Hopkins has been accepted as one of the 1200 finalists for the Galactic Sojourn. He is scheduled for an interview with Chairman Morok at 10 o'clock on Saturday at the Barclay Hotel in New York."

"Will all the interviews be held in New York?"

"No. They're also in…" He glanced at the email. "…Houston, Vancouver, Buenos Aires, London, Paris, Athens, Mumbai, Riyadh, Moscow, Beijing, and Tokyo."

"Morok is doing all that in two days?"

"That's what it says."

Penny shook her head. "That's impossible."

"Not if he appears holographically. That way, he could do an unlimited number simultaneously."

Penny gave him a stricken look. "Oh, Stephen, I don't know if I can let him go!"

Stephen sat down on the edge of the chaise and took her in his arms. "We have to be strong, Pen. Gerard would never get over it if we say no now."

#

Two days later, Stephen and Gerard arrived at the Barclay Hotel and were escorted to the Vanderbilt room where they waited with nine other candidates. There were three young men— two Caucasian, one Asian-American—who appeared to be in their mid to late twenties, a distinguished looking African-American woman with a long gray braid wrapped around her head, a young nervous-looking woman with short blonde hair, a dark-haired teenage girl dressed in a navy pantsuit, and a young Hispanic couple with a toddler wearing a blue sailor suit. Gerard was the only one in a wheelchair.

Gerard had talked nonstop the night before, speculating about life on Yxria, but he'd hardly said a word over breakfast, and Stephen could tell he was not in a mood to talk now. He opened the book he'd brought along in anticipation of a long wait.

At exactly ten o'clock a young woman stuck her head in the door. "Would Asher McMullen, Jon Wong, and Abigail Moore please come with me?"

The dark-haired girl stood up. "Oh! That's me!" she exclaimed and beamed a smile at the room. She gathered up her purse and a tote bag full of books and headed for the door. Stephen could hear her chattering excitedly with the two young men as they went out the door.

Gerard glanced at his father. "I thought the interviews were going to be one-on-one."

Stephen shrugged. "Perhaps its more efficient this way."

At ten-thirty, the young woman stuck her head in the door again. This time she called for Lucinda Clifton, Jacob Shey, and Gerard Hopkins.

Gerard turned to his father and held his hand up for a high-five, eyes bright with excitement. "Show time!"

Stephen wanted to grab his son and hug him. Instead, he slapped his palm. "Knock 'em dead, kid."

Gerard grinned and headed toward the door. Stephen started after him to open it, but the young man named Jacob Shey grabbed the door. "Allow me," he said, and held the door for the woman with the grey braid and continued to hold it open as Gerard wheeled through with a "Thanks, man."

As Stephen watched the door close behind them, he was gripped by a feeling that the weeks between now and the day of the sojourn departure were being squeezed into one long narrow day that was already half over.

"Was that your son?"

Stephen turned toward the voice. It was the man who had been holding the toddler who was now lurching around the room like a tiny drunken sailor, his mother shadowing every unsteady step.

"Yes. Is the little one yours?"

The man smiled proudly. "Yep. He's a handful, but somehow the three of us made the cut. Now we just have to see if the chairman approves of us."

"Or see if you approve of the chairman."

"Have you seen him?"

Stephen hesitated. He didn't really want to get into this conversation. "Yes, I have."

"What does he look like?"

"I think it's better if you wait and see for yourself."

"Is he scary-looking?"

Stephen thought about the question. When he had finally seen the real Morok he had been awed but not scared. Heather told him she'd felt the same. But who knows what others would think? That was precisely why Morok was doing the interviews himself. "I didn't find him scary-looking at all."

"Does he look like us?"

Stephen smiled and stood up. "My son is supposed to meet me in the lobby when he finishes. Good luck to you and your family."

He took the elevator to the lobby and sat down on a sofa to wait. He looked up when the tall dark-haired girl he'd seen upstairs walked by, her arm linked through the arm of a four-star general in full uniform.

"Daddy, he was the most *fabulous* looking creature I have *ever* laid my eyes on," the girl said.

Stephen watched the father and daughter as they crossed the lobby. The finalists and their families had taken an oath of secrecy not to talk to reporters about their interviews with Morok, and for a moment, Stephen was alarmed that the girl and her father would walk straight into the swarm of reporters and television cameras clustered outside the hotel. He relaxed when he saw two men in dark suits appear behind the girl and the general and hustle them toward a side entrance.

He tried to concentrate on his book, but his thoughts wandered. Things were moving so fast now. He wished he could rewind events to the way things were before November 5th.

But did he, really?

He thought of Gerard's excitement about the sojourn and the possibility that his son might return in twenty years, a grown man but maybe one with sound limbs. He thought of this and of the very real possibility of world peace, and he knew he wouldn't do it. He wouldn't roll the tape back to his life before GFED even if he could. The thought made him feel lighter, and he settled back to wait for Gerard.

CHAPTER 69

So, *this* was Morok, Gerard thought. *BFD,* as Gunner would say. He had expected an exotic alien creature, not the grandfatherly humanoid his father had described. The only good thing about it was that they were alone. The other two candidates had been ushered into separate rooms, presumably viewing the same hologram he saw sitting behind the desk. That pleased him, but the chairman's appearance did not. He had spent hours visualizing possible life forms that an intelligent alien species might take, and now it looked as if he was not going to see the real Morok after all. He grinned at the chairman to hide his disappointment.

Morok smiled. "It is a pleasure to meet the son of Dr. Hopkins. I am quite impressed with your father." His voice was exactly as his father had described it—low, melodious, lilting, precise, as if he had learned English as a second language.

"Yes, sir. He's a great guy."

"I am disappointed he does not want to come with us."

"He's sort of torn. He'd really like to go but he also thinks he might be more useful on Earth. Then there's my mom. She doesn't want to go at all."

Morok nodded. "That is understandable."

He clapped his hands sharply and a scene of a rocky red landscape appeared on the wall behind the desk. "We will start the interview with a video," he said, and rolled his chair to one side to give Gerard an unobstructed view.

Looks like Arizona, Gerard thought as he gazed at the landscape. His parents had taken him to the Grand Canyon when he was nine, and he had marveled at its vastness and grandeur. For weeks afterwards, he had scoured the internet for information on the Grand Canyon and the deserts of Arizona.

The camera swooped down into one of the canyons, and he caught his breath. It must have been a fifty-thousand-foot drop from the top of the peak to the canyon floor, and it made the Grand Canyon look like a shallow ditch in the middle of a prairie. The view leveled off at the bottom, then the camera soared back to the top of the mountain range and pulled high above it. As far as the camera's eye could see were pinnacles of red rock. Then, in a dizzying rush, the camera dropped to another narrow canyon floor, lifted back to the rocky peaks, then plunged again into another canyon.

He felt a rush of vertigo as the camera continued to plunge and soar. It was like IMAX, only better, infinitely better. In the distance, he saw a large bird floating on a thermal, a *very* large bird. The camera tracked the bird for a distance, and when it touched down on the edge of a rocky precipice, the camera moved around for a head-on view.

Holy shit! he breathed. Then he stopped breathing altogether.

The bird stood on the pinnacle like a giant mountaineer with its arms—its *arms*—akimbo, and behind the arms, unfurled like an enormous blue-green fan, were wings. For a moment, the wings remained extended, then they drooped downward, surrounding the bird's body like a cape.

Gerard watched, mesmerized, as the camera moved in for a close-up, bringing the bird's face into sharp focus. Its eyes were a golden green and perfectly round, with facets like a cut diamond. It looked straight into the camera with such intelligence and compassion that he was sure the bird could speak.

"We *can* speak."

Gerard stared at the screen, then realized the voice came from within the room. He turned. In front of the chair where the chairman had sat stood was the avian creature from the film. He felt a rush of…something. Excitement, maybe, or perhaps just the satisfaction of met expectations. He stared at Morok for a long moment, not knowing what to say, how to react. All he knew was, *this* did not disappoint him. "You are truly awesome," he said finally.

Morok trilled a laugh. "Do you think you could live among beings like me for twenty years?"

"Oh yes!" Gerard paused. "I have so many questions."

"Ask."

"I don't know where to start."

"Then let me give you a context in which to think about what you have seen. The video shows the predominant landscape of Yxria, my home planet. It is where you will start your sojourn.

Yxria is about the size of Earth, and it has the mountains and canyons you just saw, along with trees a thousand feet tall. The terrain was a major factor in the evolution of my species, which favored creatures that could fly. We evolved from an avian species, just as the Namuh evolved from an ape-like species you call primates."

"Do you have cities?"

"Yes. Our cities are vertical. They are built into the cliffs you saw. Before the development of cities, villages were built in the limbs of the thousand-foot trees."

"Does Yxria have an atmosphere? Will we be able to breathe there?"

"Our atmosphere is not like Earth's. We will have to make a minor adjustment to your respiratory system to enable you to breathe on your own."

Gerard was silent, processing the data, as his father called it.

"I cannot show you everything you will encounter on Yxria. My objective today is simply to observe your reaction to my planet and my species."

"How'd I do?"

"You did well. But you will meet a number of species from other planets who look very different from me. I will introduce you to one that is most unlike native Yxrians. This will give you a glimpse of the range of different beings you will encounter on your sojourn."

Morok emitted a strange sound and a large circle of light appeared on the desk, as if spotlighted from above. Gerard watched it for a moment, then looked at Morok. He repeated the strange sound.

"I'm coming, I'm coming!" The muffled voice came from the circle of light atop the desk. Slowly, an object of about one cubic foot began to take shape in the spotlight. As Gerard watched in astonishment, the object materialized into a short thick creature with a cube-shaped head and torso atop two short squat legs. On both sides of the torso, two spindly arms ended in tiny multi-fingered hands. Its face was embossed, like snakeskin, with a dark olive iridescent cast, and encircling its head were

314

small round bright blue eyes. Gerard thought it looked like a miniature army tank.

"There!" said the tank, when it stood on the desk fully materialized. It cast some of its eyes on Gerard.

"May I introduce Shulag from the planet Koveekio," Morok said.

Shulag stretched out a hand, and Gerard extended his, his heart racing with excitement. He quickly pulled his hand back when Shulag jumped backwards.

"A finger, you idiot!" Shulag's voice sounded like sandpaper stroked across wood.

Gerard glanced at Morok and extended his index finger. Shulag stepped forward and tapped it with all eight fingers on one of his hands. Gerard had once held a baby spider monkey in Mondogo, and it had tapped his neck in much the same way, as if it were playing scales on a piano. When Shulag finished tapping, he backed away and sat down, stretching his legs their full short length.

Gerard turned to Morok and gave him a wide smile. "Awesome! What does he do on Koveekio?"

"Please don't talk about me as if I weren't here!" Shulag grumbled.

Morok trilled a laugh. "There is not enough time to go into the Koveekian culture. I simply wanted to observe your reaction to a species far different from yours or mine."

"Did I pass?" Gerard asked, fearful he hadn't, and he wanted to go on the sojourn now more than ever.

Morok nodded his great head. "To put it in Namuh slang, you passed with flying colors."

#

Stephen looked up to see Gerard zipping across the lobby as fast as he could turn his wheels. He quickly scanned his son's trajectory but saw no small children in danger of being run down.

Gerard slid to a stop in front of him, eyes shining. "Dad, you won't believe it, you just won't believe it."

"You saw Morok?"

315

"Yes, and more, so much more. I don't know where to start."

Stephen stood up. "Let's get out of here first. You can tell me all about it on the way home."

The same two men in dark suits appeared as Stephen and Gerard walked toward the door. "We'll take you out a guarded entrance," one of them said.

Gerard exchanged a look with his father. "Cool!"

CHAPTER 70

Ethan Gorr walked four blocks north on Central Park West and entered the Park on 72nd Street. He followed the narrow path to the Strawberry Fields Memorial and sat down on one of the benches surrounding the mosaic that memorialized John Lennon. Ironic, he thought, that he had chosen this place to talk about circumventing a worldwide peace movement. Lennon would turn over in his grave if he'd had one.

It was early morning and he was alone except for a young couple in jeans and parkas scattering red and white rose petals on the mosaic. *Stupid kids.* How the hell can they care about a long-haired musician who died over forty years ago?

"Mr. Gorr?"

Gorr looked up. A man in khakis and a black windbreaker frowned down at him. He had close-cropped grey hair, square chin, eyes the color of steel. His hands were crammed into the pockets of his jacket.

Gorr stood up. "That's me, General."

The General towered over Gorr by at least a foot. He kept his hands in his pockets. "Let's walk."

They walked north toward the reservoir. Gorr waited for the General to speak. After all, *he* had called Gorr. He was the seller, Gorr, the buyer, and it was a buyer's market.

The General said, "I've heard you can help those of us who are conscientious, who want to protect our countries."

"Ummm…"

The General stopped. He was not used to being obsequious. "I think the United States is in grave danger if it disarms. We will be at the mercy of those who are retaining their arms—"

"But the whole world is disarming, General," Gorr said, feigning innocence.

"Bullshit! The whole world is *talking* about disarming, maybe Norway and Sweden and Costa Rica really are. But who the hell cares about them?"

"I just read that Iran and North Korea are dismantling their nuclear warheads."

"I saw the fanfare and the handshaking and the phony smiles, but what have they really done? Nothing. And what about Russia and China? If they don't disarm, we sure as hell can't. But that idiot in the White House has announced that we will destroy all our nuclear warheads as a sign of our leadership. Leadership hell! He's putting us at the mercy of any country who has the balls to keep a few Little Boys and Fat Men in their arsenals."

They walked on, the General, tall, erect, eyes straight ahead, Gorr quickening his steps to keep up.

"So, here's what I need, Mr. Gorr. I need a safe place to put our nuclear warheads. For every three warheads that are trundled into town and publicly dismantled, I want to keep one in some safe place where we can get our hands on it quickly. For every thousand M16s that we melt down, I want to send a thousand to some safe, accessible location."

"I can handle that."

"How?"

"You tell me the point of origin, give me a week, and I'll get back to you with a proposal."

"It's that easy?"

Gorr barked a laugh. "It's not easy at all, General, but I can do it. And I can do more."

"Like what?"

"This dismantling crap has the weapons manufacturers running scared. They're afraid of being left with huge inventories of weapons that no one wants, so they're discounting them like crazy to anyone who'll buy them."

"Is anyone buying them?"

"Like firewood in Alaska. I can show you some photos..." His voice trailed off.

The General stopped walking. "You have them with you?"

Gorr pulled a packet from his inside coat pocket and took out a photograph. It showed men in fatigues with rifles strapped to their backs loading large crates onto a flat-bed truck parked next to a warehouse bay.

"That's Iran," Gorr said, handing the photograph to the General. He waited a beat, then dealt out the rest of the photos like cards. "China... Bolivia...Russia... North Korea...Venezuela... Pakistan."

The General rifled through the photos. He looked down at Gorr. "Give me a proposal for that too. And soon." He brought his heels together sharply and saluted.

In all his dealings, Gorr had never been saluted. He rather liked it. Not knowing exactly how to return the salute and not wanting to look foolish, he dipped his head in acknowledgment.

The General snapped the salute, turned sharply, and walked away, looking every inch a military man even in khakis and a windbreaker.

As Gorr watched him go, a feeling of satisfaction spread through his body cell by cell. He had just made a covert, completely illegal and probably immoral deal with the head of the whole goddamned Army. He felt invincible.

CHAPTER 71

After the interview, Stephen and Gerard took a taxi to the United Nations headquarters for a tour that Heather had arranged. As they emerged from the cab, a throng of people streamed out of the glass-walled Secretariat building which soared thirty-nine stories in the center of the complex.

"We need to find an elevator," Gerard said, eying the stairs that led up to the entrance.

Stephen shook his head. "No, we're going over there." He pointed toward a long low building on the left. "That's the General Assembly Hall where you'll be introduced." He handed the guard their passes.

Inside, a young guide with long dark hair was waiting for them. "Follow me," she said with a smile. She led them through security and down a hallway to two large double doors. She held a door open and motioned them in. "This is the General Assembly Hall where the sojourner ceremony will take place in two weeks."

The hall was cavernous. To Stephen's eyes, it was half the length of a football field with rows of narrow tables cascading down to a double-tiered dais at the front of the hall.

The guide continued. "Those tables where the UN delegates sit are equipped with earphones that are linked to interpreters so that each delegate can listen to the proceedings in his or her own language."

"The interpreters sit up there, don't they?" Gerard said, pointing to a glass-walled balcony above the hall.

"You're very astute," the guide said.

"I saw it in a movie."

"Then you probably remember the gold-leaf wall from the movie too." She pointed toward the front of the hall. "It's seventy-five feet from the floor to the skylight at the top."

"What's that silver thing hanging in the middle of it?"

"It's the UN emblem, and it's not silver, it is gilded with aluminum leaf."

"And those two big video screens?"

"That's where they project close-ups of the speakers."

"Like in a rock concert!"

320

"Exactly. Would you like to go down front?"

"Sure!"

Stephen followed his son and the guide down a long side aisle to the front of the hall and its two-tiered dais where the guide continued her tour.

"The Secretary-General sits on the upper dais behind the podium, along with the Deputy Secretary-General and the President of the General Assembly, and the speakers stand on the lower dais behind the lectern."

Gerard looked at his father. "Where will we be?"

"Heather said we have a reserved space at the far end of the first row of tables."

Gerard looked around the hall. "Awesome!"

#

Stephen watched his son as he listened to the guide, his eyes shining with excitement. Granted, the hall was spectacular, but it must pale in comparison to the other things Gerard had seen today. In the taxi, he had talked about the spectacular terrain of the planet Yxria and about the exotic Shulag, but mostly he talked about the splendor of Morok.

What other marvels awaited his son on distant planets?

Stephen realized with a start that he was jealous. He had had Morok all to himself for a while; he'd been the privileged one who had seen the extraterrestrial in all his avian glory. Now his son and hundreds of others had seen the chairman, and they had seen the planet Yxria and the tiny creature called Shulag, and they would see more, so much more that he would never get to see.

"It's time to go," the guide said. She continued to chat with Gerard as she led the way up the aisle to the entrance.

Stephen walked glumly behind them, ashamed of his jealousy but unable to shake it.

CHAPTER 72

The next day, Stephen sat at his desk and tried to work but his thoughts kept returning to the sojourn. How could he not go? His life's work had been studying primitive cultures, immersing himself in the daily lives of the tribes, learning their rituals and their history and uncovering the thread of humanity that reaches back into the mists of time. Now he had a chance to study the future amid a culture more exotic than anything he could imagine. How could he not go?

He wandered down the hall, pushed open the door to Gerard's room, and looked around. Weights on the floor, school books piled on his desk, a green light glowing on the computer, all waiting like abandoned toys for the boy to come home and play with them again. What would happen to the room when Gerard left? Would they convert it to another use or leave it untouched to await his return in twenty years?

He had to pull himself out of this spiraling depression.

He went downstairs to find Penny and found a note on the refrigerator door saying she'd gone shopping. He wandered through the den and out into the sunroom where the afternoon sun had warmed and brightened the air. The birds began to shriek when he walked in. He turned on the radio to Penny's favorite classical station and they grew quiet. He watched them for a moment, wondering what evolutionary mutation had taken place on Yxria to produce an avian being like Morok.

"You could learn all about our evolution on the sojourn."

Morok's melodious voice came from behind Stephen. He turned around with anticipation and there stood the iridescent avian, his back to the wall, golden hands clasped across his chest, great wings drooping to the floor, blue-green plume touching the ceiling.

The birds began shrieking again and hurling themselves against the bars of the aviary. Morok trilled a low sound, as if he were singing, and after a moment the birds grew quiet and still.

Stephen felt a tremor of awe as he struggled to keep his voice even. "Did they understand what you were saying?"

Morok shook his great head. "No more than a chimpanzee understands your words. I saw that they responded

322

to your classical music, so I sang a lullaby that we sing to our infants." He paused. "Will you go with us?"

"I wish I could, Mr. Chairman…" He paused, then gave voice to his true feelings. Morok knew them anyway. "I am consumed with envy. I envy my son, I envy Heather, I envy everyone who's going, but I can't go and leave my wife and I don't know how to fight my way out of this debilitating miasma of gloom."

"May I sit?"

"Of course." Stephen motioned to the two wicker chairs that flanked a small table.

Morok lowered himself onto a chair. He lifted his wings and ruffled the feathers, as if trying to get comfortable. His wings drooped to the floor. Stephen took the other chair.

"I understand your devotion to your wife. Some Yxrians mate for life."

"Are you one of those?"

Morok's eyes glowed briefly, then darkened. After a moment, he said, "I think perhaps you will be more valuable here on Earth. I would like you to be the channel for all communications from Yxria during the sojourn. This will be an informal role, but the fact that you are the point of contact may result in some official appointment by your president."

Stephen felt the fog of envy begin to dissipate. It was the next best thing to going on the sojourn. "Thank you, Mr. Chairman. I can't tell you how much this means to me."

"Good. Now let me tell you what must happen on Earth before the sojourners can return. In general terms, the Namuh species must make measurable progress toward world peace. In specific terms, here is how this might be accomplished.

"Your leaders must first tackle poverty. They should make the eradication of poverty a top priority, because poverty is the underlying cause of violence. On Yxria and other planets of the Federation, there is no such thing as poverty. Some citizens enjoy more privileges than others, yes, but no GFED citizen is forced to go without food, shelter, clothing, education, or health care."

"How do we even start?"

"The money your government spends on weapons and maintaining the military could eradicate poverty in one generation. To wipe it out in a single decade, tap the money that is being spent on projects whose only function is to perpetrate a politician's stay in office—I believe it is called 'pork' in your country. Until Earth can bring all its enormous resources to bear on the specter of poverty, violence will never be erased. But your economists can solve this if they put their minds to it and think outside the box, as your business leaders say."

Stephen tried to imagine a leader strong enough to lead the dismantling of the military and the elimination of pork. The latter might be the most difficult.

Morok continued. "Another tool for eradicating violence is education. Educators have the opportunity to shape young minds and thereby shape the future of a nation, of a world, and we take that very seriously in the Federation. Our educators are charged with imparting to our youth the lessons of history and the futility of violence, and to be an educator in the Federation is to join the most prestigious and one of our highest paid professions.

"In comparison, the state of your education is shameful, particularly in the nation in which you live. Your leaders should be setting educational standards for the rest of the world, but you treat your educators like poorly paid servants, giving them neither monetary reward nor respect. It is little wonder that your populace is undereducated. Add to that the pockets of extreme poverty that we see throughout the Namuh civilization and you have a breeding ground for violence. It is beyond my comprehension that this is not apparent to a society that has, despite its young age, made extraordinary advancements in science and technology."

"I couldn't agree with you more, Mr. Chairman, but in a sprawling democratic republic like the United States, educational standards are difficult to enforce."

"Nonsense. Yxria faced similar problems in its past, and we learned to make education a priority. So can your country and all the countries on Earth. If you fail to do so—if you fail to reward and respect those who are in charge of your children's future—planet Earth will never achieve a place in the Galactic Federation."

Morok lifted his wings and readjusted himself on the chair, then let his wings fall to the floor. "You have a great reservoir of religious leaders who can sway hundreds with one sermon, millions with one broadcast. Think what they could do with a sustained directive urging their flocks toward these goals?"

Stephen gave a curt laugh. "Religion has perpetrated violence throughout our history, even to the present day."

"Even more reason it should take a leading role in the eradication of violence."

"Do you have religions in the Federation?"

"Many. But our religions offer joy and solace and transcendence to those who seek them out. The Namuh crusades and inquisitions and jihads have no counterpart in our world." He tilted his great head. "If you remember the hearing, you will know other leaders who should be at the forefront in the eradication of violence."

"Those who promote it?"

"Exactly. Your entertainment industry could stop extolling violent behavior in its games and videos and film. It could stop creating heroes out of killers and refuse to give air time to acts of violence. But even if the industry refuses to relinquish its production and promotion of violence, the people's ultimate refusal to buy their games or go to their movies or tune in to their broadcasts will achieve this goal in the long run."

Morok paused. His golden eyes glowed. "The most important, most far-reaching change will be the most difficult to achieve. You must learn to resolve your disputes peacefully."

Stephen grimaced. "That may be harder than changing our education and economic systems."

"It has to start with your judicial system. As I've said before, your judicial appointments are based too often on political expediency instead of a judge's merits, which leads to judges who are motivated by avarice and power rather than wisdom and fairness. As a result, bribes and cronyism and political favors are rife, from the lowest to the highest levels of your judiciary. This has to change, and the change can begin by establishing a merit-based system at the lowest levels and let it work its way up over time."

"As lower-level judges prove the wisdom of their judgments, they would be elevated to the next level in the judiciary?"

"Yes. That is how it works in most GFED societies. Once such a system is established in the various countries on Earth, it will eventually work its way up to the highest court in the
land—the Supreme Court in your nation. That court and similar high courts in other countries could then supply the talent and wisdom for a Supreme World Court that has jurisdiction over the entire planet.

"That, Dr. Hopkins, is the ultimate method for unifying the Namuh into a global citizenry. When individuals can pledge their loyalty and allegiance to the planet Earth, rather than to specific nations or tribes, then the Namuh will have reached the threshold for entry into the Galactic Federation."

"Will we have any guidance from GFED along the way?"

"Of course. You'll receive regular feedback from members of the sojourn and when deemed necessary, direct guidance from me or other members of GFED.'

Morok rose from the recliner and unfolded himself to his great height. His blue-green plume grazed the ceiling, the tips of his blue-green wings brushed the floor. "If, in twenty years, your world can make progress on all these fronts, the sojourners will return with the knowledge and wisdom to prepare Earth for membership in the Federation."

As Stephen gazed up at Morok, the air around him pulsed and glowed, and then he vanished.

CHAPTER 73

Two weeks later, Heather Eastlake stepped out of the shower at the Crown Plaza Hotel in New York and wrapped herself in a white Turkish towel. It was six-thirty in the morning on the day she would introduce the sojourners to the world in a special ceremony at the United Nations. It was the last public milestone before they departed on their journey across the galaxy.

Last Sunday, she had given interviews to two morning talk shows, and each host had grilled her about her reasons for going. She had given her well-rehearsed answers: to learn first-hand how a civilization became imbued with the idea of peace and how it had implemented those ideas into a practical, day-to-day, grassroots foundation. "I've been an advocate for peace my whole life," she said. "Now I have a chance to put my beliefs into action."

That usually satisfied them, but yesterday, one of them had asked, "What about the sheer adventure of it? Isn't that part of the reason for going?"

As she looked at him with her usual serious expression, she felt something light and bubbly rise from the region of her stomach, and then she was smiling, nodding her head, and then—she blushed at the memory—she had started giggling, then laughing uncontrollably. They had thankfully cut away for a commercial while she recovered. The outburst was so unlike her that she had to field phone calls all evening from concerned friends asking if she was all right. She could only attribute it to the unrelieved tension of the past few months.

Wrapped in the white Turkish towel, she studied the two outfits she had laid out on the hotel bed. One was a dark grey silk-and-wool pantsuit with a Mandarin collar and dark grey pumps; the other, a long-sleeved cinnamon-colored cashmere dress that stopped mid-calf, paired with nutmeg-colored boots. She pictured herself standing in front of the podium in each. The pantsuit made her feel elegant and supremely confident. The dress made her feel feminine and sexy. She'd worn each on different television talk shows and on some of her Sojourner interviews, and she noticed that when she wore the dress, men became flirtatious or chivalrous. When she wore the pant suit, they tended to be competitive on the one hand, deferential on the other.

That decided it. She was the sojourn leader. She must look confident and capable of shepherding some 1200 individuals on the most important journey of their lives. She hung the dress back in the closet.

Already, a butterfly fluttered in her stomach. She thought of standing before the leaders of the world in the UN General Assembly Hall and facing the television cameras that would broadcast the ceremony live around the world. One newscaster estimated that more than a billion citizens across the planet would be watching or listening to the broadcast. Suddenly, one butterfly became a flock beating their wings against the walls of her stomach.

She had to quit thinking like that. This would be a once-in-a-lifetime experience, one she could never repeat, so she had better do it right. Then another thought broke through the chatter in her mind. If she was lucky and the world was vigilant enough to follow the path to peace, she could be accepting kudos at another UN ceremony in twenty years when the sojourners returned.

"Hold that thought," she told herself. She dropped the towel and began to get dressed.

#

Stephen and Penny sat in the Crown Plaza restaurant waiting for Gerard. Penny had wanted to wait for him in their adjoining room, but Stephen insisted they meet him in the restaurant, saying he needed to get used to making his way around an unfamiliar place. Now she sipped her coffee and watched the restaurant door anxiously. "The closer it gets to the day of departure, the more fearful I become. I'm afraid that when he actually starts to leave, I'll throw myself in his path and refuse to move." She smiled a weak smile to show she was joking, though she almost thought it was possible she would do just that.

Stephen patted her hand. "You'll be fine."

"So, tell me again exactly how this is going to go today." She saw the patient look on Stephen's face, as if he were dealing with a child who wasn't very bright. "I know, we went through all this last night—"

"And the night before."

"Just indulge me, Stephen. Please."

"Okay. A car will pick us up in front of the hotel and drive us to the UN. There will actually be a red carpet for our arrival and I'm pretty sure there will be photographers and TV cameras lined up on either side."

"And those awful protestors." Protestors had been standing in front of the hotel last night when they arrived, chanting slogans, and waving placards. *MOROK IS THE ANTICHRIST... SAVE OUR CHILDREN...THE SOJOURN IS EVIL...SATAN IS TAKING OUR CHILDREN.* She had wanted to grab Gerard and head back to Georgetown and try to forget how much the world was changing.

"Them, too," Stephen said and continued to describe the day's agenda as it had been explained to them in the sojourner's Introductory Packet. "There is a staggered schedule for arrivals to smooth the flow of people into the UN building. Ours is at 9:15, and when we get there, we'll take our places in a reserved section on the main floor of the General Assembly Hall."

"And there's a special place for Gerard's wheelchair?"

He nodded. "That's why we get to sit in the front row."

"That couldn't have anything to do with the fact that you're the Earth Ambassador to GFED, could it?"

"Maybe a little." He smiled at his wife. He didn't know how Morok had done it, but a week ago, the UN had given him the official position and the Secretary-General had announced it to the world. It had pleased Stephen greatly.

He went on. "The ceremony will start with a short speech by the Secretary-General, then President Wainwright will make a few remarks, and then Heather will introduce the sojourners. When she reads a name, the sojourner will stand and wave or bow or make some kind of acknowledgement."

Penny looked at him with alarm. "You didn't tell me that! How's Gerard supposed to stand up and take a bow?"

"I didn't tell you because it would have just been one more thing for you to worry about. Gerard will move into the

329

aisle, pivot his chair to face the audience, and raise his hand in the air."

"But will people be able to see him?"

"He'll be spotlighted when his name is announced. Just as the others will be."

"Has this been rehearsed? Will the spotlight operator know where to find him?"

"Penny, you worry too much. We'll be in reserved seats, so whoever's running the lights will know where to look."

"Does Gerard know about this?"

"Yes, he knows all about it."

"What happens after the sojourners are introduced?"

"There'll be a closing ceremony of some kind."

Penny studied her husband. He and Gerard had forged a close bond since November when all this started. At the same time, her son seemed to distance himself from her. He had resented her in the beginning for refusing to believe Stephen had been abducted and had grown more resentful as she tried to prevent him from applying for the sojourn. It hurt her deeply, but she didn't know how she could have behaved otherwise. "Are you sorry you're not going?" she asked.

He hesitated. His despondency had lessened since he had been made Earth Ambassador to the sojourn, but he knew he would lose the bond that had grown between him and Gerard since last November, and for that he regretted not being part of the sojourn. And the sheer adventure of it had tugged at him when he watched Heather's mildly hysterical response on the Sunday talk show. But he was satisfied with his decision to remain on Earth. Even before his appointment last week as Earth's Ambassador to GFED, he had felt, immodestly, that he could make an important contribution here on Earth to the most important journey humans were likely to make in his lifetime. His official role simply added ballast to his decision to stay behind, and it would permit him to stay in more frequent contact with Gerard and Heather and Morok. He could live with that.

"You're sorry you're not going with him." Penny looked as if she were about ready to break into tears again.

Stephen shook his head. "Pen, I don't deny that I wanted to go at first, but staying here makes more sense. In a way,

Gerard and I will be a team working toward the same goal. He'll be out there learning how to lead our world into the future; I'll be here helping to lay the groundwork on which that future will be built."

He reached for her hand. "I'm not sorry at all that we're staying home on planet Earth."

#

On the twentieth floor of the Crown Plaza, Gerard pulled the new black cashmere sweater over his head, smoothed it across his chest, pushed the sleeves up. Black was his favorite color. If he had his way, he would wear nothing but black t-shirts, sweatshirts, sweaters, and jeans, but his mom made him promise to dress nicely, as she put it, for the ceremony, so he wore the same grey trousers that he'd worn for his interview with Morok, and the blue sports coat hung on the doorknob ready to go. But beneath the sweater was the black t-shirt he'd bought from a vendor outside the hotel. Across the front in white letters were the words that had quickly become the slogan of the day: "I AM NAMUH!" When the ceremony was over, he could take off the sweater and jacket and be himself.

He looked in the mirror and brushed his short hair, then pulled at it with his fingers, trying to make his cowlick go the right way. He wasn't usually vain. How could you be vain sitting in a wheelchair? People never really saw you, just the chair, and then they stuck a label on you and that's all they saw after that, a label that said '*Cripple.*' No matter that the politically correct term was *disabled* or *physically challenged*, the label in everyone's mind was still *cripple*. But today was different. On television, people would see his face, not the chair. It was only natural to care what he looked like.

He studied his reflection. He raised his right arm in the air as he'd been instructed to do when he was introduced, so that he could be more easily spotted by the crowd. The gesture looked lame. He brought his hand to his shoulder, pushed his arm straight up. That looked like he was raising his hand to go to the bathroom. He did it again with a sharper upward thrust. Better. He curled his hand into a fist, brought the fist to his shoulder, thrust his arm upward sharply. Better still. He did it again, punching air like the anti-Sojourn protestors in front of the hotel. His image stared back at him, angular face, square chin, blue eyes bright behind steel-rimmed glasses, fist raised boldly in the air.

"*Yes*," he said aloud, and headed downstairs to meet his parents.

#

On the floor above Gerard, the Reverend Marshall Hopkins checked himself in the full-length mirror on the back of the bathroom door. Black suit, white shirt, bright blue tie, silver-grey hair with a slight wave in front, his unlined face as tanned as if he'd spent a week in the Bahamas, thanks to the miracle of spray-on tans. He looked handsome and distinguished, if he did say so himself. Too bad he wouldn't be in the spotlight today. He had given countless invocations at inaugurations and graduations and other ceremonies. Anytime an ecumenical religious touch was needed, he was usually called upon. But this was the UN. He wasn't quite ecumenical enough for the UN. In their view, if one religious speech was given, they would have to allow a hundred to encompass the multitude of religions represented at the UN. So, today's ceremony would have no invocation of any kind.

Did that mean religious convocations at public events would die out over time? That would be a shame, but the existence of superior alien civilization had created waves of existential doubt about religion. Religious fundamentalism of any kind was being viewed as primitive, barbaric even, and Hopkins sometimes felt doubt eating away at his own faith. As far as he knew, the aliens didn't have any answers about the afterlife, and he did not want to try to reconstruct a whole new belief system at his advanced age. He was comfortable, more or less, with the idea that God was big enough to have created the whole universe. He did not want to examine the concept too closely. Some things you just have to accept on faith.

He took a brush from his suitcase and brushed the shoulders of his black suit, then gave his silver hair one last pat and headed downstairs to meet his family for breakfast.

#

Abigail Moore watched a family of four at a table across the room: a good-looking man who resembled some middle-aged actor she couldn't quite place, a small, tense-looking woman with dark curly hair, an older silver-haired man who looked familiar in the way that all gray-haired older men look familiar, and a boy in a wheelchair. The boy turned his head so that she saw him face-on. For a second they stared at each other, then the boy lifted a hand and nodded in her direction.

It was that boy from the interviews. She had noticed him the day they were waiting for their meeting with Chairman Morok. Since he was here, he must have made the cut too. She returned the wave and looked away quickly.

"Daddy!" She punched at the newspaper hiding her father's face. "Daddy, see that boy over there?"

Her father lowered the paper and looked at her over his reading glasses. He glanced in the direction she was motioning with her eyes. "The one sitting across from Marshall Hopkins?"

"The preacher?" Abby shot a quick look at the table. "So *that's* who he is. But the boy, Daddy, look at the boy."

"I see him."

"He's one of the sojourners."

Her father frowned. "When did you meet him?"

"I haven't actually, I saw him at our interviews. Isn't he cute? I mean, there were a couple of sorta cute guys at the interviews, but none as cute as him."

"Abigail! You are not going on this mission to find a boyfriend. Besides, he's a cripple."

She shot her father a haughty look. "For your information, General, he is physically challenged, not crippled. Anyway, I doubt that either label will apply once he gets off this backward little planet."

"What do you mean?"

"Surely GFED can cure something as simple as paralysis, what with their millions of extra years to work on it."

"Don't count on it, Abigail. And don't forget that you are under strict orders to behave yourself on this mission and not act like a tart."

"Daddy! When have I *ever* acted like a tart?"

General Moore gave his daughter a stern look, and she let loose with a merry laugh.

#

Across town, Ethan Gorr turned on the television and lit a cigar and waited for the opening ceremonies at the UN to begin. There had been nothing in the news about the chairman of the aliens appearing at the ceremony, but you never knew. He'd heard rumors he looked like a bird, a gigantic goddamned bird. For all he knew, it was an actor in a bird suit, part of a scheme cooked up by world leaders to take people's minds off their problems. That made a whole hell of a lot more sense than intelligent beings from another planet. Still, he didn't want to miss the chance to see the birdman if he happened to make an appearance.

He puffed on the cigar. Whatever it was, fake or real, this worldwide peace movement was a windfall for him. In a few short weeks, he had made millions helping presidents and princes and generals and sheiks hide their weapons. Then he'd doubled those millions selling them more arms that he'd bought at rock-bottom prices from panicked weapons manufacturers. *Fear and greed.* It was a game Gorr delighted in playing. By the time this silly peace movement was over, he would be one of the richest men on the planet and he could buy his brothers out of Gorr Resources and be rid of them once and for all.

CHAPTER 74

Heather Eastlake sat at a small table at the front of the General Assembly Hall and watched President Wainwright as he addressed the crowd from the lectern on the lower dais. He looked strong and confident as he talked about the hope that the Galactic Sojourn would pave the way for peace and unprecedented scientific progress. She listened for a moment, then glanced at the peaceful face of the Secretary-General, who sat on the upper dais between the Deputy Secretary-General and the President of the General Assembly, then lifted her eyes to the UN emblem on the gold canted wall, a map of the world viewed from above the North Pole and flanked by olive wreaths. And yet, in stark contrast to that emblem of peace, armed guards lined the walls on either side of the dais holding their long guns tight to their chests. She thought they were unnecessary in a world moving rapidly toward peace, but perhaps they were just for show.

She fingered the tab of the folder that held the list of the sojourners' names and looked out across the packed Hall. The Sojourners and their families sat with the UN delegates; their aides relegated to the balcony with the media. She saw Stephen and Penny at the front row of tables on the other side of the Hall with Gerard's chair pulled up at the end. She spotted Abigail Moore and her father in his dress uniform. She looked for Calvin Williams but could not see him from where she sat.

As Wainwright droned on, Heather let her mind wander. She was disappointed that Morok had declined to attend the ceremony. He'd told her that the day belonged to the sojourners and said he would make his appearance before the world at a later date. That was a week ago. She had expected to receive some kind of message last night or today, wishing her well, maybe telling her to 'break a leg,' as Stephen had done in an email, but no doubt, such rituals were different on Yxria. Face it! *Everything* would be different on Yxria.

She tensed as she heard Wainwright winding down his speech, his face projected in close-up on the twin video screens that flanked the canted gold wall. In minutes, she would be standing there with her face magnified on those screens. Her heart fluttered in anticipation as he returned to his seat amid polite applause.

The Secretary-General leaned toward his microphone. "Honored Sojourners, distinguished delegates and guests, ladies and gentlemen. May I present the Director of the Galactic Sojourn, Dr. Heather Eastlake."

Oh god! She took a deep breath and clutched the folder in one hand and climbed the few steps to the dais. She stood behind the lectern and waited for the applause to subside, amused by the undignified whistles and cheers that no doubt came from the younger Sojourners. She swept her gaze across the room and there he was in the fourth row. Calvin Williams. He caught her eye and smiled broadly. She gave him a discreet tilt of her head.

The applause faded, but before she could speak a haunting melody drifted through the Great Hall. She hesitated. *What was going on? There had been no music planned.* As she waited politely for the music to end, a woman's keening voice, mournful, full of sorrow, cut through the melody and sent a chill down her spine. She now recognized the piece as Rachmaninoff's *Vocalise,* one she had not heard since her brother's funeral. She held on to the lectern and looked out over the crowd and smiled as if the music were part of the ceremony. Inside, she was seething. How could they have done this without telling her! *And who the hell chose this funeral dirge!* If music was needed, it should have been a celebratory piece, like Beethoven's *Ode to Joy.* She waited with a sense of foreboding as the haunting voice soared through the vast Hall.

CHAPTER 75

"I am Morok, Chairman of the Galactic Federation."

The crowd burst into murmurs as the deep, melodious voice echoed through the hall. Morok was going to make an appearance after all. Heather caught Stephen's eye in the front row. He gave a small shrug, as if to say, I knew nothing about this.

"It seems we have an unexpected guest of honor," she said.

There was a ripple of applause, punctuated with a few whoops from the sojourners. When Morok materialized on the dais beside the lectern, the applause grew louder. He was dressed as always in a dark grey suit, white shirt, red tie. Heather let out the breath she didn't know she'd been holding. She inclined her head toward him, gave an 'after-you' gesture. She thought it would be impolite to leave the dais, so she sat down in a chair to the left of the lectern.

Morok moved to the front of the dais and held up his hand. "Silence!"

His voice carried such a commanding tone that the silence was immediate and total.

"I am sorry to disrupt this ceremony, but I felt it only fair to make my announcement before the introduction of the sojourners. They will be the ones most immediately affected by what I have to say." He paused. "The Galactic Sojourn is cancelled."

There was a ripple of sound from the audience, and then an eruption of protest, loud and cacophonous. Heather started out of her chair, then sat back down, confused, fearful.

"Silence!" Morok commanded, and again, silence fell over the room. "I went to extraordinary lengths to convince the Galactic Federation to withdraw its plans to exterminate the human race and to accept my proposal for the Galactic Sojourn. Our scientists wanted a chance to study the Namuh at close range because, despite its shortcomings, the human race appears to be unique in the galaxy. I believed we could teach the Namuh sojourners our advanced ways and send them back to you in twenty years to lead your planet into the future. I do not believe your leaders understood the extraordinary offer we were making."

"Here was a chance to advance your science and medicine and technology thousands of years in a single generation. Here was a chance to learn how to live peacefully and creatively together as a society, instead of expending all your resources and energy killing one another. Here was a chance to join the Galactic Federation thousands of years before you were truly ready.

The deep rich tones of Morok's voice engulfed the room. "All that was required from your leaders was to make an effort to stop the violence. Stop the killing. Prove that you can live in harmony with the rest of the galaxy. It is now clear that you cannot do this and no one is more disappointed than I."

The audience began to murmur and whisper.

Morok held up his hand and the audience grew quiet.

"Your leaders pretended to disarm," he continued. "They made motions of moving toward peaceful settlements of their disputes. Many nations signed truces, peace treaties, agreed to reduce their arms and end their conflicts. But in fact, more than half the nations represented in this room are secretly *increasing* their stockpile of weapons. Three nations are hiding nuclear warheads."

He paused as a protest swept through the audience, muted at first, then growing louder. Uniformed guards inched their way up the stairs on either side of the dais. Above the sound of the crowd, a voice rang out. "You're an imposter, old man, get off the stage!" Others picked up the chant, "Get off the stage! Get off the stage!"

Something hit Morok on the shoulder. It looked like a piece of crumpled paper, but it fell to the dais with a thud. The next missive struck his head just above his right ear.

Heather came out of her seat and stepped toward Morok, then stopped as the air around him shimmered. Another missive bounced off the air in front of his face, as if some sort of force-field now surrounded him. Then, in an instant, the real Morok appeared in all his avian majesty, arms akimbo, blue-green wings drooping floorward. The twin video screens showed a vivid close-up of his iridescent feathered face with its golden eyes, black-beak nose, and bright blue crest that reached two feet above his head.

The audience gave a collective gasp. Then came a few shouts and whistles, presumably from sojourners who recognized him from their interviews. Guards rushed at him from both sides, only to be deflected by his force-field.

He spread his wings, eliciting another gasp from the audience. Except for those who had seen the real Morok, the audience sat in deep shock. Some dropped to their knees, others crossed themselves. The lighting engineer recovered quickly at his station in the balcony at the back of the Hall. He had been instructed to lower the house lights when Heather began the introductions, then spotlight each sojourner the introductions were made. Now he lowered the house lights and flooded Morok with a bright white light.

Morok lowered his wings. "I see that some of you have fallen to your knees," he said with great sadness in his voice. "But I am not a god. I am a being who has evolved through millions of years to reach the state you now see. We have different origins—mine, avian, yours, simian—but you are on a similar evolutionary path. If we spare you—and if you don't destroy yourselves first—you could someday, on your own, develop the technology to travel the galaxy at will."

Heather saw a movement in her peripheral vision. The guards who had been standing with their backs to the wall moved aside, and in their place appeared a UN Special Ops team in full attack gear. She guessed immediately what must have happened. Already on high alert, the tension ratcheted up when the gigantic avian appeared on the dais. His words about destroying the human race must have triggered a command to attack.

One soldier lifted his weapon and screamed at Morok: "Drop to your knees!" Another fired at him. The sounds echoed in the Hall, but the bullet dropped to the floor, deflected by the force shield. Heather saw a look of bewilderment on the soldier's face.

"*I'm not finished!*"

Morok's booming voice paralyzed the audience. He raised his wings, ruffled the wingtips, and a sound like wind through palmettos rippled through the hall.

The soldiers backed away, kept backing away until they stood with their backs against the walls. They held their weapons across their chests, some of their hands shaking so hard that Heather could hear the little slap-slap sounds the guns made against the soldiers' chests.

Morok lowered his wings. "Throughout the ages your own prophets have tried to steer you onto the right path and you never listened. You might have thought you were listening but you got it *wrong* every time. You got it wrong because you heard the message through a scrim of fear and disbelief, and that fear and disbelief always led to violence."

Suddenly, standing where the avian Morok had stood was a long-haired, gray-bearded man in flowing white robes. In his hands was a large flat stone. On the video screens, his eyes blazed like fire. His voice boomed and echoed off the walls and ceiling of the hall.

"Your god commanded, 'Thou shall not kill!' and the message was written in stone so that the words would not be misunderstood as the commandments were passed down through the ages. And what did you do? You twisted the commandment into a mandate for evil and killed your brothers and sisters indiscriminately if their skin was of a different color, their beliefs a different hue. Your god's message was clear and strong—but *you got it wrong!*"

The white-robed apparition metamorphosed into another bearded man in a white robe and sandals with short gray hair crowned with a green laurel.

"In a Golden Age on Earth, I taught justice and tolerance and logic and reason. I urged you to choose leaders from the wisest and most just of your populace, to make your philosophers your kings. And what did you do? You put me to death, lost my teachings for centuries, and immersed yourselves in barbarism and violence. My message was clear and precise and imbued with reason. You listened but you didn't hear, and *you got it wrong!*"

The Greek philosopher morphed into a likeness of the Buddha, and as he spoke, the Buddha's features melded into those of Confucius, Lao-Tzu, and other Asian philosophers and teachers known only to their descendants who now sat in the UN General Assembly Hall.

"I taught that it was possible to overcome violence and eliminate killing. I taught that leaders should rule the world by moral example, not by force and violence. I taught the universal laws of cause and effect, that what you sow in this lifetime will come back to you in the next. I taught you to believe in the unity and sacredness of all life. What did you do? You ignored us, you imprisoned us, you persecuted us. Our message was clear, and you listened but you didn't hear, and *you got it wrong!*"

The philosophers merged into the persona of Jesus of Nazareth with his long flowing hair, gentle brown eyes, peasant robe, sandaled feet.

"I urged you to love your neighbor as you love yourself. I told you that the kingdom of God is within you, that the meek shall inherit the earth. And what did you do? You nailed me to a cross and left me to die under the blazing sun. Over the centuries, you have fought hundreds of wars in my name, you have tortured your sisters and brothers in my name, you have slaughtered millions of your fellow citizens in my name. My message could not have been clearer. You listened but you didn't hear, and *you got it wrong!*"

The words echoed in the Great Hall, and then the image of Jesus morphed into the bearded, turbaned persona of the prophet Mohammed.

> "I came from the same lineage as Jesus of Nazareth and I bore a similar message: That the power of peace is stronger than the power of violence. That enemies should be turned into friends. That one should treat one's brothers with mercy, equality, brotherhood. And what did you do? You have warred with your Christian brothers for centuries, each of you killing the other in the name of one god whom we called by different names. You have even warred with your own kind for more than a thousand years, warred about whether my grandchild had the right to sainthood. I brought a message of equality and peace, and you listened, but you didn't hear. And *you got it wrong!*"

The image of Mohammed transformed into a thin, barefoot Mahatma Gandhi dressed in loin cloth and shawl.

> "I taught that nonviolence is the greatest force at the disposal of humankind. I used it as a potent weapon against the evils in my country. I lived a life of truth and non-violence, both concepts as old as the hills of my beloved homeland. My message was crystal clear, but you obliterated it by murdering me. You listened but you didn't hear, and *you got it wrong!*"

Gandhi's features reconfigured themselves into the persona of Dr. Martin Luther King.

> "I had a dream that nonviolence could be a powerful moral force for transforming society. I had a dream that humans could overcome oppression and violence without resorting to violence and oppression. I had a dream that sooner or later all the people of the world would discover a way to live together in peace and equality. And what did you do? You shot me dead on a

balcony in Memphis and put an end to our dreams of peace. I spent my life speaking only of peace, and brothers and sisters, you listened, but you didn't hear. *And you got it wrong!*"

Finally, the avian Morok returned. He stood in majestic silence, blue-green wings brushing the floor of the dais. When he spoke, his voice filled the hall in a way the other voices had not. "You have had other teachers, not all well known, but all with the same urgent message: *Violence is wrong. It doesn't work. It resolves nothing.*

"Your prophets and teachers offered you a way to escape the cycle of violence, just as I have done. The dream so eloquently evoked by your most recent prophet was within your grasp—you had an extraordinary opportunity to become a peaceful society that can coexist with others in our great galaxy. Yet your leaders could not see beyond their limited horizons of fear and greed. But make no mistake—your leaders do not bear all the blame for this failure of vision. They are a product of the Namuh culture, and it is that culture that is sick to the core."

He looked out over the audience, looked directly into the television cameras that were broadcasting his image around the world. His golden eyes went soft and dark, like pieces of smoldering coal. The *Vocalise* curled its way through the Great Hall, wrapped itself around Morok, eddied up toward the skylight.

His voice rang through the hall like the tolling of a bell. "I am no prophet, but I brought you a message of peace from across the galaxy. I offered you escape from your centuries of violence. You pretended to listen, but you did not hear. For the last time, *you got it wrong.*"

In the silence of the Great Hall, he lifted his arms, spread his great blue-green wings, and vanished.

CHAPTER 76

Heather gazed out at the frozen faces of the crowd in the Great Hall. *Should she say something?* Surely some leader would take charge, the Secretary-General, President Wainwright, somebody! A murmur swept through the crowd as two Secret Service agents approached the President and hustled him toward an exit. Others were making similar exits, but the sojourners and their families sat in stunned silence.

She walked to the lectern, hoping her trembling knees wouldn't give way. She had no idea what she was going to say. She cleared her throat, tapped the microphone, which responded with an electronic ping. "Ladies and gentlemen."

Her voice came out low, almost hoarse. She could feel the focus of the crowd's attention, heavy with expectation. "I think it's safe to say that we are all in shock right now. Perhaps the best thing we can do is to go home and think about what Chairman Morok has said. Perhaps our leaders will find some way—"

Her voice broke. She felt tears well up. *Find some way to do what? Give the world back the hope it had an hour ago?* She looked up at the Secretary-General, still sitting behind her on the upper dais. She made a helpless motion with her hand.

He leaned toward his microphone. "This special meeting of the United Nations is temporarily adjourned. We will reconvene at some future date."

The crowd began to stir, stand up, shuffle toward the exits. Heather stumbled to her chair and sat down.

"Heather."

She blinked rapidly, focused on Stephen's face through her tears.

He held out his hand. "Come back to Georgetown with us. We'll stop by your hotel so you can get your things."

She saw his family lined up behind him: Penny had tears flowing freely down her face, Gerard managed a faint smile, and an older man she recognized as Reverend Marshall Hopkins was looking at her with great compassion. She knew if she tried to speak, she would break down completely. She stuffed her folder in her briefcase and took Stephen's hand and walked down the steps and out the door of the General Assembly Hall.

#

Outside the UN, protesters cheered when they learned the sojourn was canceled. Around the world, people had watched Morok's speech with the same disbelief with which they had watched the twin towers crumble two decades ago.

On *Air Force One*, the President telephoned his chief of staff. "I want you to do two things: Set up a press conference in thirty minutes and call the head of the FBI. Tell him to find out if anyone in the Pentagon authorized the stockpiling of weapons."

#

Across Manhattan, Ethan Gorr switched off the television in the middle of Heather's brief speech and walked over to the window overlooking Central Park. What he had just seen could have been a Hollywood production staged to shock people into submission, then control them with assurances that the aliens were gone. He'd never really believed they were real in the first place, never believed they were going to kill off the human race just because of a little bit of violence.

Hell, violence was part of the human condition. Nothing was going to change that. Now, with the aliens out of the way, the world would return to normal. He'd have his logging contracts and his little side deals here and there. All that had made him a rich man. Nothing to be ashamed of. But he was loath to see the weapons deals slip through his fingers. That would have made him a billionaire. Right up there with Bezos, Gates, Musk, and Zuckerberg.

He lit a cigar and considered the alternative. What if things didn't go back to the way they were? What if the UN went on a witch hunt and tried to find out which nations had the temerity to stockpile weapons? If his contacts were revealed, they might incriminate him. Hell, they *would* incriminate him. And then what would happen? Congressional investigations? Special prosecutors? World Court tribunals? But had he broken

345

any actual laws? That didn't really matter, of course, because once the names of the offenders got out, the shit would hit the fan and he would be smeared along with General Moore and Barrios and all the others.

He puffed on the cigar. Maybe he should disappear before the investigations started. His money was already safely offshore. He could go anywhere in the world. Live like a sheik. Run his legitimate companies through intermediaries. Come back when all this had blown over and pick up where he left off.

He picked up the phone and punched in a number. "Get the jet ready to leave for the Cayman Islands."

Flying to the Caymans would get him out of the country and put him in close proximity to his money. From there he could go anywhere. Anywhere in the world.

CHAPTER 77

Stephen drove in silence all the way from New York to Washington. His father, sitting in the passenger seat, had dozed off by the time they reached the New Jersey Turnpike, and Penny and Heather sat in the middle seat brooding. In the back of the van, Gerard stared dejectedly out the window. No one seemed ready to talk about what had happened or speculate on what might happen next.

Stephen replayed Morok's speech and grew more discouraged by the mile. The chairman had been GFED's primary advocate for the human race, maybe its *only* advocate, and now he had turned against them. And rightly so. If humans couldn't take even the first steps toward peace, what hope was there of transforming Earth into a peaceful planet?

He tried to shake off his despondency, tried to look at the situation from an anthropological point of view. A primitive society typically distrusts outsiders; the more different the outsiders, the greater the distrust. To gain the trust of the Abigo, he had spent several months over the course of three years, living with them, learning their customs. They had just begun to trust him when the little shaman was shot on orders of an American. The more advanced society had betrayed the primitive society, a pattern repeated throughout human history. But now the primitive society had betrayed the advanced one. Humans had tried to deceive GFED, not because a few rogue nations distrusted the Federation but because they distrusted each other. If a nation disarmed completely, it would be defenseless against its enemies on *Earth*.

A thought began to nag at Stephen as the countryside rolled by, gray and desolate under heavy skies. GFED scientists wanted to study humans' memory redundancy because, as Morok had said, such a memory structure could conceivably undermine GFED's ability to detect and thereby prevent crimes. That was the reason the sojourn had been approved by the Federation. Did the cancellation of the sojourn also cancel GFED's interest in the Namuh memory structure? If it didn't...

Stephen's right foot went slack and the car began to slow as Morok's words came back to him. *We could simply take them the way we took you and Dr. Eastlake.*

Several cars passed him in rapid succession before he realized he had slowed to forty miles per hour. He accelerated back up to seventy. The volunteers had wanted to go on the sojourn and maybe they still did. What if GFED just took them the way they took him and Heather? What if they simply went missing one morning and were never heard from again?

Stephen's gloom grew as he drove the last fifty miles into Washington with Morok's words reverberating in his head: *We could simply take them.*

#

Heather was paralyzed by the turn of events. She lay on the bed in the Hopkins' guest room and stared at the ceiling. What would she do now? Go back to the university? Try to pick up her life where she had left off? The bigger question, of course, was: Would GFED proceed with extermination, or would they quarantine the planet and leave Earth to its own violent fate?

She could not give up, she decided. Surely, she could do something to convince Morok to give them another chance. She had discovered over the past weeks that when she really needed to talk with him, to ask a question or seek his guidance about some aspect of the sojourn, he had always appeared. Obviously, he monitored her and was aware when she needed his help. Once, wondering if she could deliberately summon him, she entered into a meditative state and concentrated her thoughts on him. He had appeared in her study shortly afterward with a wry "You called?"

Maybe she could do it again. She sat on the bed in the lotus position and concentrated on her breathing. When she was relaxed, she tried to visualize Morok's avian features while silently chanting, "Talk to me, talk to me, talk to me." But his image kept changing in her head, as it had in the General Assembly Hall, into first one prophet and then another, echoing the words: *You got it wrong!* After twenty minutes, she gave up. The connection had been broken. He was no longer listening.

348

#

Gerard went straight to his computer. His dad had asked him if he wanted to talk, and all he could do was shake his head. He didn't trust himself to speak for fear he would start bawling like a three-year-old whose favorite toy had been snatched away. He logged on to KASA and saw that Gunner was online, waiting in their private chat room.

g-man	did you see morok's speech?
stargunner	yeah but moley just told me something even more dramatic he knows of one country for sure that's stockpiling weapons
g-man	really?
moleman	it's us
g-man	the united states?
moleman	yeah the good old u s of a
g-man	how do you know?
moleman	i work at the pentagon I hear things
g-man	you gotta report this to someone
stargunner	hang on to your mouse g-man I have a better plan
g-man	what kind of plan?
stargunner	one that will fulfill kasa's destiny listen closely...

After Gunner logged off, Gerard sat and stared at the screen. His plan was crazy. Ambitious. Incredible. But it might work. And if it did, the sojourn could be restored and his life would no longer be over. If it weren't for one small problem, he would be popping wheelies with excitement. But at the moment, that problem overshadowed everything else in his mind.

CHAPTER 78

The next morning, Gerard rolled down the hall to his dad's study. The door was open, but he hesitated when he saw Stephen pecking away at his computer.

"Dad?"

"Yes?" He kept typing.

"I need to talk to you."

"Can it wait a while, son? I'm trying to figure out what Heather and I can do to get the sojourn back on track."

"Dad, Moleman knew about the secret stockpiling of weapons."

Stephen stopped typing and turned toward his son. "Come on in."

Gerard rolled into the room and parked his chair close to the door. He chewed his lower lip. "Moley knew about one country that was stockpiling weapons, even before Morok's speech yesterday."

"Which country was it?"

"The U.S."

Stephen studied his son. "That's a serious allegation. How does your friend know about it?"

"He's an intern at the Pentagon. He heard stuff."

"Has he told the authorities?"

"Not yet."

"Gerard, your friend needs to report this to his supervisor."

"Gunner has a plan. He's flying in tomorrow from California to meet with Moley and me. He thinks KASA can get the sojourn back on track."

His dad was alarmed. "This is not just about the sojourn. All humanity is at stake here. It's not a matter for kids."

"But we're not kids, Dad." He corrected himself. "Well, Gunner and Moley aren't kids, they're in their twenties, and they're really smart. Gunner's smarter than anybody I know. He was a boy genius at Cal Tech, and now he's a whiz kid in the space industry."

350

"That's beside the point. Promise me you'll tell your friend to report this. If he doesn't want to go to his supervisor, tell him to call the FBI."

Another problem had been weighing on Gerard's mind, ever since his KASA friends had decided to meet. "Dad, I lied to them."

"What? Who did you lie to?"

"I lied to Gunner and Moley."

His father's face hardened with suspicion. "Did you know anything about that weapons stockpiling?"

"Oh, no, not that," Gerard said. "You see, I met Gunner and Moley three years ago on the Internet and I never thought I'd ever see them in person. Now I have to go meet them, and they'll know I lied the minute they see me—" He stopped to catch his breath.

"Slow down, Gerard. What did you lie about to your friends?"

Gerard took a deep breath. "I wanted to fit in. I was just thirteen and they were in their twenties and…I let them think I knew a lot about computer science and math."

"That part is true."

"I said I was eighteen and getting ready to start college at Georgetown and that I was on the Georgetown tennis team. Which means they don't know about…this." He motioned toward his wheelchair.

The misery on his son's face made Stephen wince. Not once in six years had he heard Gerard complain about his condition or even mention it with any hint of self-pity. Even now it wasn't his being in a wheelchair that was bothering him, but that he'd lied about it to his friends.

"I feel like a fraud. If Morok had known I lied, I'd never have been accepted on the sojourn. Now I have to confess to Gunner and Moley, and they'll probably never speak to me again."

Stephen patted his knee. "Come over here, son."

Gerard rolled slowly toward his dad, stopped a foot away.

"Your lie was just a little white one. Not a good deed, but not so terrible either. You never expected to meet them, and besides, you've always been advanced for your age. Partly because of your own intelligence, but also because your mother tutored you. I think you were even taking online college courses at the time, weren't you?"

Gerard nodded.

"You shouldn't have lied, but it's not as if you hurt anyone. And what about them? Do you know everything about Stargazer and Molegun?"

Gerard gave him a faint grin. "It's Stargunner and Moleman."

"Right. If they're really your friends, they'll understand."

"Should I have confessed this to Morok?" Gerard asked.

"I suspect he knew about it when he was interviewing you."

"Oh. That mind-scan thing you were telling me about."

"Yes."

"And he selected me anyhow!"

"That he did."

Gerard's face lit up. So maybe it wasn't such a big deal. "Well, okay." He rolled toward the door.

"Wait!" Stephen said. "Promise me you'll tell your friend he needs to contact his supervisor at the Pentagon or the FBI."

Gerard hesitated. "Can we please have our meeting first? I need to hear Gunner's plan and then—well, if it's not a good plan, I'll try to get Moley to tell someone."

Stephen nodded in agreement. Who knew whether this Mole guy really knew anything? Maybe it was just youthful braggadocio. "Okay. Have your meeting first."

His son beamed at him. "Thanks a bunch, Dad.

CHAPTER 79

Late Saturday morning, Gerard pulled the van into one of the blue-striped handicapped spaces near the front entrance of the American Indian Museum on the National Mall. He had suggested the museum as a meeting place because he was a member and because it was his favorite of the Smithsonian museums. Its curved ochre walls reminded him of photos of the cave dwellings at Mesa Verde in Colorado. Maybe that was the architect's intention.

He turned off the motor and began the arduous process of disembarking. By the time he got out and got settled in his wheelchair, he was already ten minutes late. He rolled along the curved path in the light drizzle. The Capitol loomed on his left; on his right was the Air and Space Museum. He wondered briefly how the museum would handle the discovery of intelligent aliens from another planet; then he realized there might not be anyone left to handle anything if they couldn't get the sojourn back on track. He showed his pass at the door and rolled across the broad lobby toward the first-floor museum shop. They were supposed to meet at the totem pole next to the shop.

The crowd was sparse. A couple strolled by hand-in-hand, an old man and a young girl chatted in front of the shop, a woman talked on a cell phone in front of the totem. No sign of Gunner or Moley. He rolled down to the Mitsitam Café; still no sign of his buddies. He was now fifteen minutes late. Could they have become impatient and left already? He went back to the totem pole. The old man and his granddaughter were still there. Maybe he should ask them if they'd seen a couple of young guys hanging around.

He rolled to a stop in front of them. "Excuse me?"

They stopped chatting and looked at him. The old man was built like a cyclist, thin, wiry, with a trim gray goatee and thinning gray hair pulled back in a short ponytail. The girl had on dark glasses and a red ball cap with a National's logo and a dark ponytail pulled through the hole in back. They were both dressed in jeans and sweatshirts and carrying jackets. The girl's sweatshirt was red with a small white Nike swash below the shoulder; the old man's black sweatshirt said 'Inside, I'm Still Twelve.'

"Did you happen to see a couple of guys who looked like they were waiting for someone?" Gerard asked. "I was supposed to meet them right here at 11, and now it's 11:25."

They stared at him in silence.

Gerard was chagrined. Could they *be* any less friendly?

They exchanged a quick look, then the girl put her hands on her cheeks and said, "Ohmygod!" and started laughing and the old man chuckled and said, "I'll be damned."

Gerard was infuriated. Usually, people bent over backwards to help him. Nobody had ever laughed at him, at least not to his face.

"You're G-Man, aren't you?" The girl was smiling broadly.

Gerard sat stiffly in his chair and looked at her. How would she know his KASA nickname? "Who are you?"

"I'm Moleman!"

His mouth dropped open. "You can't be! Moleman's a guy. You're a—a girl! A kid!"

"And G-Man's a college tennis player?" It was the old man speaking.

"I suppose you're Stargunner," Gerard said sarcastically.

"Yep. All the way from sunny California!" Gunner said with a wicked grin.

Gerard was stunned. Moley and Gunner had lied too. They had all lied to each other. He felt partly relieved, partly disappointed. "We all told lies about ourselves."

"Whoppers!" said Gunner.

"But this is so much more fun!" cried Moley. She stuck out her hand. "I'm Abigail Moore, you can call me Abby. Or Moley. Whichever."

"Gerard Hopkins," he said and shook her hand.

The old man said, "My name's Langston Paine. You can call me anything but that. Gunner's good."

There was an awkward silence, then Gunner said, "My friends, we're here because we have a very big problem. I have an idea on how to proceed, but first we need to hear what

Moleman has learned. Let's go to the café and I'll treat you to a coke."

Gerard nodded and started to roll away, Abby followed.

"Wait!" Gunner called.

They stopped, turned, looked at him.

"We've been friends for what, three years?"

Gerard and Abby nodded.

"Well, we may look different than we expected, but I'm still Gunner, you're still G-Man, and you're still Moley. So, let's acknowledge that bond with a big group hug!"

Gerard flushed. Abby gave a nervous laugh. Gunner held out both arms and made come-here motions with his hands. They moved toward each other and grasped arms and shoulders in an awkward embrace. Then Abby broke into laughter, and in seconds, all three were convulsing with laugher.

"You all get a table," Gunner said, as they went into the café. "I'll get the drinks. Cokes okay?"

Gerard nodded.

"Diet coke for me," Abby said. "Let's take that table by the window." She moved a chair so that Gerard could roll up to the table.

Gunner brought their drinks and sat down opposite Abby. "Okay." Gunner said. "Brief backgrounds. The truth this time." He grinned.

Abby went first. "Daddy works for the Pentagon. He's a four-star general. Actually, he's Chief of the Army. He works a lot at home, so I bugged his office. I learn a whole lot more than I could as an intern at the Pentagon."

"You bugged his office?" Gerard was getting one shock after another.

"Yes. I tapped his phone too." She caught Gerard's look and blushed. "It was just for fun," she said defensively. "But of course, now, it might save our planet."

"I guess." Gerard looked at her with confused emotions. So, this was how Moley knew so much about what was going on at the Pentagon. But what kind of person would bug their father's office and tap his phone? He couldn't imagine doing that to his father.

Abby took off her sunglasses, laid them on the table. Then she pulled off the ball cap, undid her pony tail, shook her head. Her dark hair cascaded past her shoulders.

Gerard stared at her. "I've seen you before."

"Small world, huh?"

"You guys have met?" Gunner wore a puzzled look.

"Not exactly," Abby said, "but we saw each other at the interviews last month. And again, at a restaurant in New York." She looked at Gerard. "Remember?"

He nodded. She was at Morok's interviews. That meant she'd made the cut. She was one of the sojourners.

"What kind of interviews?" Gunner asked.

"The first one was with Dr. Eastlake, the second with Big Bird himself."

Gerard shot a frown at her.

"What?"

"That's disrespectful. He's Chairman Morok, not Big Bird."

"Everybody needs a nickname." She gave him a sly smile. "If he joined KASA, I bet he'd pick that as his nickname."

Gunner was looking at them. "You both made the cut?"

"I did," Abby said. Gerard nodded. They exchanged a look. *Gunner applied and didn't make it.*

"Let's get on with it," he said brusquely. "We're here to solve the world's problems."

"Not so fast, Gunner. We need your bio, then Gerry's."

Gerry! Gerard looked at her. No one had ever called him that. He sort of liked the sound of it. But geez! She was bossy!

"Okay, brief bio. I have a Ph.D. in astrophysics. I was a strategist for an aerospace company. I'm now retired. I live in Pasadena. End of story."

"You married?" Abby asked.

"Widowed."

"Children?"

"No. Let's move on."

"Hold on, Gunner. It's Gerry's turn. All I know about him is his grandfather is that famous preacher Marshall Hopkins." She rested her chin on clasped hands, looked at Gerard. "He was with you in the restaurant in New York."

356

Gerard frowned. *She didn't miss a thing.* "I'm a sophomore at Emerson Prep. My dad's a professor of anthropology at Georgetown, my mom stays home, I like rap music and primitive art."

"Cool!" Abby said. "I go to Emerson Prep too, 9th grade. I guess we haven't run into each other because you're an upperclassman. You have siblings?"

"No." *Geez!* Moleman actually went to his school. But he was having a hard time thinking of her as Moleman.

"Me neither." She glanced down at his chair, then looked him in the eye. "What happened to your legs?"

"I was shot."

"Ohmygod! Like with a gun?"

Her dark eyes sparkled. Gunner leaned forward, interested. Gerard was somewhat pleased at their interest. Most people pretended not to notice his legs. He gave them a brief version of the shooting.

"Hell of a lot more interesting than a college tennis player," Gunner said with a wicked grin. He looked at Abby. "*Now* can we talk about the problem?"

"Okay, I'll start," Abby said. "A couple weeks ago I heard my dad talking with someone named Gorr, I think it was, about how to keep America safe during this bizarre—as he called it—obsession with laying down our weapons. He's all for peace, you understand, he just wants us to be prepared in case everyone doesn't follow the party line. So to speak. He says you can't let your guard down. Ever.

"So, he was talking with this Gorr guy about buying up the weapons that all the peaceniks—his word—were trying to get rid of. Gorr said he would store them in a secret place so our military could retrieve them if and when they were needed. Gorr kept saying that he knew for certain that other countries were stockpiling weapons and if the United States didn't do it too, we would be left totally defenseless."

She looked at Gerard, then Gunner. "Actually, he was a lot more explicit than that about how we would be left, but it would be embarrassing to repeat his exact words."

"No need," Gerard muttered. He'd heard enough about Gorr over the years.

"Anyway, after Big Bird's—" she glanced at Gerard. "Sorry. After Chairman Morok's speech at the UN, I realized how wrong Daddy was to try to hide weapons. He was jeopardizing our first real attempt at world peace. Which meant the US was giving it lip service, but that's all. Just lip service. When the chairman pulled the plug on the sojourn, I knew I had to do something. I mean, it was affecting me *personally*!"

"So you went to Gunner?"

"I went to my dad first. I didn't tell him what I knew, of course. He would have asked how I knew it and then I would have been in deep-water. I'd have been in water over my head. But I asked him if the United States was one of those countries secretly stockpiling weapons and he said *no*. He looked me in the eye and he lied to me. That's when I knew I couldn't trust him anymore. So, I told Gunner."

"All you told me is that you knew something and you needed my help."

"Yes, but I couldn't reveal this online. You know how loose those chat rooms are. God knows who's monitoring them."

Gerard said, "You know for sure we're one of the countries stockpiling weapons?"

Abby gave him a solemn look. "Cross my heart and hope to die. And I know where a bunch of them are hidden."

There was a long silence, which Gunner broke. "Fucking stupid adults." He glanced at them sheepishly. "Pardon my language, kids, but *Jesus*! What mature adult in their right mind would defy a force like GFED? Why can't they see the *opportunity*? It's spread out in front of them like a summer picnic and they're standing around with cans of Raid looking for ants. And that's why we're here. What does KASA stand for?"

Gerard and Abby looked at each other, answered in unison. "Koalition against Stupid Adults."

"Right. And who are the members of KASA? Kids, right?"

Abby tilted her head, looked at him slyly. "We thought so, until you showed up."

"Touché." He grinned again. "But I ain't one of them, despite my advanced age. I'm one of you, and I can help us solve this problem. KASA is an alliance against stupid *adults*. That's why I started—joined it, because most adults over fifty *are* stupid. We're complacent. We think we know everything there is to know because we've lived longer than everybody else, and we'll let the world go up in smoke before we support a radical idea like world peace.

"My idea is to use KASA to galvanize the kids of the world —and anybody else who can open their eyes and see the future—galvanize them to take action against the stupid adults who are screwing this thing up. It is *your* future they're messing with, and you kids should have a voice in making these decisions, not some sixty, seventy-year-old idiots who will be pushing up dandelions by the time the effects of their stupid actions are felt."

For a moment, they both stared at Gunner. Then Abby held up her hand for a high five. "Yes!" she cried.

Gunner slapped her palm, then Gerard's, then told them the details of his plan.

"Do you really think it'll work?"

Gunner nodded. "It'll work if anything will. The power of the internet has barely been scratched. But we'll need our founder behind us."

"You mean Joan-of-Right?"

"Will she do it?"

Gunner smiled. A wise, benevolent kind of smile. "I know Joan personally. She'll lead this charge like *Jeanne d'Arc* led the charge at Orleans!"

CHAPTER 80

After he left the museum, Langston Paine took a taxi back to his hotel. He went directly to his room and opened his laptop and stared at the screen. His hands trembled with anticipation. He was about to write the most important communiqué of his life. All the letters to the editors he had written over the past fifty years, pounding first on manual typewriters, then IBM Selectrics, then, glory of glories, the personal computer, all those letters had honed his skills. He had bought one of the first PCs ever made, so excited he was to have such a communication tool at his fingertips, and then he had to wait almost twenty years for the Internet to catch up with his vision of communication. Gunner grinned savagely and started pounding the keyboard. Two hours later, he stopped typing and printed a copy. As much as he loved the power of the computer, he had to have a hard copy for proofing. He grabbed the pages as the printer spit them out.

Namuh of the World, Unite!

Four weeks ago, the world was given an opportunity to take a giant leap into the future. The Galactic Federation offered twelve hundred of our fellow citizens the opportunity to travel to the stars and learn the ways of the galaxy. In twenty short years, these Sojourners would return to Earth to share with us knowledge that could catapult us thousands of years into the future in a single generation.

They would be our Prometheus, bringing back the fire of peace to light the darkened corners of our primitive world. They would deliver us from the travails of war and poverty and disease that have plagued the human race throughout the few civilized millennium of our backward little planet.

But the mere promise of peace and enlightenment was met with fear and greed, which has unleashed not one but dozens of Pandoras upon our world. I refer of course to the stupid, selfish, misguided, war-mongering leaders who have secretly stockpiled weapons and drawn a curtain of darkness on the brilliant future of which we've had only a tantalizing glimpse.

Once again, the few are imposing their stupidity and lack of vision upon the rest of us. Once again, the tail is wagging the dog.

The leaders of our planet have had decades, centuries, *millennia*, in which to change the world. And what have they done? They've polluted our rivers, our air, our food, our minds, and now our world has grown obese and uncivil, splintered and hateful.

Our leaders ignore the shameful poverty that exists even in the richest country on Earth, refusing to spend the money it takes to care for and educate the children of the poor. Then they spend several times that amount to imprison these children by the thousands when they grow up to become adult criminals.

Our leaders preach reverence for life, but in this 'culture of life,' leaders who have never experienced the horrors of war blithely sacrifice the youth of the world to the terrors of the battlefield.

GFED offered us a chance to learn the ways of a truly civilized world if only we would try to change, and what did our leaders do? They gave in to selfishness and fear and turned their backs on the greatest opportunity ever offered to humankind.

So, I ask you today: Are we going to let them get away with it?

Are we going to let the few keep us chained to the past when there are billions of us and just a handful of them?

No! I say—and I ask you to say it with me!

NO!

Let us start a chain reaction that can give the world back its destiny with the stars.

How?

For starters—stay home from work Monday

Go on strike for a single day.

Go on strike to protest the stockpiling of weapons around the world.

Go on strike to demonstrate to the people of the galaxy that the people of Earth are not violent warmongers.

Go on strike to make it clear to everyone that we want peace on Earth and we want the sojourn back. Then the leaders of the world will know they have made a terrible mistake by thwarting the world's plans for disarmament.

Our message to those leaders will be loud and clear: *Resign and make way for leaders who will listen to the people and move us down the road to peace.*

If you're with me, our one-day strike will take place on Monday, February 28. One day is all it should take if we do it together. If we act in concert, our leaders cannot help but hear us.

If you own a business, close your offices for one day. Let the world known that it can't survive without you and the jobs you create.

If you're a grocery clerk or a restaurant owner or dairy farmer or a cashier, take the day off Monday. Let our leaders know they can't dine out without you, can't feed their children without you, can't buy them milk or clothes or books or shoes without you.

If you're a pilot or a bus driver or a taxi driver or a flight attendant, call in sick. If you own a gas station, lock your pumps for one day. Let our leaders know they can't travel around the world without you; they can't travel across the country without you; they can't even travel across the city without you.

If you're a soldier, lay down your rifle Monday. If you're a sailor, refuse to board your ship. If you're a fighter pilot, ground your plane. The world can't fight its wars without soldiers and sailors and pilots and planes, so for one glorious day let's show our leaders who really has the right to decide about weapons and war.

If we do this together, we can show the corrupt leaders of the world who holds the real power. We can show them that we, not they, will make the decisions about weapons and violence and war.

For this strike to succeed, this message has to find its way around the world, which it can do in just eight hours if you will send it to ten people and ask each of them to send it to ten more.

Send it to your parents, your grandparents, your brothers and sisters and aunts and uncles and cousins and coworkers and friends and enemies. Send it to everyone you know, and urge them—BEG them—to join the Worldwide Work Strike on Monday, February 28.

Onward...in peace!

[signed]

Joan-of-Right, Founder of KASA

Spiritual Descendant of *Jeanne d'Arc*

Gunner leaned back in his chair and smiled. *Good enough!* He posted the blog to his website, then copied the text into an email and wrote a note to the members of KASA.

"We called ourselves the Koalition Against Stupid Adults," he wrote, "and for years ours was a voice crying out in the wilderness. Now we have an opportunity to make our voices heard around the world. I urge you to read this email as if your life depended on it. Because it does!"

He pressed Send and felt a tingle of anticipation as he thought of his missive landing in the email boxes of twenty thousand KASA members and then leaving those boxes to travel through cyberspace around the globe. It was the closest he could get to instantaneous worldwide communication. Now he would wait and see if it worked.

CHAPTER 81

Stephen was in his study when he heard a 'ping' signaling the arrival of an email. He glanced at the message in the corner of his screen. It was from Gerard, which was strange, as Gerard rarely sent him emails. He opened it and did a double-take at the subject line: "Namuh of the World, Unite!"

When he finished reading the email, he buzzed the intercom in Gerard's room. "Joan-of-Right?" he asked, when his son answered.

"She's the founder of KASA."

Stephen nodded with a knowing smile, "Does this email have anything to do with Gunner's plan you mentioned?"

"Yes, he asked Joan-of-Right to get involved."

"To instigate a worldwide work strike?"

"Yes."

"Do you know what chaos that will create if the plan succeeds?"

"That's the point, Dad."

"You're playing with fire, Gerard."

"Papa Marsh marched in anti-war protests in the Sixties. You marched in protests in college. This is our version of your protests."

Stephen was silent. The email had struck a chord.

"Dad, the strike is only for one day. People can't do a lot of harm by staying home from work for one day. But we can sure demonstrate that we have the power to make some changes."

Stephen thought of what Morok had said. That change should start at the grassroots level and work its way up.

"Will you do it, Dad? Will you send the email on to your friends?"

"Okay," he said finally. "I'm in."

He read the email again, clicked Forward to Entire Address Book and typed a brief note:

> My friends, this is for real and it just might work. I urge you to send this on to your family and coworkers and friends, and join me in the work strike Monday, February 28.

He hesitated for a moment. "I hope you're watching, Mr. Chairman," he said aloud, as he clicked Send.

#

Reluctant to return to California, Heather checked back into the Hay-Adams on Saturday. She had been so despondent she could hardly bring herself to get out of bed, and she wanted the privacy of a hotel. On Sunday, she was still in bed at noon, staring at the ceiling, when she heard the 'ping' on her laptop announcing a new email. She'd been deluged with messages from Sojourners who were angry or depressed or both, and she had tried as best she could to console them. She forced herself to get up.

The email was from Stephen. She read his note, then the entire email.

What a brilliant idea! She clicked the Forward button and replaced Stephen's note with one of her own. 'Please help us get the world back on the road to peace,' she wrote and sent the email to her entire address book.

#

Marshall Hopkins was revising his sermon for his Sunday night broadcast when he noticed the arrival of an email message from Stephen. That was such a rare occurrence that he stopped what he was doing and read it. He read it again and thought about the potential response if it found its way to more than two million of his devoted followers. Whenever he sent out a plea for money, the response rate was sometimes as much as thirty percent.

He thought about it some more, then clicked the Forward button and replaced Stephen's note with one of his own.

> God works in mysterious ways. I am sure He wants you to join the work strike Monday and stay home from your jobs. And if you want to do more to help me make this happen, send a small donation to the Ministry of Life, God will bless you ten times over.

He nodded with satisfaction and pressed the Send button and thought about how he could weave the message into his Sunday night sermon.

#

Calvin Williams was at home when the email from Heather Eastlake arrived. They had corresponded regularly since his interview two weeks ago but he had not heard from her since the UN debacle even though he had sent her a note immediately afterwards. He opened the email eagerly. When he finished reading it, he let out a low whistle. It was a good idea for rousting out the culprits who were hiding weapons, but he couldn't see how it could get the sojourn back on track. Still, what was there to lose?

He opened his email address book and examined the various lists. There was a list of friends and fellow players from his basketball days, a list of colleagues from his university days, a list of associates at PCAST and the White House, and a long list of media contacts.

He thought of Heather, held her image in his mind for a long moment, the copper hair, the green eyes, the lips curved into that half-smile of hers.

I'm with you, babe, he thought, and forwarded the email to every list in his address book.

#

Penny was preparing a roast for dinner when Gerard rolled into the kitchen.

"Mom, you need to check your email."

She placed the roast in the marinade and glanced at her son. "Why? I'm not expecting anything important."

"I just sent you one that I need you to forward to all your friends."

Penny shook her head. "Gerard, you know how I hate that. I simply don't forward silly emails to friends."

"This is important, Mom, just open my email and read it." He was looking at her anxiously. "Please!"

"Why don't you just tell me what it says?"

"You've got to read it."

There was a pleading tone in his voice she rarely heard. "Now?"

"Yes. It's really, really important."

"All right."

She washed her hands and dried them and went to her office. Gerard followed her. She opened her email and clicked on his and began to read.

When she finished, she sat in stony silence, her elation at the cancellation of the sojourn ebbing away. She had been so relieved that he wouldn't be leaving her after all. True, he had been despondent for two days, but he would get over it. After a while, everyone would forget about Morok and the aliens and the world would return to normal. Gerard would go back to school, he would graduate in three years and go to college at Georgetown, he would get married one day and have children and they would all be together. That had always been her dream, and for two days she'd allowed herself to dream it again. And now the major player in that dream wanted her to help get the sojourn back on track so he could leave her for the next twenty years, maybe leave her forever.

She couldn't do it.

"Mother, if you love me, you'll send the email to everyone you know."

He must have known that was the one thing she couldn't refuse. She nodded without looking at him.

"You'll do it?"

She found her voice. "Yes, my darling, I'll do it."

"Thank you." He moved closer, took her hand and kissed it, then left her alone.

She let the tears flow down her cheeks as she forwarded the email that would set in motion events that would break her heart. Again. She forwarded it to her colleagues at the magazines she wrote for, to her friends at church and at Gerard's school, to her family back in Georgia, and to the couple in Peru that she'd kept in touch with since her missionary days. It took a while because she added a personal note to each group urging them to keep the email going, and each time she pressed Send she felt as if she were sending her heart into the cold depths of outer space.

#

Ethan Gorr sat under an umbrella on the white sands beach of the Ritz Carlton in Grand Cayman and watched a parade of girls in thongs and bikinis. He was bored out of his skull. If you didn't like water sports or pedaling a goddamn bicycle around the island, there was nothing to do here but sit on the beach and he had had about enough of that. Today he had brought his laptop. He checked his email and found one from Marshall Hopkins. He read the message and muttered, "Money-grubbing prick!" Then he read the plea from Joan-of-Right.

Christ! If the damned strike worked, all of his carefully cultivated relationships would go straight down the toilet. But what could he do? He thought about it for a while, then smiled to himself. All he had to do was wait for the dust to settle because the one thing people in power had in common was a love of power. Let 'em go ahead and elect all the new leaders. Once they got a taste of power, he could have them eating out of his hand just like the ones that came before them.

#

On a cold but sunny day in Central Park, Ethan's nephew Tory was entranced by the stirring performance of a street violinist, when his cell phone pinged. The minute he read Joan-of-Right's message, Tory let out a loud 'Whoop!!'

Suddenly other phones in the audience began vibrating and pinging, including the cell phone of the violinist. After a brief pause to read the message, she transitioned from Vivaldi to John Lennon's "Give Peace a Chance."

An elderly couple turned to Tory, confused by what was happening. He forwarded them Joan's email, along with everyone else on his contact list. A long-time member of KASA, young Tory was thrilled to take part in the action. So were the elderly couple, who posted Joan's message on Twitter.

368

#

As Gunner's email made its way around the globe, people began receiving it for the second and third and even fourth time from different senders. Meanwhile, social media amplified the reach exponentially. By five o'clock Saturday afternoon, Gunner's inbox was crammed with messages of support. He grinned with satisfaction as he read each one.

"By god!" he said to himself. "It just might work."

CHAPTER 82

News of the proposed strike dominated the airwaves on Sunday. The television talk shows devoted entire hours to it, phone lines were jammed at radio talk shows, the internet was literally buzzing and KASA chat rooms were so clogged that connection times slowed to a snail's pace.

By eleven o'clock Sunday night, word began filtering into newsrooms that the work strike had already started on the other side of the globe. Melbourne and Sydney were the first to weigh in with reports of empty offices, closed stores, and vacant streets. Then came reports from Bangkok, Hong Kong, Tokyo, Taipei, and dozens of cities in the Far East. Workers were staying home in droves while management—when management showed up at all—struggled with skeleton crews to keep the wheels of commerce turning.

In the U.S., Monday dawned on virtually empty streets along the Eastern Seaboard. As the sun rose in the sky, an eerie silence fell across the land. In Boston and New York, Philadelphia and Washington, Atlanta and Miami, the streets were empty except for a few taxis and police cruisers and the occasional ambulance, its siren whining, racing toward a critical care hospital with a skeleton staff.

As the sun moved across the sky, so did the silence. In Chicago, St. Louis, Detroit, Oklahoma City, Dallas, Denver, Phoenix, city streets looked as empty as they were on Super Bowl Sunday. By the time the work day dawned in the Pacific Time Zone, it was obvious that the strike had succeeded. Up and down the West Coast, students took to the streets, marching, laughing, singing, heady on the rediscovered power of protest. They wore t-shirts and carried placards bearing the slogans I AM NAMUH and LEADERS, YOU GOT IT WRONG! They chanted WE ARE NAMUH as they marched in the streets of San Diego, Los Angeles, Santa Barbara, San Francisco, Portland, Seattle, and Vancouver.

The media had a field day. This was a story to rival Morok's UN speech in importance, and no one wanted to miss it.

By late Monday afternoon, CNN had uncovered the identity of Joan-of-Right and had hustled Langston Paine to their studio in Washington, D.C. for an exclusive interview with Walter Anderson who flew in the night before.

Cooper introduced Gunner as the voice behind Joan-of-Right and the author of the email that brought the world to a virtual standstill. "You can't mean that everyone should skip work today? You're here. I'm here. How would we tell your story?"

Gunner wore a blue sports jacket over a white open-necked shirt. His gray hair was pulled back in a ponytail. His face was lined, his beard was grizzled, "That's right Walter, I assumed that everyone would exercise common sense. If your job is essential to protect the lives, safety, or health of others, you know to show up to work. And yes, the media is crucial to keeping us all informed and spreading the word of the incredible success we're having today. The people know what's right, it's only our leaders that got it wrong."

"So, what's next, Mr. Paine?" he asked.

Gunner's blue eyes danced, "We want those leaders who secretly stockpiled weapons to resign. We want them replaced by men and women who will follow the wishes of the people—wishes that have been made very clear today. We want peace. We want the sojourn back."

Walter Anderson looked skeptical. "You might get the resignations you want, you might even get new leaders who will work for peace, but how are you going to get the sojourn back? It seems to me that GFED has washed its hands of us."

Gunner shrugged. "Maybe. Maybe not. Could be they're still watching us, and if they are, maybe they'll give us another go at it."

Cooper said, "Well, here's your chance, Mr. Paine. Wherever Chairman Morok is, he has access to our airwaves. Talk to him."

Gunner rose to the occasion. He looked directly into the camera and began: "Chairman Morok, if you've been watching us, you've seen that the vast majority of humans want peace. Everyone who participated in the work strike today wants peace. We will find the stupid, short-sighted, misguided humans who have been hiding weapons, and we will remove them from power. The violence you have seen in our past is not genetic, it is

371

a learned behavior, and we can change it. We can change it because we want GFED to be our mentor and lead us into the future.

"So, Mr. Chairman, on behalf of the hundreds of millions of Namuh who have made their voices heard today, I ask you to give us another chance. Give us back the sojourn. If we can act in concert the way we have shown we can today, there should be no doubt that we can work together to keep our end of the bargain and find our way toward worldwide peace."

"How are we going to find those who stockpiled the weapons?" Walter asked.

Gunner grinned. "I suspect we'll know their names by morning. It takes a lot of workers to transport and hide weapons—workers like those who took part in today's strike. The idiots who squirreled away weapons can run, but they can't hide."

The camera moved in for Walter Anderson's sign-off. "There you have it, folks. The man who orchestrated this unprecedented worldwide strike just issued another challenge: Find the bastards and throw them out."

He gave a wry smile and added, "I'd like to second the motion."

#

Gerard looked at his father, his face slack with disbelief. "I can't believe Gunner is Joan-of-Right."

"I can't believe that old man is Gunner. I thought he was in his twenties."

"Yeah, I forgot to tell you, he's seventy-something. And Moleman is a girl."

Stephen thought about that, then burst out laughing. "So, you *all* lied to each other."

Gerard grinned sheepishly. "I guess we did."

"Did you like Gunner any less when you found out he was old?"

"No. He's still the coolest person I know."

"What about Moleman, did she disappoint you?"

372

"I guess not." A rosy flush crept up his cheeks. "But I still can't believe Gunner is Joan-of-Right."

CHAPTER 83

The next day, most of those who had joined the strike in the U.S. returned to their jobs, and they flooded the Internet with emails demanding the resignations of the President and the entire Congress.

Empowered by Monday's success, students continued to protest. They marched on city halls and state capitols, calling leaders by name, demanding their resignation. Emails flew from campus to campus announcing a march on Washington on Saturday.

Galvanized by the work strike and the ongoing student protests, the media went to work. Investigative reporters tracked down leads and by Tuesday evening, journalists began naming names of those who had helped to stockpile weapons around the world.

In the United States, General Abner Moore, Chief of the U.S. Army, was being mentioned as a possible traitor, as such conspirators were being labeled. In a show of support, President Wainwright posed with the general in front of six American flags and called him the most loyal soldier he'd ever had the privilege to know, while leaders of both parties stumbled over each other to denounce the president and the general. The Army moved swiftly to declare the investigation a military matter, and the trial, if there was to be one, a court-martial.

By Wednesday, leaders of sixty-five-member countries of the United Nations had resigned, including all of the G-8 countries except Britain and the United States. Speculation was rife that Charles Bartlett and William Wainwright would be next.

CHAPTER 84

Two days after the strike, President Wainwright sat alone in the Oval Office and watched his old friend Charles Bartlett announce his resignation as prime minister of Great Britain.

Bartlett spoke in the crisp, clipped syllables of the British upper class and said exactly what he'd said to Wainwright in a private conversation earlier that morning: "I had nothing to do with the cache of weapons that were found in abandoned castles in Wales. Nevertheless, it happened on my watch, and that makes me ultimately responsible." His eyes misted over as he looked into the camera. "I therefore tender my resignation to Parliament and to the people of Great Britain. God save the King."

The White House filled the television screen followed by a shot of dozens of protesters outside the fence. The camera focused on one placard that urged in big black letters: THROW THE WAR MONGER OUT!

A reporter spoke off-camera. "How long will it be before William Wainwright bends to the will of the American people? The march on Washington scheduled for Saturday threatens to be the biggest in our history, an eloquent plea for his resignation. Will that convince him? Or will he dig in his heels and challenge Congress to remove him by force?"

Wainwright turned off the television. He might have been able to ride out the storm had it not been for his appearance with General Moore on the White House steps. Within the hour, Chairman of the Joint Chiefs advised him that an investigation of Moore was indeed under way, although it was clear that he didn't think General Moore had done anything wrong. If he did it, the chairman said, he was only trying to protect his country.

Wainwright agreed with him. In fact, he had taken it for granted that the Pentagon wouldn't destroy all the weapons. What else is a military for if not to protect the country? In a sane world, General Moore would receive a medal for his imagination and audacity. But the world was no longer sane.

Wainwright sighed. He could refuse to resign and force the country to go through interminable hearings by Congress, but he knew he would not emerge unscathed like Reagan. No, he

would follow Bartlett's lead and resign with all the grace he
could muster.

CHAPTER 85

On Friday evening, Stephen and his family watched the president announce his resignation in a special broadcast from the Oval Office. Wainwright looked haggard, as if he hadn't slept well for weeks.

"I will resign at noon tomorrow," the president said at the end of a long and emotional speech. "Vice President Baker will be sworn in at that time. And now I bid you farewell, my friends. May God bless our planet Earth."

The television screen blinked once, went black for a moment.

Chairman Morok's blue-green, black-billed visage filled the screen, his golden eyes luminous. He spoke without preliminaries.

"The Galactic Federation has been most impressed with the leadership of the KASA group which initiated your recent work strike. We were even more impressed by the response of millions of Namuh who joined that protest, which resulted in the resignations of your current leaders. This has led us to believe that the violence ingrained in your culture may not be irreversible.

"I still believe, as do others in the Federation, that the Namuh possess inherent qualities that will allow it to mature into a species worthy of membership in the Federation. So, I have come to announce that the Galactic Sojourn has been reinstated under the same terms as before. The sojourners whom I have interviewed will depart for Planet Yxria in eight weeks.

Gerard raised both fists high in the air.

"I would remind you that all of the conditions of my original proposal remain: The Namuh civilization must give up its culture of violence and begin to replace it with a culture of peace. You have taken an impressive step with your work strike this week. But it must be the beginning of an ongoing effort.

"If the sojourn succeeds, life on Planet Earth will be transformed, and you will owe a great debt to the man who initiated the strike that has led to its restoration. His name is now well-known, and I invite Mr. Langston Paine to join the sojourn if he so desires.

Morok paused. "One final note. Don't be too harsh with your fallen leaders. They are a product of your culture, and it is your culture that must change."

The screen blinked and Morok's image disappeared.

"It's back on," Gerard said, disbelief softening his voice. Then, as the truth settled in, he shouted, "The sojourn's back on and Gunner's going with us!" He wheeled around and grabbed his cellphone off the table to call Gunner.

Penny looked as if she had been kicked in the stomach. Stephen stood and pulled her to her feet, drew her close. With Morok's words, the uncertainties of the past tumultuous days seemed to be cohering into something solid inside him, something strong and good. "It's going to be okay," he whispered against her hair. "We have a lot of work to do."

#

When President Baker announced Dr. Stephen Hopkins would join his cabinet as the GFED ambassador, it was almost more than Ethan Gorr could bear. Sure, the bastard had dropped publication of the book, but now he was in a position where he could cause Gorr political harm. And he was practically a goddamned hero with all the alien nonsense. Gorr stewed about it for a week, then he phoned Marshall Hopkins.

"When exactly does that sojourn departure take place?"

"Hello to you, too, Ethan," Hopkins said.

"Cut the crap!" growled Gorr.

The reverend cleared his throat. "The group departs April 20. There's going to be a farewell ceremony the day before at the National Cathedral, and I've been asked to give the invocation."

Gorr paused. "Who will be there?"

"All the big shots," Hopkins said. "Our new president and just about every world leader you can name, plus members of Congress, the sojourners, of course, and my whole family."

"What about the aliens?" Gorr asked.

"I've heard some of them will attend, maybe even Morok. But hopefully, there won't be the drama we saw at the UN last month. All that 'you were wrong' stuff coming out of the mouth of Jesus was a big blow to my followers. It was a big blow to the whole concept of religion."

Gorr thought about all those people gathered in one place, one building. Too bad he couldn't just drop a bomb on it and get rid of them all, Stephen Hopkins and his kid, the sojourners, the aliens, all those newly minted peace-mongering leaders. One fell swoop, they'd be gone and the world would go back to normal and he could resume his weapons trade. Hell, after an attack like that the world would be cowering in fear and the demand for weapons would soar.

But maybe he wouldn't have to *drop* a bomb. Maybe he could bomb it from the inside.

#

It took several days and the intensive sleuthing by two private detectives, but Gorr finally located Sly Wicker in Sydney, Australia. After several long phone calls outlining his plan and the promise of an extraordinary amount of money, he convinced Wicker to come back to the States. He arrived the next day and met with Gorr in his Washington office. Gorr filled him in on the details.

"I've got some real special bombs, and I need you to hide them in the National Cathedral before the sojourn ceremony begins."

"How the hell am I going to hide bombs inside a church?" Wicker asked.

"Easy," Gorr said. "Marshall Hopkins is giving the benediction, and he's invited five of his religious buddies to bring their little kiosks into the cathedral so they can hand out literature to the crowd."

"You can do that in a cathedral?"

"Hell, they do it in the Vatican."

"So how does that fit in your plan?"

"That's where you're going to hide the bombs, inside those kiosks."

Wicker snorted. "What do I say, 'scuse me, preach, I wanna put a bomb in there."

379

"Don't be an idiot. The bombs will be in metal boxes, but the preachers think the boxes contain religious pamphlets."

"What happens once I get the bombs in place?"

You get blown up with the rest of them, Gorr thought. He wasn't about to leave any witnesses at the massacre. "You'll meet me across the street from the church, and we'll set off the bombs by remote control."

Wicker chuckled. "We'll get to watch the fireworks, huh?"

Yeah," Gorr said. "Violence will be back to stay."

CHAPTER 86

As the sounds of Beethoven's Ninth Symphony filled the National Cathedral, Stephen Hopkins gazed out over the crowd, his nerves on high alert. His father would give the invocation, followed by a few words from President Baker, and then Heather Eastlake would welcome the 1200 sojourners in the ceremony that had been aborted at the UN. Everything had been planned down to the tiniest detail, but he could not shake the feeling that something catastrophic could happen today. He had mentioned his fears to Morok during their visit two days ago.

"There have been real threats," he had said, and told Morok about Ethan Gorr and about the kidnapping attempt on Gerard, unaware that the Yxrians were the ones who had thwarted it.

"I still have nightmares that Gorr will try to harm Gerard, maybe even kill him. With the sojourners departing, Gorr may think this is his last chance to get his revenge."

"We will keep an eye on Mr. Gorr," Morok had said. "Do not worry."

Now, sitting in the cathedral with two Secret Service agents directly behind him and two hovering over Penny and Gerard, still his stomach was tense with apprehension.

He scanned the crowd but did not see Morok. His gaze lit on the blue banners that identified the religious kiosks parked around the perimeter of walls. To Stephen, it seemed a travesty to allow them into a secular ceremony, but this was a church, after all, and President Baker thought that a conciliatory gesture to religious leaders was necessary. That was why he wanted the ceremony in the National Cathedral and why he'd invited Marshall Hopkins to give the invocation.

Stephen noticed several men in dark gray uniforms standing near each kiosk, hands clasped behind their backs, eyes roving the crowd. Security guards, of course. He could make out the name "National Security" on the back of the guard closest to the dais, and felt a small wave of relief. Everything would be fine.

As Reverend Marshal Hopkins stepped up to the podium for the invocation, the guard near the dais turned in that direction. When Stephen focused on the guard's face, he caught his breath. *It couldn't be!* But the memory of that day in Mondogo slammed into his consciousness. The cadaverous face of the man walking beside Ethan Gorr in Mondogo as Stephen carried his wounded son to the helicopter was the man guarding the kiosk a few feet away.

At that moment, the guard glanced in his direction. He was sure he saw a flash of recognition in the man's eyes before he began sidling toward a side exit. Stephen's first impulse was to whisper an alarm to the Secret Service agent standing behind him, but what if he were wrong? His actions would at the very least interrupt the ceremony. At worst, he might create an event with national or international implications.

"What is wrong?"

Stephen looked around, then realized the words were Morok's voice in his mind. Morok was communicating with him telepathically. Stephen formed the thought as clearly as possible: *"The security guard heading toward the west exit is an accomplice of Ethan Gorr!"*

#

Just as she received Morok's telepathic message, Myssa recognized Sly and performed a quick mind-scan. What she uncovered was an explosion that would happen in seconds. Where? Where? She closed her eyes and saw the bombs in the kiosks.

Without waiting orders from Morok, she instantaneously encapsulated each kiosk with an invisible shield. Within seconds, the bombs exploded simultaneously inside protected by the shields.

The deafening sound sent people diving under their seats. Secret Service agents threw the president to the floor. But the bombs had simply created mini-firestorms inside the shields. When it dawned on the crowd that the explosions were contained, they stared in fascination at the debris whirling around the areas where the kiosks had stood.

At the moment of the explosions, Sly Wicker hurled himself toward the exit door. He stood up when he realized he wasn't hurt and stared at the encapsulated firestorms. "I'm outta here," he muttered and burst through the exit door. Myssa was waiting there, arms folded patiently across her slender chest, with Drakk by her side.

She gave a slow blink. "Remember me?"

#

Across the street, Ethan Gorr watched the National Cathedral through binoculars. When he heard the explosions, he lowered the binoculars to get the full impact of the great church going up in flames. But there were no flames. There were no screaming people pouring out of the building.

Something obviously had gone wrong.

He flew down the stairs out onto the street and into his Mercedes. As he raced away, Gorr caught a fleeting glimpse of Sly Wicker, hands behind his back, held there, by the long green fingers of a large lizard walking upright.

CHAPTER 87

Ethan Gorr sat under an umbrella on the white sands beach of the Ritz Carlton in Grand Cayman once again, watching another parade of girls in thongs and bikinis, but this time he wore a hat and sunglasses to avoid being recognized.

A strikingly attractive waitress approached, with a piña colada on a silver tray. "For you, Mr. Franklin."

Gorr smiled, "No need to be so formal. Just call me Ben."

She handed him his piña colada, "Of course, would you mind taking a selfie with me, Ben?"

Gorr, flattered, took a sip of his drink, "A selfie? With you?"

The waitress nodded and smiled, "Why yes, of course." She pulled out her cell phone, "Ben, would you mind taking off your sunglasses?"

Gorr hesitated, "Do I need to?"

"Not really, but I bet you have beautiful eyes, Ben."

Gorr removed his sunglasses and winked, "You know, I've been told that before."

The waitress and Gorr both smiled into the lens. She snapped the selfie and stared carefully at the photo on her phone and compared it with a screenshot she'd grabbed earlier.

"Can I see?" Gorr asked eagerly.

"One second. It came out great," she answered, as she deleted the screenshot and held the phone close to Gorr's face blocking his view. She quietly signaled a police officer standing behind them who pulled out a pair of handcuffs and quickly snapped them onto Gorr's wrists.

The waitress suddenly turned serious, "You're under arrest, Ethan"

"But my name is Ben—"

"We know who you are, Ethan Gorr. We know everything."

Gorr struggled to get out of the handcuffs, "We? Who are you? What about my rights?"

The waitress pulled out her badge, "The FBI has a legal attaché office that covers the Cayman Islands with a mutual extradition treaty. The good news is, you really do have beautiful eyes."

The police officer grabbed Gorr's arm and took him away, "You know I've also been told that my eyes are beautiful too."

#

Gorr found himself cuffed to a chair at FBI headquarters in Washington D.C. in a small room with bare walls, furnished with a table and chairs.

In an odd twist of fate, this was the same room that Stephen Hopkins found himself in, not so long ago.

The door opened and two female agents, one blonde, the other brunette, entered the room. Each carried a small bag and sat down at the table directly across from Gorr.

The blonde introduced herself as Special Agent Francine Monaco. Gorr couldn't take his eyes of her, *voluptuously attractive*, he thought with a brief grin.

"Stop staring Mr. Gorr. It's rude," she said frowning.

Gorr turned to face the brunette. She introduced herself as Special Agent Susan Randall.

"Let's cut to the chase. You're facing at least 20 years in prison," said Agent Randall curtly.

"I need to call my attorney."

Agent Randall stood up and faced Gorr down, "You have the right to remain silent, but it doesn't really matter. We know everything about you. Everything. We've had eyes on you for years. We have Sly Wicker in custody, and what he's told us could fill a book. In fact, we've already read a book that—"

Gorr looked up, "What book?"

She pulled out a copy of *Merchants of Evil,* "Look familiar?"

Gorr looked closely at Agent Randall's face, her blue eyes… "Wait a minute. Who are you?!"

Agent Randall smiled, "You hired me to steal the manuscript. Remember? And for the record, I heard you call me a greedy bitch."

Agent Monaco stood up to also face Gorr down, "Remember me?"

Gorr stared at her confused.

"Maybe this will help," she pulled a pair of binoculars out of her bag and flipped him off, "When you weren't ogling me with your telescope, my eyes and ears were focused on you. Your lines were tapped. Hell, your sorry life has been tapped for years. We know all about your illegal weapons trade, bribery, extortion... as well as the ERG Holding Company and where all your money is hidden. Your brothers ratted you out on that score."

Gorr seethed, "My brothers knew?!"

Agent Randall, "We've been waiting for a chance to bring you down, but you did it to yourself with that terrorist stunt in the Cathedral. Go ahead, call your lawyer. We've got enough on you to put you away for the rest of your life, let alone 20 years. Unless..."

Gorr squirmed in his seat, "Unless what...?"

Agent Monaco placed the binoculars on the table, "Apparently you have friends in high places."

Gorr beamed, "Well, I do have access to the President."

"Former President," she reminded him, "I'm talking about Chairman Morok. Although, I'm not entirely sure he would call you a friend."

"The alien?! What does he want from me?"

Agent Randall shook her head "Apparently, he's very interested in studying the criminal mind. Exactly how it works and if it can change. He'd like spend some time to get to know you better...for about 20 years."

"20 years?!!" Gorr shrieked.

"Would you rather spend 20 years in prison or 20 years as one of the sojourners on planet Yxria?" Agent Monaco asked, "Your nephew Tory put in a good word for you."

"Tory?" Gorr asked, "Really? Is he going too?"

CHAPTER 88

Two weeks later, on a bright spring day, Stephen Hopkins watched President Baker wind up his speech to the departing sojourners. He spoke from a lectern at the base of the Washington Monument with his image projected in an enormous close-up on a video screen. Behind him, several rows of dignitaries were seated on folding chairs. Stephen stood with his family in the special sojourner section near the center of the Mall.

Secret Service agents hovered nearby, scanning the crowds that were cordoned off by the police along the edges of the Mall. Now they all were waiting for the spacecraft that would transport the sojourners to Yxria.

Thirty minutes before the scheduled departure, the spacecraft had not yet arrived. Stephen suspected that no vehicle would show up at all. Instead, the group would be teleported to their destination, as he had been for the GFED hearing last December. It would be difficult for families to watch their loved ones simply vanish for twenty years, but he couldn't imagine how a spacecraft could land in an area the size of the Mall.

Twenty years! He felt a surge of panic as the thought of the time and distance settled in his mind. It seemed surreal. He felt as if he were in another of a series of vivid dreams that began when he came to on that bench months ago with a gap in his memory. He kept thinking he would wake up and it would still be November and he would be headed home for his son's sixteenth birthday.

Penny slipped her hand into his. She looked elegant in a white silk suit and a big-brimmed black-and-white hat. She smiled and squeezed his hand.

"You look beautiful," he said, "and amazingly serene."

"Actually, I'm near hysteria." Her smile disappeared. "Why did we agree to no good-byes here? I want to hold him in my arms one last time."

He looked at his son, who was talking with Gunner and Abby Moore. "Gunner and Abby have no family here. That's why he didn't want a tearful good-bye."

"But they'll have him for the next twenty years." Her voice broke on the last words.

He put his arm around her shoulders. "We spent all last week saying good-bye. We have to respect his wishes."

As he watched his son for a moment, he recalled their conversations over the past week. They had talked about the wave of new leaders taking office around the world and the messages of peace that each delivered. They speculated how long that mood would last and what it would take to keep the world on a path to peace. They imagined together the kind of worlds Gerard would find on Yxria and the other planets of the Federation. They'd talked about his return in twenty years. That was a long time, yes, but the future that lay ahead would be worth it.

"I'm going to talk to the reverend," Penny said.

Penny headed toward the Reverend Marshall Hopkins, who was deep in conversation with a middle-aged woman a few feet away. As the father of the new cabinet member, the reverend seemed to be taking on the air of an elder statesman.

"Mr. Ambassador."

Stephen turned to see Heather Eastlake standing with Calvin Williams, her hand tucked through his arm. Her copper hair hung loose to her shoulders; a shade lighter than the cashmere dress she wore.

"You remember Calvin," she said.

"Congratulations," Williams said as they shook hands.

"It took me completely by surprise."

Heather glowed with excitement. "Can you believe this is finally happening?"

Stephen smiled. "No, I can honestly say I can't."

A rustle of movement in the crowd was followed by loud murmurs, then a shout from Gerard. "Dad, Mom, look!" he said, pointing beyond the monument. "There's our spacecraft."

Stephen's breath caught in his throat. A transparent cylinder about the size of the Washington Monument hovered a few feet above the ground, then came to rest on its base of circular steps. Inside the craft was a tall, slender, opaque cylinder surrounded by row upon row of high-backed seats, facing outward. As the crowd watched, the outer walls of the cylinder appeared to be turning counter-clockwise, rising from its base, inch by inch, turning slowly, until it hovered about eight feet above the base. He felt Penny beside him and reached for her hand.

A low female voice emanated from within the craft: "Attention, Sojourners. Please proceed to the conveyance for boarding."

A cheer went up as the sojourners swarmed toward the craft from all directions. Ethan Gorr and his nephew Tory walked together, as they joined hundreds of others heading up the circular steps. Gorr paused for a moment to look out into the crowd of family and friends. Was that Hopkins? Doesn't matter anymore, he thought, as he took Tory's hand and continued up the steps.

Heather hugged Stephen. "I'll be in touch." She gave Penny a quick kiss on the cheek. "I'll look after your son," she whispered, and walked to the craft, arm in arm with Calvin Williams.

Stephen hadn't seen Gorr, but he caught his son's eye. He had promised there would be no tears, but he could feel Penny trembling beside him. He put his arm around her, drew her close and gave Gerard a thumbs-up. Gerard returned the gesture with a solemn look, then wheeled toward the craft, Abby on one side, Gunner on the other. When the threesome reached the circular base of the cylinder, a ramp descended for Gerard's wheelchair.

He glanced back at his family and grinned. "Cool!" he yelled, and Stephen felt tears sting the back of his eyes.

Inside the craft, the sojourners sat in the high-backed seats facing outward for a parting glimpse of their families. The cylinder descended silently in a clockwise motion and locked on to its base. The sojourners waved. The families on the Mall waved back.

Gerard leaned forward and placed his hand flat against the transparent wall. Stephen raised his hand, palm out, as if to press it against his son's hand for one last time. Gerard's face blurred as the walls of the craft began to shimmer. It kept growing more and more blurry and then vanished.

Penny gasped and hid her face against Stephen's chest. His father began reciting the Lord's Prayer; a woman standing nearby joined in. A few of the crowd wandered away. The rest stood and stared at the ground where the spacecraft had been.

Suddenly, Stephen was filled with joy. An absurd emotion at a time like this, but there it was. He knew Gorr was among the sojourners, but maybe that was a good thing. *Maybe everything was as it should be.* Stephen let everything go. The anger and guilt he had carried like an albatross all these years was gone. So was the feeling of dread that had plagued him for months. Both had simply vanished, like the spacecraft, and their absence left him feeling as light as air.

He scanned the sky for a glimpse of the spacecraft now carrying his son to his destiny across the galaxy. But he knew it was probably light-years away, maybe already on Yxria. Stephen's own destiny stretched before him in a way he had never dreamed possible. He felt he was exactly the right man for the job at hand, and he was gripped with an almost uncontrollable urge to laugh out loud.

He noticed the Secret Service agents watching him from behind dark glasses, and he summoned his professorial dignity and guided Penny toward the waiting limousine. To the millions of Namuh watching the departure ceremonies on television, the new GFED ambassador looked solemn and dignified as he walked across the Mall with his wife. Inside, he was turning cartwheels.

EPILOGUE

Inside the spacecraft, Gerard placed his hand flat against the transparent wall and watched his father raise his hand, palm forward, as if pressing back. A feeling of loss gripped him before Abby's hand found his and squeezed it. He squeezed back.

The transparent walls of the craft began to shimmer, and the families on the Mall blurred. When the shimmering stopped, the walls had turned an opaque gray with a black metal strip dotted with tiny holes encircling the room near the ceiling. Suddenly, the walls turned transparent again, revealing the blue-and-white globe of Earth suspended in black space. The female voice came over the speakers. "We are now leaving planet Earth."

Gerard watched the Earth recede until it became a speck of light in a star-studded blackness, replaced by a flash of white and in the center, a single red-tinged star. He watched as the star grew larger and larger until it solidified into a planet the color of red clay.

As the craft drew closer to the planet, it glowed red-orange like a setting sun. Then it resolved slowly into jagged, brick-red peaks and deep, sharp valleys as far as the eye could see.

ACKNOWLEDGEMENTS

For the help and encouragement received from friends and family, many thanks are owed, but to none more than Sandra Bentley for her tireless editing, revisions and commitment to getting the book right. I am grateful to and humbled by my children, Jeff Brown, Scott Brown, and Tracy Navarro, and my late wife, Carolyn. They are The First Readers.

Thanks to my brothers, Jim and Tom Brown, who cheered me on always, and my creative niece, Christina Brown, was there with great ideas and enthusiasm. And grandson, Nicolas Navarro, is credited with unbiased criticism and for grounding me.

Optimism and assurance came from many friends and professionals: Very many thanks to Dr. Karin Marin, Sharon Joyce, Kevin Reich, Brian Stuart, Barbara Castillo, Carson Dodd, and Brian Murphy of The Planetary Society. And of course, to my good friend Carl Sagan, who played a huge role by telling me to write a novel instead of the science book I was writing. I wish he were still here to read it.

Very special appreciation and thanks go to my elementary school teacher, Elizabeth Franz, who taught me the love of reading and writing lo, these many years ago. From a one-room schoolhouse in rural Pennsylvania, she taught six grades, where I was the only student in grades 2 through 5.

Last but certainly not least, two friends and professionals who got me to the finishing line, Nicky Noxon and Steven Reich. Their input, energy and guidance were the fuel that was needed to launch the book.

As a NASA engineer, David Brown designed the landing gear on the Apollo Lunar Landing Module for America's first mission to the Moon.

An author of several books on investing, and Founder of Sabrient Systems, David serves on the Director's Council at the Kavli Institute for Theoretical Physics at the University of California, Santa Barbara.

David served both as Chairman of the U.S. Science and Technology Commission, and Chairman of the New Millennium Committee of the Planetary Society. An avid avian enthusiast, his garden is filled with over two dozen bird feeders, each dedicated to a specific species, that brings him joy every time he looks out his window.

agiganticleap.com
david@agiganticleap.com

If you enjoyed reading this book, please kindly consider leaving a review.

BOOK 2 of the *A Gigantic Leap* series coming early 2024!